PRAISE FOR MIDNIGHT FOR JUSTICE

(WARREN AND CARMICHAEL LEGAL THRILLERS - BOOK 1)

"...an exceptional thriller that combines sophisticated legal drama with urgent contemporary relevance, making it a must-read for fans of intelligent suspense fiction."
—K.C. Finn for Readers' Favorite

"Perfect for fans of Scott Turow and anyone who enjoys complex, character driven courtroom drama. An easy five stars."
—James Rosenberg, author of the Verdicts & Vindication series

"Midnight for Justice involves murder, an unflinching and risky investigation and, ultimately, a deadly confrontation in the Pacific Northwest. I can still hear gunfire and the sounds of the sea."
—Mac Logan, Scottish poet and author of the Angels' Share thriller series

"...an adventure story, full of excitement and relatable characters with an interesting twist at the end that leads us right back to the beginning of chapter one. A well-deserved 5 stars."
— Lucinda E Clarke for Readers' Favorite

"A combination of legal procedural, military thriller, historical fiction, and personal drama rolled into one compelling read..."
—SPR Review

"It is clear from Charlotte and Don Stuart's narrative that they are well-versed in historical facts about the Vietnam War and weapons. The descriptions of the remote settings along the northern Pacific coast are vivid and authentic."
— Angelique Papayannopoulos for Readers' Favorite

BAD DAY FOR JUSTICE

A WARREN & CARMICHAEL LEGAL THRILLER – BOOK 2

CHARLOTTE STUART

DON STUART

COLVOS PUBLICATIONS

Published by Colvos Publications

Cover design by Chris Holmes

Interior design by Interbridge

ISBN: 979-8-9938223-0-3 (paperback)

ISBN 979-8-9938223-1-0 (ebook)

To George for his persistent and compassionate pursuit of justice. And, to all those who believe in and support our fragile and essential justice system.

*"The wheels of justice turn slowly,
but they grind exceedingly fine."*
—Unknown ancient Greek and Chinese Philosophers
(Referenced by Plutarch, First Century, ACE)

"Justice delayed is justice denied."
—William E. Gladstone
(Four-time British Prime Minister and
19th Century advocate for legal reform)

A Note From The Authors

The entirely fictional events in this book are based upon a very real financial disaster and a real military aircraft.

In January 1982 the Washington Public Power Supply System (WPPSS) halted construction on two partially completed nuclear power plants after it became apparent that the electricity they were to have supplied would not be needed. The following year, the Washington State Supreme Court relieved 88 local municipalities of responsibility for some $2.25 billion in debt incurred in the construction of those plants. This resulted in what was believed to be the largest municipal bond default in American history.

The U.S. Navy's legendary Gruman EA-6B Prowler top secret electronic countermeasure aircraft was in active service from 1968 to 2019. Many have claimed that it was one of the ugliest airplanes ever built. Still, for over forty years the EA-6B played a vital role in U.S. military operations, including those in Vietnam, Afghanistan, and Iraq.

Cast Of Characters

- Sydney Warren – protagonist
- Duncan Carmichael – protagonist
- Kate Carmichael – Duncan's wife
- Megan – Duncan & Kate's daughter
- Lilly – Duncan & Kate's granddaughter
- Mel Marshall – private investigator – 1983
- Kyle Marshall – Mel's son and private investigator – current day
- Harold Dawson – financial advisor in RDN (Ravenswood, Dawson & Nowak)
- Julia Ortez – Harold Dawson's daughter
- Daniel Ortez – Harold Dawson's son-in-law
- Andrea Rymes – Harold Dawson's administrative assistant
- Lauren Franklin-Keene - RDN receptionist
- Cecil Ravenswood – RDN Senior Partner
- Parker – Harold Dawson's loyal dog
- Allison Girard nee Ortez – Harold Dawson's granddaughter (son Jack; husband Peter)
- Jamison Nowak – financial advisor in RDN (Ravenswood, Dawson & Nowak)

- Bryce Nowak – Jamison Nowak's son
- Bonny Price nee Nowak – Jamison Nowak's daughter
- Rear Admiral Nathan Waterman, ComFAirWhidbey (1983)
- Stacy Vaughn – Waterman's Yeoman Master Chief Petty Officer
- Ross Michaels – Ortez's bombardier-navigator
- Judge Roberta Francis – King County Superior Court judge
- Walter Rice – King County deputy prosecutor
- Ginger Small – SPD detective
- Jason Brown – SPD detective
- The Bright family – Two Mountain Creek visitors (Marjorie, Robert, Jenny, and Timothy)
- Eric Gee – professional burglar
- Will – Eric's burglar partner
- Louis (Big Lou) Mitchum – Money lender and Eric's cellmate
- Grant Meade – Big Lou's collector
- The Campbell Family – Vacationers in BC (parents with Abigail and Madison)
- Mitch Brunelli – local crime boss
- Leo Marks – Brunelli's second-in-command
- Ray Barge – Brunelli's enforcer
- Lt. Commander Philip James – ComFAirWhidbey (current) legal office
- Special Agent Barlow – NCIS Silverdale
- Sara-Rose Martinson – woman who adopted Parker (Dawson's dog)
- Helen – gun expert in Sheriff's Property Management Office
- Martin Buckingham – gallery owner on Grenville Island, BC

Prologue

D-day for WPPSS

Washington Nuclear Power Project
Plant Three construction site at Satsop, WA
An early morning in late January 1982

The colossal mass of Nuclear Plant Five loomed tall against the deep blue early morning sky. At nearly 500 feet in height and 440 feet in diameter, its gigantic concrete containment structure was a monument to modern technology and a grand promise of a sustainable energy supply to meet the vast demands of the economically vital U.S. Pacific Northwest.

Twelve men in the concrete finishing crew huddled together in the chill morning air as they awaited their instructions for the coming day. For them, working on this plant was more than just a source of income. They took immense professional pride in being employed on a project this challenging and of this significance for future generations.

"Sorry to keep you waiting." Their usually punctual foreman was fifteen minutes late. "I'm afraid I have some bad news." He paused and cleared his throat as nervous murmurs passed among the men. "I don't know how else to say this other than straight out." He paused again, frowning at the anxious faces of the men in front of him. Then, in a firm but flat voice: "This project has been cancelled. You will receive two weeks' severance, but work stops *today*."

There was a moment of stunned silence before one of the workers said: "I don't understand. What do you mean 'the project is cancelled?'"

The foreman waved a hand indicating the entirety of the worksite. "This whole plant is going to be mothballed. Construction has been called off. Nuclear Plant Five is history."

"But we're just getting started." Several men mumbled agreement, with a few swear words thrown in.

"Guys, I only know what I've just told you." All the starch left his demeanor as he lowered his voice and said: "I suppose we'll learn the details soon enough."

"What about the other plants?" another man asked.

"I . . . don't . . . know. Sorry." The foreman shook his head, shrugged, turned abruptly, and headed back for his office, shoulders drooping.

They'd all heard the stories of cost overruns and mismanagement. The bond market had already suffered losses. But they'd never believed it could come to this. Before leaving, the dispirited crew members took one last look at the huge looming edifice of the Plant Five containment structure and silently shared a last depressing thought: "What an incredible waste!"

Over the months to follow, thousands of investors would be hit with huge financial losses as shockwaves reverberated throughout the municipal bond market. Nationwide, devastated elderly bondholders would demand answers and complain to politicians. Lawsuits would be threatened and initiated. And over and over again the question would be asked: *How could this have happened?*

Unlike the famous D-day of WWII known for incredible loss of life but ultimate success, this D-day would be remembered solely as a pivotal moment in a $2 billion blunder.

PART ONE

THE $2 BILLION BLUNDER

1983

CHAPTER 1

**United States Naval Air Station, Whidbey Island, Washington
Office of Rear Admiral Nathan Waterman, Commander Fleet Air
Whidbey
Monday, June 20, 1983 (8:25 a.m.)**

"We have a situation, sir," said the uniformed yeoman. She was standing in the doorway to the Admiral's office with a phone receiver held to her ear.

But Rear Admiral Nathan Waterman already knew. His short gray hair glinted silver in the morning light as he looked out through his office window with a pair of oversized Zeiss binoculars scanning the sky to the Northwest.

The Admiral's second-floor office overlooked Ault Field at U.S. Naval Air Station Whidbey Island. He had a speaker on his wall that was softly tuned to flight ops at the field below. There was no way he would have missed the controller's urgent command uttered just moments before his yeoman had appeared in his office doorway: "Abort landing. Abort! Abort!"

Each day he witnessed hundreds of takeoffs and landings. That airfield was his world. Nothing happened out there without him knowing about it. And, as Commander, Fleet Air Whidbey (ComFAir-Whidbey), whatever went on down there was his responsibility. If there was cause for concern, that concern was *his*.

The yeoman stood patiently by while the Admiral continued to assess the situation.

It was a dry but overcast Monday morning. A light southwest breeze had the day's flight traffic assigned to the east-west runway, the one that aimed directly out over Juan de Fuca Strait. The Admiral had been working at his desk while half-listening to a voice giving directions from the tower. Then another voice had broken in on the channel. One of the controllers had apparently been unable to get a response from an EA-6B Prowler. Controllers are trained to stay calm, but a non-responsive aircraft taxiing out onto the field without permission during active flight ops had definitely captured their attention. As had the controller's unmistakable request to "please identify yourself and do not proceed. I repeat: DO NOT PROCEED."

Contrary to increasingly frantic instructions from the tower, the aircraft had turned up an inactive taxiway, entered the North-South runway, powered up, and taken flight headed northwest. In the process, it had passed directly across active traffic engaged in "touch-and-go" practice landings on the properly designated east-west runway.

It was a flagrant and extraordinarily dangerous breach of protocol.

"Son-of-a-bitch," the Admiral said for perhaps the third time in the past minute.

Admiral Waterman finally lowered his binoculars and turned to face his yeoman, a first-class petty officer who had remained at the entrance to his office, watching the Admiral while listening to someone on her phone. The phone's long, curly cord led around the corner of the doorway and back to her nearby desk; a testament to the Navy's security-conscious reticence to move to the new cordless phones.

"What the hell was that?" the admiral barked the instant she took the receiver away from her ear.

"One of the Prowler teams," she said. "An EA-6B. They're flying with a 3-person crew. Apparently, the pilot sent the other two back to the ready room on some errand, misled his ground crew, and then taxied out alone and took off. Nobody knows why."

"Headed where?"

The yeoman waved her phone receiver toward the window and shook her head apologetically. "They don't know, sir. Northwest, up toward Canada. Flying low. That's all they can say for sure."

The Admiral and his yeoman stared out the window for a moment. In the wake of the flurry of hurried tower instructions to put other aircraft on hold both in the air and on the ground, flight ops had now ceased. Aside from the redirected traffic circling above, the base had gone silent.

"Son-of-a-bitch," said the Admiral once again.

"Should we notify the Canucks?" the yeoman asked.

The admiral set his binoculars aside and stared at the papers on his desk, saying nothing. This was *his* base. Everything that happened here was *his* responsibility. And there was no blueprint for how to respond to a Navy pilot taking off on some venture of his own in one of the Navy's highest tech, highly classified electronics countermeasure aircraft.

"He's probably already entering their airspace," she coaxed carefully.

The admiral looked at her and shook his head in disgust and resignation. "Make sure first. But, yes, let them know. They need to be warned. We need to have warned them."

The anger etched on the Admiral's face made his yeoman grateful she wasn't the one flying that aircraft. Whoever he was and, whatever his reasons, that pilot was in one whole hell of a lot of trouble.

And so was Rear Admiral Nathan Waterman.

~

A private residence adjacent to NAS Whidbey Island
Monday, June 20, 1983 (8:26 a.m.)

"My God!" said the woman as she stepped out of her kitchen with a dish towel in her hands. She stood there a moment, frozen in place in the aftermath of the prodigious clap of thunder produced by two mighty Pratt & Whitney P-408 turbojet engines with combined 24,000 pounds of thrust that had just rattled every door and window in their home. The plane had passed overhead at what felt to her like inches above their rooftop. Still flying low, the aircraft and the rumble of its passage were now receding into the distance.

Their home was one of several along the beach at the eastern end of the Strait of Juan de Fuca. It was only a few blocks north of Naval Air Station Whidbey, so the noise of military jets was a constant, everyday occurrence. "The sound of freedom," her husband always said.

But *this* had been different.

Her husband was a retired Navy Master Chief who'd once been stationed right there at NAS Whidbey. He joined her at the sliding glass doors facing out onto the front deck of their waterfront home. "Did you see how close that thing came?" she asked.

"Low," he agreed. "Damned low." He studied the water in front of their home where a light westerly breeze was ruffling the surface. "He wasn't even on the designated runway."

They stood there together for a moment, gazing off to the northwest after the disappearing aircraft.

"Somebody's gonna be in some deep shit over this one."

~

Royal Canadian Air Force, CFB Comox, BC, Canada
Flight Control Office
Monday, June 20, 1980 (08:40)

"What the bloody hell was that?" The sergeant looked up from his screen in alarm just as his boss, the flight operations officer, stepped through the door and quickly went over to the big east-facing windows which overlooked the airfield and beyond it the Strait of Georgia.

The Flight Control Room was the beating heart of the RCAF base at Comox, BC. It had been an uneventful morning, but now, suddenly, all that changed. Something travelling at nearly 800 klicks and with no electronic signature had just streaked close offshore out over the Strait. It had been flying no more than a couple hundred meters above the water.

The captain reached down and picked up one of the station's new cordless landline phones, but before he could call anyone, it rang in his hand.

"Flight ops, Comox," he said. And then listened. "Uh huh . . . Yes, just now . . . No sir . . . Headed north, fast and low." Long pause. "Yes sir. Will do." Then he hung up the phone, glanced over, and saw his sergeant's curious gaze. "Some idiot Yank," he said. "Hijacked one of their Navy's precious EA-6B Prowlers out of Whidbey." Not all that many years earlier an American pilot in Vietnam had defected with one of their U.S. Navy patrol planes. "They think it may be headed for Russia." The captain wiggled his eyebrows and grinned:

The sergeant grinned back. Over the years, the RCAF had experienced enough arrogance from their US military counterparts that an event of this kind, serious as it was, could not help but generate at least a trace of amusement.

As the sergeant turned back to his work, his mind refused to let go of what they had just witnessed. Russia was a long way off. That EA-6B Prowler was a carrier-based aircraft. And those jets burned a lot of fuel. No doubt its range was classified. But he had his doubts that this plane would make it anything like that far.

CHAPTER 2

Duncan Carmichael
Preston-Martin Building, Seattle
Law Offices of Warren and Carmichael
Friday, June 24, 1983

Duncan Carmichael's new client scooped up her one-year-old daughter and followed him down the long, carpeted hallway from their comfortable waiting room to his office. With a wriggling child propped against her hip on one side and balancing a small but very full backpack on the opposite shoulder, the young mother had her hands full. At his office, she paused just inside the entrance to take in the incredible view of Elliot Bay from the 35th floor windows behind the large desk in his orderly yet comfortable space. Then she quickly moved to what was obviously the client chair, dropped her backpack on the floor, sat down, and tried to settle the active child on her lap.

As was his habit, Duncan asked if he could get her anything to drink, and she declined with a shake of the head while murmuring soothing sounds to her child.

Duncan sat down and took a few moments to assess his new client's mood before getting down to business. Many who found their way to his client chair were angry or upset. They felt they'd been wronged and were spoiling for a fight. He had to wade through their anger to get to the facts. Other times, clients came to him because they needed both a reality check and reassurance that everything would be okay. However, most of his clients came with simple, personal requests. What they wanted was for him to clarify complex legal issues and walk them through unfamiliar paperwork and legalese. And, almost to a person, they were concerned about what they perceived as expensive fees for services they didn't fully understand.

In this instance, however, he couldn't identify what his new client was feeling. Julia Ortez, although somewhat distracted by her energetic daughter, appeared to be comfortable and in control. Not angry or defensive or anxious. But she wouldn't be there if she wasn't facing some kind of legal problem.

One thing he couldn't help noticing was that she was an extraordinarily attractive woman with the kind of face you might see on a TV ad for skin care or standing next to an exotic sports car with her hair blowing in the breeze. As she leaned over her daughter, her long blond hair almost touched her daughter's golden curls, an idyllic mother with child moment. He watched her longer than he probably should have before softly clearing his throat to get her attention.

When she turned toward him, her deep blue eyes locked onto his dark brown ones, and she smiled. "I can see why you keep your back to the windows. It's a gorgeous view."

"My chair swivels," he replied with a wide grin. It was hard not to return her smile. In addition to being attractive, there was something warm and magnetic about her persona. "What can I do for you, Mrs. Ortez?"

"Please, call me Julia."

"Julia."

"To be honest, I'm not sure you can actually help me," she said. "But I didn't know where else to turn."

He found himself feeling flattered that she had come to him for assistance and then chagrinned that he needed to remind himself that she hadn't turned to *him* but to a *lawyer*. "Well, once you explain your situation, I'm confident we can find some answers." Why had he said that? It was his practice to never overpromise. Especially before hearing all the details.

"Have you seen the news coverage on my husband, Danny Ortez?"

"I believe I have. If he's the Navy pilot who disappeared into Canada with a Navy aircraft. It's been on TV as well as in local papers. You husband has caused quite a stir."

She nodded, remaining composed but with flickers of distress sparking in her eyes. "It surprised everyone. Nobody has any idea why he did it, including me." Perhaps because she heard signs of stress in her mother's tone, her child reached out and put a hand on her face. Julia squeezed the tiny hand without looking at her daughter. "It makes no sense. He's a good father and a very responsible person. If the accusations about him are true, I would have known. I'm sure of it."

From what Duncan had read, Lieutenant Junior Grade Danny Ortez had made off with one of the U.S. Navy's high-tech Gruman EA-6B Prowlers, a carrier-based electronic counter-measure aircraft. An extensive search was underway, but according to local news reports, so far neither Ortez nor the plane had yet been found.

"You say that you're not sure I can help, but when you scheduled the appointment, you said it was about an urgent matter related to a Navy housing issue."

"Yes, I want to know if there is any way that you can get the Navy to restore my husband's pay and keep me and my daughter from being evicted from the Navy housing community at Maylor Point in Oak Harbor. Or, at least delay things long enough that I can make alternative arrangements, or until it's determined where he is and why . . ." Her voice trailed off, the first sign of the depth of her personal despair.

"The Navy has asked you to leave?"

"They've terminated my husband's pay and benefits and all of my entitlements as a Navy spouse as of this Wednesday. Including the right to remain in military housing. I'm supposed to move out by *next* Wednesday. I can't even hire a mover in that length of time."

"He, ah, left on Monday, right?"

"Yes. They contacted me late Wednesday with their decision to discontinue his Navy pay and benefits—effective immediately."

"Did you get the request in writing?"

"It was no *request*, Mr. Carmichael. I got a hand-delivered official letter stating that all his pay and benefits had ended pending further investigation. And directing my departure."

"Did it mention what the investigation entailed?"

"No, but I know they think he's at best a deserter and at worst possibly a . . . a defector." She had a hard time saying the word *defector*. "I don't believe that," she quickly added. "Not for an instant. There has to be another explanation."

It didn't surprise Duncan that Navy loyalties to family members would end abruptly when a Navy pilot highjacked a U.S. Navy jet and flew it out of the country to parts unknown. But he could also understand why, from her point of view, the speed of the termination seemed unfair. "Have you been questioned?" he asked.

"Do you mean, do they think I'm complicit?" Her chin came up an inch and her cheeks flushed pink.

"I'm not suggesting that's the case, Mrs. Ortez. I'm simply wondering if you have more to worry about than being cut off from benefits." He could understand how the Navy might suspect that the man's wife had some warning in advance. At the same time, he felt an obligation to try to protect her and her daughter, no matter what the circumstances.

"I've seen TV programs where an entire family turned out to be a sleeper cell. But this is not a movie, Mr. Carmichael. I can assure you that I'm 100 percent American, committed to our country." She paused, blinking as though in an effort to hold back tears. "And *so is my husband*. There's no way my Danny is a defector."

"But they did interview you?"

"They sent a guy out, an agent with Navel Investigative Service. A civilian. But I had nothing useful to say. It was obvious he thought I was holding out on him; he kept coming back to whether I had even the slightest suspicion that my husband was about to leave the country in a stolen airplane. He asked things like: *Had he mentioned anything, anything at all that was suspicious? Had he given any indication that something was wrong? Did he drink? Use drugs? Was he a gambler? Were we in debt? Having marital problems?* You name it, he hinted at it.

"I kept trying to convince him that we were a happy family and that

Danny is a wonderful husband and father. He dotes on Allison. And me. Before this, I would have said that we were *everything* to him. I still believe that, despite what has happened."

Staring him down across his desk with those penetrating eyes, she said: "I know exactly what you're probably thinking—a wife can be fooled into believing her marriage is perfect. That the very fact that he took off without saying a word to me indicates I didn't have a clue about what was going on with him. But in my heart, I know there's an explanation other than that he either had some sort of mental breakdown or that he is a traitor." She took a deep breath. "There just has to be."

Her daughter had fallen asleep on her lap. Julia brushed some hair back from the girl's full-cheeked face before continuing. "After the NIS fellow delivered the letter, they called to tell me I needed to drop off my identity card at Personnel. Now I can't even shop at the Commissary or the Navy Exchange. I'm lucky they still let me drive through the gate to my housing unit—they gave me a special 'temporary guest' pass for that.

"I just don't understand why they are doing this to us. He hasn't been convicted of anything. For all they know, he had someone pointing a gun at his head."

"Was anyone seen in the vicinity of the aircraft before he took off?"

"I have no idea. I tried to get someone to talk to me about the possibilities. But the only thing they care about is finding Danny and getting their airplane back."

In spite of feeling sorry for her, Duncan couldn't help being intrigued by the unusual circumstances she was facing. Military regulations and military justice had some special quirks, and Julia Ortez was about to learn more than she probably wanted to know about both.

Julia continued: "Given that they don't have any answers at this point, doesn't it seem rather hasty to end pay and spousal benefits so quickly? I realize his departure was . . . dramatic, but I've always understood that they don't consider someone a deserter until at least thirty days have passed. Honestly, I think they're just angry because they feel Danny has made them look bad. And they are punishing me and Allison for what he has allegedly done."

Duncan suspected she might be right—the Navy's uncharacteristically quick reaction might very well reflect their embarrassment as well as their aggravation. Her husband had stolen a valuable piece of military equipment, a plane that most likely contained technology that they didn't want to fall into the wrong hands. Nor was disobedience of any kind tolerated in the military, especially on the level of what Ortez had done.

When the deeply bureaucratic Navy wanted something to happen quickly, they had the ability to make it happen. So, he wasn't surprised that it had taken the Navy personnel office a mere three days to decide that the entire Ortez family was persona-non-grata. In fact, as Duncan thought about it, the more likely it seemed that the Navy would naturally assume Julia Ortez was in cahoots with her husband. Knowing the Navy as he did, maybe they also suspected her one-year-old daughter as well. If not the family cat.

But that wasn't her most urgent problem. "Do you have friends on the base who you could stay with temporarily?" he asked.

She shook her head. "I went shopping at the commissary the day after he disappeared, and it was as if I had the plague. No one would look me in the eye. I saw a couple of women I thought were friends. They turned their carts around to avoid running into me. It's as if both my husband and I have been tried and found guilty."

"I'm sorry." It felt inadequate to say he was *sorry*, but what else could he say?

"Besides, after next Wednesday, I won't be allowed on base. And I've even been fired from my part-time waitress job at the local deli-café in Oak Harbor. I was at work when my boss handed me my final paycheck. He told me I was a good employee but that he had 'no choice.' *This is a Navy Town, Julia. I'm sorry, but I cain't have you waitin' on my customers*," she said in a southern twang to mimic his voice. "*It's thayat simple*." She gave a short laugh. "Simple? Not for me or my daughter. Losing everything isn't 'simple.' And he didn't even sound sorry; more like he was sentencing me after a guilty verdict. He didn't even wait until after the noon rush. I was lucky to grab my purse and jacket before he ushered me out the door."

He could understand why she was bitter. It sounded like everyone had turned against her.

"Do you have family in the area?"

"My mom lives here in Seattle. It's not ideal, but I can stay with her temporarily. What I need most is more time to make the move. And I could use what he's owed for time he'd put in up to when he left. We've got very little savings." She took a deep breath. "Worst of all, I don't even know what's happened to Danny yet. I've spent the last few days trying to talk to people at the base who knew him to get some idea of what, if anything, he said to them that might explain his actions. What I'm hoping is that you can buy me a few weeks to get my life in order."

Duncan was torn about what he should say. He didn't want to give her false hope, yet he wanted to help if he could. "You made an awfully long drive, what, a couple hours, to come to Seattle all the way from Whidbey Island. Is there some reason you didn't get someone on the island to handle this?" He knew for a fact that even if she couldn't turn to a Navy legal assistance officer, there were excellent civilian lawyers right there in Oak Harbor, lawyers with strong Navy experience and local contacts.

She gave him a look that suggested he should already know the answer to his question. "Those private Oak Harbor law firms are filled with retired Navy personnel. Even if they aren't retired Navy them-selves, most of their clients are. I'm sorry, but that town is convinced my Danny is a deserter. Maybe a defector. A traitor. I'm not trusting someone from there to represent me against the U.S. Navy. No way."

"I'm a Navy Reserve officer myself. You know that, right? I'd be happy to refer you—"

"No, no. I know exactly who you are, Mr. Carmichael. That's why I came to you. You're the lawyer who brought down that corrupt admiral a few years back. That *was* you, right? You and your partner."

It wasn't exactly how he'd have described what he and his law partner Sydney Warren had done, but he had to acknowledge she had the right person. Four years earlier, when he was still in the Navy and Sydney was an ACLU attorney-volunteer, they had won a very public and bitter legal battle with the U.S. Navy. Their collaboration on that case was what had later led them to launch their new civilian Seattle law firm: Warren and Carmichael. It was also the case that had convinced him to end his own career on active duty with the U.S. Navy JAGC— Judge Advocate General Corps.

At the end of their conversation, Duncan promised to take a look at the BuPers Manual—the manual for the Bureau of Naval Personnel— and to contact the NAS Whidbey personnel office to see if there was anything he could do to get her some money and more time to transition to civilian life. Then he walked her to the lobby, promising that he would get on it right away. He had other files he was working on, but none that were as time sensitive.

As a civilian attorney as well as a Navy Reservist and former active duty JAGC officer, Duncan often received legal referrals for representation of Navy personnel when they were looking for an experienced civilian attorney in their courts martial. On a few occasions in the past, he'd also been asked for help by Navy personnel who had personal civilian legal problems unrelated to their service. The U.S. Navy did offer limited general legal assistance and advice on non-Navy matters to active-duty personnel and families. However, if it came to anything serious, if there were off-base adverse parties involved, or if there was litigation other than a court martial, the Navy lawyer inevitably bowed out. Active-duty U.S. Navy JAGC officers stayed *away* from civilian courts.

Especially if the adverse party was the U.S. Navy itself.

Duncan did not, of course, face any such constraints. But it was definitely a first for him to be representing the wife of a rogue pilot who had made off with a highly classified twenty-five-million-dollar aircraft. Had Ortez defected? Was he a traitor like the Navy seemed to believe? Or, was Julia right and there was some yet unknown reason why Danny Ortez had absconded with a high-tech Gruman EA-6B Prowler?

CHAPTER 3

Duncan Carmichael
Preston-Martin Building, Seattle
Law Offices of Warren and Carmichael
Friday, June 24, 1983

After reading and researching the military regulations on Julia's financial and residency issues, Duncan made a few calls. He started with the Navy Personnel Office at NAS Whidbey. Next, he reached out to Danny Ortez's superiors and colleagues at the base. He knowingly but carefully used his rank as a reserve Navy officer and an authoritative tone of voice to gain access—without, of course, mentioning his current inactive status. As usual, no one challenged an officer's right to make inquiries. Even so, he learned very little that was helpful.

The most interesting conversation he had was with Lieutenant Junior Grade Ross Michaels, a bombardier-navigator electronics counter-measure officer—an ECMO who'd been scheduled to join Ortez on his flight that day. Michaels told Duncan that he and Ortez had been partnered up together for some time and that one other person, another ECMO, would have flown with them that day as well.

According to Michaels, touch-and-go training was mostly just about the pilot. So, there were only the three of them rather than the usual crew of four.

"We all three started out together that morning," Michaels said. "But then the sonofabitch lied to our face. We were about to board the plane when he told us he'd left his flight manual and checklists back on one of the chairs in the ready room. He insisted that we both go back to look for them while he prepped the plane for take-off.

"We weren't in any particular hurry, so even though we thought it was strange, we did as he asked. But then, while we were gone, he apparently convinced the ground crew that he'd been directed to practice an abbreviated active combat pre-flight check-through. It was a long walk, so by the time we were on our way back from the ready room, without finding the supposedly missing flight manual I might add, he was disconnected. The ground crew had him unchalked, and he was rolling off down the taxi-way alone. The son-of-a bitch took off without us. Un-freaking-believable."

When pressed, Michaels had no explanation for why Ortez might have done what he did. Nor did he seem to have much concern for his former partner's fate. Then, as Duncan was preparing to end the call, Michaels volunteered some last licks about the man. "Good riddance, as far as I'm concerned," he offered, unsolicited. "Crappy pilot. His days were numbered anyway."

That caught Duncan's attention. "Was he in some kind of trouble?"

"About to wash out, as I understand it. Don't have a clue how he made it through basic flight training. Didn't have what it takes, you know."

Duncan was aware that Navy Pilots were intensively trained and needed to be extraordinarily skilled and well-practiced at what they did. Landing on an aircraft carrier at sea wasn't for the faint of heart. But he didn't know exactly what Michaels was referring to. He asked for more details, but that was all the man was prepared to say.

As for the Navy itself, they believed they owed Julia Ortez nothing. Her husband was a deserter. Maybe even a traitor. And he'd stolen a hugely expensive and strategically important aircraft in the bargain, one with electronic components that could be of immense value to America's enemies. As far as the Navy was concerned, that definitely cancelled out a few days of unpaid back pay.

From the Navy perspective, the loss of that aircraft seemed almost personal. Taking it was the worst kind of disloyalty. And its loss was a huge public embarrassment that had captured the attention of the news media. Worst of all, they had absolutely no idea where Ortez had gone, so with every passing day they looked more and more incompetent as well.

According to news reports, the Navy had lost track of their aircraft almost immediately. Ortez had apparently shut down his transponder and any other potential identifiers and had flown literally under the radar. The aircraft was soon lost to civilian and military flight control.

It did not go entirely undetected though. A loud, low flying jet, especially one with U.S. Navy markings, attracted attention in Canada. Sightings suggested that Ortez had followed the BC inside-waters coast-line north over some sparsely populated areas. Once the plane had cleared the northern end of Vancouver Island, the population thinned even more, and there were no further reliable eyewitness reports of its passing.

From personal experience, Duncan knew that the BC coast was a literal maze with hundreds of largely uninhabited passages, islands, and long narrow inlets up which a plane might easily fly, low and invisible. So, he wasn't surprised that no sightings had been reported further north along the coast. Or up in Southeast Alaska. Nor were there any credible sightings inland. But that didn't mean Ortez hadn't made it to Alaska. Or even beyond. It just meant that no one had reported seeing the aircraft.

Various "experts" happily offered their "informed" speculation in otherwise brief newspaper reports concerning the plane's likely destination. But the bottom line was, the damned thing had simply vanished.

Duncan learned that the Canadians had been quick to offer their assistance in the search. They delegated some local RCMP and military resources to the effort. They also offered the help of their Coast Guard, a civilian agency in Canada. But from the accounts that Duncan saw, it appeared as though the Canadians were more peeved than anything. A U.S. military aircraft had encroached upon their airspace without warning or permission, had ignored their flight regulations, and had quite possibly landed without authorization somewhere in their territory. Ortez was lucky not to have been shot out of the air.

For the Canadians, Duncan guessed that preventing the aircraft from falling into the wrong hands was probably not a priority, but locating it so they could make a point of how their airspace had been violated seemed to figure prominently in their response. With all their characteristic Canadian civility intact, they still managed to make it absolutely clear that accepting help from the U.S. military vessels and aircraft was out of the question. They were not about to allow free reign to the U.S. Navy to do an intensive search of their sovereign territory.

Duncan ended up speaking with a civilian U.S. Naval Investigative Service agent stationed at NAS Whidbey whom he understood to be one of several individuals launching an intensive but low-key aerial examination of the BC coastline using private civilian chartered aircraft. That type of civilian search had apparently been approved by the Canadians, although they'd made it clear that any findings, reports, or arrests must pass through Canadian authorities. The NIS was also doing some discreet ground searches by talking to witnesses. They planned to follow up on any sightings of a landing or signs of a crash.

When Duncan asked whether any progress had been made on the search for the missing plane, the NIS agent said: "Nah, we haven't found a thing, sorry. And I don't have much hope. Those carrier-based aircraft like the A-6 Intruder and the EA-6B Prowler are specifically designed for low landing speeds on short runways. The tides were down at the time, so he could easily have ended up on an exposed beach somewhere. Although it's more likely that he used some small dirt strip inland."

"Are there many such places?" Duncan asked.

"Oh yeah. There's been a lot of logging in that region. Lots of logging roads. And some people have taken advantage of the access those roads have provided to move to the outback. There are literally scores of places to land an airplane, mapped and otherwise, in use and abandoned. Hell, he could have put the thing down on some open meadow somewhere and simply covered it up. Those planes are surprisingly small. Once on the ground, it wouldn't have taken much to make it difficult to spot from the air. On the other hand, if he wasn't able to land and crashed into an area of heavy forest, unless it caught fire, it could also be very hard to find.

"Who knows, maybe he even ditched it in the water—Navy planes are equipped for emergency landings at sea. And their crews are trained for it. For all we know the damned thing could be at the bottom of one of those Canadian fjords. If that's the case, I doubt it will ever be found. Might have been an oil slick from its fuel tanks. But that wouldn't have lasted long."

"Assuming he landed it safely," Duncan said. "And given your knowledge of the area, any ideas about the most likely places to look?"

The man laughed. "Who the hell knows?" he said. "There are thousands of abandoned logging roads out there. It depends on what he wanted to do with the plane. Leave it behind or sell it. If he wanted a fast getaway, he could have stashed a motor vehicle somewhere up one of those logging roads—a car or a motorcycle. Or he could have had a small boat hidden along the shore. All he had to do was pull it up the beach and into the trees in one of those inlets. That's what I'd have done."

"You've obviously given this some thought," Duncan said.

"Yeah, assuming he just wanted a new life, once he disposed of the aircraft, all he'd need is a fake ID and a change of clothes. He could drive his car or motorcycle or his boat into the nearest town, pay cash, and fly out on the next shuttle.

"Or, with a cache of fuel left somewhere, he could have flown that thing all the way to Vladivostok. Or, who knows, maybe he met up with some Russian somewhere and exchanged cash for the plane. The Russian could have stripped it of its goodies or flown it to who knows where."

"But you definitely think it would be possible to hide the plane after landing it on some remote landing strip."

"Let's face it, if he landed the plane safely and camouflaged it in some way, I think it would take some serious luck to find it by air or land. At least to do so quickly. There's just too much territory to cover. That's what I told them, but they want us to check out as much of it as we can anyway. Can't give up without putting in some effort. I hate to fail, although I guess it's worth a try. As long as the weather holds, anyway."

~

As interesting as the NIS agent's speculation was, none of what he'd learned from talking to people about Danny's theft of the aircraft helped Duncan figure out how to argue Julia Ortez's case to the Navy. Nor was his initial research into the relevant sections of the BuPers Manual at all encouraging. It looked like the Navy had plenty of discretionary authority to act as they had in her case. Especially if they labeled the case a matter of national security because of the EA-6B's high-tech components.

Just to be certain, he made one more call to a friend and former colleague, a JAGC officer who was still on active duty. His friend confirmed his fear: if her husband was thought to be a deserter, neither he nor his family would get much love from the U.S. armed forces. So long as Lieutenant Junior Grade Ortez was missing without any credible explanation, there wasn't going to be much Duncan could do to help his abandoned wife and daughter.

Feeling like he had reached a dead end on legal options, Duncan finally made a call to plead Julia Ortez's case on humanitarian grounds directly with the base commander, the officer responsible for the Navy base itself. He was a Navy Captain whose official role was as a kind of "landlord" in that he had physical jurisdiction over the airport, the base, and other facilities, including housing. The squadrons that made up the air wing known as "Fleet Air Whidbey" were, in effect, his "tenants." Their crews were housed at the base while they honed their skills and awaited deployment overseas aboard the Navy's various aircraft carriers around the world.

After explaining that he represented the wife of Daniel Ortez, Duncan got straight to the point: "Captain, all she asks is that she and her one-year-old daughter be allowed to stay a few more weeks in her assigned base housing unit. As I understand it, there are a number of empty units at present, so she isn't creating an inconvenience. And, while I know people in small communities can't help but speculate when something like this occurs, there is absolutely no reason at all to suspect her personally of any involvement. Or to fear that she represents some kind of security risk. She's a 22-year-old dependent spouse with a year-old daughter whose husband has just run off leaving her in the lurch. She's a victim, just like the Navy. I'm assuming your decision on this is discretionary. Can't you make some kind of short-term accommodation for her?"

In the end, Duncan was able to gain Julia and Allison Ortez an additional week to find a mover. But that was it.

Even though he'd spent time trying to find answers, Duncan felt he'd provided so little assistance that he decided to waive his fee. It seemed unlikely she'd be in a position any time soon to pay him anyway.

Chapter 4

New owners of Harold Dawson's former home
East Madison District, Seattle WA
**A private residence in the Broadmoor gated residential
community**
Monday, June 20, 1983

The dog was back.

The woman looked out her window at the small, black-and-white spaniel with the sad, intelligent eyes. He seemed to be standing vigil on the edge of their front porch, staring down the quiet residential street as if waiting for someone to return. The dog had a collar, but it was too frightened to let her get close enough to read what it said. She put some food and water outside the door and retreated back inside. Looking out between the living-room curtains she saw the dog warily approach, drink some water, and look nervously around before wolfing down the food.

Then he went back to the front edge of the porch and sat, as if waiting.

The house was in one of Seattle's most exclusive gated residential communities. She and her husband had moved in a little over a week ago. The instant her husband saw the bedraggled animal he insisted she call animal control. But she couldn't face the idea that the poor dog might be caged or put down in return for what was most likely loyalty to the last owner of the house.

The next morning, she didn't call the pound as instructed. Instead, she paused at the guard house at the entrance to the Broadmoor community on her way back from a trip to the grocery store and asked the security guard if he knew whether the former owner of their home had a black and white spaniel.

"Yeah, that sounds like Harold Dawson's dog Parker. A nice dog. Him and Dawson are inseparable. Dawson's an investments advisor at a big firm downtown. The Seafirst Building, I believe. He always took Parker to work with him. I used to keep a bag of dog treats here so I could give him one in the evening when they'd come through on their way home." He paused. "You say that dog's here? At your house?"

"On our porch. Can't get it to leave."

"That's doesn't sound right. Dawson would never let Parker out of his sight. Maybe it's a different dog that just looks like Parker."

"Maybe," she agreed, but deep down she felt certain this *was* Dawson's dog. When she got home, she called their realtor, explained about the dog, and got a new address and a phone number for Harold Dawson. According to the realtor, Dawson was recently divorced. He now lived in a smaller place, a rental in North Seattle near Sand Point. The ex-wife lived in West Seattle.

When she called Dawson's number, the call went to a machine. She left a message and impatiently waited for a call back, but it never came.

That evening she had another unpleasant exchange with her husband about the dog, but she held firm. "Well, if the guard's right, at least it's not really a stray, I guess," he finally conceded.

Early the following day, she drove to the address she'd been given by the realtor. Dawson's new home was a plain, middle-class house, a great deal smaller than the place he'd sold them. No one answered when she knocked. She'd decided in advance to leave a note on the front door if he wasn't home. But looking around, she thought that Dawson was probably more likely to use the side door, the one adjacent to the driveway and a detached garage. She went to the side door and knocked again, just in case. But no one answered.

She taped the note to the door. Uncomfortable about leaving too much personal information on a stranger's door, all it said was to call her if his dog was still missing. Her mission accomplished, she was about to leave when she decided to take a look at the back yard, just in case someone was out there.

The cement walkway from the detached garage to the back door also led to a gate between the house and the garage. Peering over the gate, she could see that there was no one in the large back yard, but next to the fence was a covered kennel with a good-sized doghouse and a variety of well-used dog toys scattered about. The kennel gate was open. From where she stood, she could see two large bowls of uneaten dog food and a lidless plastic tote filled with water.

There was also a hole that had been dug in the dirt under the chain link fence. At least now it was clear why Dawson's dog was on the loose.

Parker was on her porch when she returned home. As usual, he retreated till she'd refreshed his water and went back inside.

She tried to put the matter out of her mind, but it nagged at her. After lunch, she got on the phone and, with a bit of help from the phone directory's Yellow Pages, she identified the financial consulting firm where Harold Dawson was a partner.

"Mr. Dawson is no longer with this office," she was told. "Are you a client?"

"No. But I do need to get in touch with him. It's rather urgent. Do you have a new number?"

It seemed like a simple request, but rather than providing a number, the receptionist put her through to someone who identified herself as Harold Dawson's former administrative assistant.

"And you are . . .?" the administrative assistant asked.

"I have his dog, Parker."

"Ah. So, you're not one of Harold's clients?"

"No, no. We bought his former house. I just have his dog. I want to return him to Mr. Dawson."

"Oh. I see." She paused, as if carefully considering her response. "We all know Parker. Harold used to bring him to the office. But returning him to Harold is going to be a problem."

"If Mr. Dawson is away for some reason, perhaps someone there would take him temporarily."

"Well, you see, it wouldn't be temporary. I'm sorry to say, Harold Dawson died last week. And his ex-wife is definitely not a dog person."

"Oh, how sad. Was it sudden?"

After a brief pause, she said, "He was murdered."

"Oh."

"I'm afraid poor Parker is on his own."

CHAPTER 5

Sydney Warren
Preston-Martin Building, Seattle
Law Offices of Warren and Carmichael
Friday, June 24, 1983

S ydney Warren's potential new client shook her hand heartily, his ostentatious gold pinkie ring pressing uncomfortably into her fingers. At the same time, he flashed his perfect white teeth in a smile that she thought screamed "hustler" and "egocentric." While her first impression wasn't all that positive, she told herself that you didn't choose your clients because you liked them. Besides, the small Seattle law firm she and Duncan Carmichael had started together three years earlier was still in the early growth stage; they couldn't afford to turn away paying clients. And Jamison Nowak, a financial consultant in an expensive looking suit, appeared capable of managing a substantial retainer. She would hear him out and then decide.

"I had an unpleasant visit with a couple of police detectives yesterday afternoon," Nowak told her as they entered her office. She shut the door, offered him one of her client chairs, and then took a seat behind her desk. "I didn't like the sound of what they had to say, and

I'm hoping you'll look into it for me. See if you can keep me out of trouble." He gave her another toothy smile.

"It's what we do," she said with a slight head nod. "At the very least, I should be able to assess the seriousness of your situation."

Sydney's legal assistant brought in a coffee service, set it down on the front corner of her desk and, with a nod from Nowak, poured him a cup and withdrew. Sydney watched as Nowak adeptly used the little stainless-steel tongs to add a cube of sugar before leaning back in his chair. He was maybe 50 years of age, on his way to baldness, and modestly overweight. But he moved like a man who'd been an athlete in his youth. Someone who had slowly surrendered an earlier active life to the demands of a more sedentary profession.

"A friend of mine has died," Nowak said. "A friend and business partner." He paused, as if awaiting an acknowledgement of his loss, continuing when Sydney nodded in sympathy. "Apparently he was murdered."

"Murdered?" It wasn't what Sydney had expected. She'd been thinking it would be about some kind of suspect business deal gone south.

"Yes, and the feeling I got from those two detectives was that they think I did it." He looked directly at Sydney. "Let me assure you right off. I did *not* kill my friend." He took a deep breath. "But it turns out I *was* right there, nearby, at the scene of the crime. And I was alone. So, I don't have an alibi. Moreover, there *were* some issues between him and me."

Motive *and* opportunity, Sydney thought as Nowak took a sip of his coffee. Two out of three.

"It's not as if Harold was a saint. He had plenty of people mad at him. I wasn't the only one."

Sydney didn't know what to make of this guy. His overall demeanor was off-putting, more salesman than financial guru. Even so, she found herself wanting to hear more. "Harold?" she asked.

"Harold Dawson."

"I'll want to know the details of his death, but first, tell me more about your business."

"He was one of the partners at RDN—Ravenswood, Dawson, and

Nowak. We're a small independent financial consulting firm with a half dozen associates and a fair number of well-to-do clients. You've heard of us?"

When Sydney indicated that she hadn't, he continued. "You're probably familiar with Charles Schwab. Or Edward Jones. We're like them only much smaller. Kind of a local 'boutique' version. We manage investment portfolios for people who have assembled enough wealth that they need a safe, properly diversified, and productive place to put their money. At the same time, we cater to clients who want a more personal touch than a giant company offers.

"It's a winning formula. We've been a very profitable company." He suddenly pursed his lips, hiding his gleaming teeth. "Before Harold's screw up, that is."

"Harold's screw up?"

"I'll get to that. First, let me give you a little more background. Harold and I were partners for over ten years, and I considered him a friend as well. Although I wouldn't describe us as exactly close, I liked him. He was a decent guy who really cared about his clients. Maybe a bit too much.

"The thing is, most of our clients are conservative investors. They're usually older professional people who have worked hard and built up their savings over time. They're not comfortable with high-risk, speculative opportunities. They mainly want to protect what they've saved while adding more to it than they could get from CDs. That's why a lot of them love investments like municipal bonds. Muni-bonds pay a decent return, and they're usually very safe. They typically have an entire community's tax base or hundreds of thousands or even millions of ratepayers behind them. If things go sour, the municipal government can simply raise taxes or nudge up water or power bills. Clients rely on this; losing big money on a bond fund is not something they understand or easily forgive. That's why WPPSS was such a disaster for our firm."

"I'm aware that a lot of people lost money on WPPSS," Sydney said. It would have been hard to miss the extensive news coverage about the fiasco that was colloquially referred to as *Whoops!* "But tell me more about how your firm was impacted. And why the police think *you* might have a motive for killing your partner. Although, as you may know, when people are murdered, it's often by a friend or relative. So, it's no surprise that the police would be questioning you as a suspect."

"How much detail do you want?"

"Enough context for me to understand how the WPPSS failure connects to the screw-up you mentioned."

"Well, as you probably know, WPPSS was created by the state legislature as an independent municipal corporation. For many years, it had been the public agency responsible for anticipating the regional need for electrical energy and then for creating the supply infrastructure required to meet it. Its aim was to keep Washington and the Pacific Northwest energy independent. We've been blessed with clean, inexpensive energy resources, like Columbia River hydropower. WPPSS was the public agency everyone relied upon to make sure that blessing continued."

Sydney was impressed with how business-like and professional Nowak sounded when explaining the situation with WPPSS. Maybe he wasn't all sell and no substance, after all.

"Not surprisingly, WPPSS invested heavily in nuclear power," Nowak continued. "Public utilities throughout our region signed up to purchase the energy that would be produced by five new nuclear power plants. Bonds were issued to finance the cost. And construction was well underway on three of the plants when things started to turn sour.

"As the risks and complications of nuclear power became increasingly apparent, progress slowed down, and the cost of construction skyrocketed. When the Three Mile Island incident happened in 1979, everything got way more complicated. The price for building those plants soon looked like it would run as much as ten times over budget. Meanwhile, a less-than-impressive economy, new energy conservation practices, and a more realistic assessment of demand made it clear that a fraction of the energy produced by those plants would actually be purchased. As a result, only one of the five planned plants looks like it will now be completed.

"Eighty-eight local public utilities around the Pacific Northwest had signed on to the WPPSS nuclear enterprise. When they realized that the electricity to have been produced by those nuclear plants would never be needed or delivered, those utilities sued to terminate their financial obligations in the whole enterprise. The trial court ruled against them, and they appealed. If those utilities were held responsible there would have been dramatic increases in local ratepayer energy bills, but the bondholders would have gotten their money back.

"But the Washington State Supreme Court recently reversed the trial court, and WPPSS alone became responsible for payback on all those municipal bonds. A $2.25 billion loss. Without ratepayers or a tax base, they don't have any way to pay that money back."

Nowak paused to take a sip of cooling coffee. "It looks like it's going to result in the largest municipal bond default in U.S. history."

"I take it you had a lot of clients who'd invested in those bonds?" She thought she knew the answer, but she still wasn't entirely clear where Nowak was going with the story.

"You could say that. In Harold's defense, back when those bonds came out, they seemed like gold. Our clients loved them. And so did we —they appeared to be exactly the kind of secure investment the majority of our clients preferred. They were financing a public response to the massive electrical energy demand for one of the most prosperous, rapidly growing, robust regional economies in the world. Needless to say, when things started falling apart and it all made the news, quite a few clients naturally wanted to sell their bonds. But just because a bond —or stock—has lost a lot of value doesn't mean it's necessarily wise to sell. In fact, it can be the exact opposite.

"After the initial trial court ruling, those eighty-eight public utilities were still on the hook. And, despite the expected ratepayer unhappiness, there was reason to believe that our clients would at least get repaid at face value, or at some price that would minimize their losses. A lot of people, including Harold, thought it made sense to hold onto those bonds, especially considering their greatly diminished market price. The hope was that if the bondholders stuck in there, there was the genuine possibility they could recoup most of those losses later.

"Then the State Supreme Court granted what they call 'discretionary review' and bypassed our state's intermediate Court of Appeals. If the State Supreme Court had affirmed the trial court, like Harold expected, there'd have been a sizable bump in the value of those bonds. Harold had a friend who was one of the lawyers on the appeal. The friend told Harold not to worry. That there was no way the State Supreme Court was going to throw all those investors out of the boat. So that's what Harold told us. And, idiots that we were, we didn't question his assessment. After all, he was our municipal bond expert. He was telling us to stand our ground. And that's what we did—

"By then, many of our clients were panicking and dumping their WPPSS municipals. Some were even threatening to leave our firm. Including a few of our group retirement and investment plan groups. When a group leaves, it's a serious blow. They account for a big chunk of our income. And they usually take with them a lot of individual investors as well. Fortunately, as is our policy, our clients had fairly diverse portfolios, but their losses were still unsettling.

"During that time period the firm took some major hits, but it was even worse for Harold. For him it was a financial disaster. Municipals were his specialty, and most of his clients were heavily invested in them. His client base was evaporating by the day, even clients he'd represented for years. When they decided he couldn't be trusted on WPPSS, they inevitably concluded that he couldn't be trusted on anything else either. He'd made a classic mistake by not sufficiently diversifying.

"At the same time all this was happening, Harold's wife of twenty-seven years decided to divorce him. They owned this big, expensive home in Broadmoor. They had a nice boat moored down on the Ship Canal at the Seattle Yacht Club. And they owned a valuable collection of some amazing antique jewelry—the kind of historical pieces that you show off in a glass case but no one ever actually wears. Harold was really proud of his collection. Unfortunately, all of it was divvied up in their divorce, and whatever Harold ended up keeping for himself was placed at risk by his business mistakes.

"For us at RDN, things got really tense at the end of May, a couple weeks before the Supreme Court decision on June 15. I'd heard that our receptionist was upset because she was getting a lot of calls from Harold's disgruntled clients. People were seen storming out of his office. Or they'd come in without an appointment and demand to see him immediately, and when told he was 'unavailable,' they would insist on waiting in reception until he became 'available.' For a while there, we had a reception area filled with angry people unwilling to leave without talking with him while he, apparently, was hiding in his office, door closed, afraid to come out. At one point, this big bruiser of a guy came in and threatened our receptionist when she refused to show him where Harold's office was. She had to call building security.

"Our senior partner, Cecil Ravenswood, asked me to take a closer look at Harold's accounts, and his numbers turned out to be far worse than he'd been letting on—worse than any of us imagined. I called and spoke with several of his clients, and that's how I discovered how unbelievably stupid he'd been. In anticipation of a positive Supreme Court decision, he'd actually made false representations to some clients about the real market value of their WPPSS bonds. He was outright lying to keep them from selling out their WPPSS holdings and almost certainly dumping him in the process. Then I discovered that in several cases he had, believe it or not, purchased their WPPSS bonds personally, with his own money, at an inflated price. Just so they wouldn't catch on to his lies when they insisted on selling.

"He must have borrowed a shit-pot of money to cover those lies and was obviously incurring a huge personal debt even before the court decision. Given his financial situation and how he was trying to keep it secret, I doubt very much that he got a bank loan to cover his losses. I'm pretty sure he went to a loan shark. That would explain the gorilla who threatened our receptionist—probably some kind of enforcer."

Nowak drained the rest of his coffee and shook his head "no" when Sydney offered him a refill. "I'm sure Harold believed that he'd be able to pay it all off after the Court ruled. Not an unreasonable expectation, but not a sure thing either.

"I braced him about the situation a couple of days *before* the Court's ruling. That would have been about the 13th of June. A Monday, I believe. I'll admit, I was pissed. We all were. He was engaged in a kind of fraud—a sort of backward pyramid scheme. He had to have known it would all fall apart if the Supreme Court decision didn't uphold the trial court ruling. By then, I'd discovered he'd already sold off everything he still owned after his divorce. With all that debt and no backup plan, he'd put us all at risk as well.

"We had a heated argument about it at the office. I told him I had to advise Cecil Ravenswood of his situation. After all, Cecil and I had to look out for our own clients. And for our associates and their clients. He begged me to hold off till after the court ruled. As a friend, I wanted to support him. But I couldn't. The whole point was that we needed to fully inform and make this right with *our* clients *and with his,* and do that *before* the court ruled. That was the legal and ethically right thing to do. I told him that he needed to fully and fairly explain the risks to his clients and give them the informed opportunity to bail if they wanted to do so.

"Clearly, he'd bet *everything* on that court decision. He knew that if he was wrong, he was going to lose it all. He wanted us to save him by making the same bet.

"During our confrontation, he got really angry with me. Even though we were in the conference room with the door closed, I knew some of our staff could hear us—it got pretty loud. I'm guessing that's why those Sheriff's detectives are convinced that there was bad blood between us. I tried to explain the situation to the detectives, but they apparently have limited capacity to endure complexity. So, when they started asking me about my hunting rifle, I finally said I wanted a lawyer. That seemed to irritate them and make them even more suspicious.

"When they finally cut me loose, one of them poked me in the chest with his finger and told me: 'We'll be *seeing you again,* Mr. Nowak.' I didn't like the way that sounded one bit. That's when I decided to come to you."

"I can see why you felt threatened. But let's go back to what happened after your argument with Dawson."

"It wasn't good. Harold stopped coming into the office, and he wouldn't answer his phone. We were all worried about him. He was in a desperate situation. I wanted to help, if I could. But the firm was in trouble, too; that had to be my first priority."

"Did you go by his home to find out what was going on?"

"I wish I had, but I was busy at work and, I confess, like Harold, I thought things would improve after the State Supreme Court Decision. Were we wrong about that!

"The day the Court decision came down, we were all in shock. I tried to get in touch with Harold, but he wouldn't answer his phone. Then, the next morning, he picked up and said he wanted to meet and talk. That made me hopeful that he hadn't given up on me as a friend. Of course, everyone at RDN was furious with him, so when he suggested a time and place to meet outside of the office where, as he said, we could talk freely, I agreed."

"Where did he ask to meet?"

"Two Mountain Creek parking lot. That seemed a bit strange, but it's only a half-hour drive from downtown in light mid-day traffic. And we used to go up there to hunt, so I was familiar with the area."

"That's where they found the body?"

"Yes, some hikers found him Friday afternoon, just before noon. The police say he died a couple of hours before that—somebody shot him on one of the wooden footbridges that crosses the creek. It was a through-and-through head wound. They think the weapon was a rifle. I read in the Times that, at least as of yesterday, they haven't found the bullet, the shell casing, or the gun.

"If they're right about the timing, I was there when it happened—in my car in the parking lot. At one point, I thought I heard a gunshot. But in the woods, it isn't that unusual, so I didn't pay much attention."

Sydney wasn't easily surprised by what clients told her. But Nowak's revelations were startling. And hugely concerning. He'd agreed to meet at a wilderness park. He knew his friend was there somewhere because his car was in the parking lot. Then he hears a gunshot but isn't concerned when his friend doesn't show up?

"OK, so I have to ask," she said. "What did you think was going to happen when you met?"

"Well, the day when we'd had that argument in the office, he'd been really mad. He called me a 'traitor.' Said I'd betrayed our friendship. That kind of thing hurts, you know. But when he called that morning, he seemed calm. Said he'd given the situation some thought and told me he still had a few personal assets to liquidate. He said he thought he could cover some of the firm's losses too, and we needed to talk about options."

That seemed reasonable, but the place and timing still seemed off to Sydney. There was a key question she needed him to answer. "What did you think when he didn't show up?"

"He hadn't been behaving normally for a while, so I wasn't sure what to think. Maybe he'd arrived early and gone for a walk up one of the trails and lost track of time. Or he'd had second thoughts, changed his mind about how he wanted to proceed and wasn't ready to talk about it yet. I just didn't know what his game was. But I was frustrated and didn't want to hang around all day waiting for him to show."

"Did you tell anyone else about the meeting?"

"No one. I wanted to hear what he had to say before mentioning it. And there was no one around when I talked with him on the phone."

"Do you think he could have told someone about your planned meeting?"

He shook his head. "Doesn't seem very likely, does it? I mean considering why we were meeting and what we planned to talk about, I'm guessing he kept it to himself, like me. Still, someone must have followed him up there and shot him. Maybe one of his disgruntled clients. Or maybe the loan shark enforcer. Like I said, there were lots of people upset with him. Unless it was totally random, which seems unlikely."

"So, how long did you wait?"

"Almost an hour. I mean, his car was there, so I kept thinking he was going to show up. I was pretty upset, but then decided that if he'd changed his mind and didn't want to talk, it was on him. Finally, I gave up, drove back to the office, and worked late. I half expected a call from him apologizing for not showing. I didn't hear about him being killed until I went home that night and saw it on the news."

Sydney contemplated what Dawson had told her for a few moments. His story was odd in places but seemed plausible overall. There was, however, one more thing she needed to know. Something that might make it three out of three: motive, opportunity, *and* means. "You mentioned that the police asked you about a hunting rifle?"

"Yeah. I own a Marlin 336. It's a .30-30 lever-action hunting rifle. It was them asking about my rifle that made me start to worry." Nowak suddenly blinked several times, shook his head, and said, "Damn."

"What is it?"

"Probably nothing. My rifle. I keep it in a locker at a shooting range. Use of a locker is included in the membership fee. That way we don't need to carry our firearms with us coming and going. Harold had a locker there too."

"The two of you were members of the same sportsman's club?"

Nowak nodded. "It's not exactly a club. More a commercial shooting range. They call us 'members,' but we basically pay a monthly rental and usage fee."

"Do you know any of the other members?"

"Kind of. In passing. People come and go, some are regulars, but they're all there to shoot, not to socialize."

"You and Harold would shoot there together?"

"Not often. Sometimes."

"You're sure your rifle is there?"

"I can't see why it wouldn't be. But I should check."

"Actually, Mr. Nowak, I don't think you should go there. Let's have you stay away from that club and from your rifle for now. You have a key for the locker on you?"

"It's a combination lock."

"Why don't you give me that combination. And the location of the club. I'll have one of our people stop by and secure your rifle."

"Then you'll represent me?" He sounded as though he'd had some doubts in spite of his generally over-confident demeanor. Perhaps he'd sensed her initial hesitancy. However, during their conversation, she'd started to see things from his perspective. She still didn't care for the man, but she thought he just might be telling her the truth. Unfortunately, a good story without facts to back it up didn't necessarily count for much in a criminal trial.

"Yes," she said, wondering even as she did so whether she was making a big mistake by taking on Nowak as a client.

After giving him detailed instructions on the nature of their attorney-client relationship and the confidentiality of their communications, she told him in no uncertain terms not to speak with the police without her present. She had him sign their firm's standard representation contract and another form that provided authorization to access his locker and to take possession of his gun. The sizeable retainer he paid was more than sufficient to cover her preliminary investigation.

Unfortunately, the next time she saw Jamison Nowak he was a guest at the King County Jail.

Chapter 6

Sydney Warren
Preston-Martin Building, Seattle
Law Offices of Warren and Carmichael
Friday, June 24, 1983

Immediately after Nowak left her office, Sydney made two phone calls. The first was to a firearms analysis company and the second was to Mel Marshall. Sydney had first met Mel when she was a new associate attorney at the Seattle law firm of Steiner, Bentley, and Waterhouse, and since she and Duncan had started their firm, they had come to rely heavily on him for his investigative skills.

Mel was a former Tacoma cop who'd quit the force 20 years earlier to start the Seattle firm known as First Class Credit and Collections, now one of the more successful collection agencies in the region. Although Mel still owned the business, he had a general manager in charge of operations. Mel wasn't directly involved anymore, but he had held onto his former CEO office and ran his PI business from there.

"Mel. There's something I'd like you to take care of," she said. "Any chance you've got some time this afternoon or tomorrow? I realize it's the weekend."

Mel laughed. "Worry not—weekdays, weekends, it's all the same to me. I'm well past having a life of my own."

"Good—for me if not for you. I'm going to messenger over a signed 'authorization' form. I have something I need you to do— today, if possible. Tomorrow morning at the latest."

"This afternoon will probably work. Um, authorization for what?"

"I'm representing a man named Jamison Nowak. He owns a 30-caliber hunting rifle. It's in a locker up at a shooting range near Issaquah. I need you to drive up there and pick it up."

"OK." Mel sounded puzzled but didn't interrupt with questions.

"You'll need to show the authorization to the people at the shooting range. Then go to Nowak's locker and retrieve the rifle. The combination will be in the envelope with the authorization form, along with a telephone number for Jonesy from Jones Brothers in case you can't do this until tomorrow."

"The firearms analysis people?"

"Yes. It's important that you deliver it directly to Jones Brothers immediately after you retrieve the rifle. Get a receipt from them. If you can't make it till tomorrow, call Jonesy and let him know. After you pick it up, he will meet you at Jones Brothers to log it in."

"If chain of custody is important, you must think a crime may have been committed with this rifle."

"I'm hoping that isn't the case." Sydney knew what Mel was thinking. He didn't want to end up suspected of tampering with evidence. "You shouldn't have anything to worry about, Mel. Not if you're following my instructions. And not if you're delivering it directly to an unimpeachable expert seeking bona-fide services in good faith. At this point, it is our understanding that it is NOT a weapon used in a murder. We just want to make absolutely certain of that before the prosecution seizes the gun and we end up having to fight for the privilege of having it properly assessed by *our own* experts."

"This sounds like an interesting case, Sydney. I will deliver it as instructed. But some day I hope to hear more of the details. Fair enough?"

"Fair enough."

Sydney forked the last few pieces of lettuce from the take-out salad she had eaten to carry her over until she could finish up a few things and head for home. She was surprised to see that she managed to also devour almost half a container of mixed nuts she had opened only yesterday. Tall and thin, she didn't need to worry about calories, but she did think it was good to eat a healthy diet. With her busy schedule, that wasn't always easy.

It was almost 6:00 when Sydney got a call from Mel. She answered it on the first ring.

"Bad news," he said the instant she answered.

Sydney had feared there might be a hitch, but she still felt a surge of disappointment even before Mel gave her the details.

"I stopped by that shooting range/sportsman's club like you asked. And, once the manager saw the signed 'authorization' from your client, he was completely cooperative. Showed me the locker himself."

"And . . .?"

"No rifle."

"Damn."

"Um, sorry, Syd, but that's not the really bad news. Unfortunately, the police were there ahead of me. With a warrant. Which suggests they're circling the wagons around your client as a suspect. And now they know his rifle is missing because the locker was empty when they looked earlier. The manager gave me the full story before showing me the locker but let me look inside in case there was something left to find. There wasn't."

"How about the victim, Harold Dawson. He supposedly had a locker there too. Did the manager mention anything about the police checking his locker?"

"Yes, he told me all about it. He's quite the gossip. And apparently a believer that any publicity is good publicity for the shooting range. He told me that they found a rifle in Dawson's locker, and he heard them say it was clean and unfired. The police impounded it, though I'm not sure why. Covering all their bases, I'd guess."

"What kind of place is it, Mel? What's there?"

"It's in an area that's surrounded by National Forest. Modern. Decent layout. Has first-class firing ranges, indoors and out. A comfortable coffee-shop that seems popular with their members. A modest gun and ammo shop. A couple of nice big conference rooms for classes, meetings, and the like. Freshly paved entry road and parking lot. And busy—even on a weekday afternoon."

"How about the lockers? They look secure?"

"I'd say so. I think I'd feel quite comfortable leaving a weapon there. The locker area is the other side of a wall behind the reception desk, so nobody but members get in. Lockers are heavy steel—tougher than what you find in a school or a gym. Customers bring their own locks— as you know, Nowak's uses a combination. A sturdy-looking lock. Be pretty tough to break into, I'd say, unless you knew the combination. Although it could be done.

"Then there's the fact that it's a gun club, right? Not a place you'd want to get caught tampering with someone else's locker. Of course, someone could have broken in after hours. I didn't check their overall security, but given the look of the place and the fact that they provide lockers for guns, I'm guessing they have something top-of-the-line."

"Cameras in the locker room?"

"None that I saw; they may consider it a privacy issue or somehow related to the Second Amendment. I walked around outside; any cameras out there were well hidden. My guess is that their members might not be happy about Big Brother watching them. But I'm still fairly certain there's some surveillance system in place. I didn't think you'd want me to ask about it, but you might want to check with your client about the last time he was there."

"How about the location of Nowak's locker. Is it fairly visible? Public?"

"Yes and no. The lockers are in a series of alcoves. Not everyone who passes through would be looking right at them, but they aren't exactly private." He paused, and Sydney could almost "see" him visualizing the locker room. "I guess if you were a member, or did a good job of pretending to be one, and waited for the right opportunity, you could probably open someone else's locker without anyone noticing. Especially if you had the key or a combination."

"How would someone get his combination though? He told me no one else has it."

"Reconnaissance. If you knew what you were doing, it wouldn't be that hard to look over someone's shoulder to cop their combination—either directly or with a mirror or even with a camera if you could do it discreetly. People in familiar surroundings like that are often way more trusting than they should be."

"That makes sense. You get focused on what you're doing and lose track of what's going on around you. I've done that."

"All in all, the place seems good. I'm thinking about getting in some practice time there myself. Do you and Duncan still shoot?

"Not often. Duncan and his wife Kate shoot sometimes—self-defense prep, that kind of thing."

"Sorry I didn't have better news."

Sydney was more disappointed than she wanted to admit, but it hadn't changed her mind about taking the case. "By the way," she said, "I know I didn't ask you to investigate the victim, Harold Dawson, but in talking to the manager, did you happen to learn anything interesting about him?"

"Nothing much from the manager, but, I confess, I couldn't resist doing a little research—nothing extensive, just checked to see if anything big popped up. Nothing you probably don't already know, though. Like the fact that the guy was in deep financial trouble. It wasn't that long ago that Dawson and his family were living large in this big mansion in Broadmoor. Then it all fell apart. His business went sour. He and his wife got divorced. They sold off assets. Wife managed to buy a condo in West Seattle. Husband ended up in debt and living in a rental house in North Seattle. Pretty sad story, really."

"Ending in murder, so 'pretty sad' is an understatement."

"Anything else I can do for you to make your life miserable?"

"Yeah, one thing. I'd like to know more about the ex-wife. Why don't you bill me for what you've already done, and then take a look at her and a closer look at him. Divorces can be messy. Maybe there's something there."

"Okay, how deep do you want me to dig?"

"Not too deep, unless you find something suspicious. Then check with me before putting in a lot of time on it."

"Will do."

Chapter 7

Sydney Warren
King County Superior Court
Arraignment: Judge Roberta Francis presiding
Wednesday, June 29, 1983

"State vs Jamison Nowak. Murder one."

"Walter Rice for the State of Washington, Your Honor."

"Sydney Warren for the defense, Your Honor"

"How does the Defendant plead, Ms. Warren?"

"Not guilty, Your Honor. And we move for the defendant's release on his own personal recognizance. Mr. Nowak is a lifelong Seattleite. He is a partner of many years in a respected local financial consulting firm whose clients and colleagues will suffer if he is jailed for an extended time. He has family who reside in this area. He has a clean record. And the case against him is highly circumstantial. There is no physical evidence, no eye-witnesses—and they haven't yet found a likely murder weapon. The police were clearly premature in making their arrest.

"Furthermore, Your Honor, we strongly suspect this murder was committed by criminal elements linked to the decedent, Harold Dawson, and to his deeply compromised financial situation resulting from the recent messy WPPSS bond default. The police have stumbled upon a simplistic answer to what seems likely to have been a very complex crime. My client needs to be out of jail so he can assist with his own defense."

"Mr. Rice?" The judge looked at him over a pair of half-frame readers balanced on her long, straight nose.

"The State opposes bail, Your Honor. If the defense feels the case lacks probable cause, they're free to argue that in a proper motion to dismiss. But we know they won't do that because the defendant admits he was physically present at the time the decedent was killed. It happened in a wooded public forest reserve east of Seattle. The victim was likely killed with a hunting rifle, and the defendant, an excellent marksman, owns such a rifle. Naturally, it has 'mysteriously' gone missing from a secure, undamaged locker at a shooting range in Issaquah. Just three days before the killing, the defendant was overheard in a bitter argument with the victim over business matters which have caused considerable financial losses to the defendant who, I might add, has more than enough wherewithal to easily leave this jurisdiction at any time he may wish."

Sydney held her breath. Judge Francis had a reputation as pro-defense. But Sydney knew that reputation had arisen because Francis mistrusted the "system" to protect the rights of minorities and the poor. Jamison Nowak definitely did *not* fit that description—rather, he was a poster boy for the exact opposite. Sydney had advised him that bail might be a long shot. Unfortunately, she was right.

"The defendant will be held without bail," said the judge, shaking her head. She looked in Sydney's direction: "Counsel, I assume you will want a speedy trial?"

"We will, Your Honor."

"Very well, let's get a trial judge assigned and get this matter underway."

❧

After the hearing, Sydney waited out in the hall for the prosecutor to exit the courtroom. She'd been told that Walter Rice wasn't just handling the arraignment; he had also been assigned the prosecution itself. It was good news and bad. The good news was that Rice was relatively young and inexperienced to be taking the lead on a murder case, especially one with a public profile like this one. The bad news was that he was smart, capable, and very ambitious. Sydney had dealt with Rice before. She'd found him to be professional and competent. This case could be an important benchmark for him as a career prosecutor.

When Rice exited the courtroom, he was on the phone. She waived at him, and he nodded, holding up a finger for her to wait. Then he stepped to one side of the hall to complete his call, joining her when he was through.

"Ready to change your plea so soon?" said Rice with a smile. His clean-shaven face was lightly tanned, as if he'd recently spent a few hours in the sun. He looked and acted like he was ready to take on the world.

Sydney ignored the jibe. "Ready to see some actual evidence," she replied. "You know that everything you have is circumstantial. My client voluntarily, willingly even, aided your detectives' investigation. Answered their questions. Treated them with respect. All because he has an interest in finding the *real* killer. In exchange, I would hope that you and your team remain open to other possibilities and follow up on alternative theories. The least you can do is give my client the benefit of the doubt. And the sooner you get me some serious discovery, the sooner we can help you identify who really did this."

"We wouldn't have filed charges if we didn't have a case, Syd. You'll get your evidence by the omnibus hearing."

She didn't think they knew each other well enough for him to call her "Syd." She chalked it up to male arrogance. His frat boy geniality didn't play well with her, and the exchange convinced her that there would be little accommodation or flexibility from the prosecution. Now that the case was in court, any further investigation on their part would undoubtedly be a search for whatever might prove them right, nothing more. Why waste your time looking at other suspects if you already had the guilty party in a cage?

In the two weeks following Harold Dawson's murder, even before Nowak's arrest and preliminary hearing, the case had become big news. Then, following his arrest, media interest became even more intense. As did the apparent, if attenuated, connection with the WPPSS default. In the days preceding the arraignment, media interest had become downright frenzied. "Victim and partner argued over WPPSS DEBACLE" screamed one headline in bold caps. "Luxury Broadmoor home of WPPSS victim sold for $2.7 million," announced another. Before long, the media tagged the high-profile case as "The WPPSS Murder." The shooter was labeled the "WPPSS Killer." Jamison Nowak become a sensationalized, public villain. In addition to being accused of murdering Dawson, media coverage of the case strangely implied that Nowak was somehow personally linked to the WPPSS default as well. The absurdity of the connection wasn't addressed. Nor, of course, was any possibility that Nowak might actually be innocent.

Even given all the publicity, Sydney did not anticipate the fusillade of flashbulbs and the onslaught of questions she encountered following the arraignment. As she stepped out through the courthouse door onto a crowded third Avenue sidewalk, she found herself surrounded by a cluster of determined reporters. For a fleeting moment she was glad she'd worn her stylish grey pin-stripe pants suit and had taken care to pin up her long dark hair.

"The judge denied your client bail. Does that mean he's a flight risk, Ms. Warren?" yelled one reporter as he elbowed people on either side of him and shoved a microphone in her direction.

"Of course not. Mr. Nowak is a responsible citizen, a family man, and he is innocent of these charges."

"What does your client have to say to the Dawson family?" called out another.

Sydney simply shook her head to indicate she had nothing to add and continued wending her way through the crowd.

Suddenly, a well-dressed, pleasant looking young man stepped in front of her and held a microphone just inches from her lips while a colleague to his left pointed a big TV camera directly at her: "Will Mr. Nowak be paying back all of his firm's bondholder clients who lost money in the WPPSS collapse?" He made it sound like that was something Nowak *should* do. It made no sense, and this was not the time or place for that conversation.

"No further comment." Syndney waited for the man to step aside.

When he didn't, she tried to maneuver around him. He sidestepped to stay squarely in front of her, and the camera kept staring. "That was what your client argued about with the victim, correct?" His voice was louder than it needed to be given that he was standing so close.

"Would you mind stepping aside?" She kept her voice calm and low, but it wasn't a request. He hesitated only briefly before lowering the mic.

Before she could escape, he leaned toward her and asked: "Any chance of an interview with you later? Maybe over coffee?" He spoke softly, like the exchange was just between the two of them, but she knew from experience how sensitive those microphones were.

She put her lips close to his ear and whispered: "No chance in hell." Then she smiled to the crowd, sidestepped abruptly, and managed to slip away.

Thankfully, none of the reporters followed.

CHAPTER 8

Duncan Carmichael
Preston Martin Building, Seattle
Law Offices of Warren and Carmichael
Friday, July 8, 1983

"We need to talk."

As usual, Duncan had knocked on the closed office door before immediately pushing it partly open and peering in. He caught Sydney at her desk surrounded by paperwork with her Dictaphone mic in her hand. Wispy strands of hair had escaped from the clasp that held it back. Her jacket was slung across the back of one of her client chairs, and there was an open container of almonds nestled amongst her papers.

"This a bad time?"

She smiled, laid down the mic, and waved him in. "Now's fine. Just pulling together a brief in my civil rights case."

Duncan couldn't help grinning as he pushed the door open, stepped inside, and closed it behind him. Sydney always seemed to have at least one active civil rights case in the works. As well as a few criminal defenses—usually they were cases for defendants who were being unfairly treated by what she feared was a deeply biased and unfair criminal justice system. She was the crusader in their office. Dealing with grieving survivors, angry families, disillusioned true believers. The kind of things that would have kept him up at night.

He, on the other hand, after leaving the Navy had avoided criminal defense work. Several years in Navy JAGC had confirmed his preference for handling civil matters. His was a general practice specializing in maritime law and insurance defense as well as estate planning and probate. The cases he handled tended to focus on factual evidence and didn't feel as morally fraught to him as Sydney's criminal cases.

"I have a client we need to discuss," Duncan said, taking a seat across from her. "I've been asked to handle her father's estate. I told her yes, but conditioned it on us not having a conflict of interest. Her father was Harold Dawson, the investment consultant who died. I gather you're representing Jamison Nowak, the man accused of Dawson's murder."

Sydney sat back and laid down her mic, her sharp blues eyes alert. "When did this happen?"

"She came in at 10:00 this morning. I helped her last month with a 'pay and allowances' issue with the Navy. But now she needs someone to handle her dad's estate. Her mother, Dawson's ex, is willing to foot the bill—as long as it doesn't get too complicated and take too many hours to resolve.

"She doesn't actually know Nowak, but she of course knows who he is. I think they both may have been here in our office at around the same time a few weeks ago. This morning I told her I had to talk with you about whether there's a conflict of interest that would prevent me from handling her case. For my client, it's mostly a matter of closing the door on a clutch of hungry creditors. She keeps getting calls and demands for payment. She wants to clean the slate so she can shut down the harassment and move on."

"Is there anything specific that you think could become a conflict of interest?"

"Not that I know of, but I wanted to check with you before I make any commitment."

"Well, I can certainly raise the issue with *my* client, but it seems to me that if anyone has an objection, it would be *your* client. After all, it's her lawyer's partner who is defending a man charged with murdering her father."

"She said she's fine with it and is willing to sign a disclosure and release statement. She's staying with her mother here in Seattle, so she can easily swing back by. I think she doesn't want the hassle of finding a new lawyer. And I've been working cheap. She's a Navy wife facing some financial challenges and needs to get her father's estate settled."

"OK, I'll ask Nowak, but I'm sure he'll agree. He has bigger things to worry about."

Duncan stood, then paused. "There is one further bit of information I wanted to share that might be helpful."

"Something you learned from your client?"

"Yes. Nothing confidential though. It's about someone who paid her mother a visit at her condo over on Alki Way while my client was there. A debt collector, apparently."

"A collection agency is already going after Dawson's assets? That's fast. He's only been dead for, what, just over a week?"

"Yeah, well, that's the thing. The way she described it, he sounded to me more like a loan shark enforcer than a legitimate debt collector. She described him as a big muscled bruiser. Pushed his way into her mother's apartment. Walked around like he owned the place. Then he showed them what he said was a signed promissory note for two hundred fifty thousand dollars. He told them that, with interest, they now owed a lot more—over five hundred twenty thousand dollars. Both agreed that it looked like Dawson's signature, so they were understandably upset. The guy made it clear that the person he represented wasn't about to wait around for probate only to be put on some list with other people Dawson owed money to. He insisted they give him the money *right away,* all five hundred twenty thousand . . . *or else.*"

"That's not good."

"Both of them were scared out of their wits."

Sydney paused in thought. "A loan shark enforcer? Interesting."

"Does that mean something to you?"

"Well, before Dawson was murdered, someone came to Dawson and Nowak's business office, RDN Financial Services, demanded to talk to Dawson and didn't want to take no for an answer. He was described by the receptionist as a big tough guy, and she felt threatened enough to call security. Do you think it could have been the same person?"

Duncan shrugged, gave her a broad smile, and wiggled his eyebrows. "My gift to you. A 'some-other-dude' defense."

She knew he was referring to a common fallback criminal defense in which the claim was that the crime was committed by "some-other-dude," someone it might or might not be possible to specifically iden-tify, but a person who also had motive and opportunity. The "some-other-dude" defense was used when nothing else would work to provide "reasonable doubt."

"It doesn't really surprise me," Sydney said. "Dawson was in some serious financial trouble. He had a lot of people mad at him. My client suspected that he may have borrowed money from a loan shark to fore-stall going belly up. But no way to prove it. Did your client or her mother have any ideas about who this guy represented?"

Duncan handed her a sheet of paper. "He gave them this copy of the signed note from AA Best Bet Bail Bonds. It's pretty standard. Twelve-percent annual interest. Lawful on its face. But sometimes these places don't limit themselves to lending bail money. They also have a separate corporation, a registered lender that makes consumer and other loans. AA Best Bet has offices on Third Avenue not far from the King County Courthouse. You'll also notice this signed note is only for two-hundred-fifty thousand. Whereas the guy's demand was for over twice that. Prob-ably vig. They were carrying the loan for about six months, a long time for a loan shark. I'm guessing they'll end up making a claim against the estate for the two-fifty plus legal interest. And then try to intimidate the women for the rest of it."

"If you're right about there being nothing left in the estate, what good will that do?"

"The daughter's husband ran off, and she lost her job, so there's no way she can pay even part of that loan. But the mother is in a slightly better position. She owns a two-bedroom condo and has some modest savings. And, as you can imagine, the two of them are terrified. They don't know what to do."

"It's probably a bluff. Once the holder of the note realizes there's no money, or very little, they'll likely back off."

"That's what I told them. They called the police, but according to them, the responding officers didn't seem impressed. My client told me that her mother has purchased a gun for self-protection. We both know all the reasons why that was a bad idea. But you can't really blame her."

"No, but I don't see anything good coming out of any of this."

"At least you have a potentially plausible back-up shooter now. The 'other dude.'"

"Thanks for that. I may well use it, though I hope I don't have to. It reeks of desperation. But at this point, all I have is a client who claims he's innocent. That isn't likely to sway a judge or a jury."

"If there's any way I can help . . .?"

"Not sure how, unless you have a more solid legal defense strategy in your jacket pocket. Something better than the 'other dude.'"

"I left my jacket in my office; I'll check the pockets when I go back, just in case."

Sydney's shoulders drooped, as if she suddenly felt the weight of what she was facing. "Nowak's trial is only a couple of months down the road. I'd hate to let an innocent guy down."

"You think he's innocent?" As usual, Duncan was doubtful.

"I'm not convinced that he's guilty."

"Spoken like a true criminal defense attorney."

CHAPTER 9

Sydney Warren
Preston-Martin Building, Seattle
Law Offices of Warren and Carmichael
Later Friday, July 8, 1983

As soon as Duncan walked out of her office, Sydney called Mel Marshall to ask him to investigate AA Best Bet Bail Bonds, Inc. as part of the "some-other-dude" defense based on the paperwork Duncan's client received. Mel didn't answer his phone, so she had to leave a message and said that if he needed more information to call her back.

Mel returned her call a little after seven that evening. The office receptionist was long gone. As usual, after hours, Sydney answered the call herself.

"Glad I caught you," Mel said. "Working late on a Friday evening—what a surprise." He chuckled. "Your message said you wanted me to take a look into AA Best Bet Bail Bonds. I've done some digging, and I think you'll find it interesting."

"Where are you?"

"Right now I'm in a phone booth outside the 5 Spot Diner at the top of the Queen Anne Counterbalance. I've got the file with me. I'd be glad to drop my report by your office in the a.m."

"How long do you think you'll be there?"

"I'm working a domestic. Husband and girlfriend are inside. They just ordered dinner, so . . . a while, I'd guess."

"Stay put—if you can. Traffic permitting, I'll be there in fifteen minutes. If I miss you, I'll look for it tomorrow morning." Sydney was ready to call it a night, and the 5 Spot was only a matter of blocks from her home. She rented the second floor in an older Queen Anne Hill house overlooking Puget Sound.

"Come inside when you get here. You can join me for coffee. It'll help my cover."

Sydney had parking karma and arrived at the 5 Spot almost exactly fifteen minutes after they talked on the phone. Mel was on a stool at the 5 Spot's long lunch-counter, his back to her when she entered. In the years since she'd first met him, he'd gone from black curly to close-cropped greying hair. But he still wore neutral-colored clothing that did not stand out; she guessed that was the point. He was just finishing a slice of apple pie, chatting with the waitress while she refreshed his coffee. She removed his plate and left as Sydney slid onto the empty stool beside him.

"Your 'party' still here?"

"In the booth over there." He nodded slightly in the direction of the booth. "But I think not for long. They've almost finished their food, and I'd say their minds are not on dessert. At least not here."

Sydney took a surreptitious glance. The happy couple were leaning toward each other, intimately picking at what remained of their food with one hand while holding hands across their small table with the other. They were engaged in what appeared to be soul-searching and flirtatious eye contact.

"I see what you mean." She waived at the waitress and pointed at Mel's coffee and then at herself. "I feel sorry for the wife."

"I don't think the girlfriend is in it for a 'forever after' relationship either. That's not usually the way it works with situations like this."

The waitress came over with a cup of coffee for Sydney and quickly departed. Sydney turned to Mel and asked, "What 'cha got for me?"

Mel pulled a thin, number 10 manila envelope from the inside breast pocket of his well-worn brown sport coat and handed it over. "AA Best Bet is fairly well known around town. They do sell bail bonds, but according to my sources, that's mostly cover. They're lenders. I hope you're not looking to borrow money."

"Not nice people?"

"Not if you can't repay."

"They capable of violence? Would they consider 'eliminating' someone who wouldn't or couldn't pay?"

Mel gave that some thought. "They're certainly capable of diminishing a debtor's quality of life. Killing, on the other hand, isn't typically a sound business practice for a lender. And it's risky. I don't think that's as popular in real life as it is in the movies."

"Did you find out anything about their collector, or if they have more than one?"

"They may use different people for collections, but they have one they use a lot. His info's in the envelope. Name's Grant Meade. He's their official leg-breaker."

"Tell me about him. What kind of witness would he make?"

"Well, I'm not sure what you're looking for here, Sydney, but he wouldn't be someone whose credibility I'd count on to make my case. That what you mean?"

"Not exactly. Just trying to figure out where he fits in on a couple of cases. So, a tough guy?"

"He was arrested for assault several years back. Was in a bar brawl and beat a guy senseless. Got a deferred prosecution because he was underage and the other guy had it coming. He may not be as mean as he looks, but he definitely looks mean. He's maybe six five and weighs, at a guess, 280. Big muscled arms. A scar on his chin. Tats on his fingers. Probably all assets for the kind of work he does. Not someone a jury's likely to take to, but he could definitely be an alternate suspect."

"You've read my mind." Sydney took a long drink of coffee. "You know where he lives?"

"No. But if you're looking to serve a subpoena, he'll be easy to find. He spends a lot of time playing pool at that little bar across Third from the courthouse. When he isn't playing pool, he's out visiting one of the firm's debtors, or chasing down a bail-jumper. Most times you can probably catch up with him at Best Bet. When I dropped by to check it out, I noticed they have a back room, probably a place for their *employees* to hang out when they aren't busy harassing people. As you know, I don't serve process, but whoever you ask to do this, you might suggest that they not hang around for a 'thank you' after handing over the paperwork."

While he was talking, she'd opened Mel's envelope and was scanning his written report. "He looks perfect. Hope he doesn't have a solid alibi."

"Sounds like you don't think he's a likely prime suspect."

"I have no idea if he's a viable suspect, but he made a visit to the victim's office and intimidated the staff, and he also threatened the victim's daughter and ex-wife. My goal is to take the heat off of my client and to get the police to consider other suspects. Like him. Which they haven't done to this point."

Mel nodded. "Happens all the time. The police are swamped. If someone looks good for a crime, it's hard to keep searching for other suspects. Just makes things more complicated and arrest records look bad."

"But when they know the victim is a financial advisor with serious money problems, you'd think they'd take a good look around at who they may have ticked off instead of going for the easiest target."

"And who he'd borrowed money from. They wouldn't have had to dig too deep to discover his connection with AA Best Bet."

"He signed what looks like a legal note at 12% interest. Then the lender demanded repayment for a lot more. Does that make sense to you?"

"Perfect sense. Profits from loan sharking can be laundered through 'bad debts' in the bail bond and lending business. As a business plan, it probably works great. The signed note is cover. It makes everything look legit if the authorities come sniffing around. After all, AA Best Bet is a licensed lender. Completely legit on their face. It's the extra fees a needy borrower agrees to orally or with a handshake where the real money is made. The actual loan amount may have been for the $250,000 shown on the note. But I guarantee the debtor will have owed one whole hell-of-a lot more in weekly vig than a mere 12% annual interest."

"As ruthless as a real shark."

"And a lot more dangerous."

Sydney tapped the envelope with two fingers. "Thanks for this," she said. "This Grant Meade sounds like he could be the one I'm looking for."

"You'll get my invoice. Payment will be all the thanks I need."

Mel glanced over in the direction of his target. They were still lingering over the remains of their dinner.

"You must like your work," Sydney said, taking a sip of coffee. "Here you are, late on a Friday night, staking out adulterers."

"What can I say? It pays the bills."

She hesitated. "Come on, Mel. You don't need to do surveillance work. You could hire someone to do it and save the fun stuff for yourself."

"There's not much on TV on a Friday evening. And I'm between wives at present."

"You have someone lined up for number two?"

"It isn't easy for a middle-aged black man to find the perfect woman. But there's always hope."

"Not if you spend your Friday evenings like this."

"I guess your date must be outside waiting for you in the car . . ."

"If that's a question, no, I can't seem to find the time to meet anyone. Besides, I like being cover for a covert op." Sydney laughed. "Okay, changing the subject. It's none of my business, but I'm curious: how did you go from being a police officer to running a collections company? You've never said."

"Well, both are in the law enforcement business. Cops deal with criminals, and collections professionals deal with debtors. Unfortunately, in both instances, it can sometimes be easy to forget that people in trouble are still people. When I first started the business, I frequently felt bad about going after some of the debtors we were hired to collect from. Some poor sod whose every spare dime goes to keeping a roof over his family's heads gets his wages garnished and then misses a rent payment. Or, we have to repossess the three-year-old Ford pickup truck needed for the landscaping business of a hard-working immigrant whose wealthy clients can't be bothered to pay him in a timely manner. Or, we put pressure to pay some late bill on a single mom trying to raise three kids on what she can earn from her waitress job. On the other hand, these people may be down-and-out, but they *do* owe someone or some company money, quite possibly someone who deserves to be repaid.

"You'd be surprised who some of our clients are—hospitals, nonprofits, funeral homes, a neighborhood grocery, all kinds of small businesses . . . you name a service or product and someone has tried to stiff them. For all sorts of reasons. Over the years, I've had to remind myself that these organizations and people owed are sometimes barely getting by too.

"At least my employees are trained to treat people with respect and go by the book. As for me, I appreciate that it's been a profitable business. And it's allowed me to branch out and do some work that I find a bit less morally challenging."

He nodded ever so slightly in the direction of the extramarital couple happily eyeing each other at their table in the adjacent dining room. "Not that this PI stuff is all white-hat work. But at least I can pretend it's somehow in aid of 'truth and justice.'" He made air quotes with his fingers to make his point. Then he looked at her with a sardonic grin and one raised eyebrow. "Your case, for instance. It's all about the pursuit of justice—even if you have to sometimes color outside the lines, right?" He pointed a finger at the envelope in her hands that contained his report. "A month from now, when you defend your *innocent* client accused of murder, you're going to use that to make sure the truth rises to the top." He gave her a tight little grin.

Sydney nodded. "I admit there are some grey areas I have to navigate. And truth doesn't always rise to the top. But someone has to hold people, even the authorities, accountable for their actions." Sydney smiled and pushed a strand of long hair behind an ear. "I guess we're in our jobs for similar reasons. And we face similar challenges."

"The bail bonds people would probably make the same argument about accountability, but I'd like to think we are a bit higher up on the ethical ladder." He took a sip of what must have been cold coffee and nodded as if that settled the matter.

Mel's targets suddenly stood and began gathering their belongings, reaching for their coats piled on an empty chair at the table, getting ready to leave.

"Coffee time is over," Mel said with a grin. "The fight for truth and justice calls."

They walked to the door together. Once outside, she headed back to her car. She knew exactly how she planned to use Mel's information. But how that might help advance the cause of truth and justice was a good deal less clear.

CHAPTER 10

The Bright family
Central Cascades
Two Mountain Creek
Sunday, July 10, 1983

"Timothy . . .! TIMOTHY!" Marjorie Bright scanned the picnic grounds, searching for her son, sounding increasingly frustrated as her voice got louder. "Where on earth has that boy gotten to now?"

"It's fine, Mom," her daughter Jenny said. "He's fine."

Jenny and her parents were seated at a picnic table next to a trailhead parking lot some distance off I-90 in the Central Cascade Foothills. Jenny was only sixteen, but she knew her role in this family. She patted her mother's arm comfortingly. "He went back up the trail, exploring. He won't go far."

"Where?" Marjorie asked. "Not up toward that river. That river looked dangerous."

"It's just a creek, Mom." Jenny rolled her eyes. Sometimes her mother was so hopeless. Ten minutes before, Jenny had seen Timothy slip away from the table and head for the trail where the entire family had earlier taken a brief stroll. Her brother was like that—always going off on his own, preferring to be alone rather than with his family.

Sometimes, she understood him perfectly.

"Robert." Marjorie turned to her husband who was just biting into his second grilled hamburger they'd bought in North Bend on their way to the park. "Put that down. You don't need a second burger."

Her husband hesitated, then took another quick bite before setting the hamburger aside.

"You may have noticed that Timothy isn't here," Marjorie said. "Aren't you worried?"

"He'll come back when he's ready." Her husband knew better than to roll his eyes. But he also knew what was coming. He picked up the burger and took another bite, wiped his mouth with a paper napkin, and stood, resigned to the inevitable. Robert played poker with friends in a monthly game back home in Othello. Those games, along with fifteen years of marriage, had taught him when to stand his ground. And when to fold.

"He's gone up that trail to the river. I don't like that place, Robert. It's dangerous."

"Come on, Jen," he said, reaching out his hand. "Let's go see what your little brother's gotten up to this time."

Jennifer smiled at her father as she took his hand. She agreed that her brother would show up when he was good and ready, but a walk up the trail with her father was preferable to sitting around and waiting for him to return, especially with her mother all hot and bothered.

As they approached the wooden footbridge over the rushing creek, Jenny ran ahead. Next to the concrete pad that held the supports at the near end of the bridge, there was a worn footpath that led down to the rocks below, beside the creek. There, as she'd expected, was her little brother, down on his knees, bent over one of the rocky pools beneath the bridge abutment. As she approached, she saw him reach his hand down into the water and come up with something small and brassy looking. When he looked up and noticed her scooting down the steep path from the bridge, she saw him quickly slip it into his pants pocket.

"What'd you find?" she asked.

"Nothing." He scowled at her.

"Fine. Keep your piece of junk. But come on. We gotta get back. It's time to head for home. Mom's going bonkers."

PART TWO

THE TRIAL

1983

CHAPTER 11

Duncan Carmichael
King County Courthouse, 3ʳᵈ and James, Seattle, WA
Office of the Court Commissioner
Wednesday, September 14, 1983

D uncan Carmichael was the last person still waiting in the hall outside the Court Commissioner's office in the King County Courthouse at the very end of a long day. He needed an ex-parte judicial signature on his order in the Harold Dawson estate directing "Final Payment of Debts and Distribution of Assets." There was no longer any need for probate to remain open. The paperwork was all fairly pro-forma. It was a matter of getting an ex-parte judicial signature.

The probate had been simple. Dawson had died intestate with his daughter Julia as his only heir. At the end, Dawson had owned no assets other than a few mostly worthless furnishings and personal belongings and a four-year-old Mercury Monarch with 65,000 miles on it. Its value didn't even cover court costs. Technically, probate hadn't really been needed. But it had allowed his daughter to clearly discharge that $250,000 loan, which, with interest came to $287,000, as well as to decisively close the book on any pointless legal claims from Dawson's angry, die-hard clients. Since the estate was broke, claims would have been pointless; instead, former clients would have to negotiate with the firm's malpractice insurance carrier.

While standing there waiting, Duncan reflected on a recent conversation he'd had with Julia about how the WPPSS disaster had affected her parents. She'd told him that growing up, her life had been one of privilege. One thing in particular that she remembered fondly was her father's amazing collection of antique jewelry. He'd kept it in glass display cases in a "secure room" in their basement. Julia used to tag along when guests came over and he gave tours of the collection. As a youngster, she'd not only been fascinated by the jewelry itself but by the stories associated with some of the items. It had made her proud to be part of a family that owned such a precious collection. Although she couldn't remember her mother ever showing much interest in the collection or the tours.

Her father had been especially fond of an incredible brooch called the "Tsarina's Spider." When describing the piece to Duncan, Julia's voice had become wistful with memory. Even without seeing a picture of it, Duncan had no trouble visualizing the brooch with its twisted gold lace-like web, the deep green of the spider's emerald abdomen, the smaller body segment consisting of a spinel of bluish green, and eight thin legs extending from the body that were encrusted with diamonds and tiny gold granules. And, of course, the eight round ruby eyes.

"*My father made me learn the anatomy of the spider,*" she'd told him before naming the parts: "*Cephalothorax, scapulae, pedipalp, fang, abdomen, spinneret, and anal tubercle.*" From her child's perspective, she'd considered the brooch "*kind of scary,*" but intriguing. Her father let her hold it from time to time, always reminding her that it was a "*priceless heirloom.*" Although she remembered him mentioning at one point that it was worth a million and a quarter.

When she was younger, Julia had assumed that their way of life and their lifestyle was normal—end of story. But even before WPPSS became "Whoops," she was aware that her parents were experiencing some tough times in their marriage as well as financially. By then she was married to Danny, and the Navy was moving them from one place to another, so she was focused more on her own life than on theirs. It was her parents' divorce that was the first shock.

From the divorce settlement papers, Duncan knew that Dawson's wife got the cash from whatever was left of their equity in the house, its contents, and what remained of his jewelry collection—with the exception of the Tsarina's Spider. Dawson had kept that. Because of his attachment to it, Julia assumed the Spider was the last thing he finally sold to cover his mounting debt.

While continuing his long wait to see the commissioner, Duncan also mentally went over another conversation he'd had with Julia about her husband's relationship with her father. She'd explained that after Danny got transferred to COMFAIR Whidbey that Danny and her father had become tight friends. For some reason that she found hurtful, her father didn't want to share his troubles with her; instead, he'd turned to Danny for emotional support. Almost everything she knew about the details of her father's fall from grace, she had learned indirectly from Danny. Even her mother hadn't known the depths of the challenges her father had faced toward the end.

"*He was doing his best,*" Julia had said to Duncan. But her mother couldn't face the steady decline of assets. She wanted out before everything was gone.

"*It must have been painful to watch,*" Duncan remembered saying.

Julia had broken down at that point and cried.

Trying to console her, Duncan recalled saying that *it sounds like your father was trying to do the right thing.*" In fact, he believed that it was Harold Dawson's foolish obsession with those bonds and his unprofessional commitment to his clients that led to a preordained tragic downfall. To Duncan, it was just another example of how the "mighty" can fall. And now Julia and her mother were living with the consequences.

He'd asked Julia if she thought that her husband's disappearance with that airplane could have in any way been related to her father's situation and death. For instance, had her father's death depressed Danny to the point of making *him* emotionally unstable? Did he start to become fatalistic about hard work not being sufficient to guarantee a good life? Were there any changes in his mood that she might in retrospect wish she'd paid more attention to?

She'd appeared to consider his questions, but in the end said that she hadn't noticed anything unusual in her husband's behavior. And she didn't see how the two events could possibly be related.

One thing Duncan didn't mention to Julia was what Danny's bombardier-navigator had told him about Danny being on the verge of washing out of flight training. Duncan felt uncomfortable bringing it up in case she hadn't known. If it became relevant in the future, he could deal with it then. The family had gone through so much already. But at least there would be some closure once Duncan got this signature from the court commissioner.

In any case, earlier that same day, Duncan had finally been able to deliver some good news to his client, a very pleasant surprise. Duncan had been in his office when his receptionist buzzed him on the intercom and asked if he'd like to take a long-distance phone call from a claims adjustor from the San Francisco office of Universal Amalgamated Life and Casualty Company. He considered refusing the call because he was wrapped up in writing a complex appeal brief in a federal admiralty case. But, the name of the company sounded vaguely familiar, and it was possible the call might be a request for legal services. At this stage in their law partnership, he and Sydney couldn't afford to be cavalier about such things. So, instead of asking the receptionist to take a message, he reluctantly had her put the call through.

Afterwards, he was very glad he had.

The claims adjuster was calling about a two hundred-thousand-dollar whole life policy they had on file for one Harold Dawson—now apparently deceased. The sole beneficiary shown on the policy was a daughter by the married name of Julia Ortez.

"Might that be your client in the probate currently underway there in King County, Washington?" the agent had asked.

"It might indeed," Duncan had told him.

"We'd have called earlier," the adjuster said. "But we've been looking at the circumstances of Mr. Dawson's death."

The adjuster unnecessarily explained that they'd had to be sure that Julia was not a suspect in her father's murder before making a distribution. Now that there was a suspect under arrest, they were ready to move forward with payment on the policy. There were some papers requiring her notarized signature. That was the reason he was calling Duncan. He didn't have a current address for her and assumed that as her lawyer, Duncan could provide that. Once the papers were returned, they would send her a check for the full amount.

The agent emphasized that the check would be made out to her alone. Duncan assumed that this was the agent's not so subtle way of making clear what Duncan already knew: that these insurance proceeds would *not* be a part of Dawson's estate. And, therefore should not be included in the calculation of any probate lawyer's fee. What the agent had no way of knowing was that, because the estate was basically bankrupt, Duncan was being paid a modest hourly fee covered separately by Julia's mother.

Being perhaps overly cautious, Duncan was reluctant to give the agent Julia's mother's address. Instead, he asked for the papers to be sent to his office. Meanwhile, he intended to check on the company before asking Julia to sign the papers. She'd recently suffered too many losses to face another one on his watch.

At first the agent resisted the idea, but when Duncan insisted that because Julia was in the process of moving and therefore sending it to his office was the safest option, the man relented.

Finally, Duncan wanted to make sure that the windfall wasn't going to be snatched by the loan shark's enforcer, so he asked for verification that the payment would not be a matter of public record. The agent sounded somewhat insulted at the thought. He'd said rather forcefully: "We here at Universal Amalgamated are nothing if not discreet. And, as I'm sure you may know, life insurance payouts are not considered income, so no 1099 form is required."

With that, Duncan had thanked the agent, assuring him that "Ms. Ortez will be delighted with this good news." He added that he felt it likely that she'd been entirely unaware that her father even had this life policy, so the agent's effort to track her down was greatly appreciated by both of them. He could almost feel the man puff with pride for being thanked that he had gone the extra mile in this instance.

The call ended by the agent offering his condolences for Julia's loss and their appreciation for her father's business.

Later that day when he'd dialed Julia's number to tell her the good news, it crossed his mind that she would be doubly pleased. She would certainly be thrilled with the money, but the fact that her father had continued to pay the insurance premiums to the very end was a remarkable act of love for his daughter.

Now, as he waited in line for his turn before the Court Commissioner and reflected on his conversations with Julia and the insurance adjuster, Duncan sincerely hoped things were turning around for her. She had gone through so much, all things outside of her control. She deserved better from those close to her.

Finally, the lawyer ahead of him concluded his business, exited the office, and briskly disappeared down the hall. Duncan immediately stepped inside and laid his unsigned court order down on the commissioner's desk.

"Looks like you're about to close this one down," said the commissioner after glancing at the document.

"Yes sir. We're close."

"Just this one outstanding unpaid debt?"

"Yes sir. Nothing for it. The estate is bankrupt."

"Uh huh. Yeah, I see," he said. But he still hesitated to sign his name to the order.

"Is there something further you need?" Duncan was certain he had jumped through all of the necessary hoops to complete the process.

"No. Not really," the Commissioner said as he finally leaned in and signed his name to the order, turned it around with his fingers, and slid it back in Duncan's direction. His fingers still on the order, the Commissioner locked eyes with Duncan across the desk. "Between us, about that note for, what is it now, $287,000 with interest, outstanding to AA Best Bet Bail Bonds. Can I assume you and your client know exactly who these people are?"

Now it was Duncan's turn to hesitate. "Yes, I think we do, Your Honor."

"I hope you don't mind me asking—none of my business really. But does she have any assets of her own—beyond this estate, that is?"

Duncan didn't really want to answer that question even though the Commissioner would know this was confidential information. He settled on: "Some, perhaps, but not much, I'm afraid." It was, at that moment, both true and untrue at the same time.

"Um. I see. Well, you'll do what you think is best," said the Commissioner. "But I've seen notes just like this one discharged in probate before. Unless I miss my guess, this lawful $287,000 debt probably reflects a handshake obligation for a good deal more. If your client, um, this Mrs. Ortez, plans to leave this debt unpaid, which she has every right to do, you might consider advising her to use some special care in the weeks ahead. Just sayin'. Off the record."

His order signed and filed, Duncan left the courthouse with a grim smile on his face. One never knew where, hidden within the complex universe of an urban courthouse, a secret truth might unexpectedly reveal itself.

CHAPTER 12

Sydney Warren
Central Cascades
Two Mountain Creek
Friday, September 16

A s Sydney parked her aging yellow Porsche in the gravel lot at Two Mountain Creek, she was surprised to see two other vehicles. The trails there weren't particularly wonderful Cascade Foothills hikes, but it wasn't far from Seattle. And there were multiple trailheads. So, on a typical weekend, the place would be filled with hikers' cars, and often with picnickers occupying the cluster of outdoor wooden tables at the far end of the alternately muddy or dusty parking area.

On this cool, post Labor Day weekday morning, however, she'd half expected to have the place to herself. Taking a closer look, she noted that one of the vehicles was a non-descript, dirty brown, bare-bones Ford Crown Vic, exactly the kind of "unmarked" vehicle typically driven by King County Sheriff detectives. The other was a plain white van. It had "exempt" clearly printed on the rear-mounted license plate, identifying it as a government vehicle.

Something was up.

She'd taken the time to drive there out of desperation. Mel had already made a thorough search of the area that hadn't produced anything helpful for the case. If *he* hadn't found anything, it was highly unlikely that *she* would. Still, the Dawson trial started next week, and she felt a strong need to do something, anything, to shake up her thinking a little.

It was unsettling to see two official vehicles in the parking lot, one that probably belonged to detectives from King County Major Crimes and the other which could have been transport for a crime scene team. Why would they be there if they weren't still investigating her case? If they were, why were they doing so now—on the eve of the trial?

And why the hell hadn't she been informed?

Sydney started down Two Mountain Creek Trail through a deeply-forested path that departed from the western end of the parking area. After only a couple-hundred yards, she saw the narrow wooden foot-bridge where Dawson had died. There was a pile of aluminum equipment cases and miscellaneous scuba gear beside the trail at the near end bridge abutment. Ahead, out on the bridge itself, stood the two King County plain-clothes detectives who had worked the case: Ginger Small and Jason Brown. They were both leaning against the wooden railing, arms resting on its flat surface, staring downstream away from her.

The bridge spanned a narrow gut where the creek flowed between two rocky banks. It wasn't exactly a waterfall, but it could definitely be described as a rapid. Even now in mid-September, the creek was rushing with water. The noise of it covered her arrival right up to the moment she joined the two detectives and leaned casually on the railing beside them, looking downstream to check out what they were seeing.

"What's up?" she said, smiling at their surprised faces when they turned toward her. Their surprise quickly faded to what she interpreted as discomfort. That confirmed her suspicion that they were up to something she wasn't going to like.

Ginger Small was the older, more experienced of the two. Ironically, she was neither red-headed nor short. Her brown straight hair ended at her neck, more efficient than stylish. Sydney always felt as though Small considered her the enemy, inevitably remaining tight-lipped about evidence until legally forced to provide it. Her younger partner, Jason

Brown, was an Alaskan Native who'd grown up in a small town in Southeast Alaska and who carried those community values with him into law enforcement. He seemed to see even those who broke the law as people, individuals with a life story that influenced their behavior.

Sydney had dealt with Brown on a case a few years earlier when he was a patrol officer who'd busted her 18-year-old female client at a party where there'd been some underage drinking. The police showed up on a neighbor's complaint. While Sydney's client and immediate friends had not been drinking, the matter became complicated when it turned out that some of the alcohol consumed at the party had been transported to the event in the trunk of her client's car. The young woman had driven several friends to the party, including the 21-year-old male who had purchased some of the booze and had supplied it to others, including some underage partiers.

The possession and conveyance of alcohol in her client's car put the young woman on the hook for supplying alcohol to persons under the age of twenty-one. Being charged with a gross misdemeanor, in addition to perhaps being hit with a hefty fine, would have been extremely damaging to the young woman at that stage in her life. She freely admitted to being aware that the alcohol had been placed in the trunk of her car, but not that it was later to be handed out at the party without regard to age. It was a defense that hadn't apparently sounded credible to the prosecuting attorney who was inclined to punish her to the extent possible.

Fortunately for her client, Officer Brown interceded. He argued that convicting the teenager wouldn't make the community safer and helped get the charges reduced and deferred. It was a kind move by a guy who had teenaged kids himself and understood how easily a teenager could mess up their lives with one small, unthinking act.

Ginger Small was another matter entirely. It was she who answered Sydney's question about what they were doing there.

"Just some routine follow-up," she said, matter-of-factly. "Nothing to be worried about." Then, looking down at the work underway in the rocky creek-bed below: "I guess you could say," she added, "*no stone unturned.*" She grinned at her own cleverness.

But Sydney *was* worried. There had to be a reason for all this new activity. But, since Small clearly wasn't going to tell her anything helpful, she decided to ignore them and complete the task she'd come for. Let them wonder what *she* was up to.

After a quick walk across the bridge, she paused to have a closer look at the surrounding area. The creek was running vigorously even now in September, but it had lost a great deal of the tumult she'd noted in June when she'd first visited this scene. The shores were heavily forested on both sides with the trail at each end of the bridge disappearing quickly among the trees. As Mel had noted, a shooter could conceivably have hidden in the woods upstream or downstream of the bridge and shot Dawson when he'd stepped out into the open to cross over. Or, they might have simply followed him here and shot him from the path behind—from the general area upstream of where the Sheriff's team was conducting its search.

If, as the Medical Examiner had reported, the wound was a through-and-through, where that bullet might have landed would depend on how much velocity it had retained as it exited Dawson's skull. Everyone had assumed that the most likely scenario was that the bullet had dropped into the creek and settled among the rocks, but they hadn't been able to locate it in the fast-moving water. Another possibility was that it had gone as far as the trees on the other side of the creek. The trees and vegetation in the area had been thoroughly searched. With negative results.

Given how intensive the original search of the creek and woods had been, Sydney was puzzled as to why they were checking out the stream and surrounding area again. If they hadn't found the bullet before, what made them think they could now? Unless they were looking for something else. Or unless, like her, they felt desperate and were hoping against hope to find something, anything. But why *now*?

When she saw the team packing up, she lingered at the far end of the bridge until they were gone. Brown turned to wave at her as they left, but Small didn't. They were probably as curious about what she was doing there as she was about them, but they hadn't asked. Maybe because they didn't want to open the door to that discussion.

As soon as they were out of sight, Sydney started back across the bridge, slowly, examining the wooden railings on each side as she went.

She wasn't surprised not to find anything aside from a good deal of wear and tear from the weather, public use, mishaps, casual "artwork," and the initials and messages carved by lovesick teenagers.

Near the spot where the body had been found, she noted a shallow scar angling across the flat surface at the top of the railing. Its direction was consistent with the possibility that it might have been made by a rifle bullet coming from the direction of where Dawson's body had fallen. If so, such a bullet might have just skinned the top of the railing before disappearing into the water below. She pulled out her camera and took a couple of pictures.

Pausing to consider the height of the flat railing, it seemed obvious that the trajectory of the bullet that had killed Dawson would have been much too high to have made the mark on the railing. The entry wound was in his forehead, so the police had speculated that he might have been alerted and turned back in the direction of his assailant when he was shot. Or his killer might have been ahead of him, partway across the bridge and killed him as he approached. Sydney was obviously trying too hard to find something suspicious. The scar was probably attributable to idle vandalism, similar to what she'd seen at other places on the bridge.

On the other hand, it was possible but extremely unlikely that someone had shot him when he stopped to tie a shoelace or stooped down to pick up something. Either way, the bullet would have ended up in the water or on the other side of the creek.

Sydney looked around, picturing her previous visit to the site nearly three months earlier. She remembered how surprisingly clean everything had been at the time. Unlike today. Today, the area was littered with signs of human recreational usage: coffee cup lids, paper napkins, a child's mitten. Of course, at the time of her original visit, the site's neatness was likely in large part due to the crime scene team having gathered up anything that could conceivably be of interest in the investigation. She recalled the inventory that had been among the documents included in discovery; nothing had seemed worthy of further examination.

Taking one last look around, she mentally scolded herself for making the trip. Given all the people who had scoured the area looking for clues, she'd been kidding herself to think for even a minute that she'd had a snowball's chance in hell to come up with something no one else had discovered or thought of. On the other hand, she *had* learned that the prosecution was nosing around. She wondered what, if anything, they had found. The more she thought about it, the more anxious she became.

An hour and a half later, Sydney was back in her office and on the phone, arguing with Walter Rice's aid about putting him on the phone no matter how busy he was at the moment. When she finally got through, she didn't bother to hide her irritation.

"When were you planning to let me know that there was a tech team searching the streambed up at the Dawson crime scene today?" Without waiting for him to reply, she added: "And when can I expect timely disclosure as to what they found?"

"Easy, tiger," Rice replied, irritating her even more. "Just some routine follow-up. Making sure nothing has been overlooked."

"Routine? Right. And you just chose to do this 'routine' search two days before our trial begins because your detectives suddenly had some extra time on their hands?"

"No, no. No need to get excited. It's nothing like that. We just had a few details to chase down. You'll be looped in first thing next week."

Sydney had to try hard to keep her voice steady and not shout into the phone: "It's Friday, Walter. Noon on Friday. Our trial starts on Monday morning. So please take note of my specific question for the record: *What 'details?'* Is there something about which I should be 'looped in' as counsel for the defense? Because if so, I'd like for us to get that 'looping in' done *right now*. Not Monday. *Now*. We both know your discovery obligations. I want to know why you committed two detectives and a crime scene team to what was obviously a search for new evidence."

When Rice didn't respond immediately, she'd had enough.

"OK," she said. "How about I put down this phone and walk the three blocks to your office. You can 'loop me in' and turn over *in person* —*today*, whatever it is that you've got. Or I can serve you with expedited notice of hearing and then continue on up to the eighth floor and have a chat with Judge Francis."

"Now look, Sydney. There's no need for you to come storming over here all angry and het up. It's no big deal. Just the usual last-minute stuff. Stuff like this happens in every case. What if I message something over to you?"

That convinced her—he was definitely withholding information. "Walter, I'm putting down this phone right now. And I'm on my way. I will be there in your office in five to ten minutes. If you're not there with the answers I need when I arrive, I will be immediately heading upstairs to talk to our judge. We'll see what *she* has to say about all this."

She hung up the phone without bothering to hear his response.

When Sydney arrived at the King County Prosecutor's office and checked in with the receptionist, she half expected to be told to take a seat. Instead, she was immediately escorted down the hall to a large conference room. Walter Rice was waiting for her, seated at a long white oak table, a slight frown creasing his otherwise smooth skin. On the table in front of the chair that was directly across from where he sat was a single brass spent cartridge case.

When he caught sight of her, he greeted her with what she considered an obnoxious, condescending grin.

"May I?" Sydney asked, pointing at the cartridge case.

"Sure," Rice said. "No relevant fingerprints."

As she picked up the cartridge case, he slid a photocopied document across the table. She studied the casing a moment, then turned to the document. It was a signed witness statement from a 9-year-old boy by the name of Timothy Bright of Othello Washington. It referenced the boy's discovery of a brass cartridge case in a rock pool beneath the wooden footbridge across Two Mountain Creek. This had occurred on July 9, approximately three weeks after Harold Dawson's death.

Sydney held up the document. "What is this?" she asked.

"At this point, Sydney, you know everything we know. As the boy's statement indicates, he found this item under the footbridge at the scene of the crime."

"And I'm just seeing this now because . . .?"

"The boy found the cartridge case when his family stopped off for a picnic lunch at the trailhead near the crime scene. He apparently kept his discovery to himself. But his older sister knew about it. Recently, they saw mention of our case going to trial on the news. It was the sister who put two-and-two together. She realized that her brother found his 'treasure' at the scene of a crime that had occurred not long before their family had a picnic there. She told their parents what her little brother had found. The parents demanded to see it. Then they contacted the King County Sheriff's office."

"So, you've known about this for several days?"

"Hours, Syd. Several hours. Small and Brown drove over to Othello yesterday to interview the family and pick up the cartridge case. I received it just this morning."

"And no fingerprints were found on the cartridge?"

"Correct."

"Not even the boy's?"

"Unfortunately, he'd polished it."

"I take it you still haven't found the gun."

"Nope."

"So, this spent cartridge could have come from any gun? Maybe it has nothing to do with our murder."

"Correct."

"And, you were planning to inform me of all this, what, on Monday morning the day of trial?"

"Syd, the detectives just tracked this down and got their hands on the cartridge yesterday. As you say, it could have come from any one of untold numbers of thirty-caliber rifles. It may have nothing whatever to do with our case. At this point, I'm not at all sure it's actually evidence of anything."

Each time he called her "Syd" she felt her jaw clench, but she was determined to keep her irritation in check. About that at least. "Right. Sure. Totally insignificant. That's why your detectives were at the scene this morning, two work days before trial, with a bunch of folks in wetsuits scouring the streambed where a kid found a cartridge case. Looking for the gun or the bullet, perhaps?" She held up the cartridge case. "So, I guess you have no intention of making any use of this at trial? It's totally insignificant, right?"

He raised his eyebrows slightly and smiled. Sydney could picture him using the same expression to let his mother know he was innocent of eating a cookie before dinner. "Well, let's just say the significance of whatever evidence we have is for each of us to figure out, isn't it? Why don't we share our thoughts on that matter on Monday when the trial begins."

"I guess that means the answer is 'yes.'" Sydney was barely able to quell her anger. She pointed across the table at the corner of a photo peeking out from the file folder from which Timothy Bright's written statement had been taken. "That a picture of this cartridge?"

Rice sighed as if to let her know she was making a big thing out of nothing. Then he pulled out the photo and showed it to her. It was a close-up shot of the brand name information imprinted on the base of the cartridge.

"How about you let me have a copy of that photo as well? Or, since it is so clearly irrelevant, maybe you'd like to provide me with a guarantee that you won't be using any of this at trial?"

By way of response, Rice slid the photo across the table. "Take this one. It's a copy."

She silently slipped the statement and the photo into her zippered case. Then she stood and shrugged on her jacket. "See you Monday, *Walt*." she said as she headed for the door.

There was a great deal more Sydney would like to have said, but thankfully, she was able to restrain herself. Monday! That's when she'd have her chance to even up the scales with this self-involved SOB.

It would all have been a lot easier had the man she was defending not been someone who, against all odds, she somehow still believed was innocent.

CHAPTER 13

Sydney Warren
King County Courthouse, Seattle
Courtroom of Judge Roberta Francis, Eighth Floor, Room 808
Monday, September 19, 1983

"Are we ready for trial?" The judge squinted over the top of her readers at the two attorneys. As a matter of pure chance, Judge Roberta Francis, who had presided at Nowak's arraignment, had also been assigned as his trial judge. Sydney wasn't disappointed. Despite the decision on bail, Sydney considered Judge Francis to be both capable and fair.

"The prosecution is ready," said Deputy Prosecutor Walter Rice. He stood tall, his back straight, a warrior ready for battle.

"Defense is ready," said Sydney Warren. She knew her voice sounded more confident than she felt. Sometimes it was impossible to control inner turmoil, but it was important not to let it show. "We do have a new pretrial motion for Your Honor."

"Proceed, Counsel. Let's get started."

For Sydney it had been a busy weekend filled with urgent planning and intensive briefing. For most of it, she had been in her office accompanied by her legal assistant and helped along in the research and brief-writing by Duncan. On Sunday afternoon she'd gone into her office and spent several hours behind a closed office door writing and then practicing her opening statement.

When she'd entered the courtroom and greeted her client, she also met his wife for the first time, as well as their twelve-year-old daughter and fourteen-year-old son. The boy looked bored, but the girl seemed eager to take in all the details of what was happening. Both were dressed in what Sydney thought of as their "Sunday best." Their mother also looked as though she had dressed for the occasion, conservative yet put together. As instructed, they'd arrived early and taken seats in the front row of the spectator section immediately behind the defense table. Together they were intended to provide the perfect image of an appealing, caring family unit—hopefully humanizing the defendant and perhaps providing some insulation from whatever rhetorical poison might be directed his way over the course of the trial.

Sydney gave copies of her motion and the supporting brief to Walter Rice and to the court clerk who, in turn, handed them to Judge Francis. "On Friday afternoon, Your Honor, I was first informed by the prosecution of some questionable new evidence in this case—a spent thirty-caliber Winchester rifle cartridge case said to have been found near the scene some three weeks following the crime. It has no particular connection to our case and will, the defense believes, simply serve to confuse the jury and prejudice our defense. We ask that this cartridge case and any mention of this supposed evidence be suppressed at trial for two reasons: First, because of its irrelevance and prejudicial nature, and, second, because its existence was unnecessarily withheld from the defense for several days." She wanted to say that the detectives had taken their "sweet time" to turn over the evidence to the defense, but she didn't want to start off the trial sounding like she had a chip on her shoulder.

"Mr. Rice?"

"Your Honor, we do plan to offer this material in evidence at trial. And we feel it is entirely relevant.

"Harold Dawson, the victim in this case, appears to have been shot with a rifle while crossing a wooden footbridge at Two Mountain Creek located between Seattle and Snoqualmie Pass. While the bullet has not been found, the medical examiner will testify that the death wound is consistent with the victim being shot with a thirty-caliber hunting rifle. The defendant, Jamison Nowak, owns such a rifle. Not only is he an experienced rifleman, but according to witnesses at a shooting range he frequents, he is an excellent shot. He admits keeping his rifle at the shooting range in a secure, password protected locker. However, pursuant to warrant, the Sheriff's' detectives looked for the rifle in his locker, and it wasn't there. The locker showed no sign of having been improperly opened. When asked about the missing rifle, he refused to talk with us about it. The whole matter is deeply suspicious.

"Also in this locker, at the time of their search, the police seized a partially empty box of thirty-caliber rifle cartridges of exactly the same type and brand as this one found at the crime scene just three weeks after the murder.

"I will be the first to acknowledge that our case is circumstantial, Your Honor. But that does not make it any less powerful and persuasive. Those 'circumstances,' taken together, are going to prove this defendant's guilt beyond any reasonable doubt.

"To make that case, however, the prosecution must be allowed to offer *all* of the factual circumstances, any one of which, taken alone, might not be sufficient to prove guilt. For example, the discovery of this thirty-caliber cartridge at the crime scene following the murder. This cartridge *is* one of the factual building blocks in the edifice of the prosecution's case. When taken together with all the other evidence, I guarantee this cartridge case will become profoundly relevant."

"Ms. Warren?"

Sydney moved back to the center of the courtroom.

"Your Honor, there are literally *millions* of thirty-caliber rifles in this country. It is far and away the most common caliber for hunting rifles in America. Moreover, there are many millions more of other brands and types of rifles and handguns out there that have a sufficiently similar caliber as to be completely indistinguishable from a thirty-caliber when examining a wound.

"Furthermore, this cartridge case was found in an area frequented by hunters. Near a trail hiked by thousands of people every single year.

The prosecution has provided no meaningful evidence that links this particular cartridge to Dawson's murder, or to this defendant—other than where it was found. Given these facts, this supposed piece of evidence should not be admitted in this case.

"Moreover, Your Honor, the prosecution knew about this cartridge several days before being forced to reveal it to the defense. I only discovered its existence by accident. The prosecution knew that withholding this piece of information in the critical days immediately before trial would put the defense at a disadvantage. It should be omitted for that reason alone."

Judge Francis leaned back in her chair, steepling her hands on her desk. "Mr. Rice, I want you to tell me when, exactly, you first become aware of this evidence."

"I first learned of the possibility that this evidence might exist on Tuesday, Your Honor. That's when the Sheriff's detectives contacted me to ask if it might be a matter of interest in the case. At that time, I told them I believed it might."

"And when did your Sheriff's Office detectives acquire this evidence?"

"I believe they were contacted by the parents of the tender-age child involved on Monday morning. Then, based on their conversation with me on Tuesday, they drove over to Othello on Wednesday, secured the casing, and took the youngster's written statement, returning after business hours Wednesday evening. They called me Thursday morning and asked for my views on sending a team out to the crime scene to look for the gun in the stream beneath the footbridge where the crime occurred. I agreed that was a good idea.

"I personally had my very first look at the actual evidence on Friday morning and provided it to Ms. Warren at around noon on the very same day it came into my hands, Your Honor."

To Sydney, his chronology of events seemed contrived, but she had to admit that he sounded like a reasonable man who believed he had complied with the letter of the law. Walter Rice was going to be a formidable opponent.

Judge Francis turned to Sydney. "I'm sure you'd like to have seen this evidence sooner, Ms. Warren. But it sounds to me like they basically did the best they could to secure it after they learned of its existence early last week. I'm having trouble finding fault with that."

"With all due respect to the prosecution, Your Honor, I would like to emphasize that the Sheriff's detectives learned about this evidence a full week ago today. They then went well out of their way to slow-walk the entire process, hoping to slip by this past weekend before having to reveal it to the defense. I would not have seen this item until today had I not, through pure luck, happened upon their search at the scene on Friday morning. We can have no doubt that Mr. Rice authorized that search knowing full well that the evidence was entirely circumstantial at best and on very shaky ground overall. So, the longer he delayed providing the defense with that information, the better for the prosecution. He did so specifically *because he appreciated the potential significance of this evidence for our trial prep.* The detectives knew everything relevant that there was to know about this item on the previous Tuesday. They should have told us about it then. I'd hate to see them rewarded for that kind of conduct." She hoped she hadn't gone too far in pointing a finger at the sincere sounding prosecutor.

The judge smiled indulgently: "Still, the fact remains that you *did* get this evidence in hand mid-day on Friday. You've had all weekend to look it over. And frankly, it's pretty straightforward evidence. It either exists or it doesn't; I find it hard to see how your client has been prejudiced here."

She turned to her clerk and the reporter. "The court finds the boy's testimony and the cartridge casing he found to be relevant and admissible. Furthermore, that there has been no harmful breach of the prosecution's duty to disclose." She looked at Sydney. "Is there anything else to bring before the court ...?"

"Just one further thing," Sydney said. "By way of anticipation and fair notice, Your Honor. In view of the purely circumstantial nature of the prosecution's case, at this time I want to notify the court and the prosecution that the defense will be asking questions and presenting evidence of alternative suspects in this case. We hope the court will be as forthcoming in allowing us to present circumstances that suggest the possibility of other suspects in this crime as it is in allowing the prosecution to present circumstances that might implicate the defendant."

It was a warning as much as a notice of intent.

"Very well. Notice acknowledged. Let's get on with the selection of our jury, shall we?" The judge's tone was completely neutral, but Sydney thought she detected a slight edge beneath the surface. She may have gone a bit too far, but what was done was done.

~

Aside from the obvious, Sydney had one particular strategy for jury selection—it was in support of her "some other dude" defense. Hopefully AA Best Bet Bail Bonds enforcer Grant Meade was as much of a bruiser as she'd been told. If so, she wanted jurors who might find him intimidating.

The very first juror they questioned, Juror No. 1, was a young woman who worked as a pharmacy technician, assisting a pharmacist in filling prescriptions. She was not a juror Sydney would normally have chosen for this kind of case. For one thing, her profession called for detail and precision, and she might therefore not be forgiving of mistakes or ambiguity. Although it was Dawson rather than Nowak who had created most of the problems for their WPPSS client accounts, technically, Nowak had let it happen. In addition, as a self-supporting single woman with no children, there was also the possibility that she might have less sympathy for Nowak as a family man.

That was two strikes against this potential juror, and ordinarily Sydney might have asked that the woman be excused. Perhaps not "for cause" but, more likely, using one of her peremptory challenges. Still, the woman's demeanor suggested she was introverted, perhaps even somewhat timid. She seemed to avoid eye contact whenever possible and spoke in a soft, barely audible voice.

Sydney glanced down at her juror information form and asked another question: "So, you live in Carnation, in Eastern King County?"

"That's right."

"How did you get to court, today? Did you drive in?"

"Oh no. I'd never make a drive like that in morning traffic! No way. I took an Uber."

"So, does that mean that your employer isn't here in Seattle?"

"Thankfully not. I work at the pharmacy in Carnation. It's an easy walk from my apartment."

Hoping her intuition was right, Sydney told the Judge: "Defense has no objection to this juror, Your Honor,"

"None from the prosecution," Walter Rice intoned as he smiled at Juror No. 1. Too bad for Rice, Sydney thought—the woman was looking down and didn't see the good-looking prosecutor's attempt to make a personal connection.

The rest of the jury selection went fairly quickly. Sydney approved without challenge anyone who struck her as potentially being open to accepting Grant Meade as the "other dude" simply because he was intimidating and therefore possibly aggressive. She wasn't one hundred percent sure of the strategy, but with so little actual evidence to support her case, it seemed like a chance worth taking.

Sydney had only one peremptory challenge left when Rice used up his. In the end, she didn't have to use her final challenge. With one juror to go, they both quickly agreed to accept a man who might arguably go either way.

The stage was set. Those on the panel not chosen to be on the jury were excused, and the judge launched into the jury's introductory instructions.

"What happens next?" Sydney heard Nowak's daughter Bonny ask her mother. Her twelve-year-old voice echoed off the high ceiling. There were a few snickers from the gallery.

"Shush, hon," said the girl's mom softly. Then Sydney heard a further whispered response; she couldn't make out all the words, but it must have satisfied Bonny because she remained quiet after that.

Minutes later, the judge announced the beginning of the trial.

There were no particular surprises in the prosecution's opening statement to the jury. But Walter Rice had been right about one thing: while each of the specific small circumstances he offered as proof of Nowak's guilt was unimpressive on its own, when you added them together, they did feel persuasive. Sydney, on the other hand, focused on Nowak's personal history, trying to make the jury see him as a sympathetic figure who had been unfortunate enough to get caught up in a web of random circumstances and emphasizing that there was a huge difference between *speculation* and *facts.*

The stage was set; the lines drawn.

$\sim$

After a noon recess, Rice launched his case in a traditional fashion, presenting the evidence in the order in which it had appeared to the detectives, as a chronology of the investigation rather than as a story of the crime.

The first witness was Detective Ginger Small. She walked to the witness stand with the stride of someone used to being in command; her plain dark suit and utilitarian hairdo reinforcing her no-nonsense approach.

Small was introduced as one of two detectives who had responded on June 17th to the report of a body found at a hiking trail in the Cascade Foothills about twelve miles east of North Bend and not far from Interstate 90. Rice asked her to tell the jury about what she and her partner Jason Brown found when they arrived on the scene.

"The dead man turned out to be Harold Dawson," Small testified. "He was a partner in a Seattle financial services firm. His body was discovered on a wooden footbridge across the Two Mountain Creek located about 230 yards from the trailhead. He appeared to have died from a bullet wound to the head.

"The absence of powder burns suggested Mr. Dawson might have been shot from some distance away—perhaps by a hunting rifle. This raised the possibility that it could have been some kind of hunting accident. There was, however, no hunting season open in that location. And the death had occurred on the wide-open area of a footbridge with none of the line-of-sight restrictions typically associated with most hunting accidents.

"There were also no signs of a struggle. And no sign of theft following the shooting—Mr. Dawson's wallet containing his driver's license, credit cards, and other identity documents plus $83 in cash was found on his person—all undisturbed. A ring of keys was in his trouser pocket. They were for his home, his office, and his car, a four-year old Mercury Monarch parked in the lot at the trailhead."

"What did you do after examining the scene?" Rice asked his witness.

"A crime scene team was called in to search the area for evidence. The medical examiner was called in to examine the body. And detective Brown and I proceeded to contact and interview his family, friends, and colleagues at work." Rice then walked Small through each of the various ensuing stages of the investigation leading up to their interrogation of Jamison Nowak. He stopped there, leaving what Nowak had told them for later.

Following Small's testimony, three employees of RDN's financial services firm—Ravenswood, Dawson, and Nowak—were called to the stand. All three testified to having overheard an argument between Harold Dawson and the defendant, Jamison Nowak. Rice emphasized that the argument had occurred in a conference room at RDN just three days before Dawson's death.

One of these three witnesses was Andrea Rymes, Harold Dawson's Administrative assistant. A week or so before trial, Mel had caught up with her outside the office and tried to assess what kind of witness she would make. Although she seemed to lean toward being protective of her former immediate boss, she didn't express any particular animosity toward the defendant. She apparently considered him one of her bosses, too, and they had a longstanding employer-employee relationship. Based on what Mel told her, Sydney felt that Rymes' testimony could go either way, depending on what she knew and was asked by the prosecution.

Unfortunately, it was soon clear that Rymes' testimony wasn't going to go as Sydney hoped it might.

"They'd just completed a partners' and associates' meeting in the conference room at the office," Rymes explained. "When the others left, Mr. Nowak and Mr. Dawson stayed behind. The door was shut, but the room has these big interior glass windows. Normally you can't really hear much. But if people are speaking loudly, it isn't all that hard to hear what's going on."

"How *loudly* were Mr. Dawson and Mr. Nowak speaking that day?" Rice prompted.

The witness glanced guiltily in Nowak's direction. Then: "It was pretty loud," she said. "And we could all see them in there. There's a curtain thingy, but it's never really used, you know. And they were really angry. Especially Mr. Nowak."

"Objection, Your Honor . . ."

"I know, Counsel." Judge Francis turned to the witness. "Ms. Rymes, we'd like you to confine yourself to answering Mr. Rice's questions." Then, turning to the prosecutor: "Mr. Rice, do your best to elicit testimony concerning what this witness actually observed. Let's avoid getting into conclusions she might have drawn about those observations. And, ladies and gentlemen of the jury, you're instructed to disregard any conclusions this witness may have expressed concerning the defendant's state of mind. We need you to rely solely on what she actually observed."

She then turned back to Rice and, with a wave of the hand, indicated that he should proceed.

"As he spoke to Mr. Dawson, what did you notice concerning Mr. Nowak's actual behavior? What did you *see*, Ms. Rymes?"

"Well, um, he was flushed, and he waved his arms around a lot." She hesitated a moment, then continued: "He was standing close to Mr. Dawson, kind of leaning toward him."

"You said they raised their voices. Were you able to hear what the argument was about?"

"Yes. My desk is not ten feet away from the conference room. I could hear almost every word." The witness paused, glanced at the Judge, then back at Rice. "Do you want me to tell you what they said?"

"Please, Ms. Rymes. What did you hear them say?"

"Well, I can't repeat their conversation word for word. But the gist of it was that Mr. Nowak accused Mr. Dawson of 'putting the entire firm at risk' by encouraging his clients to hold onto those WPPSS bonds even though they were declining in value. Mr. Dawson tried to convince Mr. Nowak that despite their losses, the value of the bonds would spike when the court ruled against the appellants. But Mr. Nowak wasn't having it. Personally, I thought it was rude of him to keep Mr. Dawson in that room and just dump on him like that."

Before Sydney could object, Rice asked: "Keep him in the room? How so, Ms. Rymes?"

"You know, block his way. Mr. Dawson kept stepping to the side, trying to get around him. But Mr. Nowak wouldn't let him by."

"Thank you, Ms. Rymes. No more questions."

On cross, Sydney trod lightly. This woman had been Harold Dawson's admin for several years. She was obviously still loyal to her deceased boss in spite of the mistakes he'd made that had cost him and the firm huge financial losses and damage to their reputation. And Sydney was going to need her in a friendly frame of mind in a day or two when she might be called again as a witness for the defense.

"During the meeting that preceded this conversation in the conference room between Mr. Nowak and Mr. Dawson, where had the two men been sitting?"

"Well, Mr. Dawson would have sat where he nearly always did, down near the end on the far side of the table with the outside windows behind him. He liked having the light at his back."

"And Mr. Nowak? Where did he sit?"

"I believe he was late to the meeting. Things had already started when he showed up. He sat in one of the empty chairs near the door."

"So, when everybody else left the room, and as Mr. Dawson headed toward the exit, Mr. Nowak was already between him and the door, isn't that right?"

She gave the question some thought before replying. "Yes, he was."

"How wide was the aisle between the table and the windows where Mr. Jamison and Mr. Dawson were standing when they spoke?"

"I'm not good estimating in terms of feet, but maybe about like the distance between me and that table there." She pointed.

"So, four feet, perhaps. Your Honor can the record reflect the space indicated by the witness is about four feet?"

"The record will so reflect."

"And there were chairs there, right? Chairs that had previously been occupied and some that may have remained pushed away from the table?"

"Sure. The chairs were all there."

"So, considering the setting, Ms. Rymes, isn't it inaccurate to imply that Mr. Nowak *deliberately* blocked Mr. Dawson's way and 'wouldn't let him go' as you described it, when in fact, he was already between Mr. Dawson and the door at the end of the meeting. Correct?"

"Well, yes, I suppose so. It just seemed to me that he could have moved aside to let Mr. Dawson pass." Her words and tone suggested she wasn't totally buying Sydney's interpretation of the situation. Sydney left it there, hoping she'd made her point to the jury. Because of Rymes' response, Sydney couldn't help wondering if the woman had been prepped for the question. That may have been why Rice hadn't objected to Sydney's line of questioning; he knew that nothing Rymes said would hurt his case nor particularly help hers.

Two other witnesses had heard bits and pieces of the same argument between the two men and made similar observations. One used the word "fight" to describe the exchange. Sydney objected, and the judge had sustained her objection, but Sydney knew that image most likely lingered in the minds of the jurors. There was simply no way to get around the fact that the two men had a serious, public disagreement over Dawson's decisions regarding the WPPSS bonds.

CHAPTER 14

Sydney Warren
King County Courthouse, Seattle
Courtroom of Judge Roberta Francis, Eighth Floor, Room 808
Tuesday, September 20, 1983

First thing Tuesday morning, Rice called the medical examiner to testify. She confirmed what everyone already knew: Dawson had been killed by a bullet through the head. The bullet had entered near the center of Dawson's forehead and had exited somewhere a few inches behind his right ear. It had been a through-and-through with massive and fatal damage to the brain. Dawson would have died instantly.

The medical examiner concluded that: "The size and nature of the wound were 'consistent with the bullet having been fired from a typical thirty-caliber rifle of the kind commonly used by hunters.' And, since there were no powder burns or residue in evidence on the body, the weapon that killed him was at least two feet away. Although it could have been much farther."

In her cross examination, Sydney vigorously attacked that statement: "I'm wondering why you specifically mention a thirty-caliber hunting rifle as a type of weapon potentially used in this shooting—it couldn't be because you were made aware that the defendant owns a thirty-caliber hunting rifle, could it?"

The ME looked shocked at the idea. "Absolutely not. Of course not," she said, her voice a blend of indignation and confidence.

"Then why? Why mention that caliber in particular?"

"Because that's the most common rifle used for hunting, and the area is a well-known hunting location."

"I see. So not because a thirty-caliber round fired from a rifle was the *only* possibility." She paused briefly before asking her next question. "How many thirty-caliber hunting rifles do you assume are owned by people in Western Washington?"

"I'm sorry; I don't know the number."

"How about nation-wide ownership?"

"Again, I don't know the number."

"Would you be surprised to learn that there are likely tens of *millions* of thirty-caliber hunting rifles in the hands of Americans today?"

"No, I suppose I wouldn't."

"And, as I recall your testimony, you said the head wound was 'consistent with' a thirty-caliber bullet, am I right?"

"That's right."

"So, it's also possible that his wound could just as easily have been caused by a rifle of a caliber somewhat larger? Or somewhat smaller?"

"Yes. Possibly. It isn't an exact science when you don't have the bullet."

"And I assume that you know there are, in fact, also several handguns that employ ammunition of similar caliber."

"I'm aware of that, yes."

Rice rose quickly to his feet. "Your Honor, the witness is being asked to testify on matters that are clearly speculative."

Sydney jumped in. "I'm almost done with this witness, Your Honor."

"Wrap it up quickly," the judge said.

Turning back to the witness, Sydney summarized: "So we can't even know if this victim was in fact shot with a rifle, can we?"

"Not with absolute certainty, no." Her words agreed with Sydney's conclusion, but her tone told the jurors she thought the theory was far-fetched.

Sydney decided to have one more try to plant doubt in the minds of jurors, in spite of the fact that she had told the judge she was almost through with the witness. "We're not just talking about a mere million or even ten million possibilities out there. The number of weapons that could have caused this wound is actually many times larger than that that. Maybe it's 50 million. Maybe 100 million, for all we know."

Rice dragged himself up again. "Your Honor . . ."

Before he could finish his objection, the judge said, "I believe the witness has already answered the question you're leading up to. Move on."

"Yes, Your Honor." She smiled at the witness. "Do you own a passenger car?"

"I do."

"So, saying that Mr. Dawson is guilty of murder because he owns a thirty-caliber hunting rifle would be like suggesting that if someone was struck by a motor vehicle and the injuries they sustained were consistent with that vehicle being a passenger car, *you* could be implicated as the driver in that accident."

"Objection, Your Honor." Rice sounded angry. Perhaps somewhat mad at himself for not seeing the point until it was obvious.

"I'm sorry, Your Honor. I'll rephrase the question."

"I didn't hear a question," said Judge Francis sternly.

"The bottom line here is that you don't know for certain what kind of gun killed this man, isn't that right, Doctor?"

"I'll say what I said initially: the wound was consistent with a thirty-caliber hunting rifle as the murder weapon."

Sydney turned and gave the jury a look to confirm the absurdity of this answer, and to let them know that she assumed they were savvy enough to understand the witness was biased by having access to information about Nowack's rifle.

In the moment, it felt like a winning point. Unfortunately, on the heels of that cross examination, Sydney had to face some much more difficult evidence that the detectives had learned from the defendant himself.

Rice next recalled Detective Small to reestablish her observations from the initial visit to the crime scene and to confirm witness testimony regarding the tension observed between the two men prior to Dawson's death. Small was clear and decisive, someone Sydney knew would be seen by the jury as credible even if not likeable.

Approaching the core of his case, Sydney anticipated that Rice would want to cap things off with the defendant's own statement to the police. For that, he opted to use a less experienced but more relatable witness.

"The prosecution calls Detective Jason Brown, Your Honor."

Sydney knew the jury was going to love Jason Brown. He was the ultimate nice guy, the clean-cut, decent young man you'd be overjoyed to learn was going to marry your sister.

Then again, he was a police officer. And a lot of people didn't trust the police no matter how polite or nice they seemed. Furthermore, maybe he was a bit too honorable and would acknowledge gray areas instead of painting everything in black-and-white. That was what Sydney was counting on.

"In the course of your investigation," Rice began, "did you have occasion to interrogate the defendant, Jamison Nowak?"

"Yes sir. We did that early on, shortly after we learned of the argument he'd had with the deceased."

Rice next took Brown through the preliminaries leading up to them taking the defendant's statement. As far as Sydney could tell, Small and Brown had done everything by the book. Besides, if the jurors sensed that she hoped to prevent them from hearing what her client had initially told the police, they would assume he had something to hide. Instead, she would act as though she welcomed this testimony. She was still undecided about whether to put Nowak on the witness stand, afraid that he'd seem too "slick" to some jurors. And he was a financial consultant, perhaps a profession that some would doubt for its total honesty. For her to succeed, she needed this jury to trust her client. And that all started with his recorded *voluntary* statement to the police.

"Detective Brown, following the defendant having waived his rights to counsel and his right to remain silent," Rice continued, "did he complete and sign a written statement concerning this matter?"

"He did."

"Is this that written statement? All, um, seventeen pages of it?"

"It is."

"Is this the defendant's signature at the end of the document?"

Brown examined the last page. "Yes."

"And his initials at the bottom of each page?"

"That's right."

"And to the best of your knowledge, this was all done willingly and after having voluntarily waived his right to remain silent?"

"Absolutely."

"Your Honor, the prosecution offers this signed, sworn, written statement of the defendant into evidence at this time." Rice laid the document on the small table beside the clerk.

This was a moment of truth. Sydney had intentionally avoided any challenge to the admissibility of this statement *before* the trial. She'd preserved her opportunity to put on a small show for the jury now. Followed by an attempt to get what she really wanted from this exchange.

"Your Honor," she said, "We're happy to have this statement come into evidence. But could we please flesh out a few matters on the record before we agree to its admissibility? Nothing acrimonious, Your Honor. The defense would like to ask a few further questions on voir dire."

"Very well, proceed, Counsel."

"So, Detective Brown, you testified that this statement was completely voluntary, is that correct?"

"Absolutely correct."

"No coercion involved?"

Brown seemed genuinely surprised that she'd ask such a question. "Absolutely not," he said.

"You didn't deprive him of food and water?"

"No ma'am, In fact, we offered, but he refused our offers of food and water."

"Was he lied to during the interrogation?"

"Never."

"Was he threatened with being charged with a crime?"

"Well, he was advised of his rights—if that's what you mean. But we did not 'threaten' him."

"You're sure he understood his right to legal counsel?"

"Yes."

"And his absolute right to remain silent—to refuse to answer your questions?"

"Definitely. That was all spelled out for him when we read him his rights. He specifically declined to exercise those rights. And he signed a written waiver. Quite happily, I might add."

"Do you have that waiver?"

Brown looked toward Rice who pulled a document from a file folder on his table and held it up.

"I'd like to get that waiver admitted as well, you honor." Sydney stepped over to Rice's desk, Rice handed over the document, and she carried it back to the witness stand and showed it to Detective Brown. "This the waiver you're talking about? The one the defendant signed?"

"Yes, it is."

"Your Honor, we'd like to offer this waiver in evidence at this time."

"Mr. Rice?" the judge inquired.

"No objection, Your Honor," Rice said, sounding slightly confused.

Sidney then turned back to the witness. "So, in addition to being quite willing to answer your questions in this interview, what was the attitude of Mr. Nowak during this interrogation? His demeanor?"

It was a non-leading, open-ended question. The kind every fledgling lawyer is told never to ask an adverse witness. But Sydney believed she'd sufficiently set the stage. And that Jason Brown would respond consistent with his character.

"Cooperative, I'd say."

"Helpful even?"

"Sure. Considering the circumstances."

"Relaxed?"

Rice stood up, "Judge, the defense is leading the witness."

"He's your witness, Mr. Rice," the Judge said. Then to Detective Brown: "You may answer the question."

"Oh, he wasn't fidgety if that's what you mean. It was a fairly comfortable exchange."

"So, if that's true, if Mr. Nowak was cooperative and willing—and I believe your assessment; you're an experienced officer. I assume you also have some evidence that could demonstrate his demeanor, isn't that right, detective?" Sydney's client had mentioned to her that the detectives had audiotaped the interview. It was a practice that was becoming common in police interrogations across the country. She'd seen a typed transcript of the recording, so she was hopeful her strategy would work.

"I'm not sure what you . . ."

"I'm referring to the audiotape you did of this interview with Mr. Nowak." Sydney turned to Rice. "You do have that recording, Mr. Rice?"

"Um, well, yes. We do. I don't have it on hand here in court at the moment. I do have the transcription of it, however." He held it out in Sydney's direction.

Sydney didn't take the document. "I already have this transcript, Your Honor," Sydney said, turning to Judge Francis. "What I'm asking about is the audiotape itself. The transcription is fine for some purposes. But, as a part of my interrogation of this witness, I'd like for us to hear the *actual tape recording* of the police interview with my client. This witness has just testified that Mr. Nowak's interview was totally voluntary, and that he was also very cooperative. But unless there's film of the event, the *best* evidence will be the actual audio recording. I believe the court and the jury should hear that recording to gauge for themselves the credibility and demeanor of my client." She turned to Rice to make sure the onus of any objection would rest on him. "I assume you have no objection to the jury hearing the *actual* recording, right?"

Rice was taken aback. "Your Honor, we have the defendant's signed, written statement right here. And I'd be glad to offer the transcription as well. I'm not sure what the recording adds." Clearly, he was finally "getting" what Sydney was trying to do. "I object to admitting the recording at this time."

Sydney feigned surprise at Rice's objection. "Seriously?" she said with a tinge of disbelief. "You're saying you don't want us to *hear* the *actual* recording that shows just how 'voluntary' and 'cooperative' Mr.

Nowak was when giving his statement? How he perhaps had no idea he was a suspect because he knew he had done nothing wrong?"

Before Rice could intervene, Sydney turned to the judge. "Your Honor, I realize that what we're discussing here is a matter of law. But it seems to me that both you *and* the jury would benefit from listening to the actual recording. I don't hear any reasonable explanation from the prosecutor for why you shouldn't. And even if *you* don't feel the need, it seems like something the *jury* might want to hear. I'm surprised the prosecution would try to suppress it. Maybe he has a reason to keep it from the jury that he hasn't shared."

Rice glanced self-consciously at the jury. "Perhaps this is a matter that should be heard *outside* the presence of the jury." Sydney was gratified to see puzzled looks on the faces of a couple of the jurors at Rice's comment as he continued: "If the defense wishes to offer this as a part of their defense case, we can consider it at that time. The defense had the chance to ask about the admissibility of this statement during pretrial. They didn't, and I don't see what has changed."

Sydney was ready for his argument. "It was the prosecution that raised the voluntariness of my client's statement in *their* direct examination of *their* witness. It's a little late for them to argue that this should now happen in secret and away from this jury or at a later time. Regardless of the statement's admissibility, the jury still has the right and obligation to independently assess its truthfulness for themselves. I don't want to presume, Your Honor, but I suspect you're going to rule that Mr. Nowak's signed statement is admissible—as it should be. But I seriously doubt that Your Honor intends to rule on its credibility. The jury must decide *that* matter for themselves."

Sydney was completely conscious of having intentionally complicated the issue. But she had also intentionally not challenged the admissibility of Nowak's police statement in her pretrial motions for this very purpose. It was a way to avoid calling Nowak as a witness in his own defense. At the same time, she very much wanted in evidence what he'd had to say in that initial statement to the police. And she wanted it to come into evidence now, in the middle of the prosecution's own case. The recording of his interview not only had the big advantage of avoiding a cross-examination, but it was a chance to show Nowak in a favorable light at a point where the prosecution's flow would be disrupted. She was betting on the judge to do the simplest and most expeditious thing and let it in.

Judge Francis ruled after only a moment's hesitation: "Well, Mr. Rice, I do believe you opened the door here. You asked Detective Brown whether the defendant had given his statement freely and voluntarily. The defense now wants to elaborate on that. You've offered the written statement as evidence. If it comes in, I don't see why the recorded one shouldn't. This witness can authenticate the tape recording of that interview."

The judge turned to Sydney. "Ms. Warren, are you saying you'd like to play this audiotape for the jury?"

"That is exactly what I'm asking, Your Honor. If they want the defendant's statement in evidence, surely the best evidence of that is the actual recording of the interview itself."

"Mr. Rice?"

Rice apparently saw how the wind was blowing and, with a quick glance at the jury, decided to fold. "I believe the tape is downstairs in my office, Your Honor. I can have it here shortly."

"Very well, the court will be in recess for fifteen minutes. Will that be sufficient, Mr. Rice?"

"Fifteen minutes will be fine, Your Honor."

"Mr. Rice, along with the tape, would you also bring a tape recorder machine for us and the jury to play it on, please." The judge turned to the jury and said, "Ladies and Gentlemen of the jury, we're going to take a brief recess. We'll reconvene at 3:20 p.m."

Sydney's strategy with the audio tape was a success. By 3:30 p.m., the jury was paying rapt attention to a recording of Jamison Nowak's actual interview with the police. The full tape took most of an hour, and by the time it was over, the court day had run out.

The jury was sent home for the night with Jamison Nowak's completely cooperative and credible voice in their heads. Yes, the recording included Nowak's admissions that he'd had a significant disagreement with the decedent. And that he'd actually been present at that Two Mountain Creek trailhead at the time of the murder. But both of those admissions would have come in as a part of the signed written statement in any case. Or in the written transcript. And when you *listened* to that tape, what came through was Nowak's willingness to cooperate with the police and his seeming truthfulness when he told them that he'd gone to that trailhead to make amends and clear the air. Furthermore, he freely stated that he had initiated the call, and it sounded like he was being honest when he said that it was Dawson who had suggested where they should meet.

Perhaps the most significant and convincing comments came near the end of the tape where he addressed their friendship and his concerns as a business partner.

"Harold was a friend," he said. "He was a really decent guy who cared about his clients so much that he allowed himself to fall victim to wishful thinking. Of course we disagreed—no financial advisor should be personally buying up their client's investments at more than they're actually worth just to keep their clients happy. He'd bankrupted himself trying to keep things afloat until after the court decision, and he wanted the rest of us to go along. It was tragic. We were watching him come apart in real time.

"When the Supreme Court ruled against his position on the Wednesday before he died, I knew he'd be devastated. I called him several times and left messages, so when he finally answered, I was hugely relieved. It wasn't an issue that was going away any time soon, and as his friend and partner, I wanted to work out a solution. I understood why he didn't want to come into the office and face everyone. Even so, when he suggested the trailhead east of town, my first thought was *why there?* Still, it wasn't that far away, and we'd been there together in the past during hunting season. Frankly, I'd have gone anywhere he wanted to meet. We really needed to talk."

There was a slight pause before he continued in a soft and emotional voice. "I can't believe that he's dead. He was a good man who deserved a lot better. I'll . . . I'll miss him." He paused again as if to gain his composure. "It's hard to believe somebody killed Harold. He messed up, but he was basically an honest man. Even the stuff he was doing wrong he did because he thought it was the right thing to do."

Sydney watched with inner glee as she saw the impact of the recording on the jurors. Hearing Nowak's description of Dawson conjured up images of a man heartbroken by the loss of a friend. She wouldn't need to put her client on the stand and risk him looking too glib or getting defensive or angry. They'd just heard his explanation of events. And none of it was subject to cross-examination by the prosecution. Best of all, it had all come in as a part of the prosecution's own case.

Although the tape closed on a less personal note, it was a great way for the day to end.

CHAPTER 15

Sydney Warren
King County Courthouse, Seattle
Courtroom of Judge Roberta Francis, Eighth Floor, Room 808
Wednesday, September 21, 1983

The full recording played for the jury the hour before adjournment on Tuesday was undoubtedly still fresh in the minds of jurors when they returned on Wednesday morning. With detective Jason Brown still on the stand, however, Walter Rice tried to erase that positive memory by questioning Brown about the specific portion of the interrogation that happened at the end. And then by replaying that selected portion of the recording to "clarify" his questions. It was the point at which Nowak started to realize that the police were thinking of him as a *suspect* rather than as an innocent witness. Two things stood out in that part of the recorded interrogation: First, Detective Small, who'd done most of the questioning, wasn't pleased that Nowak was catching on. You could hear it in her tone and in the repetition of key questions as she blatantly tried to find a crack in Nowak's story. Second, Nowak's comfortable, conversational manner turned into wariness and felt less transparent than earlier.

Even though they'd heard the entire interview the day before, the jurors seemed completely engaged as they listened to Detective Small ask: "You admitted earlier that you are an experienced hunter and rifleman, right?" The comment wasn't really a question, and by Nowak's response, it was clear that it set off some red flags for him.

"Well, I like to hunt, and I, ah, enjoy practicing at the shooting range. So, ah, I guess you could say I have experience." Then he quickly added, "It was something Harold and I had in common. We used to go to the range and shoot together when we could. Have a beer or two afterwards."

Ignoring the reference to their friendship, Small asked another repeat question. "And, you own a hunting rifle, right?"

"Yes, I think you already asked me that."

"Where is that gun now, Mr. Nowak?"

"I keep it locked up."

"And you have no problem with letting us examine it?"

Nowak was slow to answer. "I'm not quite sure what you're asking here, Detective. Are you implying that you think *I* had something to do with Harold's death? Because if that's where you're going with these questions, you're way off base." His voice sounded tight and slightly higher pitched than it had.

"Come . . . on, Mr. Nowak." She drew out the first two words to emphasize her incredulity. "If you had nothing to do with this murder as you say, you should be happy to let us examine your hunting rifle. I'll tell you what I think. I think you're not being truthful with us. Prove me wrong. Let's have a look at your rifle. See what kind of story *it* has to tell."

There were then several seconds of silence on the recording. Finally, Nowak said: "Look, Detective Small, I've spent the past hour telling you everything I know about what happened before Harold was shot. But I've got to say, right now, I don't much like the sound of what's happening here. I came in on my own because I want to help you find my friend's killer. Now it's starting to feel like you haven't been listening to what I've been telling you. It sounds to me like you think *I* killed Harold."

"Did you?"

"Absolutely not. Of course not."

"Then prove it. Tell us where your rifle is and let us take a look at it."

There was a long audible sigh—presumably from Nowak.

Rice paused the recording, and then asked Brown a direct question: "In your experience as a detective, does an innocent man refuse to turn over his rifle if he didn't use it to commit a crime? What other explanation could there be?"

Sydney felt like she should have a snappy response to his rhetorical question; she didn't want it hanging there for jurors to come to the conclusion Rice was dangling in front of them. Of course, she could have objected that it was argumentative, it was two questions, and it called for a conclusion. But objecting wouldn't have made it go away in the minds of the jurors.

"Not in my experience," Brown predictably replied.

"So, detective Brown," Rice asked, continuing his direct examination. "Yesterday afternoon, we heard the full tape of your interview with Mr. Nowak. But let's clarify one thing: The defendant admitted having a rifle and using it at the shooting range where he allegedly kept it locked up, is that correct?" Rice was apparently going to let the likeable Brown carry the water on this one.

"Yes, that's correct. As you heard yesterday, he admitted that he owned a hunting rifle and that he's reasonably proficient in its use."

"Based upon that response, what did you do next?"

"Well, we wanted to see the rifle. See if maybe it could have been the murder weapon. I mean, given the argument he'd had with the victim a couple of days before the murder, it seemed like a logical thing to do."

"And . . . ?"

"Well, we looked back over the witness statements. In one of them, Harold Dawson's secretary had told us that her boss and the defendant were members at a rifle range up near Issaquah. She couldn't remember the name, but there was only one place that seemed to match. At this point we had plenty for a warrant. Not only did the two men have a loud, bitter argument a couple of days before the killing, but . . ."

"Objection, Your Honor. This witness didn't observe that argument, and he is in no position to characterize it. The jury has already heard from witnesses who were actually present. I think we should stick with what the witnesses saw and said about the exchange." Sydney noted to herself that Detective Brown might come across as a nice guy, but he was obviously quite willing to put a thumb on the scales of justice when he thought it was justified.

"Sustained. The jury is instructed to disregard the witness's characterization of the argument as 'bitter.'"

Rice continued: "Ignoring the argument, Detective Brown, what did you learn from the autopsy about the weapon used in killing Mr. Dawson?"

"The autopsy report referenced a hunting rifle as the likely murder weapon. Since we had the defendant's admission that he owned such a gun, and since he also admitted that he was physically present near to the scene of the crime at the time of the murder, locating his rifle was a priority."

"And?"

"We drove up to Issaquah to the shooting range, showed them our warrant, and asked if Jamison Nowak was a customer of theirs, and if he was, did he keep a locker on their premises. It turned out he did. His locker was secured with a combination padlock owned by him, the user. We cut the lock open with bolt cutters. It turned out the locker did *not* contain a weapon. It did, however, contain half a box of thirty-caliber rifle ammunition which we seized as evidence. Upon further inquiry, one of the personnel at the rifle range who was familiar with the defendant advised us that, ordinarily, the defendant did in fact keep a .30-30 Marlin 336 lever action hunting rifle in that locker. The employee indicated some surprise that we hadn't found it in there because, in his words: 'He keeps it here all the time, except when he goes hunting.'"

This was more hearsay. But Sydney didn't want to call any more attention to this evidence by requiring the prosecution to bring in the actual witness. So, she made no objection.

"Did the gun range keep any records of this rifle?"

"Yes, they did. It's a voluntary system, but the gun range's insurers will cover theft or damage to any weapon kept in one of the lockers on the site if the owner provides the serial number and description of the weapon as a part of their locker rental agreement. Mr. Nowak had signed up for the coverage."

'Based upon that information, what did you do next?"

"We communicated with Ms. Warren who had by then been retained as the defendant's legal counsel. She told us that the defendant no longer wished to assist in our investigation."

"Objection, Your Honor." This one was too much. "Detective Brown has badly misstated what was said in that conversation. And, even if it were true, which it is not, I believe what he's just testified to is also hearsay. I don't believe I ever talked with him on the matter. The only conversation I had about this was actually with Detective Small.

"More importantly my client has been entirely willing to assist with the investigation into this crime. Never have I, nor has he, *ever once* indicated otherwise. From the very start he was eager to help these detectives find the actual killer. He just wasn't prepared to help them pin it—falsely—on him. I am quite sure that there is not a single person in this room, including Mr. Rice, who would have continued answering the increasingly acrimonious questions of these detectives under those conditions. Nor would I advise them to."

"Sustained. Jury will disregard the witness's comments concerning what was allegedly said by Ms. Warren."

Moving right along, Rice asked Brown: "Has this rifle been found?"

"No sir."

"And this locker you mentioned, Mr. Nowak's locker at that Issaquah shooting range, I think you said it had a combination lock. Did anyone on staff at that range have its combination?"

"No sir. They also have no surveillance cameras in the locker area. It's their policy to respect the privacy of their clients. The holder of each locker provides their own padlock. If it's a combination lock, only the owner has the combination."

"Objection, Your Honor. "That last statement about *only* the owner having the combination—this witness simply cannot know that. And, as we plan to show, it is quite obviously not true." The statement was also based on hearsay, but that wasn't the objection she needed to make.

"Sustained. Jury will disregard."

"Well, when we were there, certainly no one there had the combination," Detective Brown commented a bit defensively, without waiting to be asked. "If they had, they'd have told us instead of letting us destroy the lock."

"Objection, Your Honor. May we please wait till final argument to hear the prosecution's arguments and conclusions about this matter?" Sydney was restive and unhappy with the direction of this testimony.

"Sustained."

In spite of the Judge's ruling, Rice continued to press the witness: "So, at this point, Detective Brown, the absence of that gun, how it might have been used, and its current location is a mystery, am I right?"

"Objection, Your Honor. That's a conclusion for the jury to decide. It is also a leading question. And, it is argumentative. It is intended to highlight the point the prosecution is trying to make—not to elicit factual testimony."

"Sustained. Focus on the facts, Mr. Rice."

"Yes, Your Honor."

Sydney knew the ruling had come too late; Rice had made his point. The jury had to be wondering: Where, indeed, was Jamison Nowak's hunting rifle? Why was it missing from his locker? And if, as seemed likely, he was the only person with access to that locker, didn't it have to be him who had removed it?

Sydney rose for her cross examination, resisting the urge to clear her throat in case jurors interpreted that as a sign of nervousness. Shoulders back, chin up, she said to herself.

"Someone else *could* have had the combination, that's possible, isn't it, Detective Brown?"

"I guess anything is *possible*."

"Or, someone good with picking modestly priced combination locks could have gained access. Isn't that also possible?"

He paused momentarily. "Well, I *suppose*."

"My client could even have left it unlocked by accident and the rifle was stolen—that's also possible, isn't it?"

"Objection," Rice said. Sydney was surprised he hadn't objected earlier. The questions were clearly speculative, although under the guise of simply exploring options "She's asking for evidence outside the purview of this officer."

Sydney noticed frowns on some juror faces at his use of the word "purview." Before he could explain, she said: "Your Honor, I withdraw the question." Without missing a beat, she continued. "Detective Brown, how long did the investigation by you and your colleague, Detective Small, take to complete? How many days, weeks, months did you spend on it?"

"Well, we were full time on it initially. For a couple of weeks. But we've actually been working on it off and on right up to coming in here today to testify."

"Anybody else working on it?"

"Well, sure. Lots of other people."

"Could you be specific, please."

"Well, we've had a substantial crime scene crew involved. The medical examiner and their staff, of course. Technical people doing their analysis. Officers searching the scene for the bullet for a couple of days at the outset. And they were back out there again a few days ago to look for the gun. Like I say, lots of people, off and on, over the past three months plus."

"How many people? Roughly?"

"Um, I don't know. All told, might be as many as thirty or so."

"That's thirty professionals, right? These are people who are generally experts in their field?"

"Absolutely."

"And, would I be correct in saying that, at this point in time, you feel you know everything of any importance that there is to be known about this crime?"

"Yes, I'd say that's correct. It's been a thorough investigation."

"Now I'd like you to go back to that interview you and detective Small did with Mr. Nowak shortly after the murder. To the written statement he signed. And to the recording we've all recently listened to. We know, of course, that you don't agree with Mr. Nowak's statement that he was innocent. But other than that, tell me, Detective Brown, based on all of your investigation, all of your work, plus the work of all those thirty professionals extending over the entire last 'three plus months' that you've been investigating this, did you find *any* fact or assertion from Mr. Nowak, *anything at all*, about which you concluded he had lied?"

"Other than his claim that he was innocent, you mean?"

Sydney smiled and turned slightly toward the jury. "Of course, Detective. We can assume that is what *you* believe. If you believed he was innocent, we wouldn't be here, would we? No, I'm asking about everything else he told you. Everything in his written and oral statements. Everything in that interview that was recorded, and that we all recently heard for ourselves. What I want to know is, after *all* the investigation by *all* those people over *all* that time, have you found *any* other detail in anything he told you or anyone else working on the case that turned out to be proven false? Anything at all?" She knew she was taking a risk, but she also knew that without a bold move, her client would probably be convicted.

Detective Brown pursed his lips and gave her question some thought before responding. "Well, he claimed Harold Dawson asked that they meet and chose the place of the meeting. That seems highly unlikely."

"Were you on that call yourself, Detective Brown? Do you have a witness who overheard that conversation?"

"Of course not."

"So that statement by Mr. Nowak has not been proven to be false, has it?"

"Well, it sure seems highly unlikely given what else we know."

"Given, you mean, because you believe he is guilty."

"Ah. That's right."

"Anything else. Any statements he made in that interrogation that were later *proven* to be untrue?"

Emphasizing the word "proven" was an implicit warning to stay with the facts. After a brief pause, he replied: "I can't think of any at the moment."

"Come on, Detective. You were there when that interview was conducted. You listened to it in its entirety again yesterday, along with the rest of us. And you're telling us that you can't *think* of any particulars that were proven false? Or . . . or, is it possible Mr. Nowak has been telling the truth?"

"I guess, other than him claiming to be innocent, I don't know of any specific false statements he's made. However, he did stop cooperating when he realized he was a suspect."

"So, to make sure I understand, after three months of intensive investigation by some thirty or so professional investigators, in an investigation that you and Detective Small led, you're saying . . ."

Rice stood. "Objection, Your Honor."

"You didn't let me finish my sentence, Mr. Rice. How do you know what you are objecting to?"

The judge nodded for her to continue.

"You're saying that to the best of your knowledge, everything Mr. Nowak has told you has been completely and totally truthful, other, of course, than in *your opinion,* you don't believe his claim that he is innocent."

"Objection, Your Honor." Rice was on his feet again. "Asked and answered. Counsel is making an argument here, not questioning a witness."

"Sustained. The witness has already answered your question in the affirmative."

Sydney couldn't have been more pleased with the judge's response; she had just answered the question for Brown. "OK, Detective Brown, let's take another look at your *opinion* about his guilt. Let's talk about all the other suspects in the case. The ones other than Mr. Nowak. The ones that you eliminated from your inquiry when you decided to arrest Mr. Nowak. Perhaps you could list out their names for us."

Brown looked confused: "Names . . .?"

"Yes, the names of the other persons of interest in your investigation, Detective Brown."

Rice leapt up. "That would not be appropriate to name other suspects that have been cleared."

"Overruled," The judge said.

"Detective Brown?"

"Well, I'd say no one was of sufficient interest that put them on the suspect list."

"OK, then let me rephrase that for you, Detective Brown. How many other people who might have done this did you eliminate in the course of your inquiries? No names, just a number."

"Well, um, there really weren't any others. It was completely clear to us from the start that Mr. Nowak was the guilty party."

"I see. So, does that mean you didn't take a look at *any* of the people who'd lost all or a substantial part of their investment portfolios because of advice they got from Harold Dawson on WPPSS bonds?"

"Well, no. I mean we didn't think . . ." He paused, as if realizing what he was about to say wasn't a good idea.

"None had a motive for murder, is that what you thought? Losing a life savings didn't seem worth killing for?"

"That's not what I meant. There were no serious threats or anything to point to a particular person, so when we learned of the argument Dawson had with Nowak, we focused on him."

"There were *no* angry clients?"

"I didn't say that. What I said . . ."

Sydney held up her hand to stop him. "Let me make sure I understand: you believe that losing your life savings because of flawed professional advice isn't a potential motive?"

"I'm saying that Nowak became the prime suspect early on; he had motive, he owned a likely weapon, AND he was at the scene at the time of the man's death."

"How much effort did you and your team of thirty or so professional investigators make to determine that no one else had means, motive and opportunity?"

"We did what we thought was necessary." Brown was fast losing his Boy Scout persona by sounding defensive and slightly ticked off about his professionalism being challenged. She almost felt sorry for him. Almost.

"Which was basically *nothing*, isn't that right? You didn't *seriously* look at *any* other suspects, did you?"

"Objection, Your Honor," Rice said. "She's badgering the witness."

"Overruled. It's cross, and I'm sure Detective Brown can handle it."

"Please answer the question, Detective Brown. How much time did you and your team spend investigating other suspects?"

"We try not to waste time and resources when we see no reason to pursue other options."

"So, once you decided my client might be guilty, you concentrated on proving that he was?"

"Yes. Successfully, I might add."

"With nothing more than circumstantial evidence though, isn't that right?

"Not every crime has an eye-witness, Ms. Warren. It's entirely possible to draw sound conclusions from an accumulation of circum-stantial evidence. You're making it sound like we based our conclusions on insubstantial guesswork."

"'Insubstantial guesswork.' Right. Your words, not mine, Detective."

Both Brown and Rice were scowling. She was fairly certain that neither would be asking her out for a drink in the near future. But she wasn't trying to win a popularity contest; she was trying to prevent an innocent man from going to jail.

"Moving on. You were absolutely certain that no one among the dozens of people who lost money because of Dawson's bad advice was present at the scene?"

"From what Nowak himself told us, there was *no one* else there. It was a chilly weekday in June. The only two cars he saw in the lot were his and Dawson's. He even told us he *heard* the gunshot."

"And you're quite confident that he told you the absolute truth about all that, aren't you?" Her implication hung in the air like a storm cloud ready to explode.

"He had no reason to lie about any of it."

"And no reason to admit he was there in the first place, other than to be truthful." Before Rice could react, she added. "Did you ask around to see if anyone else was reported to be in the area?"

"Not specifically, but we kept the possibility in mind."

"You kept it in mind?" Sydney invested her words with sarcasm "What I asked was if you actually *investigated* to establish whether there was anyone else in the area. Maybe one of those angry clients, for example."

"If there had been other people in the area at the time of the murder, I have no doubt we'd have learned about it."

"How, Detective? By not asking?"

"Objection, Your Honor. Now Ms. Warren is simply arguing with this witness."

"Sustained."

Sydney shifted gears slightly, but her next question indicated that she wasn't letting Detective Brown off the hot seat yet. "At the time of Mr. Dawson's death, he'd also borrowed a lot of money that he hadn't repaid, isn't that right."

"He was in debt, as I understand it. Yes."

"Did you talk with any of those creditors to whom he owed money? See if maybe any of them were unhappy, even angry, about not being paid?"

"Nobody like that came to our attention. Lots of people owe money, Ms. Warren. I myself am paying off a home loan. Doesn't mean I'm worried that my lender might hunt me down and kill me with a hunting rifle if I miss a payment."

"I assume your home loan is through a bank." She paused to let the jurors consider other options. "Under the circumstances, didn't you wonder whether there might be a lender who was more than a little upset about not being repaid?"

"People default on loans. Lenders know that." Brown was sounding less certain; he hadn't missed her hint.

"You did investigate who Dawson had borrowed money from and how much he had borrowed from them?"

"No ma'am. There wasn't any need."

Sydney let that sink in with the jury for a moment. Then, turning to face the jurors, she said. "Why bother, I guess. After all, you'd already made an arrest, right? You wouldn't want to muddy the waters by conducting an actual investigation into the crime, would you?"

"Objection," Rice said.

"I withdraw the question, Your Honor. I believe the jury already knows the answer."

That concluded Sydney's cross. And from the expressions on the faces of the jurors, she felt certain that she had created doubt about the credibility of the investigation.

Rice opted, wisely in Sydney's view, not to redirect.

As Brown stood and stepped down out of the witness chair, Rice announced: "I have just one further witness, Your Honor. The prosecution calls Timothy Bright to the stand."

A young boy appeared from where he'd been seated with his family in the very back of the crowded courtroom. He was dressed in what might have been best described as fresh "back to school" clothes—a crisp plaid shirt, spotless denim trousers, and dark blue running shoes. His hair had been carefully combed, but there remained a notable cowlick sticking up at the back of his head.

Once the oath was administered and young Bright had identified himself, Rice began the questioning: "Did you recently have occasion to visit a picnic area at a place called Two Mountain Creek in July of this year?"

"Yes sir. It wasn't, you know, anything special like. We just had lunch there. Me, my parents, and my sister, too."

"While you were there, did you happen to find anything that you considered unusual? Something that you kept?"

"Uh huh. It was right there under the bridge. In the water. It didn't seem like it belonged to anybody, you know."

"And what was that?"

"A rifle cartridge. An empty one—like without the bullet."

"Is this the rifle cartridge case you found, Timothy?" Rice picked it up off the corner of the prosecution table and held it up for the witness.

"Yeah. Well, I guess, I mean it looks like the one I found. Some police came and took it with them."

"Defense will stipulate that this was the correct cartridge case found by this witness on the prosecution's representations." Sydney didn't challenge the find; there was no sense dragging this out on some chain of custody issue. "But, as Your Honor knows, we firmly object to the introduction of this completely irrelevant cartridge case into evidence, since it was found weeks after the crime in an area where guns and ammunition are not uncommon and has no apparent connection whatever to the matter at hand."

"Your objection is noted, Ms. Warren. And overruled."

"And exactly where did you find it?" Rice asked the boy.

"It was right there in the water. In one of the pools at the edge of the creek. Like under the bridge at the end you come to first from the parking lot. And, well, not exactly under. But close, you know. Right there in the water. Partly covered by sand. I just looked down and saw it."

"And you found this when you were there in July, is that correct, Timothy?"

"Um, we were coming back from my aunt and uncle's house in Tacoma. It was a Sunday. My mom says it was July 10th that we were there and when I found it. It was just there in the water. So, I kept it. Then everybody saw on the news about the man who died, and my sister told me this might be important. So, I gave it to my parents. And I guess they called the police. Is that what you wanted to know?"

Rice glanced in Sydney's direction to see if she had any objections. She shook her head and remained seated.

"That's perfect, Timothy." Rice turned to the judge. "That's it for me, Your Honor."

"I have no questions, for this witness, Your Honor," Sydney said.

"Thank you for your testimony, Timothy," Judge Francis said. "We appreciate when a young person comes forward to do their civic duty and help the course of justice. You're all done, here. You can go back and join your parents."

The boy hopped down from the witness stand and took several steps before turning back to Judge Francis. "Can I get my shell casing back now?" he asked.

"I'm sorry young man, but it is evidence. I'm afraid it is unlikely you'll get it back any time soon. But, again, thank you for your testimony."

"That's all I have, Your Honor," said Rice. "The prosecution rests."

CHAPTER 16

Sydney Warren
King County Courthouse, Seattle
Courtroom of Judge Roberta Francis, Eighth Floor, Room 808
Wednesday, September 21, 1983 (3:00 p.m.)

When Andrea Rymes first appeared on Walt Rice's witness list, Sydney was conflicted. Mel had interviewed her, found her willing to cooperate, and didn't sense that she would be a hostile witness. Of course, that was *before* she had testified for the prosecution, and *before* Sydney had asked her a series of moderately tough questions on cross-examination. Although Sydney had been careful not to push too hard, she was no longer certain that she could count on Rymes to have an open mind as to Nowak's guilt or innocence. Whatever her bias, however, Rymes was still in the best position to have detailed knowledge of Dawson's client accounts, so Syndey reluctantly recalled her to the stand as her first witness.

Without any preliminaries, Sydney went directly to the point. "For the record, you were Mr. Dawson's personal administrative assistant for several years, including *throughout* the *entire* period of the collapse of bond values with the Washington Public Power Supply System, what we all now refer to as Whoops, and right up to Mr. Dawson's death. Is that correct?"

"That's correct."

"How many of Mr. Dawson's clients were invested in those bonds?"

"Most were. Nearly all."

"Were any of them unhappy about Mr. Dawson's promotion and continued support for investments that lost them significant amounts of money?"

"Relevance, Your Honor. And hearsay." The witness hadn't even had time to draw a breath before Rice had bellowed out his objections. "Are we now going to be forced to suffer through some kind of extended effort to discredit the victim?" Rice, who knew exactly where this testimony was actually leading, was shaking his head as though the whole idea of it was offensive.

"The relevance is obvious, Your Honor," Sydney quickly responded. "We are here because someone shot Harold Dawson. The prosecution wants us to believe that Mr. Nowak is the *only* person with a motive for murder. There quite clearly may be many others with similar or even stronger motives. Mr. Rice has spent most of three days offering up what barely qualifies as circumstantial evidence to imply that Mr. Nowak is the guilty party. A good example is the miscellaneous rifle cartridge found weeks after the crime—a cartridge they have not been able to link either to Mr. Nowak or to Mr. Dawson's death.

" *We* do *not* agree with the prosecution's single-minded claims, Your Honor. Now it is *our* turn to present *our* evidence of who *we* think may have committed this heinous crime. They've had their chance. Now it's ours. As I explained right at the outset, we will be offering evidence that clearly shows that parties *other* than Mr. Nowak had motive and opportunity."

"Objection, Your Honor." His tone suggested that he knew he would be overruled, but he most likely wanted it noted for future reference.

"Overruled. Keep it short, Counselor."

"Your Honor, if the court please, I have just one more point to make related to this topic. At the beginning of the investigation, Mr. Nowak did his best to help the police. He freely shared facts that weren't always in his best interest to reveal. But because he wanted them to find his friend's killer, he held nothing back. And, as attested to by one of the detectives working the case, every word of what he told them has either proven to be completely true or remains uncontested by other evidence. Sadly, however, the detectives took the easy path and failed to investigate the many other possible suspects. After all, they had someone who admitted being upset with the victim and who had argued publicly with him. What more did they need?"

"Your point, Counselor?"

"If we are to prove Mr. Nowak's innocence, we have no choice but to pick up the ball where the sheriff's detectives dropped it. We ask that *we* now be allowed the same leeway in making *our* case as the prosecution was allowed in making *theirs*."

Rice was on his feet, on the verge of interrupting with another objection, but Judge Francis beat him to it.

"That's sufficient, Ms. Warren. I understand your position. Let's finish taking the evidence before we actually argue the case. The objection is overruled, for now. But you're going to be on a tight leash here. Keep your evidence relevant."

"Yes, Your Honor." Sydney turned to the witness: "Do you recall my last question, Ms. Rymes?"

"Un huh. You want to know about clients who were angry because of their Whoops losses."

"Yes, and please limit your response to what you have reason to know from personal contacts and conversations." She wasn't about to give Rice a reason to object to the testimony as hearsay.

"I filtered phone calls to Mr. Dawson and kept track of clients who withdrew their accounts. Is that the kind of thing you mean?"

"Yes. Please continue."

"Well, there were quite a few upset clients. For many of our clientele, the WPPSS bonds were a small part of their portfolios. But even some of these modest investors didn't like losing *any* money on what they'd previously considered a very secure investment. There were also a fair number of individuals who were heavily invested in WPPSS bonds. Although the company advocates fund diversity, the WPPSS bonds seemed like a really good deal. Some clients were encouraged to invest heavily in these bonds. And they lost a lot of money. They were definitely not happy about that. They frequently gave me an earful when they called to talk to their advisors.

"Then there were group investors. A number of them had large losses that impacted good-sized memberships. The members of those groups were mad at both their financial managers and at our company." She paused. "I know that because I talked with some of the managers, as well as with a few individual members of their groups." She looked at Sydney and asked, "Should I continue?"

"Yes, please." She was surprised Rice wasn't jumping up with an objection; Rhymes had managed to readily mix opinion and facts.

"Well, the financial managers were doubly mad at us because we'd not only lost their money, we'd made them look bad with their membership."

"For the record, when you refer to a 'modest investor,' what are we talking about—a few hundred dollars, a few thousand, tens of thousands, hundreds of thousands?"

"Mostly a few thousand or even tens of thousands, I'd say. Maybe into the hundreds of thousands for a few clients and groups, but, again, how significant that is depends on the size of their overall portfolio."

"So, if one of those several clients that lost, let's say, fifty or sixty thousand, had a relatively small investment portfolio, for them that would be a *very* significant financial loss, wouldn't it?"

Before Rice could object, Sydney changed the subject: "Did any clients leave your firm because of their losses?"

"Yes, some did. Several. Quite a few, actually."

"Even some who had been with Mr. Dawson a long time?"

"Yes." Rymes looked uncomfortable making the admission, but she didn't try to avoid a direct answer.

"Was it your understanding that Mr. Dawson always advised his clients to diversify?"

"Objection, Your Honor. The witness can only guess about whether the deceased encouraged his clients to diversify."

"Sustained."

"Let me rephrase that, wasn't it company policy to suggest portfolio diversification?"

"Yes."

"So, if Mr. Dawson was following company policy, he would have informed his clients about the risks of non-diversification?"

"Yes, but they may not have taken the WPPSS warning seriously. Initially, those bonds were thought to be a safe investment."

"And even if they'd been informed about risks, that didn't necessarily keep them from being angry when things went south, did it?"

"Objection, Your Honor. Speculation."

"Sustained."

Sydney felt she had already made her point and was not unhappy to move on. "In your earlier testimony, you were asked about the argument that you overheard between Mr. Dawson and Mr. Nowak. In the weeks leading up to the final Supreme Court decision on June 15, the one that decided the fate of the bonds, can you recall any arguments or disagreements between Mr. Dawson and any of his clients?"

"Well, I wouldn't exactly call all of the exchanges he had with clients during that time period *arguments*. But there were definitely a number of unpleasant conversations. Mr. Dawson believed the bonds would recover much of their earlier value once the court ruled, so he tried to convince clients that just because their investment had lost value, it wasn't necessarily the best time to sell."

"Objection, Your Honor. Lack of personal knowledge."

"Sustained."

"Did you personally hear complaints from any particular clients about their losses on the WPPSS bonds, Ms. Rymes?"

"Yes, several."

"Objection, Your Honor. Again, there is no reason to provide the names of disgruntled clients." Sydney was gratified to see that Rice's face was flushed, and there were tiny beads of sweat on the tip of his nose and upper lip.

"You opened that door, Mr. Rice," Judge Francis said. "You may answer the question, Ms. Rymes."

Rymes smiled nervously at the judge before continuing. "I don't like to name names . . ." She hesitated.

"You're not accusing anybody of anything," Sydney said. "With that in mind, can you describe anything you directly observed to indicate a client was unhappy with Mr. Dawson?"

"Well, I sat in on a meeting with the directors of the Cartwright Trust in which they complained pretty forcefully about their losses. And there was Mr. Moss."

"OK, let's start with the Cartwright Trust. Who are they?"

"Well, James Cartwright, a wealthy architect, left behind a trust for his two minor children—twin boys. It was to be distributed when they reached twenty-five. Karen Cartwright, the boys' mother, is the trustee. She was a big believer in municipals, something she had in common with Mr. Dawson."

Rice leaned forward like he was about to object, then slumped back in his chair.

"The boys are approaching twenty-five, so Mrs. Cartwright and her two sons had set up an appointment with Mr. Dawson to talk about the trust disbursement. I was there to take notes, but the conversation quickly veered off topic and was all about how much money they had lost with the WPPSS bonds. They blamed Mr. Dawson for their losses and berated him for the advice Mrs. Cartwright had been given."

"After Mr. Dawson's death, do you know if Detectives Small and Brown talked to Mrs. Cartwright or her sons?"

"I don't know for sure, but I doubt it. No one asked for a list of clients who lost money in the WPPSS collapse."

Sydney paused and looked at the Jury to let them know that they had just heard something significant. Then: "You also mentioned a Mr. Moss. What was his story, Ms. Rymes? Why did you bring up his name in particular?"

"Well, he had a lot of personal money in WPPSS." She stopped, as if mindful that she needed to carefully word her response to comply with court rules.

"And . . .?"

"In those last few days, Mr. Dawson was dodging all of his calls. And I'm pretty sure Mr. Moss knew it."

"What makes you say that?"

"He sounded frustrated when he called and, you know, mad. One time he even yelled at me over the phone because I wouldn't put him through to Mr. Dawson."

"You said that Mr. Dawson was 'dodging' all of his calls?"

"Yes. He told me that he was busy working on a plan to recoup their losses, and as soon as he could get the plan together, he would contact his clients."

"So, there were a number of very angry clients, and as far as you know, the police did not consider them suspects."

Rice was on his feet. "Hearsay, Your Honor."

"Sustained."

"My apologies, Your Honor." Sydney turned back to Rymes. "Did the police contact you or ask you for information about any of Dawson's clients?"

"No, they did not."

"How about the firm's associates—were any of them upset?"

"Again, Your Honor, hearsay." Rice complained.

"Let me rephrase my question, Your Honor."

The judge nodded.

"Based on conversations with the firm's associates, did you observe or learn anything that made you believe that any of them were upset about the way Mr. Dawson had handled the bonds?"

"I did. And they were. Understandably. The entire firm ended up on the hook for the losses. And the associates often have their own clients. Some of their clients were unhappy as well, though they wouldn't necessarily have known it was Mr. Dawson who was responsible."

"But the associates would?"

"Yes, of course."

"The initial WPPSS losses occurred over time though, not all at once, correct?"

"Yes, over a period of about eighteen months."

"And how did Mr. Dawson respond to client and associate concerns during that time period?"

"As I said, Mr. Dawson encouraged clients and associates to stay the course. And, as we now know, he was buying some of his clients' bonds back at above market with his own money to camouflage losses. But during that time, he still lost a fair number of clients. Even some who had been loyal for years jumped ship."

"And associates? What did he tell them?"

"Objection. No foundation. Hearsay."

"Were you present for any conversations between associates and Mr. Dawson?"

"Mr. Nowak was acting as the liaison between Mr. Dawson and the associates."

Sydney hesitated. Obviously the "angry associate" argument was a dead end. There was still one more angle to try, but it was risky. "Ms. Rymes, you said something a moment ago that seemed unusual. I'd like you to explain it for me."

"OK."

"You said that your boss was buying back bonds to camouflage losses."

"Uh huh."

"Would you say more about that?"

"Well, the thing is, Ms. Warren, you'd need to have known Mr. Dawson to understand how all these bond losses affected him. He was a truly nice person. He really cared about his clients and went way out of his way to look out for their interests. When all this was happening, and his clients started deserting him, he saw it as a kind of personal defeat and got really depressed.

"I know it's easy to see him as some kind of villain in all this. Sure, he was wrong about that court ruling, there's no getting around that. And the bonds were worthless after that. But that isn't actually when most of our clients lost their savings. Most of the harm was done many months earlier, back when the WPPSS folks called off construction on those two nuclear plants. Or even before. That's when the bond values really tanked. And it wasn't fair to blame that on Mr. Dawson. It took everybody by surprise."

For several minutes, Sydney had sensed Rice getting impatient. And maybe the Judge was as well. Rymes' story was interesting, but it wasn't getting Sydney where she knew she needed to be. Doubtless Rice had held off objecting because the part about Dawson caring about his clients painted his murder victim in a favorable light. He was probably hoping that would harden the jury toward the man who might have killed him.

Andrea Rymes had barely paused long enough to draw a breath between sentences when Rice finally had enough. "All this is well and good, Your Honor, but sooner or later there's going to need to be a point here. Objection. Relevancy."

Judge Francis apparently had a slightly different view. "I think we need to see where this is going, Mr. Rice. Objection overruled. But do move this along, Ms. Warren."

Sydney nodded and turned back to her witness. "I think we all get that. He felt bad about losing money for his clients."

"He not only felt bad, he felt *responsible.* Personally. As I mentioned, he started buying their bonds with his own money, at above their market price. He'd tell his client that he'd found a buyer who thought the bonds were a bargain. Or that things were starting to look up. When he did that, it was often enough to keep a client on board a little longer."

"It sounds like a plan that couldn't last."

"Well, the thing is, when his client base began to evaporate and he started buying up bonds to keep more from leaving, it was a huge risk. If the Supreme Court had ruled differently, the price would have gone up, and he might have recovered. Instead, he ended up buying high and selling low. It was, essentially a kind of ill-fated Ponzi scheme. Mr. Dawson basically spent himself into bankruptcy."

Out of the corner of her eye, Sydney saw Judge Francis reach for her gavel.

"Any idea how he tried to stay afloat financially?" To Sydney's relief, there was no rap of the gavel, but it remained poised.

"Loan sharks," the witness answered. "Mr. Dawson borrowed money from a loan shark."

The gavel was put to rest.

"How do you know this?"

"One day, about a week before the Supreme Court decision came down, this big guy came into the office. Insisted he see 'Harold.' Got really pushy and demanded that our receptionist show him which office was his. Said it was 'time Harold paid up.' Mr. Dawson was actually out at the time. Even so, the receptionist, bless her, wasn't going to let this unauthorized person into the office area. She stood her ground, but the experience really unsettled her."

"Objection, Your Honor. This nonsense has gone on long enough. Now we're being fed more hearsay. The prosecution objects to this whole line of questioning. We ask that the witness's last answer be stricken. And that the jury be instructed to disregard it."

"I can't disagree, Ms. Warren," said the judge. "Sounds very much like hearsay to me."

"Sorry, Your Honor. I'll remedy that hearsay objection very shortly, Meanwhile, I'm finished with this witness. Subject to recall."

"Mr. Rice? Cross examination?"

It looked to Sydney like Walter Rice had been caught flat-footed. More likely, however, he was struggling to decide whether cross-examining Rymes would benefit or hurt his cause. Rymes had proved to be a transparent, likable person with information that had held the jurors' attention all the way through her testimony.

After a moment, Rice conceded: "I have no cross examination for this witness."

"You may stand down, Ms. Rymes," said the judge. "But please return tomorrow and remain available. There may be more questions for you then."

It was the end of the day. As in any trial, the tide of evidence ebbed and flowed in favor of one side then the other. Sydney hoped that tomorrow the tide would again flow in her favor.

CHAPTER 17

Sydney Warren
King County Courthouse, Seattle
Courtroom of Judge Roberta Francis, Eighth Floor, Room 808
Thursday, September 22, 1983

"Defense calls Lauren Franklin-Keene," Sydney announced. For a moment, she suffered a stab of fear that perhaps the formidable RDN receptionist introduced by Andrea Rymes might fail to appear. Then a stylishly dressed, petite woman rose from one of the benches in the back of the room and stepped tentatively forward.

"Ms. Franklin-Keene?" Judge Francis asked. The witness nodded. "Please come forward and take your place at the witness stand," the judge said with a wave of her hand.

For Sydney, this was one of those trial moments every lawyer prayed would happen—she experienced a rush of confidence that everything was about to come together. Suppressing a smile, she waited impatiently while the witness was sworn. Then she inhaled deeply and squared her shoulders. She was ready.

After the preliminary introduction of her witness, Sydney knew exactly what she needed to accomplish: "Can we correctly assume, Ms.

Franklin-Keene, that you were in the courtroom yesterday afternoon and that you observed much of the testimony of the previous witness, Andrea Rymes?"

"Yes. I believe I saw all of it."

"And are you the RDN receptionist Ms. Rymes described in her testimony?"

The witness produced a winning smile. "I believe I am."

"Do you recall the event she described as an encounter in the reception area at your place of employment with a large, intimidating male? That would have happened about a week before the Washington Supreme Court announced its WPPSS decision on June 15. Roughly, about the 8th of June."

"Well, I don't recall the exact date. But the timing you describe sounds about right. And, yes, I *definitely* recall the encounter. Not something I'm ever likely to forget."

"Please tell us what happened, Ms. Franklin-Keene."

"This really big, tough-looking guy wearing an ill-fitting suit came in looking for Harold Dawson. I told him Mr. Dawson was out, but he apparently didn't believe me. He loudly demanded that I show him to Mr. Dawson's office. I told him I couldn't do that, but that I'd be happy to take a message or make an appointment. That didn't satisfy him, though. In no uncertain terms, he said that he would find him on his own.

"By then I was punching intercom numbers trying to get help from anybody who was in the office at the time.

"Then this guy came around behind the reception counter, shoved me aside, and started thumbing through the printed appointments calendar I keep there. He had a gun. He didn't pull it out, but I could see it there. Under his jacket. The office directory with all of the staff and office numbers was on the desk right there beside the calendar, but thankfully he didn't know what he was looking for. I reached over past him and tried to pick up the phone receiver, but he pushed me away, like I was an annoying child.

"That was when I panicked. I was trapped behind the counter, and I was really scared.

"Thankfully, that's when Mr. Ravenswood, our Senior Partner, happened to step in through the glass entry doors coming from the elevator lobby. He is not a young man. And he isn't very big, but, bless his heart, he hurried over and got right up close to this bully and demanded to know what he was doing there. That guy could have picked up Mr. Ravenswood in one hand and pitched him across the room if he'd wanted. But Mr. Ravenswood sounded like he meant business.

"At the same time, Jerry, the bookkeeper, and Melinda, one of the firm's associates, showed up. Jerry and Melinda had heard what was going on over the intercom. The man stopped in his tracks and looked around. With me, Melinda, Jerry, and Mr. Ravenswood, there were four of us staring him down. I think Andrea came into the reception area about then too.

"For a minute, I thought he might try to take on all of us. Given his size, he might have succeeded. And if he'd drawn his gun . . . Instead, he put his hands in the air and backed away. As he came out from behind the desk, he told us that he had a message for Harold Dawson, that he'd better 'fulfil his obligations' or he, his family, and anyone else that got in the way would have some very serious regrets. He used those exact words: 'Very serious regrets.' Then he took off.

"Jerry had called building security—which, in retrospect, I should have done. But I was so scared that I wasn't thinking clearly." She smiled apologetically before continuing. "Unfortunately, there was a down elevator just opening in the lobby as the man left, so before the security people showed up, he was already gone."

Although her voice had remained strong throughout her testimony, Sydney noticed that her hands were clenched tightly to the arms of the witness chair. She hoped the jurors noticed, too. "Have you seen him since then?"

"No, and I sincerely hope I never do."

"In the months before Mr. Dawson died, was that the only encounter you had with angry people coming into the office to see him?"

"No, it wasn't."

"Can you describe any other incidents?"

"There was all this pent-up frustration with Mr. Dawson over those WPPSS bonds that looked to be headed for default. Clients would come into the office without an appointment and demand to see Mr. Dawson. When that happened, I was instructed to tell them that Mr. Dawson was out and encourage them to leave a message and Mr. Dawson would get back to them. They claimed he never did.

"Sometimes when they showed up in reception, they'd refuse to leave. On several occasions I had people sitting around in the waiting room staring daggers at me for hours before they finally gave up and left. It was extremely uncomfortable."

"Did anyone tell you why they wanted to see Mr. Dawson?"

"Oh yes. They weren't shy about that. They let me know in no uncertain terms how upset they were about their WPPSS losses and insisted I tell them what was going on. I felt bad that I didn't know any details and usually suggested that they also contact Mr. Nowak, the managing partner for the firm. None of them got physical like the big guy, but it was unnerving."

When Sydney completed her questioning, Walter Rice took a long moment to apparently consider what he might achieve on cross examination, before announcing: "I have no questions for this witness." His tone suggested that her testimony wasn't worth the bother.

Sydney reserved the right to recall the witness and asked that Lauren Franklin-Keene remain in the courtroom.

"The defense calls Julia Ortez to the stand," Sydney announced next.

Julia was present pursuant to a request from Duncan Carmichael. She was dressed casually in slacks and a subdued jacket over an ivory blouse. An attractive woman who didn't flaunt her appearance but still got admiring looks as she took the stand. Three months after her husband's disappearance, she was still staying with her mother near Alki Point in West Seattle. Nothing had returned to anywhere near "normal" for her. Sydney was grateful that she had agreed to testify.

"Ms. Ortez, what is your relationship with the victim in this case, Harold Dawson?"

"Harold Dawson was my father."

"My condolences, Mrs. Ortez. I am very sorry for your loss. And we appreciate your willingness to testify today." Sydney wanted to make it clear to the jury that the decedent's own daughter was willing to testify in her client's defense.

"Thank you. He was a good man."

"We've asked you here today to tell us about an event that happened a couple of weeks after your father died. A visit you had concerning a debt your father owed to a firm by the name of . . ." Sydney made a show of looking down at a document she held in her hand: "AA Best Bet Bail Bonds. Do you recall such a visit?" She was well aware that the firm's sketchy name and its association with the bail bonds business might seem unsavory to some of the jurors.

"I certainly do. Not much chance I'd forget."

"Tell us what happened."

"I'd moved in with my mother at her condo on Alki Beach. Then, on Friday morning before the July 4th weekend, this big bruiser shows up at the door. When I answered he forced his way inside and checked the place out like he owned it. I had no idea why he was there and what he wanted. My one-year-old daughter Allison was there with me. She immediately started crying. I picked her up to keep her away from the man. I was really frightened."

"What happened next?"

"Well, he asked me if I was Julia Ortez, the daughter of Harold Dawson who'd died recently. I was tempted to deny it, but I assumed he already knew who I was. As soon as I admitted that I was my father's daughter, he demanded that I pay him a huge chunk of change. I've forgotten the exact amount he mentioned, but it was over $500,000. He said my dad owed the money to his employer, and that the amount was accruing interest every day. And, now that my dad was gone, he claimed that I was responsible for paying off his debt."

"How did you respond to that?"

"I told him he was crazy, and that I didn't have anything like that kind of money. That my dad had been broke when he'd died.

"I'd just come back from doing some shopping and had thrown my jacket over the back of the couch. He reached down, picked it up, and handed it to me. Said I should 'leave the kid' and that I was coming with him. Said I was going to take him to my bank where we would see exactly how much money I had. That's when Allison started screaming. I didn't know what to do."

Sydney kept her eyes on Julia as she spoke, but she could almost feel the jury members empathizing with Julia's situation.

"I can see why you found that upsetting. Tell me more about this man who showed up demanding money. What did he look like?"

"Oh, well, mostly he was just big, you know. Like pro-football-player big. Way over six feet—I'm not sure exactly, but I think he had to duck to get under the door jamb when he came inside. And he was all muscle." She pointed to a place on the underside of her right jaw. "He had a small scar on his chin. And long brown hair pulled back in a pony tail."

"So, what did you do?"

"Well, I sure wasn't going to go anywhere with him, let alone to the bank. And I wasn't going anywhere without Allison. I thought about yelling for help, but I doubted anyone but my mother would hear. And I wanted to avoid involving her if I could. Then I saw her coming toward us from down the hall.

"The man was yelling at me to put on my coat, but I was still resisting, trying to decide if it was safer for Allison and Mom if I did what he said. I yelled for her to 'stay back,' but she ignored me and came right up to him and demanded to know his name and what he was doing in her home. I remember thinking that she looked like a little toy doll standing up close to him like that.

"He told her his name was Grant and that he was a collection agent who worked for one of my father's creditors. My mom told him that there would be a probate filed with the King County courts and, if his employer had a legitimate debt, they'd be notified of the probate and would be able to submit their claim against my dad's estate.

"That's when he pulled out this document—the note thing you have there in your hand. Instead of giving it to her, however, he turned and handed the paper to me. He told me to 'forget the amount it says on that note. It's way too late for that now.' Then he added something about the 'longer you wait to pay, the more it's going to be.' Then he turned to my mother and said that his employer didn't bother with courts and probates.

"I remember him looking down at my mother and sort of sneering. Then he looked at me and my screaming baby and told me I had three days to pay. His last words before he tossed my coat on the couch and left were: "Otherwise, I'll be back and you and that kid of yours *will wish you had*.""

Sydney glanced at the jury—they were all watching Julia, wide-eyed, as if mesmerized by her fear.

"Was this man, Grant, armed?"

"Well, he didn't take it out, but he definitely had a gun. I saw it under his left arm when he was trying to get me to put on my coat."

"Could you tell what kind of gun it was?"

"I don't know anything about guns. But this one just looked really big to me. Maybe because I was scared. It was in this leather holster with the handle pointed out. It crossed my mind that he'd let his jacket come open to make sure I saw it, you know. Help him make his point."

"Is this the promissory note he gave you?"

She took the document from Sydney, looked at it, and handed it back. "Yeah, that's it. It's for $250,000 plus 12% interest; not the amount he demanded."

"Is that your father's signature?"

"I believe it is, yes."

"Did you see this Grant fellow again?"

"No. But we did file a probate a few weeks later. That company, the one on the note, made a claim against dad's estate. Of course there wasn't any money in the estate to pay it. Let alone the amount this 'Grant' was demanding. For months since, mom and I have been terrified that he might show up again."

"Thank you, Mrs. Ortez." Sydney turned to the judge. "That's all I have for this witness at the moment, but I'd like her to stand by in the courtroom with the others, and to reserve the right to recall her later if the need arises."

Julia Ortez left the stand, went through the little gate at the front of the spectator area, and took an empty seat.

Throughout the testimony of Lauren Franklin-Keene and Julia

Ortez, Sydney had been glancing from time to time toward the back of the courtroom, hoping to see Mel Marshall arrive. Just moments before Julia Ortez was done, Sydney was deeply relieved to see Mel step into the courtroom, give her a nod, and wait for her to signal that she was ready for the next witness.

"We call Grant Meade to the witness stand."

CHAPTER 18

Sydney Warren
King County Courthouse, Seattle
Courtroom of Judge Roberta Francis, Eighth Floor, Room 808
Thursday, September 22, 1983

There was a flurry of interest as everyone turned to look at the door at the back of the courtroom. Timed perfectly for a dramatic entrance, one of the doors opened, and in came Mel Marshall followed by a massive man, at least six-foot-five, with a bodybuilder physique. His wide shoulders strained against the seams in his blue blazer, and his plaid flannel shirt looked like it had been tailored for Paul Bunyan. He carried a zippered portfolio under a muscular arm that, next to his impressive size, looked like a child's toy attaché case.

As he approached the front of the courtroom, Syndey noted that he matched Julia's description perfectly—his size, his long brown hair pulled back in a pony-tail, and the scar on his chin.

Neither woman had mentioned the prison tats on his fingers, but Sydney guessed that all the jurors noticed them as he took the oath.

"Please state your name for the record."

"Grant Meade," he said. Then he settled into the witness chair like a man who had done it many times before, his massive presence dominating the witness box. From the way jurors were sitting upright and eyeing the man, they were clearly anxious to hear what he had to say.

Sydney wasted no time getting to the main point. "Who is your employer, Mr. Meade?"

"I work for AA Best Bet Bail Bonds. Here in Seattle."

"And what is the nature of your employment?"

"I'm a collection agent. I sometimes serve legal process and interview delinquent clients. I also assist with the apprehension of the occasional fugitive who absconds and forfeits bail." The description of his job was more articulate than she'd anticipated. It sounded like something memorized from an advertisement for his employers.

"So, not free-lance like a bounty hunter, but similar work, right?"

"You could say that, *ma'am*. I am a salaried employee."

Sydney hated being "ma'amed," especially when accompanied by a mocking tone. She suspected he didn't care much for "lady lawyers," perhaps not for lawyers in general. "Does AA Best Bet Bail Bonds also make loans other than for bail?"

"Yes, we do. We are a 'consumer lender' licensed by the State of Washington."

"Did your firm make a loan to one Harold Dawson in the year preceding his death on June 17 of this year?"

Meade reached down, opened the zippered case he'd laid on his lap, and withdrew a paper document which he placed on the broad surface of the low wall around the witness stand. "Yes, we did. Mr. Dawson signed a personal note with us in the amount of $250,000. This is a copy of that note."

Sydney came over and picked up the document. "This is a copy of the signed paper document that reflects that obligation?"

"Yes. That's a copy of the original promissory note. You'll see it is signed by Harold Dawson. And dated January 6, 1983."

"I'd like to offer this document in evidence, Mr. Meade. I assume you can produce the original if requested?"

"Yes, of course." He sounded insulted that she would even ask such a question.

"This copy is fine with the defense, Your Honor."

"And with the prosecution." Rice sounded as though he didn't like where this seemed to be going. But he didn't have any real grounds for objecting.

"Was collecting on this note one of your assignments from your employer, Mr. Meade?"

"Yes, it was."

"How did that go?"

"Well, I was unable to obtain payment. In the end, we submitted our claim to Mr. Dawson's estate after he died."

"But the debt was never paid."

"That's right. The estate was without funds."

Despite his somewhat brutish appearance, Meade seemed both professional and relaxed. Mel had told him that he was needed to verify that Harold Dawson had borrowed the $250,000 reflected in the note and that, following Dawson's death, it had proven to be uncollectable. End of story.

However, it was not.

Sydney was about to pull back the curtain on her real reason for wanting his testimony. And she doubted that neither Meade nor Rice was going to be happy about it.

"So what security was provided by Mr. Dawson for this loan?"

"Security. Um, this was a personal note."

"Really? Wow! $250,000—even at today's prices, that's enough to buy a very nice house or . . ." she smiled ". . . a small fleet of super-luxury cars." Maintaining her pleasant tone, she asked, "So, you're saying there was no mortgage placed on his home to cover this loan?"

"Not that I'm aware of."

"As the agent assigned to collect these funds, you'd surely know if there had been some sort of security provided, yes?"

"Yeah, I guess."

"How about investment securities? Did Mr. Dawson offer any stocks, bonds, or other secondary notes to back up this loan?"

"Not that I'm aware of." He was starting to sound irritated by Sydney's questions, shifting his bulk in a chair that was made for someone much smaller.

"How about undeveloped real estate? Or . . . valuable personal property of some kind?"

"Not that I know of." He didn't flinch, but he suddenly sounded less sure of himself.

"And as the man responsible for collections, you would be aware of anything like that, I assume." Without waiting for a response, she added. "Otherwise, you wouldn't know how to squeeze anything but money out of your employer's clients."

Rice stood: "Argumentative."

"Sustained."

Meade spoke before she had a chance to reframe her question. "Like I said, this was just a personal note based on Dawson's credit record."

"So, back in January, Mr. Dawson must have had an excellent credit record for your company to loan him that much money."

"Well, I don't make the loans, but I suppose that's probably right."

"Sure, you don't *make* the loans. But you do *collect* them, though."

"That's my job."

"So, you'd definitely have seen any credit report your company had on Mr. Dawson. If you were going to collect this debt, you'd need to know everything there was to know about his assets. About his real-estate, motor vehicles, stocks or bonds, bank accounts. Anything you could attach. Like the name of his employer so you could garnish his wages, if needed. That all falls under your job description, am I right?"

"Well, yeah, sure. But Dawson didn't offer anything like that as security."

Sydney picked up the document which had now been marked as Defense Exhibit 1. "Please take a look at this promissory note, and tell me, Mr. Meade, when did this financial obligation come due? When was Mr. Dawson supposed to have paid it back in full?"

Meade took the note, pulled a pair of reading glasses out of his jacket pocket, put them on, and began scanning the page, suddenly transformed by the glasses into a very smooth-skinned but studious bear.

"It's right here, I believe Mr. Meade." Sydney reached over and pointed at the appropriate place in the document as he held it in his oversized hands.

"Yeah, so it looks like he had to pay us back on June 6, 1983."

"In full."

"Uh huh."

She reached out and Meade handed her back the note.

"Let's recap to make sure we're getting this right. In January of 1983, just after Christmas, your employer made an unsecured personal loan of $250,000 at 12% annual interest and all that was required of Mr. Dawson was his signature on this promissory note payable in full after a period of five months? Have I got that right?"

"As far as I know." Meade's stoicism was tinged with doubt.

"And I take it that after five months had passed and the note came due on the 6th of June, Mr. Dawson defaulted on this note because he didn't have the funds, am I right?"

"That's what he claimed."

Sydney paused at the word 'claimed.' "Did you think he was hiding assets?"

"They always try to do that."

"But you had no proof that Dawson had any assets hidden away."

"No proof."

Again, she paused as if struck by his wording, but then moved on. "Did your company go to court, secure a judgment, and then seize or garnish payments he was receiving from this professional partnership?"

"Not that I know of."

"But before that, before he died, he started not answering your calls? Avoiding your visits?"

"Well, yeah. It's not uncommon."

"Must have been frustrating?"

"All in a day's work."

"Did you, on or about June 8, visit Mr. Dawson's place of business at the offices of RDN Financial in the Seafirst Building here in Seattle in an effort to meet with Mr. Dawson in person and demand payment on this note?"

"No, ma'am. I did not."

"You didn't?" Sydney didn't have to feign looking incredulous. After admitting everything else, why was he denying the visit to Dawson's office?

"No, ma'am."

Sydney only paused a beat before moving on. "About two weeks after Mr. Dawson died—that would have been on Friday, July 1st—did you visit the private home of Mr. Dawson's ex-wife and daughter at their condominium unit on Alki Avenue in West Seattle?"

Meade was clearly troubled by this question. He'd denied the earlier confrontation at the offices of RDN. But, now, he was hesitating to similarly deny the visit to the home of Julia and her mother. Finally, he said: "I'd have to check my calendar on that one. Don't recall."

"Are you saying you *might* have gone there on that date? Or that you're not sure of the date you went there?"

"Both I guess. Just don't recall."

"But it might have happened? May I remind you that you're under oath."

"Could have. I make a lot of collection calls."

"Objection, Your Honor," Rice interposed. "Counsel is badgering the witness—her own witness."

Sydney was standing a good ten or fifteen feet away from the witness at the time of the objection. She turned to the judge with an incredulous smile that was also visible to the jury. She had anticipated the objection. An attorney badgered a witness to intimidate and put them off guard. The physical contrast between her and the man on the stand made it seem highly unlikely she could intimidate this particular witness. Hopefully, the judge would see that, too—and if she didn't, surely the jury would.

"Overruled. Ms. Warren, you have permission to treat this as an adverse witness. Proceed with your cross."

Sydney turned back to Meade. "Because if, as you seem to be saying, you might have made such a visit, that raises another question, Mr. Meade. That other question is *why*? If Mr. Dawson was dead and your recourse was to file a claim with his estate, *why* would you visit his ex-wife and daughter at their home in your continued efforts to collect Mr. Dawson's debt? Why did you go there that day, Mr. Meade?"

"Like I said, I don't remember."

"It was a pretty memorable meeting, Mr. Meade. At least from their point of view. You're sure you don't remember it?"

"Objection. Asked and answered," Rice said.

"Actually, I think Mr. Rice is absolutely right. I think you actually *have* answered my question, Mr. Meade. And everyone in this courtroom knows it." Sidney then turned and looked significantly at the jury, hopeful they'd followed her ironic conclusion.

"Sustained. Move on, Counsel."

With that, Sydney returned the document to the clerk before turning to face the witness. She was about to head into uncharted territory. As every experienced trial lawyer knows, you *never* ask a question of a witness unless you already know the answer. There had not, however, been any way to meaningfully interview this witness before trial. If she didn't make the most of this opportunity to point the finger at the "other dude," her client would very probably never again see the outside of a jail cell.

"Mr. Meade, could I ask that you stand and open the left side of your jacket?" She'd noticed a slight bulge in his jacket when he'd entered the courtroom and took the stand.

Rice was instantly on his feet. "What is this," he demanded. "I object. This witness is not some kind of plaything for Counsel to parade about for the jury. She needs to tell us where she's going with this."

"Ms. Warren?" the judge inquired.

"Of course, Your Honor. I'd like for the jury to see the empty holster under his left arm. I have no doubt that he has complied with state law prohibiting the carry of firearms in a courthouse and has left his handgun behind or downstairs with building security. But I'm reasonably certain that the bulge in the front of Mr. Meade's blazer is caused by the holster in which he carries a gun when not testifying in court." She hoped she sounded more confident than she felt. Both Lauren Franklin-Keene and Julia Ortez had testified to seeing a weapon, and she was counting on the holster being a part of his everyday attire. If that "slight bulge" turned out to be a package of Twinkies left over from the man's lunch, she was going to feel quite foolish.

The judge turned to the witness: "Do you ordinarily carry a concealed handgun, Mr. Meade."

"Yes, judge. I do. But I have a permit."

"I take it you do not have your weapon with you today."

"I do not, Your Honor. I know the rules."

"You are, however, wearing an empty holster?"

"I am, Your Honor."

The Judge turned to Sydney: "I think that should suffice, Counsel. Move on."

"Thank you, Your Honor." Then, turning again to the witness. "Do any of your handguns fire thirty caliber ammunition?" She asked her question directly, forcing either a yes or a no, hopefully before Rice objected.

"Yes," he said hesitantly, perhaps feeling the trap closing in on him.

"Objection, Your Honor," Rice said—a bit slow off the mark. "Relevance. Haven't we gone far enough down this rabbit hole already? How much more time do we need to waste arguing about how many weapons out there use thirty-caliber ammunition?" Rice sounded irritated, and like someone on the losing side of an argument.

"Your Honor, I think the court knows these questions are about a great deal more than how many potential weapons are out there. I'd like to point out that if Mr. Rice's stray thirty-caliber rifle cartridge and the testimony of his medical examiner are admissible, then so should be the testimony of *this* witness."

"Overruled."

"What firearms do you have, Mr. Meade, that use thirty-caliber ammo? I remind you, you're under oath."

A brief look of anger flashed in his eyes before he responded. "Well, I have an older M-1 rifle. Practically an antique by now. And I have a Smith & Wesson super-carry that fires a thirty-caliber round. For which, as I said, I have a carry permit."

Even though Meade hadn't plead the Fifth and his answer had been matter-of-fact, Sydney knew it was more gold. She paused a moment and again glanced meaningfully at the jury to drive home her point.

For a moment she reconsidered whether it was wise to ask the next question she'd planned to ask. She couldn't be sure how he would answer, but once again, it seemed like a risk she needed to take. If she didn't ask, Rice probably would. If Grant Meade had an airtight alibi for the morning of Harold Dawson's murder, there went her "other dude" defense. But from what Mel Marshall had told her about Meade's lifestyle as a loner, she thought the odds were low that he'd be able to produce a convincing alibi.

"Mr. Meade, where were you at about 10:00 a.m. on Friday, June 17 earlier this year?"

"Objection, Your Honor. Lack of foundation. Now Counsel is just being pointlessly insulting to this witness. He shouldn't be expected to answer that question."

Sydney sensed a certain lack of conviction in Rice's argument. He knew where this was going as clearly as she did. And so did the jury. "Your Honor, this answer is as close to the mark as any I could ask in Mr. Nowak's defense. If I can't ask this question, I basically can't defend my client. I think the jury needs to hear his answer. I might add that, if the police had done their job, Mr. Meade would have been asked this question months ago."

Judge Francis knew exactly what she meant. She looked in Rice's direction with a slightly disdainful shake of the head. "Overruled," she said.

"Mr. Meade?" Sydney raised her eyebrows expectantly.

And he provided the inevitable answer: "I don't remember. That's three months ago."

Sydney shook her head as if in frustrated disbelief. "No further questions of this witness, Your Honor."

The prosecution had but one question on cross: "Mr. Meade, did you have anything to do with the death of Harlod Dawson? Anything at all?"

"No sir. I did not. I never met the man. And I certainly don't go around killing my employer's clients. Wouldn't make any damned sense at all."

That concluded Rice's cross.

Sydney knew Meade's testimony had been helpful, but she wasn't sure how effective it had been in establishing him as the "other dude." When he stood, however, rising above the elevated witness box to his full, towering height and then stepped down and passed close in front of the jury box, his impressive muscular frame and the angry scowl were impossible to ignore. A couple of the jurors in the front row actually leaned back in their chairs as he walked by. One of them was Juror No. 1, the timid young pharmacist assistant from Carnation.

As Meade went through the gate and headed for the exit, he caused a similar stir from the spectators seated there. Her examination of Meade may have been inconclusive on the surface, but she was fairly certain most of those present were at least considering whether it was possible that he had played a role in Dawson's death.

As Meade disappeared through the courtroom doors, Sydney noticed Lauren Franklin-Keene, the RDN receptionist, rise from her seat at the back of the courtroom and move forward with a little wave to get Sydney's attention. She appeared distressed.

"May I have a moment, Your Honor?" Sydney said. Judge Francis nodded and waived her hand in acquiescence. Sydney met Lauren Frankin-Keene at the gate.

She leaned in close: "That's not the guy," Franklin-Keene whispered softly. "That guy that just left. It was somebody else who came to our RDN office that day. I've never seen that Meade fellow before in my life."

"Let's talk later," Sydney whispered back, trying to keep her face neutral. Franklin-Keene nodded and returned to her seat.

Thus far, the trial had been short, taking just four full days. She glanced up at the clock. It was three-thirty p.m. on a Thursday afternoon. She'd been watching the clock all day, carefully timing her defense so she could rest right about now. Everything was going to plan, Until Franklin-Keene's revelation.

It seemed almost unbelievable that there were two huge men trying to squeeze money out of Dawson, one before and one after his death. But then, Dawson had been desperate for money. Maybe there were two different collection agencies after him. Or maybe the second man had personally loaned Dawson money. It was even possible there was more than one intimidating collection agent who worked for AA Best Bet Bail Bonds. In some ways, the more "other dudes" who might have committed this crime the better. But it would be embarrassing to admit to this jury that what she'd assumed was one man actually turned out to be two different men. Especially when she couldn't identify the second man.

Meanwhile, a full weekend might be plenty of time for Meade to come up with an alibi. Or for the prosecution to come up with some kind of explanation for Meade's testimony, other than the one she wanted to push in her final argument—namely that Meade was obviously a great deal more threatening than a mere collection agent and that AA Best Bet Bail Bonds was one heck of a lot more than your usual consumer lender.

At the moment, she could argue that Meade seemed every bit as likely to have committed this crime as Jamison Nowak. It would have been easy for Meade, or someone else, to have followed Dawson from the city out to that trailhead, to have parked their vehicle out of sight on the road and then followed him along the trail to that bridge, to have shot him there, and then simply returned to town the same way they'd come.

But if Rice had the weekend to rehabilitate Meade, he would make good use of it. She couldn't take the chance. She had a powerful sense that she needed this trial to end. Needed to get the matter in the hands of the jury now. Before a weekend recess.

She considered whether she had an ethical duty to inform the court and the prosecution of what she'd just been told by Franklin-Keene. The powerful implication of the testimony, as things now stood, was that Meade may have been the same "big tough guy" at Dawson's office and at his ex-wife's home, and that he'd simply lied about the one. She now knew that he'd been telling the truth, insofar as that one visit, that is. Still, everything she'd done so far had been in good faith.

The decision had to be made in the moment. If she revealed that there were two men instead of one, it could delay final arguments. With ethical doubts hovering overhead, she opted for leaving things as they stood.

Suddenly, she realized that she'd been standing there for far too long. The entire courtroom was silent, looking in her direction, no doubt wondering what on earth she was waiting for.

She turned to face the court. "The defense rests," she said.

She saw Rice, take a brief, longing look at the clock, before announcing: "The prosecution has no evidence on rebuttal, Your Honor."

Judge Francis excused the jury till 9:00 a.m. the following morning. And, turning to the two lawyers, said: "So, let's hear any motions that either of you may have and take a look at our instructions to the jury. Then, first thing tomorrow we can instruct the jury, complete final arguments, and, with any luck, have this matter in their capable hands by tomorrow afternoon."

With that, the die was cast.

CHAPTER 19

Sydney Warren
King County Courthouse, Seattle
Courtroom of Judge Roberta Francis, Eighth Floor, Room 808
Friday, September 23, 1983

Prosecutor Walter Rice began his final argument to the jury on a personal, human note.

"Ladies and gentlemen of the jury, we've now come to the point in these proceedings when it's up to you to make a decision. Harold Dawson is dead before his time. By all accounts Mr. Dawson was a good and a decent man, someone who made mistakes in life, like all of us do. But who, in the face of difficult circumstances beyond his control, was doing his very best to do the right thing.

"What you do next will determine whether he now gets the justice he so obviously deserves.

"Throughout this trial, the defense has done everything they can to talk about the things we cannot know. But I would submit that, now as you begin your deliberations, what you must do is to focus on what you *do* know. So, let's summarize. Let's take one final look at what we know absolutely for certain. Because when we do, I think you'll agree that there isn't any real doubt at all about what happened here. And based on those facts, you'll do your difficult but unavoidable duty and find the defendant Jamison Nowak guilty as charged."

Rice took a long look at the jurors from left to right, taking time to let them know he was aware of each and every member of the jury. Then he began his chronology of what was known.

"This case began with the discovery of a body on a wooden footbridge along a remote hiking trail in the Cascade Foothills east of Seattle. The decedent was identified as Harold Dawson, a partner in the small financial consulting firm of RDN whose offices are right here in the city, just up the street from this courthouse. We know from the testimony of our medical examiner that Mr. Dawson died of a gunshot wound to the head inflicted at about 10:00 a.m. on Friday, June 17, earlier this year. Nobody has challenged any of that. Those are facts.

"We also know that, at the time of Mr. Dawson's death, the defendant was present at the scene of this crime. He admitted that right at the outset. It was at a location far from his office, his home, or any place else he might ordinarily have been expected to be. And there has been no effort whatever to disprove it. That is a known and accepted fact.

"And, as a matter of fact, there were only two cars in the nearby trailhead parking lot. Just two. No more. And the two cars present in that lot were Mr. Dawson's and the car belonging to the defendant, Mr. Jamison Nowak. We know that there were only those two vehicles in that lot because the defendant himself admitted it. The rest of that large lot was empty—lots of room for another car to park had there been another car present. Remember that fact: Just the two cars, no more.

"Another fact we know is that no one would expect Harold Dawson to be at this out-of-the-way location at 10:00 in the morning, unless they knew about it in advance, of course. And, the defendant *did* know. He even admits that he arranged it with Mr. Dawson."

"Objection, Your Honor." Sydney hated that she was interrupting her opponent's final argument. And she knew judges hated these interruptive objections as well. As did juries. But she felt this was critical. "Counsel is misstating the evidence. The only information we have on the arrangements for this meeting comes from Mr. Nowak's statement to the police. And in that statement, he is very clear that it was Mr.

Dawson who arranged the meeting place with Mr. Nowak. Not the other way around. There is no other evidence on the matter."

"I believe you'll find, Your Honor, that Mr. Nowak made that call," Rice replied.

"And," Sydney responded. "In that call, Mr. Dawson suggested that they meet, and also suggested the time and place. Your own police witness, detective Brown, confirmed that Mr. Nowak's statement was, to the best of their knowledge, true. Your Honor, the prosecution doesn't get to make things up as they go along."

"Very well," said Judge Francis. "Sustained. Proceed with your argument, Mr. Rice."

Sydney wasn't sure whether her objection had hit home or not as Rice, refusing to be thrown off stride, picked up his argument exactly where he'd left it as if there'd been no interruption.

"We also know that there was the nearby sound of a gunshot at what was later confirmed by the medical examiner to be the approximate time of Mr. Dawson's death—right at that point in time when those two cars were the only ones in that lot. And when the defendant was present at the scene and even claimed to have 'heard' the shot. Like the other facts I've reviewed, this fact has never been challenged."

His repetition of the word "fact" to refer to everything that had happened was annoying Sydney, but there was nothing she could do about it. She'd already tried her best to remind jurors that these so-called facts had originated in Nowak's voluntary statement.

"I would submit that, based upon just those uncontested facts alone, you'd have more than enough to strongly suspect this defendant of guilt in this murder. But that isn't all you have to go on. There is a great deal more.

"There is also the fact that the wound that killed Mr. Dawson could likely have been—*not that it could only have been*, but that it very likely *could* have been caused by a thirty-caliber hunting rifle. And that the spent casing from a thirty-caliber hunting rifle was found at the scene of this crime only a short time after its commission. Then, there is the fact that the defendant is an experienced and skillful hunter who personally owns a thirty-caliber hunting rifle. We also know that the defendant kept his rifle at a shooting range not far from this crime in a secure locker that was protected by a combination lock owned by the defendant. And we know that, when the detectives opened that locker, the defendant's gun was missing. Those are all uncontested facts. And, as of today, we still do not know where that rifle is or why it is missing. But we can make an educated guess on the basis of the facts we *do* know."

Sydney considered the "educated guess" argument prejudicial, but she didn't think it was worth addressing through another interruption.

"Finally, and significantly, there is the matter of motive. We know for a fact that the defendant had what witnesses described as a 'knock-down-drag-out fight' with the deceased just a few days prior to the killing. An argument in which the defendant expressed a good deal of anger toward Mr. Dawson. And we know for a fact that this argument was related to the financial status of the business enterprise of which the defendant is a partner. A fight about a large sum of money just days before a murder. Remember these facts—they are at the heart of this matter.

"The only defense offered in this case has been the bald and unconfirmed supposition that, gosh, maybe someone *else* committed this crime. The defense would have you look away from all those uncontested facts I've just related to you and, instead, speculate that maybe, just maybe, someone else was involved. But when we ask who, the best they can do is to suggest that maybe one of Mr. Dawson's clients was unhappy with him. Or maybe someone who loaned him money and wasn't repaid ordered a hit on him.

"The best they could do was to call in a debt collection agent whose only crime, as far as any of us knows, is that he's a tall, muscular guy who has a tough job. Did he have the opportunity to commit this crime? Who knows? No evidence was offered of that. Yes, he owns a thirty-caliber handgun, but has it gone missing? No. Is it connected to the scene of this crime? There's absolutely nothing to indicate that. Maybe our poor Mr. Meade even has an alibi. We'll never know—all we have is his inability to remember where he was when hit with a surprise question about a random date over three months ago. I venture that most of us wouldn't be able to properly answer a question like that either. I know I couldn't. Pulling Mr. Meade into this courtroom and asking him a question like that was a *stunt*, ladies and gentlemen, a *stunt*. It should be dismissed with the disgust it deserves.

"I submit that if you look to the cold, hard, uncontested facts in this case, you will not go wrong. If you do that, I have complete confidence that you will come back with a verdict of guilty as charged."

Sydney had given a good deal of thought to how the prosecution would argue their case. And Rice hadn't disappointed. His repetition of the word "fact" was memorable. The only question now was whether she had the ammunition to deflect it.

She stood up, took a few seconds to compose herself, hoped that there weren't too many wrinkles in her dark blue pants suit, filled her lungs with air, and stepped out into the space before the juror box.

"Ladies and gentlemen, there is one very large problem with the prosecution's argument in this case. It is something you might not at first notice, but the prosecution knows better. Their problem is that it is not up to the defendant in a criminal trial to prove his or her innocence. As you'll be told in no uncertain terms when this court instructs you on your duties in this case, Mr. Nowak is *presumed to be innocent* in this matter. It is up to the *prosecution* to *prove* their claim that Mr. Nowak committed this crime. Not the other way around.

"The requirement that there be proof, that actual evidence be required, is only logical. When someone makes a serious accusation against another, especially when that accusation can deprive a person of their life or liberty, no rational person will simply take that at face value. We naturally expect the person making that claim to 'prove it.' If they can't, we disregard the claim. That is what we lawyers call the burden of proof. And in a criminal case, if the prosecution fails to carry that burden, their case must be dismissed.

"After all, what kind of a world would we live in if someone could simply assert that you were guilty of something terrible, and then force you, on pain of imprisonment or other punishment, to prove your own innocence. It's not hard to see how that would lead to chaos.

"But there's more. As you'll hear the judge explain in a few minutes when the court instructs you on your duties as jurors. In a criminal case like this one, the prosecution's burden of proof is actually elevated. And for very good reason. When someone is accused of committing a serious crime, and when the vast powers of the government are arrayed against them, there's far too much at stake to allow for any doubt. Our laws recognize that no one should be adjudged guilty and be deprived of life or liberty unless the rest of us can be *absolutely certain* that they *are* in fact guilty. Here in America, we don't send someone off to prison simply because there are suspicious circumstances or unanswered questions. We don't convict people of crimes just because we think: *maybe* they *could have done it.* We don't convict someone even if we think: *the chances are* they did it.

"No. In a criminal case, 'likely' doesn't cut it. In a criminal case like this one, as you'll soon hear the judge explain, the prosecution has the burden and responsibility not only to *prove* guilt, but they must go further and must prove that guilt *beyond any reasonable doubt.* We don't throw people in jail because they had the misfortune to find themselves surrounded by a set of suspicious circumstances that were hard to explain. The prosecution needs to prove more than that. If they fail to live up to that elevated burden of proof, if we have *any reasonable doubt* about the defendant's guilt, that defendant must go free. It is one of the important ways our nation's laws protect every single one of us from bias, passion, ignorance, hate and government overreach. It is a critical concept in our justice system. And one that we must live up to every single day. It is a concept in our democracy that we must count on every juror like you to scrupulously honor.

"So, let's look at the evidence in this case, and ask ourselves: has the prosecution removed our doubt?

"I would argue that their failure to do so is visible in every single one of those so-called 'facts' they just presented to you.

"First of all, consider their argument about the two cars in the parking lot, a 'fact' given them by the defendant. But what if, *for obvious reasons,* someone parked off the road nearby and walked in? Or arrived there via a hiking trail from another site and left the same way they came? Or, perhaps there was another person in Mr. Dawson's car with him when he arrived and who later left the scene on foot via one of the many trails in the area. It's even possible that the killer could have been dropped off by someone else, by a friend or by a taxi even. Or perhaps they had a motorcycle hidden in the trees.

"One of the most obvious alternatives is that the killer had a vehicle parked off the road at some location outside the lot. I didn't hear the prosecution mentioning any of these very real possibilities. Or offering anything to contradict them. It sounded very much to me like these options weren't even considered. Let alone investigated. When the prosecution leaves an important line of inquiry like that unexplored and unexplained, that, ladies and gentlemen, is what we mean when we say they have failed in their burden of proof. That they have left you with 'reasonable doubt.'

"Next, let's consider their argument about the thirty-caliber rifle that was allegedly used to shoot Harold Dawson. They say, 'Oooh, the defendant owned a thirty-caliber rifle.' But they fail to consider how common these firearms truly are. There are quite literally millions of them out there. Thirty caliber is the single most common rifle caliber in circulation in the country today. But that's not all. It also turns out it might not even have been a rifle that fired the fatal bullet. And it might not even have been a thirty-caliber weapon at all. Apparently, there are many millions more guns of similar caliber out there that could just as easily have done the job. Again, remember, it is the prosecution's responsibility to make their case—to remove this kind of reasonable doubt.

"Then there's the argument that Mr. Dawson had with Mr. Nowak. Do let's start by being honest with one another. Based on our own life experience, every single one of us knows that merely because two people have a disagreement, even a serious one, does *not* mean one of the two will be likely to kill the other. Especially when that argument takes place in public. We humans argue with one another *all the time*. Right now, today, in this very courtroom, I have a very powerful disagreement with Mr. Rice over the evidence in this case. But that doesn't mean I'm likely to kill him. Thankfully, we humans *very seldom* commit murder. Think about it, when you hear an argument, how often to you come away thinking: 'Wow, I bet that person is going to commit murder.'

"Yes, there's evidence here that Mr. Nowak and Mr. Dawson had a heartfelt disagreement, maybe even a 'knock-down-drag-out' argument, whatever that means. The two men were partners in a complicated and fragile business enterprise. And, it appears Mr. Dawson might have been putting all that at risk. If I'd been his partner at the time, I think I might have argued with him too. As might any of us in this courtroom. It is only natural that his partners would call him to account.

"But not one of the several witnesses who saw that argument was worried at the time that one of the two men would resort to physical violence. Quite the contrary. Everyone who witnessed the exchange, simply went on about their work. And were it not for Mr. Dawson's subsequent death, not one of them would have given that argument a moment's further thought. That's *doubt*, ladies and gentlemen. *Reasonable* doubt.

"Now, consider what you were told about the defendant's demeanor when he was asked by the detectives to assist with their inquiries. He readily and voluntarily, on his own steam, came into police headquarters and spent over an hour answering their every question. He was scrupulously truthful in every regard—not one word of what he told them has been claimed to be false; other than his assertion of his own innocence, of course. It needs to be noted that, if he were guilty, several of those truthful answers would have been contrary to his own self-interest. But he made those truthful answers anyway. He'd been told he was not required to answer their questions. Why did he volunteer this information? Because he was innocent. Because he knew the detectives needed *his* truth if they were to discover the greater truth of who actually committed this crime.

"Unfortunately, finding the actual culprit was not the detectives' intent. It was not until it became completely evident to Mr. Nowak that the detectives weren't interested in the greater truth, but rather that they were interested only in implicating him, that he, as would have *any one of us*, finally told them enough was enough. For them to now rely completely and unquestioningly on everything he told them as the absolute and undeniable truth and label it as *fact* in every single instance *except* for his protestation of innocence; that is hypocrisy at its highest level.

"What Mr. Nowak did during that hour of his interrogation was to openly and honestly answer the detective's questions. That was the very kind of behavior that you'd hope for and only expect of a good citizen and an innocent man. I submit to you, ladies and gentlemen, *that* constitutes reasonable doubt.

"The heart of the prosecution's case is nothing but circumstantial evidence. Based loosely on 'facts' freely shared by the defendant in the pursuit of justice. Now they're asking us to look at what they consider 'suspicious circumstances' and to accept their conclusion that, taken together, they sure do make the defendant *seem* guilty.

"The problem is that, while each of those supposedly 'suspicious' circumstances may seem *consistent* with guilt, not one of them—not a single one—when you look closely, is actually *inconsistent* with innocence. They are not proof. Even a cluster of suspicious circumstances does not necessarily constitute proof. Especially not when, for every single one of them, there is totally reasonable doubt.

"In addition to the circumstantial evidence offered by the prosecution and the information provided by the defendant himself, you need also to consider the evidence *we* presented in Mr. Nowak's defense. Evidence regarding the host of other people, some more likely than others, who *also* had the means, the motive, and the opportunity to have killed Harold Dawson.

"Harold Dawson was a man who'd been drawn into a deep, deadly spiral of debt and deceit. There wasn't just one other person who might well have wanted Mr. Dawson punished for his actions; there were, quite literally, *dozens of them*. People who lost their life savings, people who felt cheated, people who may well have wanted revenge. Who is to say whether one of them may have decided on the ultimate punishment of death for the person they blamed for their tragic personal losses? Unfortunately, we'll never know for sure because the police didn't bother to learn more about them. To actually investigate anyone other than Jamison Nowak.

"Mr. Nowak is simply the one unlucky guy who got sucked into the maelstrom of this prosecution by investigators early in their inquiries because he was present at the scene and because he was honest enough to have told that to the police. Once they knew that, they made up their minds before considering any of the countless other possibilities.

"We would have investigated all of those other people who had been cheated by Mr. Dawson if we'd had the time, the personnel, and the resources to do that. We did our best, as you've seen here in this court-room. Unfortunately, the people who *did* have the time, the resources, the personnel, and the *responsibility* to investigate further—the prosecu-tors, the specialists, and the detectives assigned to the case—well, they didn't bother. They had Mr. Nowak in their sights. That was enough for them.

"Whether it was through a desire to get the case over with quickly, simple short-sightedness, or because they had too many other demands on their time and resources, they made *no effort* to look into other suspects who might just as plausibly, maybe much more plausibly, have been guilty of this crime. They settled on the defendant as the guilty party and refused to even consider anyone else. You heard that in the testimony from the detectives themselves who were assigned to the case. You can see it in the circumstantial evidence the prosecutor has relied upon as proof." Sydney paused for dramatic effect before concluding: "From listening to everything that's been presented, you know that the prosecution has failed to meet their burden of proof. That is the very essence of reasonable doubt."

This was the point at which she had intended to point the finger directly at Grant Meade, but that was no longer possible without actively misdirecting the process. But whenever she mentioned that there were others who should have been considered as suspects, she hoped a vision of Meade in that witness chair came to mind. That image might be enough to put a face on the other possible suspects that should have been investigated before settling on the defendant as the guilty party.

"Thus, I submit to you that when you actually look closely at all the evidence presented in this case, you're going to have a great deal of doubt about what happened that day on the bridge at Two Mountain Creek. Enough reasonable doubt to confidently acquit Mr. Nowak of these unproven charges."

Half an hour later, at 11:30 a.m., following the court's instructions to the jury, the twelve jurors retired to the jury room for their delib-erations.

CHAPTER 20

Sydney Warren
King County Courthouse, Seattle
Courtroom of Judge Roberta Francis, Eighth Floor, Room 808
Friday, September 23, 1983

I t was late afternoon when Sydney received the call that the jury had reached a verdict. There were theories that a relatively fast decision favored the prosecution; others believed it favored the defense. Sydney's stomach was churning with anticipation as she raced to the courthouse. It took her but a spare ten minutes to get to Judge Francis's courtroom from her office, just a few blocks up Third. She was still the last one to arrive.

The gallery was full. Most of the spectators looked to be media. The trial hadn't caught the interest of the national press, but there were reporters from all over the Pacific Northwest. The entire region had been affected by the WPPSS collapse, and Harold Dawson's death resonated with newshounds and with those who followed crime in the area.

Jamison Nowak was already seated at the defense table. His wife, son, and daughter were in their usual spot in the front row immediately behind the bar. Nowak had turned his chair around, and he and his family were engaged in what looked to be a serious conversation. Walter Rice was standing behind his prosecution table in a deep discussion with his second. As Sydney made her way down the aisle, Rice glanced in her direction and gave her a smug grin. She couldn't help thinking how pleasing it would be to wipe that look off his face with a defense verdict.

Sydney gave Judge Francis's bailiff a nod as she swung open the gate in the bar and stepped through. Nowak turned to her as she put her unopened briefcase on the table. She leaned down and asked, "Are you ready for this?"

Nowak and his family looked anxious, as they had every right to be. Before he could respond, the bailiff's voice filled the small room.

"King County Superior Court Department Three is now in Session," the bailiff announced. "Judge Roberta Francis presiding. All rise."

With the return of the judge to her elevated bench, the final steps in the ponderous but inexorable court process resumed.

"Anything for me before we bring in the jury?" asked the judge."

"No, Your Honor," Sydney said, her voice sounding hollow to her. The stress of waiting for a verdict to be announced was almost like a near death experience, you could sense something momentous was about to happen, but you weren't sure whether you would emerge into light or dark.

"Nothing from me, Your Honor." Rice sounded confident. Sydney experienced a pang of dislike and jealously for his self-assured hubris.

As the jurors entered and took their seats, Sydney scanned for any sign that they were avoiding eye contact with the defense. A few looked her way, but others were perusing the media, and a couple were taking in Nowak's family. There were no obvious tells that she could discern. That they'd agreed upon a verdict in the three short hours since returning to their jury room after lunch seemed quick, but not terribly unusual. They'd very likely all wanted to get the trial over with and put it behind them before the weekend so they could get on with their lives.

Sydney put her hand on Nowak's arm as they stood to receive the verdict. His face was pale, almost colorless. He returned her brief smile of reassurance with a nod. The jury decision was called for, and everyone fell silent as the foreperson, a kindly-looking older woman handed over the printed jury's verdict form to the bailiff. All eyes were on the bailiff as she walked over and passed the document to the judge.

Although Sydney was carefully studying the judge's face as she perused the verdict, she became aware that Juror No. 1, the young pharmacy assistant, was looking at her rather than at the judge. She glanced over and noted the timid smile on the woman's face. Then she noticed that two or three of the other jurors were looking calmly and comfortably in Nowak's direction. Even the foreperson ventured a quick peek at the defense table.

Sydney had heard of jurors signaling their verdicts in this manner, but actually seeing it was a first for her. At least she hoped she was reading their nonverbals correctly. She prayed that she was. For Nowak and for his family. She noticed Nowak was clenching and unclenching his fingers, so she leaned close and whispered to him to "stay calm."

It was ironic that she was telling her client to stay calm when she could barely control her own emotions. She had to force herself to breathe normally as she waited for the words: *guilty* or *not guilty*. Suddenly, she realized that she was squeezing Nowark's arm, hard. But he seemed oblivious as he stood rigidly by, staring at the foreperson, silently willing her to say two words instead of just one.

"Not guilty" the foreperson said when asked for the verdict, the phrase ringing loud and clear in the still room.

The words hung in the air a brief moment before everyone started reacting. Nowak let out a huge sigh as if he had been holding his breath. Behind him his wife and children were literally squealing with joy. Suddenly he turned toward Sydney and pumped her hand up and down while repeating "thank you, thank you, thank you." Then, while the judge was making her final comments, he turned to hug his family across the divider.

Slowly Sydney became aware of the excited voices coming from the gallery, especially from the media at the back of the room. A number of spectators were rushing to the exit. Then Judge Francis called for order and moved to conclude the proceedings. She thanked the jurors for their service and excused them.

Next, the judge turned to the defendant and spoke those fateful words: "You are free to go, Mr. Nowak," she said. "This court is in adjournment." With that, she rose and promptly disappeared into her chambers.

Rice was no longer wearing a smug smile when he came over and shook Sydney's hand. His "congratulations" were perfunctory, but at least he was gracious enough to make the effort. He could have simply skulked off without saying anything. Sydney's "thank you" was similarly flat. Her brain numbed by everything going on around her, she couldn't think of a witty comeback or manage a gloating smirk. She was just thankful it was over.

Duncan waved to her from the back of the room, grinning his happiness for her win. As she headed toward him, she stopped to say a few words to Nowak's ecstatic wife while he was busy hugging his kids. She squeezed Sydney's hand and twice said: "I can't thank you enough."

Out in the hall there was a string of reporters waiting impatiently for Nowak to come out. When they saw her, they circled and shoved microphones in her face. She mumbled a few words about the "wisdom of the criminal justice system." They didn't press harder; it was Jamison Nowak they wanted to hear from, and he had just burst out of the courtroom, beaming, his happy wife and children in tow.

After he said how pleased he was that the jurors were able to see through the lies told by the prosecution, he wisely turned it over to his wife to speak. She said they were thankful to the jurors for their careful consideration of the facts and were pleased that the family would finally be able to put this ordeal behind them. She was as radiant as a new bride, and Sydney had no doubt that news coverage about the trial verdict would include pictures of her and their two children who were standing to one side, gazing with wonder at all the attention the family was getting.

Sydney wished her client hadn't criticized the prosecution, but as someone just found innocent of a serious crime, she felt like he had earned the right to complain a little. But she was relieved when they quickly ended the exchange with the press.

Reporters hurried off to make sure their stories made the late edition or the evening news. Sydney and Duncan followed in their wake and walked back to their office together. They were met by their two legal assistants with applause and happy faces. Then, a few minutes after five, they closed up shop and everyone headed home for a much-deserved weekend off.

~

Sydney decided to treat herself to a weekend staycation. She lounged around her Queen Anne apartment in sweatpants and an old Fleetwood Mac T-shirt, let her answering machine pick up calls, took a long bath, read a thriller that had been on her nightstand forever, and ordered takeout instead of cooking. It was a glorious, isolated weekend of rest and self-pampering. She didn't leave once, occasionally simply standing before her living room window looking out at the view of Elliot Bay with its ships and piers and the Seattle waterfront, her mind at peace.

By Monday morning, she felt renewed and ready to face the world.

She stopped to pick up a Seattle Post Intelligencer at the coffee shop on the first floor of their office building. As she stepped into the elevator, she opened the paper to check out the front page. The top headline struck her like a fist in the center of her stomach.

"MURDER WEAPON FOUND!" There was a picture of the bridge at Two Creek Mountain below the headline. The full story started just above the fold. As soon as she got off the elevator, she hurried to her office and read the article.

> *"The likely murder weapon in the so-called 'WPPSS Murder' case appears to have been recovered—too late to be of use in the trial that concluded with an acquittal on Friday. The rifle, a .30-30 Marlin lever-action hunting rifle was discovered several hundred yards downstream in the creek that runs beneath the footbridge where financial advisor and WPPSS promotor Harold Dawson was found dead this past June. His murder occurred days after the fateful Supreme Court decision relieving local power companies from responsibility for WPPSS bonds.*
>
> *"On Saturday afternoon, a private club that calls themselves the 'Citizen Detectives' searched the scene of the murder. 'We knew the murder weapon had never been found,' the president of the group told*

the PI. 'We figured if the killer was somebody other than the man the jury found not guilty, they'd have had to leave the scene on foot because there were no other cars in the lot. It would have been hard to carry a rifle and keep it hidden. So, it seemed to us that the killer might have decided to leave it behind or maybe hid it somewhere nearby. Or threw it in the creek.'

"Just days earlier, shortly before the trial, the police had made what Detective Ginger Small said was a 'very thorough' search of the area, but nothing was found.

"Knowing that Two Mountain Creek fills with rapidly running water in the early summer but late in the year diminishes considerably, the Citizen Detectives felt it was possible that the police underestimated how far downstream a rifle might have traveled in the current. The president of the group concluded 'We got lucky.'"

Sydney laid down the paper and immediately dialed Detective Small and was relieved when she got through to her.

"Sorry to bother you, but can you tell me if you've identified the owner of the rifle the Citizen Detectives found?"

"I can. The question is whether I will."

"Come on, Detective. You know why I'm asking."

"And, how will you feel if I tell you that it's your client's rifle?"

Sydney felt her throat tighten. "Is it?" she asked, her voice sounding strangely thin to her own ears.

"Yeah, it's definitely Nowak's rifle." Small sounded gleeful, as if she had been the one to find it. "Serial numbers match the records up at the gun club. But that's not the kicker. The casing that kid found at the scene matches this rifle. So much for your 'millions of thirty-caliber firearms out there' argument. Not much doubt that this is the murder weapon."

Sydney's chaotic thoughts refused to coalesce into a coherent and appropriate response. She'd been so sure of her client's innocence, and so pleased with her victory in court. When she didn't respond, Small spoke up.

"I guess you can feel pretty proud of yourself. Oh, and in case you're wondering, there are also trace prints on some unfired rounds still in the magazine. The crime lab's working on them now, but you and I both know what they're going to find."

Sydney ignored the jibe, thanked Small politely for the information, and ended the call. Small's bitterness was understandable. But, while Sydney was not exactly pleased to learn she had successfully defended a murderer, she could not help reflecting on how fortunate had been her decision to get the trial wound up before the weekend.

That split-second courtroom decision had kept Jamison Nowak from spending the balance of his life in prison.

PART THREE

LEGACY IN MOTION

A GLIMPSE OF THE PAST AND
A LEAP TO THE PRESENT

CHAPTER 21

Two Members of the Russian Nobility
Saint Petersburg, Russia
Private Residence
July, 1762

T he two men were seated in a dark wood-paneled drawing room surrounded by walls covered with pictures of religious icons set in gilded frames. Candlelight from hanging lanterns cast a golden haze over the room. The host sat on a bench covered in brocade-encased pillows. The other man relaxed in an elaborately carved and upholstered chair reserved for important visitors. Both wore long, richly embroidered kaftans. Two silver goblets filled with Georgian wine sat on a stout wood table off to the side within easy reach.

"Is it true? Peter III has been replaced by his wife?" The speaker sounded incredulous at the notion that she had been able to carry out a successful coup d'état within months after her husband became the emperor.

"It's said she had the support of the Imperial Guard. Apparently, Catherine's lover Grigory Orlov was involved."

"Serves Peter right—he never even bothered to learn how to speak proper Russian."

"No one will miss him." The two men nodded in agreement.

Then, the first man lifted his goblet, and before taking a swig said, "To the Grand Duchess Catherine."

The second man corrected him: "To the Empress."

"She will always be 'Catherine' to me."

"Ah, was she once your lover?"

"I was one of many, I'm afraid. And it didn't last long. But while it did—" He smiled at the memory, or possibly for dramatic effect.

"She and Peter were never happy together. She was fortunate not to have been sent to a convent like his grandfather did to his first wife."

"Peter was weak, whereas she has always been ambitious. It will be interesting to see what changes she makes."

"One thing for sure, since she loves jewelry, I have no doubt she will commission an impressive crown for her coronation. Probably one with thousands of diamonds and accented with ruby spinel."

"It's said that she has a passion for emeralds. Among other passions." The two men laughed and sipped their wine.

"I've never seen it, but there's gossip about a brooch called the Tsarina's Spider that has been passed down with the Crown Jewels. It's alleged to have an amazing emerald body. Studded with rubies, diamonds, and spinel. Sounds quite remarkable."

"A spider? Aren't they considered bad luck?"

"Not in the Western world. Catherine's modern that way. Some consider spiders a marvel of engineering."

"No doubt this one is modeled after a deadly female that casts a web to catch unsuspecting prey." The two men laughed again.

"There's nothing more frightening than a powerful and ambitious woman."

"Well, she better enjoy it while she can. Power and wealth can slip away when you least expect it."

CHAPTER 22

Eric Gee
Washington State Penitentiary
Walla Walla, WA
February, 2020 - evening lockdown

Eric Gee counted himself lucky.

Eric's cellmate was Louis Mitchum, or "Big Lou" as he was known in the criminal world. Big Lou was getting old, but he still had a physique that matched his name and a reputation as someone you didn't mess with. It was common knowledge among the inmates that Big Lou looked out for his friends, so for a resident of the State Penitentiary at Walla Walla, Washington, it was singular good luck to be assigned as his roommate. As long as you didn't tick him off.

Many years earlier, before originally being sent to prison, Big Lou had been the proprietor of a highly successful if corrupt bail bonds, consumer lending, and loansharking operation in Seattle. Ending up in Walla Walla on a conviction for extortion, as well as assault and battery, was not an uncommon fate for someone in his line of work. He'd have been back out on the streets long ago, but on the eve of release he had killed another prisoner in a yard fight. That had added another twenty-five years to his sentence—

enough that, given his age and declining health, it seemed likely Big Lou Mitchum would never again breathe outside air beyond the prison yard.

Lou was extremely well-connected, however, and because of his size, reputation, and those connections, Eric was determined to keep Lou sweet. Lou was Eric's ticket to survival among the prison's general population. In addition, Eric felt like he had a lot to learn from an old-timer like Big Lou Mitchum. Sometimes, if you wanted to better your-self in the world, you just needed to listen up, know your place, do as you were told, and be respectful.

One particular evening, shortly before lights out, Lou laid back in his lower bunk and carefully adjusted his considerable bulk to minimize the continuing discomfort in his lower gut. Eric climbed into the upper bunk, intending to make himself comfortable.

"What the fuck?" he said when he noticed his pillow was missing. A quick glance over the side of his bunk answered his unspoken question. Lou's head rested gently against two pillows; one was his own; the other was obviously Eric's. Lou looked back without a word, but his fake, sleepy-eyed stare was the only challenge Eric needed.

"Oh yeah, sure, good," Eric said. "Hey, no sweat, man. You need that pillow a hell-of-a-lot more than I do." It was probably true. Lou was suffering with some kind of painful low grade internal infection, and he wasn't getting much help from the prison physician who seemed to think he was malingering.

Maybe it was because he was feeling low, or maybe it was to acknowledge Eric's good-natured response about the pillow—for what-ever reason, Lou fell into a talkative mood. "So, I guess you've only got a few months left in here," he said. "What you got planned when they let you out?"

Eric leaned over the side, hanging on with one hand. "Not much. Probably look up Eileen. See what's happening with her." Back when Eric was arrested for residential burglary, Eileen had been his girlfriend. She had not, however, troubled herself to visit him even once in the more than four years since he'd been incarcerated. Big Lou knew that.

"Uh huh," was Big Lou's only comment.

When he didn't add anything, Eric said, "When I was a kid, my dad had a boat. We used to go fishing in Puget Sound. I liked that a lot. Maybe I'll try for something in the maritime trades. Maybe work as crew on the ferry boats. Something like that."

"That's a union job, isn't it?"

"Yeah. Good pay. Tie up the boat when it lands. Direct the traffic. Seems like something I could do."

Neither man said it out loud, but both knew a job like that would be tough to land with a criminal record. And it would also require some kind of Coast Guard credentials and a lot more experience than a few fishing trips as a kid on your parents' outboard boat. But neither man seemed ready to taint Eric's freedom dreams with reality.

"I don't guess the burglary game worked out all that well for you," Lou said, matter of fact.

"Naw, although it was fun while it lasted. I didn't like getting caught, though."

Everyone in the prison knew the stories of most of the other inmates. What they were in for. The length of their sentence. How much money they had for barter. Eric had taken a lot of crap initially about getting caught by the owner of the house he'd broken into. The homeowner not only had very astute hearing, he also had a gun. He'd forced Eric to lie down on the floor on his stomach and put his hands behind his head in a "citizen's arrest" while the two of them waited for the police to get there. It had been embarrassing in the moment and even worse when retold by a reporter in the local paper. It had also made him the butt of crude and mean-spirited jokes among his prison companions.

"Well, you ain't the only one that has some regrets, my friend. I once let the biggest single score of my life slip through my fingers. Still think about it and wish I hadn't been so stupid."

"Hmm." This was something Eric hadn't heard before. He was really curious, but he knew better than to ask questions. If Lou wanted to tell him about it, he would. If not—

Lou inched over so he could see Eric better. "Would have cleared well over a million. Maybe more. A lot of cash back in the day. If I'd just followed through."

"Yeah. I hear ya," Eric said, trying to sound like a man who understood regrets.

"Thing is, Eric, knowing what I do sure as shit's never going to do me no good sittin' in here."

"Uh huh." Eric didn't know what to say. Was Lou about to share a secret with him? Why would he do that? Was it some sort of trick?

"Happened a few years before I got arrested," Lou said. "Loaned a quarter of a mil to this guy with a fancy office in the Columbia Center. Had a really nice home in Broadmoor. A big power cruiser at the Yacht Club. Swanky wife. Pretty young daughter. Full of himself. Till he had to come to me to save his butt.

"Guy was a financial advisor. What a laugh. He got himself and a bunch of his clients in trouble. Lost a ton of money. Had to sell everything to stay afloat. I mean *everything*. But while it was all going sour, he still hung onto this one piece of fancy jewelry that was worth a fortune. He refused to sell it, even though he was desperate for cash. Came to me instead.

"It was a pin thingy, like women wear on their clothes. Only this one was old, I mean, really old. Belonged to some Russian princess or something. He called it the 'Tsarina's Spider.' Showed me some paperwork telling who had owned it and how much it was valued at. Said the Spider was the first pricey piece of jewelry he'd ever bought and he couldn't bring himself to part with it."

Lou took a moment to adjust Eric's former pillow. "Acted like he was the la-de-da professional while I was only a money lender. Yet, HE was the one going belly up, while I was the one sitting on a pot of cash.

"I checked around. Turned out the Spider was as big a deal as he said. Worth at least a couple mil, probably more if you found the right buyer. So, I loaned him a quarter of a million with the Spider as security. My mistake was to let him keep the damn thing. Didn't seem risky at the time. He had it in a vault in his basement. Besides, guys like that scare easily. Didn't think he'd have the cajónes to scam me."

Lou stopped and studied Eric's face. "I know what you're thinking. But when you're in the business I was in, you don't rely on some kind of formal security agreement for collateral like that. That pin was worth a lot more than my loan, and I figured it wasn't going anywhere. Soon after, his house went on the market—wife took whatever cash they got from the sale and anything else she could lay her greedy hands on. Typical bitter bitch. But he hung onto that pin. That's when I should have insisted on him handing it over until he paid up.

"Why I trusted him I can't tell you. He was a bigger con than I was, I guess. You know the type. Overpaid white-collar job. Wore a pressed shirt and silk tie to work every day. They never really get that it can all go away in a flash . . . until it does.

"When I realized he wasn't going to have the money to pay me back, I figured I'd take that Spider off him and make out like a bandit. Should have been easy. Guys like that are usually easy pickings. Push comes to shove, they always fold. Don't like pain. Way too much to lose.

"I started calling him, but he wouldn't answer. So, I went to his office, but they wouldn't let me in to see him. It became obvious that I was going to have to do it the hard way.

"Bottom line—I waited too long. He ended up getting himself murdered. He'd lost too much of other people's money; he was on everybody's shit list. The partners in his firm were pissed as hell. One of 'em plugged his ass somewhere up in the mountains east of town.

"Even when he died, I wasn't too worried at first. My guess was that his daughter would have the Spider, and I thought collecting from her would be a piece of cake."

Lou sighed regretfully.

Eric held his breath and said nothing. He sensed that he was about to learn something useful, and he didn't dare say or do anything that could queer things before he knew where this was going.

"The daughter was married to this Navy pilot stationed up at Whidbey. They lived on the Navy Base, so I figured it would be easy to find them. Then, couple of days after the murder, her husband goes AWOL. 'Unauthorized absence.' Takes off with a multi-million-dollar Navy jet, flies up into Canada, and disappears. Maybe headed for Russia. Can you believe it?

"The Navy's understandably pissed. The pilot's wife—the stiff's daughter—gets kicked out of Navy housing. She and her baby end up moving in with her mother down in Seattle in a condo on Alki. I sent a guy with a nose for sniffing out money over there for a visit. He wasn't impressed. The mother was working as a clerk at Costco. The daughter was driving a six-year-old Toyota and had been a waitress in some dive up in Oak Harbor. She'd got fired because of what her husband did. Grant said it looked like they didn't have squat between them; there was no way she had that Spider or any extra cash from selling it. He figured he'd scared the shit out of both of them and that they'd have paid up if they could."

Eric waited. Lou had gone silent. Perhaps he was reflecting on the whole messed up situation. Or on life's lost opportunities. Finally, Eric worked up the courage to ask: "So . . . what do you think happened to the Spider?"

"Well, hell, it's obvious inn' it, Eric? At least that's what I thought back then. When my client got himself popped, I figured that damned son-in-law saw his opportunity, grabbed that Spider thing and took off for parts unknown. Looking for a life of leisure without a squalling kid and having to live in base housing. The pin alone would of set him up for life. All he needed to do was land the airplane somewhere remote, strip it, sell the electronics to the highest bidder—the Ruskies or the Chinese or some shit country with oil money. They'd have paid him plenty. Then, when the time was right, he could of hocked the pin and be set up for life.

"What I didn't see coming was that the wife must have been in on it all along. It looked to me like he'd run out on her and the kid. Left them behind to look out for themselves. But then, a few months later, she and the kid disappeared. Probably joined her husband up in Canada some-where. I really messed up. I should of gotten to that Dawson guy a lot sooner and got my money. Later, I could of put more pressure on his daughter, got my share of the Spider out of it then."

Again, Lou paused. After a few minutes of silence, Eric said: "I guess it's probably too late at this point, though. They could be anywhere. New IDs. New lives."

"Yeah, maybe. But, you know, all those years of chasing down bail jumpers taught me a few things. If there's one thing I know, it's that people don't change. They always go back to their old ways. They have habits. They like certain things. Have weaknesses that don't go away. You just gotta get inside their head. See the world through their eyes.

"Take Ortez, the son-in-law, the guy that sole the airplane. I could of tracked him. He'd of been an easy mark. Would of done it too if I hadn't got arrested. That's what I'm telling you for. So's when you walk out of here, you got something to think about, you know. Somethin' other than that no-good girlfriend of yours. Or directing traffic on some stupid ferryboat."

He didn't pause after dissing Eric's plans but went on to offer up his own suggestion for Eric's future. "Odds are, that Navy pilot and his family are still living right under our noses up there in Canada. If you could find them, all you'd have to do is threaten to turn them in. No way they're going to risk everything after this long. They'd happily pay you to keep quiet."

Eric's mind was racing. Lou was right. Be hard to find the guy, but it might be worth the try.

Then Lou sighed again. "Thing is, Eric. I'm never getting out of this place. Except in a box. And even if I did, it would take too much time and effort to find the Ortez family and pull it all off. I'm too damned old, too sick, too tired.

"You, hell Eric, you're just a kid. You got a whole life ahead. I'm just saying—you want to do this, go for it."

"I don't know what to say, Lou." And that was the truth. It wouldn't be easy to find the Ortez family, maybe not even possible, but he couldn't say that he wasn't interested. Lou was giving him a gift he had to accept. "I'll owe you big time if I find them. Whatever you want—"

Lou waved a hand and shook his head. "Forget that shit. I know how the world works. Once you walk out those doors, you're not going to give me and the rest of us poor toads still couped up in here a second thought. And you shouldn't. That's not why I told you about this. If you can find that guy, you just keep whatever you can get for yourself. Someday, when you're sitting on a sunny beach in Tahiti with a drink that has one of them little umbrellas sticking out of it, you tip that glass and say 'thank you, Big Lou.' And I'll give you a little nod from my perch down in Hell, or wherever I end up. At least I'll have done one good thing for someone else in this crappy life."

"Lou . . ." Eric's voice cracked with emotion. "I don't know how to thank you. I mean, even if I don't find them, I really appreciate you telling me about this."

"One other thing, Eric. Just a bit of advice from someone who knows. When you get outta here and go back to burglary, get yourself a partner, OK? Get some help from someone that knows the game. Knows how to not get caught. Better yet, set yourself up with the Italians in Seattle. They'll take a cut. But it'll be worth it. You don't want a repeat of what got you in here."

Ten weeks later, Eric Gee walked out through the prison gate, hitched a ride into town, and caught a Seattle-bound Greyhound at the Walla Walla bus station. Soon he was back cruising his old haunts in Seattle. He didn't call his old girlfriend; nor did he apply for a job. Like Big Lou had predicted, he was planning a residential heist.

His stint in in Walla Walla had taught him a lesson or two, however. And he'd caught the wisdom of Big Lou's words of advice. Not only did he plan on being more careful in future, he also started looking around for a few well-placed friends to partner with. He needed a reserve if he was going to make a serious effort to find the Ortez family and grab that Spider.

CHAPTER 23

The Campbell Family
North Pacific Coast of British Columbia, Canada
An Isolated Inlet
Midsummer, circa 2002

Abby was the first to notice the bulkhead. "Hey, Dad. Check that out over there," she said, as their small cruiser motored slowly up the quiet inlet. She was pointing at a couple of rotting, weathered logs beneath the overhanging trees along the nearby beach. The logs looked to have been laid atop one another and cabled into place a very long time ago.

"You're right, hon," her father said. "There could have been a logging operation here at one time. Look at those old piling stubs in the shallows up ahead. I bet they were used for log collection."

"Can we go ashore and have a look around?"

"Sure." Her father turned their small, twenty-eight-foot cruiser in toward shore. The Campbell family did vacation trips every summer to explore the wild, mostly uninhabited fjords and inlets along the northern BC Pacific Coast. Twelve-year-old Abigail loved the trips; her younger sister, Madison, not so much. Madison didn't care for the bugs and would rather have stayed home. But she wasn't given that choice.

"This place would have been ideal for logging," their father said. "This whole area was seriously logged at one time or another. Do you know why?"

"Calm water," Abby said, looking up and down the beach.

"It wouldn't always be this calm," said their father. "But it is pretty well protected."

"Steep, wooded hillsides," Abby noted. "It would have been easy for gyppo loggers to skid logs down into the water." Abby loved the whole idea of "gyppo loggers." Loved the sound of the label. Even though her father had told her it wasn't a nice thing to call someone. Still, she relished the idea that small groups of independent loggers had once explored this wilderness searching for precious and accessible timber whose harvest could make them rich.

When their boat was securely anchored, the family went ashore two at a time in the tiny inflatable they towed along behind. They kept a long line attached to the inflatable so they could pull it back to the cruiser for the next two to row ashore. Then, starting from the flattened off area atop the aging bulkhead, they began to bushwhack their way up the hill to see the view from the top, Abby in the lead.

"Oh great," said Madison. "Nettles!" She glared at some tall green plants and rolled down the sleeves of her shirt.

"Hey," Abby said, stopping and pushing the toe of her shoe into the dirt. "There's gravel under the brush. There must have been a trail here." She turned back to her parents and sister. "Let's see where it goes." Abigail surged ahead.

"Wait up," her father called. "Stay together." He didn't add "there could be bears," but that's why he carried a pump-action 12 gauge shotgun loaded with slugs.

Slowly, with Abby in the lead and her younger sister coming up behind, the four of them made their way up what did definitely seem to be a long-unused pathway which traversed up the hillside to where the land flattened out at the top.

"Wow," Abby said as she turned to look back down toward the inlet. It was an incredible view. The whole place seemed both wild and peaceful at the same time. Below, you could see their boat, *Daddy's Girl*, at anchor in glassy water just offshore. Their small grey Avon skiff was visible through the tress where they'd pulled it up and secured it at the top of the beach.

The long, low ridge on which the Campbell family now stood extended for some distance to the southwest in the direction of the mouth of the inlet, tapering out against a forested hillside to the east. The ridge itself was covered by a low forest of young conifers. Abby kicked at the ground near where she stood. "Look here, Maddy," she said, hoping to get her sister involved. "It's more gravel."

Their dad joined the two girls and bent over to look. "More like crushed rock," he said. "a well-packed surface. Interesting."

"I bet there was a town here," Abby said.

"I'm not so sure about that, hon." Her father straightened up and studied the area with an eye familiar with the stages of growth and development in forested terrain. "More like a landing strip," he said. "And judging from the size of these trees, maybe only a couple of decades old. At most."

"Packed crushed rock. Seems pretty extravagant for a logging camp airstrip," his wife said.

Abby strolled over to the edge of the hill, had another look at the view below, and decided to see how far she could throw a rock out toward the beach.

Madison started wandering off to the east.

"Don't go too far on your own, sweetie," called her mom.

"I'm looking for some Dock Leaf for my nettles," Madison called back.

The girls' mom looked at her husband and grinned. "Dock Leaf? I guess you've trained your kids well," she said.

"Maybe a bit too well." He looked at his mobile phone. It had taken quite a while to climb that hill. "We should be getting back down to the boat. I don't want to spend the night anchored here. It's too exposed. What do you say we run back to where we saw that anchorage near the mouth of the inlet?"

"Sounds good to me." She called out again to her daughter. "Madison. We need to start back; I've got some ointment for your nettles on the boat."

"There's something here," Madison yelled. "Some plastic netting and stuff with something under it. It looks really big."

"Come on, Maddy. We need to head back down to the boat," her father said.

Madison reluctantly returned to her family. As they began their journey back down the hill toward the beach, Madison turned to her sister: "There was something big covered up there in the trees, really big. It had all this plastic netting over it."

"Yeah," Abigail said, less than enthusiastic. From her perspective, anything that involved a plastic net wasn't all that old and therefore no big deal. The previous year, they'd run across an actual abandoned logging camp on one of their jaunts ashore. One that might have been operating before World War II. It had shacks that were still standing. Rusty hooks and choker chains. And an outhouse with a half-moon cut into the door.

Now that was exciting stuff.

CHAPTER 24

Eric Gee
Seattle's Central District
A Capitol Hill Bar
Current day

Eric had been out of prison for less than two years when the news of Big Lou's death reached him. Apparently, he'd died of some sort of undiagnosed health issue after a short time in the prison hospital. At least it hadn't been from a shiv in the back, Eric thought. That evening Eric met a friend and business partner to tip a few brews in the back of a favorite bar on Capitol Hill. He proposed a toast to his mentor and former cell mate, and as he held up the glass, he thought of Lou saying he should toast him with one of those drinks with an umbrella in it.

There had been a number of times since Eric's release from prison when he'd thought about trying to locate the Tsarina's Spider. The most recent was when he saw a story in a local Seattle blog that dredged up all that history about the murder of Harold Dawson, the guy who'd borrowed the money from Big Lou. But something had always come up to prevent him from following through.

He had, however, followed through on Lou's advice to find someone to work with.

Eric and his friend Will shared a territory and supported each other's efforts in the preparation and execution of home break-ins in the city. It wasn't big money, but it paid the bills. Will also had other associates Eric would never have dreamed of approaching directly. They were pros with criminal support at a level of play that Eric could only imagine. It was part of their deal that Will's connections were separate from his dealings with Eric.

As they made their toast to Lou, Eric's thoughts went back to their conversation about missed opportunities. If he didn't make use of what Big Lou had told him, maybe one day he would be reminiscing about *his* lost opportunities.

"You know," he said to Will, "I have this information I've been sitting on for a while now. A lead that could amount to something pretty big. The longer I wait, the less chance it'll be worth anything, though. Thing is, it's going to require some prep and resources that I can't manage on my own."

Then he filled Will in on the story he'd been told about the wealthy expat American family probably living as fugitives under false ID in Canada. He explained that they'd either have an incredibly valuable piece of jewelry in their possession, a pin called the Tsarina's Spider, or, if they'd sold it, they'd most likely still have a wad of money from its sale, maybe also some serious money from selling contraband military electronics, too.

"All we need to do is find them, and they're going to have no choice but to play ball."

"How much we talking?"

"At least a couple of mil. Maybe a lot more."

"From what you're saying Lou told you, it sounds like this all happened some time ago. The money's probably long gone by now."

"Maybe. Maybe not. Three or four million bucks is an awful lot to simply blow, especially if you're looking to keep a low profile. And people that have that kind of money aren't like you and me. They don't spend it all. Most likely they invested it and now have twice that much.

Or, maybe they found the pin thing hard to sell and still have it. As you and I know, selling hot property can be tricky."

"Which raises a good point. If we actually did lay our hands on that Spider, we'd need a serious fence to unload it—not just some shifty dude in a neighborhood pawn shop. And what makes you so sure this guy stayed in Canada? Maybe he did fly all the way to Russia. Or maybe he flew somewhere else—some other country entirely. Like Tahiti. Or Italy. Or some country that would refuse to extradite them."

"Extradition laws can be tricky. I looked into that. And besides, he had a wife and child." Eric took out a map of the Western Hemisphere, unfolded it, and placed it in front of Will. "Here, Look at this map. It's possible to make a pretty good guess about where he went with the plane. Whidbey Island is a hell of a long way from any foreign country other than Canada. And this plane wouldn't have had full tanks. I've looked it up. When the Navy does touch and go practice, they do it on partially full tanks. It makes the planes lighter and more agile. And safer."

"OK, but why would this Ortez stick around? Seems like he could have bought an airline ticket out of Vancouver for him and his family and gone anywhere in the world. All he'd need is some fake ID. Just have to go someplace where nobody knows or cares about what he'd done."

"Stealing a navy airplane was a pretty big deal at the time. Seems to me that once he's shed the airplane and is off on his own, he'd want to lay low for a good long time. Stay unnoticed. Be somewhere that people speak his language and where he can fit in. Then, after his wife and kid join him, maybe they settle in and decide they're happy where they are. We don't know all the reasons he left in the first place. And we won't know if they're still around unless we look into it."

Eric was pleased that his friend seemed to actually be considering the job, so he hit him with one more thing he'd been thinking about. "One lead is to contact people who might have bought the Spider from him. I don't know anyone who handles big-ticket stuff like that. And, I don't know how to go about finding someone who does. But here's the thing, Will. You've got connections. I been thinking maybe you could pass the idea along to your friends in the organization? Maybe to that Arturo guy you're always talking about. See if they might be interested in making something out of it themselves. Cut us in if they make some money on the tip."

Will took a long swig of beer before replying. Then he nodded. "Sure, buddy. Why not? All they can do is say no."

With that, Eric went over the story again, filling Will in on some details he hadn't covered already. The bosses should at least be impressed with their initiative. Who knew? Maybe this could boost their budding criminal careers to a whole new level.

Three weeks passed before Will reported back: "Sorry, Eric, it's a no-go on that thing with the Spider and your friend who died. They did look into it, though. There's some Canadian private eye they had do a search for the guy you mentioned, but they came up empty."

CHAPTER 25

Sydney Warren
Preston-Martin Building, Seattle
Law Offices of Warren and Carmichael
Current day

E ven before the Nowak "children" made their appointment to meet with her, Sydney had heard that her long-ago client Jamison Nowak had recently died. She assumed that his surviving son and daughter had called because they planned to ask her to handle his estate. People didn't always realize that lawyers, like other professionals, had fields of expertise. If they knew a lawyer, of any kind, that's often who they reached out to. Her plan was to commiserate with them about their father's death and then hand them off to Duncan.

When she'd last seen Nowak's two offspring, Bryce and his younger sister Bonny had been tender-age children. She remembered them sitting respectfully with their mother in the front row of the spectator gallery during their father's trial, well-behaved children impressed by the formality of the courtroom and by the seriousness of what was happening to their father. Now they were both married with children of their own, and Bonny's last name was Price.

When the receptionist let her know they'd arrived, Sydney went out to the lobby to meet them. She was immediately struck by how much Bryce looked like his father had at the time of his trial. Both siblings had light brown hair, not as blond as it had been when they were younger. Bonny's long hair was straight and tucked behind her ears. Bryce's hairline was starting to recede. Both were well-dressed and healthy looking. People you might run into in a yoga class or on the tennis courts. Not that Sydney had time for either.

After shaking hands and exchanging a few pleasantries, Sydney walked them to her office, got them settled in the two chairs in front of her desk, and asked if they wanted anything to drink. They both declined.

Since they had mentioned their father's estate when making the appointment, she was completely unprepared for the blast of sentiment when she asked what she could do for them.

"That murder case ruined our father's life," Bonny said in a firm, emotional voice. "Bryce and I remember what he was like *before* the trial. He was a kind, thoughtful, loving father. He cared about people, including his partner, Harold Dawson. But afterwards? Let's just say that Dad became a bitter, defeated man."

Bonny paused to let Bryce pick up the story. "He was thrilled when he was found not guilty at trial," Bryce said with feeling." He took a breath, moderated his voice, and added, "He never forgot what you did for him, Ms. Warren; he was deeply grateful. But after the trial, when those 'justice' people found his rifle in that mountain stream and matched up the bullet, everything went downhill."

After a brief pause, he continued in a voice tinged with angst. "Nobody wanted anything to do with him. Friends, colleagues. As you may have heard, his senior partner, Cecil Ravenswood, forced him out of the firm. With dad gone and with Harold Dawson dead, RDN became Ravenswood and Associates. Dad ended up renting a storefront office on Northgate Way, not far from the old Northgate Shopping Center. He did his best to make it on his own as a financial advisor, but most of his clientele had already abandoned him, and his business was never the same. The whole ugly affair followed him for the rest of his life."

"A couple of years after the trial, our mom divorced him," Bonny added. "Even when we were young, Bryce and I understood. He was consumed with anger and had become impossible to live with. After their divorce, we lived with our mom, but we'd see dad occasionally. He made an effort to be upbeat when he was around us, but we sensed even then that it was an act, and we dreaded those visits. Mom insisted we be nice about it, but it was painful to be around the person he'd become."

"That's why we're here, Ms. Warren," said Bryce. "When he died, Dad was involved in one of his endless pro se lawsuits. The case is here in Seattle. In the King County Superior Court. We'd like you to represent us. We want you to win that case. For us, and for him."

Now she understood why they'd asked to meet with her rather than an estate lawyer, and she felt sorry for these two people who'd more or less "lost" their father under horrible conditions and at such a young age. Still, she wasn't at all sure it was something she wanted to take on. One thing she'd learned in her years as a lawyer though was to never say either "yes" or "no" before getting all the facts.

"Tell me about the case," she said.

"It's a defamation lawsuit," Bryce said. "Dad filed it shortly before his death. It's against the Seattle Report. Are you familiar with them?"

"Yes." Sydney didn't read their weekly "underground" news blog on a regular basis, but upon occasion a story caught her eye. Their focus was on offbeat local news, interesting characters, and, very often, the gossip and the local Pacific Northwest history that sometimes surrounded such stories.

"The case was outstanding at the time of his death," Bryce continued. "He filed it about four months ago when the Seattle Report published a historical retrospective on the WPPSS bond default back in the early 1980's. The story was less about the facts of the case and more about local personalities. I suppose it was inevitable that they include stuff about Harold Dawson and our father.

"The story referred to Dawson as a man who 'never lost faith' in the WPPSS bonds. They described Dad as the man who'd been acquitted of Dawson's murder only to have 'critical and dispositive forensic evidence of his guilt' come to light two days after the jury's verdict. That use of the term 'dispositive' was bad enough. But if the writer had left it with that, Dad might have let it go. Instead, in her summary at the end, the writer referred to the WPPSS default as having . . ." He took a notepad out of his shirt pocket and flipped a few pages. ". . . 'left behind an inheritance of disappointed investors, failed policy, wasted tax revenues, mothballed nuclear plants, and a *freed killer*.'"

Bonny jumped in. "Our initial reaction was to simply settle or dismiss the case. It was just another in a string of defamation claims and lawsuits Dad brought over the years following his acquittal. We decided if they retracted the bit about 'a freed killer,' that we *would* drop it. We called, talked to them, figuring that they'd happily agree. Instead, they blew us off and, in yet another 'report,' they doubled down and basically repeated all of the prosecution's evidence of Dad's guilt. They probably assumed that we wouldn't pursue it now that he was gone.

"That's what changed our minds. It seems to us like this final lawsuit presents us with a last chance to help clear our father's name. We want you to follow through and see this thing resolved. To put to rest all the ugly controversy that ruined his life. To finally set the record straight."

Sydney was not enthused by the request. "Realistically, it's probably not be possible to accomplish all that with one small defamation lawsuit," she said.

"We still want you to try. Even if all you do is make them admit they shouldn't have called him a 'killer.'"

"He refused to give up," Bryce said. "Every time he came across someone writing about him as though it was a fact that he had murdered Harold, he sued. Always representing himself. He was his own avenging angel.

"After a few cases, he became quite knowledgeable on the law of libel and slander. As he explained to me after his first few claims, the investigative materials, briefing, and legal documentation had all been done; it was easy for him to simply adapt and recycle them."

"He must have become fairly good at it," Bonny said. "Not one of Dad's cases ever went to trial. All inevitably settled—typically in exchange for a modest but meaningful sum; large enough to make settlement worthwhile for Dad."

Sydney recalled that one of her lawyer friends had been in the courtroom the day of the summary judgment hearing on Nowak's first defamation case, one she'd declined to handle because it didn't seem winnable to her after the rifle was discovered. According to her friend, the defendant's attorney had obviously gone in thinking it was going to be a slam-dunk to win against some poor sap acting as his own lawyer.

Apparently, Nowak submitted no brief. Nor even a single affidavit in advance of the hearing. Then, after the publisher's lawyers completed their argument and the judge turned to Nowak for his opportunity to be heard, all Nowak did was stand, raise his right hand, and make a statement: "My name is Jamison Nowak. I am the plaintiff in this case. I hereby swear under oath and upon penalty of perjury that I am not guilty of the murder of Harold Dawson, so help me God."

"That was it . . . all there was," her friend had said, somewhat gleefully. "The attorney tried to argue the inappropriateness of oral testimony in a summary judgement motion, but the judge dismissed the issue by simply asking Nowak to write down what he had just said on a pad of paper provided by the clerk, sign it, and have the bailiff put the case file number on the top and notarize it." In a summary judgment motion, that would have been all that was needed to require the case to go to trial.

After that, according to Sydney's friend, Nowak became notorious as a pro se litigant in the courthouse. Everyone knew that he jacked lawyers around on providing exchanges of Interrogatories and Requests for Production by photocopying what they sent him, changing the headings to make them his, and sending them back for them to respond to. That and a few other clever maneuvers were enough to drive up costs and billable hours for the attorneys involved. It was not surprising that defendants always came up with settlement offers.

"He really hated being called the 'WPPSS Killer,'" Bryce said. "I hated it too; I was the 'son of the WPPSS Killer.'"

"I think being labeled like that was one of the main reasons he kept fighting them in court," Bonny said.

"The bottom line was that, between his financial consulting and modest lawsuit settlements he made enough to live on," Bryce said. "His estate is solvent, but not by much."

"But it isn't about the money," Bonny interrupted. She looked down at her hands resting on the table and frowned. "I admit, I didn't do a lot to support him over the years. When I was a kid, I was embarrassed by the publicity and, later on . . . if I'm being honest, it was hard not to have doubts about what happened back then. But I believe he didn't kill his friend. And I want us to do this one last thing for him."

Sydney felt herself losing her resolve to say "no." Even if their father had committed murder, these two didn't deserve to continue suffering. She would do it for them, if not for her former client.

"I'll admit, I've got some serious doubts," Sydney told Duncan the following day. "But I do think Bryce and Bonny may have a shot. The article mentions Nowak by name. And it refers to the later discovery of 'critical and dispositive evidence of guilt' and then refers to Nowak as 'a freed killer.' That's probably a libel per se."

Duncan was frowning as he listened to her. "I don't know, Syd," he said. "I'd be awfully careful about this. That rifle and its connection to the case are pretty convincing evidence of the man's guilt." He had learned to value her ability to analyze and come up with winning strategies in cases, but in this instance, he felt like she might be leading with her heart.

"I've told them that. They want to take their chances in court."

"So, you're confident that they know what they're getting into."

"I painted a pretty bleak picture, Duncan." She ran her hands through her naturally graying hair, a habit she had when she was feeling uncertain about something. "I said I'd look into it mostly because I feel for Bryce and Bonny. Their dad just died, and understandably, they're looking for some kind of vindication. Even if they win this case, they're probably not going to get that much satisfaction. The rifle will still be on the record as the murder weapon."

"You know, Syd, it can be hard to end up with a happy client if what they want is to right some perceived wrong. Even if you tell them success is a long shot."

Sydney thought for a moment before responding. "They seem like truly decent people—both of them. They've suffered through a lot with their father over the years, not only because of the rifle evidence that made the 'not guilty' verdict seem like a farce, but because of how it changed him from a loving parent to a bitter man obsessed with getting 'justice.' I can't imagine how it must have felt to grow up with a father who was so consumed with anger that he spent most of his life suing people who besmirched his reputation."

"I get it." He did understand the "why," but still thought it was a bad idea. "Are you doing this pro bono? Not that I care; just curious."

"I didn't want it to be about the money; we agreed to an hourly fee."

"And you may not count all the hours you spend on it . . . I know you."

"Well . . ."

"Honestly, I think you pulled off a miracle for a guy who was almost certainly guilty. He was damned lucky. But I'm not sure another miracle is in the cards."

"You know, Duncan, even after all these years, I still find it hard to accept that the Jamison Nowak I knew was actually guilty of that murder." She held up her hands. "I know what you're thinking, especially given the rifle evidence, but I've never been able to shake this feeling that he was telling me the truth."

CHAPTER 26

Sydney Warren
Preston-Martin Building, Seattle
Law Offices of Warren and Carmichael
Current day

Two days later, Bryce and Bonny were back in Sydney's office. After talking with Duncan, she wanted to make absolutely certain they understood the consequences of moving forward with the lawsuit.

"You haven't changed your mind, have you?" Bonny sounded anxious.

"No, it's not that. I just wanted to make sure you know what to expect. We've already talked about it being a long shot, but I hope you've also considered that the trial will once again put a public spotlight—however briefly—on the original trial and verdict. You're OK with that?"

"Yes," Bonny said without hesitation.

"We definitely want to go ahead with it," Bryce agreed.

"You two have indirectly lived with libel and slander law for years, but I want to go over a few key points." Bonny and Bryce nodded. "The truth is a defense in a defamation case. And, as you know, the burden of establishing that truth is going to be on the defendant. That's going to be more difficult if your dad is seen as a public figure—voluntary or not. They will be trying mightily to prove that your father was indeed guilty, in spite of the jury verdict. If they succeed, not only will you lose, but we'll also have torpedoed any real hope you might have had to rehabilitate your dad's reputation. Not that there's a clear path to do that even if we win. But losing could end up making things even worse. So, before we proceed, I need to feel confident that you understand the consequences of a potential loss. Because, given the evidence that's out there, losing is a very real possibility."

Sydney was fully aware that this wasn't the pep talk they might have been hoping for. But she wanted to be as honest as possible.

Bryce and Bonny looked at each other. Sydney couldn't tell what they were thinking. After what seemed much longer than the few seconds that it actually was, Bryce asked: "Does the jury verdict in Dad's criminal case carry *any* weight in this lawsuit?"

"Unfortunately, not in the way you might hope. In that criminal case, the prosecution had to prove that your dad was guilty *beyond a reasonable doubt*. In this civil case, all these defendants will have to do is prove that your dad was guilty by a *preponderance of the evidence*—basically to convince the jury that it is more likely than not. That is a great deal easier to do. Moreover, the discovery of your dad's rifle at the scene, his partial fingerprints on the cartridges, and the match between the gun and the shell casing all came after the trial. If presented correctly, it does seem to support the truth of the statements made by the Seattle Report."

"But how about all those cases Dad brought where he was paid a settlement? He must have had something going for him." It was clear how desperately Bonny wanted to believe in her father's innocence.

"As we discussed before, in most of those cases he was a pro-se litigant whose every move in court cost him next to nothing but required his opponent to pay thousands of dollars in legal fees to respond. The hard truth is that those settlements were likely made to forestall further costs of litigation. Not necessarily because there was any particular merit in his claims."

There was a moment of silence. Then Bonny said: "We more or less knew that was the bottom line, but we think he made some good points on his own behalf too."

Bryce reached out and put a hand on his sister's shoulder before asking Sydney: "So it sounds like you're saying we can't win this."

"No, it's *possible* we can. The passage of time will make this harder for both sides. Recollections fade. Some of the witnesses may well have died or disappeared. For instance, one of the reasons we won back in 1983 was because we were able to posit the possibility that the crime might have been committed by someone else. We had the loan shark collector in the courtroom as exhibit A for that theory. But Grant Meade is no longer with us. On the other hand, the transcripts from the original criminal trial might be admissible under one or another exception to the hearsay rule. They would be helpful.

"What I'm saying is that it's complicated. While it is hard to predict, the discovery of your dad's rifle makes this a huge uphill battle. And, even if you do win, the damages we can claim on your behalf are probably minimal. If you're asking my advice as a lawyer, it would be not to do it."

"As we told you before, we don't care about the damages," Bryce said, his tone firm. "But let me just ask you straight up: if you had to predict the outcome, do you think we will lose?"

Before she could respond, Bonny interrupted. "Actually, I don't think that's the question we should be asking. You already said losing is a very real possibility—maybe the most likely one. I think both Bryce and I understand that it's a tough case and that we could easily lose. What I want to know is: What do you *believe*? Do *you believe* our father was guilty?"

Sydney wanted to be transparent, but there were always so many shades of gray when dealing with the legal system and the "truth." "I think you need the answer to *both* of those questions, Bonny. As to the first, the most I can say is that I don't know what the odds are, but I have serious misgivings. One can never be sure beforehand what will happen in a fight like this. But, at the moment, my best professional judgment is that, even if we put up a very good fight, losing does seem like the most probable outcome. If we go ahead with this, I think you need to face that. And, as I said earlier, a loss could easily end up actually making things much worse."

Sydney waited a moment to let that sink in. "But as for *your* question, Bonny, back when we tried you dad's case, I believed him. Even now, despite the discovery of that rifle after the trial, I still find it very difficult to believe that he murdered his friend and colleague. I must add, however, that what I personally believe doesn't carry any weight in a court of law. Nor should it sway your decision. The facts are the facts. If we're going to launch this project, I need to know that you're doing so with a clear head and a realistic vision of the risks and possible outcomes."

Bryce exchanged another look with his sister. If they were communicating nonverbally, it was pretty subtle. Too subtle for Sydney to make a guess about what was going through their minds. Finally, Bonny nodded and Bryce responded on behalf of the two of them.

"Here's the thing, Ms. Warren. Bonny and I are on the same page on this. We discussed it at length before we ever called your office. And we had another intense conversation over dinner last night. We both feel we'd be betraying our dad to simply ignore this case and let it die. We know in our hearts that our dad was innocent of that crime. And, frankly, it sounds to me like you do too. Yet, even after he was found not-guilty by a jury of his peers, he spent the whole balance of his life engaged in a never-ending battle in which he was constantly trying to prove his innocence and was never able to do so.

"Now, his official legacy to us turns out to be two things. First, there's his bank account with maybe seventy or eighty thousand dollars left in his estate, what remains of his hard-earned savings from a lifetime of uphill effort. And second, there's this unresolved lawsuit. Honestly, it's hard for us to see that set of circumstances as anything other than a cosmic message, as a plea from him, maybe from beyond the grave, to use that money to see this through. To finally get him the justice he deserves. Or at least a small piece of justice by presenting his side of what happened one last time."

The two shared another look, and Bryce continued: "We believe you're the best possible lawyer to handle this. So, please consider us fore-warned. And know that we *are* prepared to be practical and reasonable as we learn more down the road. But, at this point, we want to proceed."

CHAPTER 27

Eric Gee
Downtown Seattle
A bar on 1ˢᵗ Avenue
Current day

"They're not going to like it."

Eric could tell that Will wanted to do it. But he was afraid of the "bosses." It made sense to be wary, but, as Eric saw it, the bosses had given it their best shot, and they'd come up short. He didn't know exactly how much effort they'd put into it, but as far as he was concerned, now that they'd said "no" to the project, the whole thing felt like it was again his baby.

The more he thought about it, the more he was glad it had gone the way it had. If he could locate that Ortez guy on his own, he wouldn't have to split the proceeds with anybody other than Will. It was like an inheritance. Lou had given him this gift; he owed it to him to try.

When he looked back, he was very aware of just how good Big Lou had been to him. Without Lou's protection, Eric might never have made it through his prison term. And Lou's mentoring had been like a mini-university course in crime. One thing in particular Big Lou had hammered home was the need for careful preparation. Now, before ever setting foot inside any target for one of his burglaries, Eric did his prep. He investigated the online profile of the owners and their habits as well as doing a Google Street View scan of the neighborhood and a parcel search in the local county real property records. In addition, he reviewed local real estate websites for the address in question. It wasn't uncommon to find detailed interior photos and even the occasional video "virtual tour" still posted from the last time those same premises had been on the market for sale.

As it turned out, however, researching Danny Ortez wasn't as easy as he'd hoped. In 1983, when Ortez had disappeared into Canada with that Navy jet, there wasn't much online information on individuals available. No Facebook pages. No LinkedIn profiles. No sophisticated search engines. No digitized public records.

He began by going to the Seattle Public Library to look for old newspaper stories published in the days following Danny's disappearance. Records for the Seattle Times and Post Intelligencer had been digitized from microfilm, and he did find articles related to the loss of the aircraft that identified the pilot as Danny Ortez, but there weren't many details about Ortez. It seemed pretty clear that the Navy had been less than transparent in responding to press inquiries.

In talking to a librarian about where he might find more information on the plane theft, he found out that there was an established local weekly serving the Oak Harbor community, the small town where Naval Air Station Whidbey was located. He decided it was worth a try. For Oak Harbor, that Navy plane theft would have been a very big deal. Maybe some enterprising local had managed to dig up a few facts not released to the larger papers.

It wasn't a long drive, but it involved a ferry ride. He actually enjoyed the trip. But when he arrived, he discovered that while the paper was in the process of digitizing their archives, papers from as far back as 1983 were still on microfilm at the local Oak Harbor Public Library. The good news was that since the paper was a weekly instead of a daily and was focused solely on local news, there weren't that many pages to scan per weekly edition. He quickly became proficient at using the microfilm reader, and before long, he found a brief front-page article published the week following the aircraft theft. The article confirmed that it was Lt. J.G. Daniel Ortez who stole the Navy aircraft and said that he and his wife Julia and their 1-year-old daughter resided in family housing at the Naval Air Station. It also mentioned Ortez had been in Fleet Replacement Training—whatever the hell that was.

When he looked it up, Eric learned that fleet replacement training was for training new pilots on the specific airplane they'd be flying in combat. With that in mind, Eric started calculating how long Ortez may have been in the Navy. Ortez would probably have been transferred to Whidbey for the specialized training. To get to that point, Eric guessed he'd been in the service about two years, give or take.

The next question was when Ortez got married. Eric had browsed wedding announcements for wealthy people in the past, looking for when family members would be away from their homes. They were often a goldmine of information. And he knew from Big Lou that the wife's family had started out with money. Surely they would have announced their daughter's marriage in one or both of the Seattle papers.

The final issue was timing. It seemed unlikely Ortez would have met a Seattle woman *after* he signed up. Not impossible, but very unlikely. And, given the age of their child, he guessed that they got married around the time Ortez first joined the service. If he was right, he knew about when to start looking for wedding announcements. Eric felt like patting himself on the back for being so clever.

The next morning he was back at the Seattle Public Library when it opened. It took some searching, but he found an announcement of the "marriage of Julia Dawson to Daniel T. Ortez." Danny was described as the son of "Santiago and Bethany Ortez of Astoria Oregon," with no other family mentioned. Danny had graduated from the University of Oregon in 1981. Sure enough, Julia had also attended the University of Oregon—so there was the connection.

It wasn't much, but it was a start.

When he Googled "Daniel Ortez, Astoria, Oregon," he came up with nothing. But there, among the results for that search, was an obituary in the Daily Astorian for one "Santiago Ortez of Astoria Oregon, 1938-2022," who was referred to as a "respected Astoria salmon troller."

Eric had no idea what a "salmon troller" was and at first thought it curious that an obit would mention that someone was a sports fisherman. He soon discovered that salmon trolling was a commercial fishery conducted in all four Western U.S. states: California, Oregon, Washington, and Alaska. Trollers fished out of relatively small boats, often alone, with limited entry fishing licenses that were bought and sold among private individuals but that were registered by the states.

If Danny Ortez's dad was a commercial fisherman, Eric thought his son might know something about salmon trolling as well. He recalled what Big Lou had told him about people always going back to their old ways and what was familiar. And, if there were salmon trollers up and down the U.S. coast, it seemed logical that there'd be salmon trollers in Canada, too. To Eric's way of thinking, fishing on your own out on the ocean seemed like a pretty good occupation for somebody who wanted to stay off the radar. IF Ortez was in Canada. And IF he wasn't simply living off of money from his thefts, maybe somewhere far away.

He started researching Canadian salmon trolling and, sure enough, Canada had a limited entry commercial salmon troll fishery just like the U.S. He called the Canadian Department of Fisheries and Oceans' offices in Vancouver, BC, but they refused to give Eric any information. There was some kind of privacy issue. It appeared to be a dead end.

But Eric wasn't about to give up. He decided to make a trip to Vancouver BC. Even with Customs, it was an easy three-hour drive from Seattle. He started early and arrived before noon. At the main office for the agency, he asked a few innocuous questions about the process for getting a salmon troll license and about how the limited-entry licensing system worked. Then, when lunchtime came, he followed a couple of employees to a nearby café. It was one of those places where you ordered at a counter and picked up your food when they called your number. It didn't take long for him to pick his target: a young man who needed a haircut and who was dressed in what looked like inexpensive off-the-rack clothes that weren't a perfect fit. Eric saw him look in his wallet and finger some bills before choosing what he wanted for lunch. Of course, it was possible the man didn't care about appearances and was trying to decide whether to pay with cash or a credit card. But Eric had to start somewhere.

After lunch he followed the young man back to the office and waited at the entrance for him to leave at the end of the workday. He'd come up with what he thought was a good cover story. His brother had been a druggie, was involved in a hit and run, and disappeared. The family thought he might have gone to Canada and had looked for him to no avail. It had been a while, but Eric had decided to try again to find his brother. And he had a lead—he thought his brother might have purchased a salmon troll license under an assumed name.

At first the man was hesitant to talk to Eric, but when he heard that Eric was looking for a brother who had run away from home years ago, the young man was willing to listen, although he said right off that he wasn't sure how he could help. Eric made a passionate plea and offered the man a small fee for his "trouble" in providing a list of license purchases over the five years following Danny Ortez's disappearance with that airplane. It didn't take long for the man to agree to ignore the agency's privacy policy and see what he could find for Eric.

The next day, Eric had a printed short list of possibilities.

Most fishermen held on to their licenses for a long time, so there were only about half-a-dozen first-time license purchases during the time period in question. One of the names on the list leapt out. The license had been purchased less than two years after Danny Ortez's disappearance. The buyer was one Vincent MacDonald whose mailing address was a P.O. box in the small First Nations village of Bella Bella, BC. No physical address or email was listed. The name of the boat to which the license was issued was the "*Liza M.*" Since it was a commercial fishing vessel, Eric did a search in Transport Canada vessel registration website and found a commercial fishing vessel by that name. It was 38' in length, a carvel planked wooden hull with a single screw and was powered by a diesel engine of 120 horsepower. The owners were shown as Vincent and Elizabeth MacDonald. The date of registration was only weeks before the date of purchase of the limited entry troll license. And the mailing address shown was the same PO Box in Bella Bella. A quick check showed that the post office was located within a block of the Bella Bella, BC Ferry terminal.

It had to be them.

Once armed with this basic information, the going got easier. Eric called the Canada Post Office in Bella Bella and asked if someone there could confirm that the Vincent McDonald who held a P.O. Box there was the same "Vince" who owned the salmon troller, "*Liza M.*"

"I'm a troller myself," Eric told the postal clerk. "I live in Vancouver and met Vince last summer on the grounds. He mentioned he lived near Bella Bella, and I have something I want to send him, a framed picture of his boat out on the water. My wife took the picture, and it's so nice, I couldn't resist framing it for him. But I thought I'd better check for sure that I have the right address before I ship it."

"No problem," the clerk told him. Then she turned chatty. "I've known Vince and Elizabeth for years. They come in for mail and groceries every couple of weeks. He sells his fish here in town during the season. Vince and Elizabeth are the salt of the earth," she said. "Really nice people. Their daughter, Allison, lives in Vancouver, but that doesn't keep her from stopping by to say 'hello' whenever she's in town for a visit. She's married now. Girard, I think is her married name. Like you, she lives in Vancouver. Has a grown son in school down there. Lovely family. I'd be happy to pass along a message if you'd like."

Eric thanked the woman profusely but added, "No message, thanks. I'd like the picture to be a surprise. I'll send it along the next time I get to a post office."

The first thing he did when he put down the phone was to silently pump his fist in the air a few times in celebration. He couldn't believe he'd actually done it. He'd hit the jackpot. Now, his biggest concern was the possibility that after going to all the trouble to track Ortez down he would discover the well was dry. He was also unsure what he would actually do if Ortez refused to cooperate.

When he told Will he'd located Ortez, his daughter, and his grandson, Will was impressed. But he was still concerned that they might be exceeding their authority to act on their own given they had originally shared the potential idea with his bosses. Eric assured him that the bosses would never find out. "Everything we need to do will happen in Canada. This Ortez guy sure as hell isn't going to be talking about it. Nobody else needs to know except for you and me. We just contact the daughter by email. Maybe send her a picture of her son to show we mean business—that'll get their attention. After that, we use a burner phone to arrange for a handover."

"I don't know, Eric. We need to get our hands on that Spider thing without revealing who we are. That's where kidnappers always go wrong. How do we do that and make sure we don't get caught?"

"That's why this is so beautiful," Eric said. "We aren't going to kidnap anyone. It will be a straightforward exchange—the Spider for our silence. The main thing to keep in mind is that sending someone a picture of their grandson isn't illegal. They're the ones hiding from the U.S. government; we haven't done anything wrong. If they still have that Spider, they'll probably be happy to turn it over to us to keep quiet about where they live. If they've sold it, we can negotiate how much it's worth to them to stay hidden. Unlike a kidnapping, these folks won't want us to get caught afterward. They can't involve the authorities without having some awkward explaining to do. And if they report us for anything, anything at all, they know we'll expose them. Its foolproof."

"Unless they are ruthless and take us out."

"No one is going to 'take us out.' We just need a simple way to avoid giving them the opportunity. I got something in mind. Something very cool that doesn't involve any risk. I'll do it myself. This is going to be a walk in the park."

CHAPTER 28

Duncan Carmichael
Preston-Martin Building, Seattle
Law Offices of Warren and Carmichael
Present day - three weeks later

"Thanks for taking the time to meet with me." Allison Girard shook Duncan's hand with a firm grip when he came out to the reception area to meet her. Her dusky blond hair was set off by large dark brown eyes and smooth tanned skin. Casual clothes: denims, sneakers, and checked flannel jacket. A middle-aged woman who favored comfort over fashion, perhaps from a rural community. He also thought he detected a Canadian accent.

There was something vaguely familiar about her. "Have we met before?" he asked.

She smiled broadly as if there was humor in his question. "Actually, I believe we have. But it was a *very* long time ago. I have no personal memory of the meeting."

He took a second look and tried to envision a younger version of the woman, but he still couldn't place her.

As they entered his office and took their seats, she explained: "I'm told I take after my mother, Mr. Carmichael. As I understand it, I was with her on the day, many, many years ago, when she drove here to Seattle from Oak Harbor to meet with you after my dad stole a jet airplane from the U.S. Navy."

She broke into a wide grin when he did a double-take. "As I said, it was a long time ago. 1983. I would have been around a year old."

Duncan smiled back. "I'll be damned. Yes, I definitely remember the meeting with your mother. And I recall that a few months later, she and you vanished without a trace. Now here you are." He wanted to ask, *where the hell have you been all these years?* But he held back. It sounded like he was about to find out.

She nodded. "I can see why you might have a question or two about that."

"I do." He was especially curious about the coincidence. Less than a month ago, Nowak's adult children had come in to see Sydney, and now, as if on cue, here was the daughter of Julia and Danny Ortez.

"Well, Mr. Carmichael, my family is in trouble," Allison Girard said rather abruptly. "I'm here because we need your help."

"Perhaps you'd better start from the beginning. I'm sure a lot has happened since first your father, and then you and your mother, left the state."

For the better part of the next hour, Duncan mainly listened, occasionally inserting a question or asking for clarification, enthralled by the tale of a family's makeover after leaving their former lives behind. He found their story both heartbreaking and inspiring at the same time.

"After my parents fled to Canada," Allison told him, ". . . we lived off-the-grid in a float home. It was basically a self-sufficient floating barge that my parents anchored up for extended periods of time in different places in Northern British Columbia. I'm sure you know that there are literally thousands of tiny, uninhabited coves tucked in among the multitude of rocky inlets in the BC coastal wilderness. Float homes aren't strictly legal in unincorporated areas in Canada, but they're not uncommon either. Because they can move around so easily, they're not so very different from pleasure yachts. They don't do any particular harm so, unless there is some complaint, there is very little effort to regulate them.

"When I was young, my folks first drove the barge with an outboard motor. Then Dad became a commercial fisherman and used his fishing boat to tow our barge to new places. We moved around a lot because Dad was afraid of getting caught. He would usually pick up anchor if other boats or float homes showed up, and off we would go to our next hideaway. In some ways, I think he loved the adventure. He always seemed able to discover some picturesque, uninhabited protected nook or cove somewhere. Sometimes there'd be someone nearby eking out a living ashore, but more often than not, even if there was a cabin, it was abandoned.

"I think a lot of people fantasize about living in the wilderness, but the fantasy often fades as reality sets in. Not for my dad, though. And not for Mom and me, either. As a child, I loved the life, loved the water and always having some new place to explore. And I was oblivious to the worries my parents had about the government catching up with us.

"After Dad bought a commercial salmon troll license, he mainly sold his fish to packers on the grounds, but occasionally, if we needed supplies, he would sell in town. I considered that a real adventure. Then, at the end of the fishing season, he moored his boat alongside our float home. We had a small outboard skiff to run into some little village for groceries and the like.

"We were happy. Dad could build or fix anything and was always tinkering with one project or another. Mom was a musician and a poet, and an avid reader. She taught me to play the flute, and we always had lots of books around. It was a great life for a child.

"When I was old enough to be useful, I got to go out with him on his boat during fishing season. Mostly, he caught salmon but also black cod and halibut. Being part of the commercial fleet brought me in contact with more people who, like us, were earning their living from fishing. I thought my life was not really that different from how other people lived.

"Although I was being home-schooled, I occasionally interacted with other kids who lived on boats or float-homes like ours or that I ran into when we went into town. A lot of them, like me, didn't attend school regularly. So even though I got glimpses of how others lived, I still didn't think we were all that different.

"Eventually, I started asking questions about our lifestyle and about the future. At first, my parents didn't want to talk about why we lived on a float home or whether we were ever going to settle in one place. But I persisted, and when I got older, they finally told me about their past and made me promise to keep their secret. I loved my parents and didn't want to see anything bad happen to them, so I buried their past just like they had.

"It wasn't until they began preparing me to go away to college that it slowly became clear just how unusual our situation was. When I finally left home, it was a real shock. But then, going away to school can be traumatic for kids who grow up in normal homes too, so I have no complaints.

"Anyway, they'd apparently done a good job at home schooling me, because I aced the American SATs. Canadian Universities depend mostly on high-school grades and don't use the SATs, but I took the test because I didn't really have normal grades for the admissions people to see.

"My dad goes by the name Vince MacDonald. And my mom goes by Elizabeth. It wasn't till I was in my early teens that I learned those weren't their *real* names. According to Mom, they picked their names off of tombstones in a cemetery someplace outside of Prince Rupert. They looked for the graves of children who'd died young and who'd be about the right age had they lived. It was something they'd seen on TV back when they lived in the States. She picked the name Elizabeth Martins with Martins as her maiden name. As they tell it, there was no particular reason for choosing the names they did, other than that they belonged to children who died young and were buried in that graveyard.

At that time, and despite the law, birth and death records weren't always reliably matched up, especially in rural BC. So, if you could get a birth certificate, you could also get a National Social Insurance number and build an identity from there. That's what they did. MacDonald became Mom's married name. It became my surname as well on a birth certificate that was forged and filed—I am actually almost two years older than it says on my official birth certificate. Fortunately, I've never needed to use it. At least not yet."

She paused to take a sip of tea that his admin had brought in for her. "Sorry this is taking so long."

"I want all the details," Duncan assured her. "It's fascinating. And it's a bit like finally reading the last chapter of a book you never got to finish."

Allison smiled. "That I can understand. There were times when I was kid that I had to leave library books behind when we moved on. It took me several years to finally read all of *Anne of Green Gables*." She laughed. "Not everyone would consider that traumatic, but at the time, that was the worst thing that had ever happened to me. Mom didn't want to do anything that could call attention to us, like not returning a library book, I guess."

"I can see how that could leave an impression in a small community."

"Anyway, their approach apparently worked because nobody ever suspected that Dad was actually the infamous fugitive pilot who stole an airplane and deserted from the U.S. Navy. Or that all three of us were illegal immigrants. Over the years there have been amnesty opportunities for illegals to become citizens, but we couldn't take advantage of them because if anybody ever found out who Dad was, he'd be extradited to the U.S. and thrown in prison as a Navy deserter. Mom could have been charged with being an accessory. We'd have all been deported."

Duncan was amazed at how calmly she explained those missing years, as if they hadn't begun with an extraordinary event that could have easily been the plot for a made-for-TV movie. She seemed so well-grounded, but he wondered if she was as unaffected by her strange upbringing as she appeared to be. After growing up so isolated, he couldn't imagine how she'd made the transition to college and then, when she married, to a "normal" life in a Vancouver, BC suburb.

When she came to the end of her backstory, Duncan asked: "How's your mom, by the way. Is she OK?" When Allison's mother, Julia, had joined her husband in Canada, she'd gone from being a young Navy officer's wife living on a navy base to an isolated life on a float home in Western Canada. For a young woman with a privileged upbringing, it couldn't have been easy.

"Mom's fine. She said I should tell you 'Hi.' As you know, not long before she left to join Dad, she received some money from Grandpa Dawson's life insurance. That's what they used to start a new life together. When I went away to college and got married, she started fishing with Dad in the summertime. They're pushing seventy and in good health, but I worry about what happens as they get even older. I've been telling them they should retire, but moving into a senior living community or some public retirement home obviously has legal complications." She took a long breath as though preparing to plunge into the deep end of a pool. "That brings me to the present. Everything was going along just fine . . . until recently.

"I'm here because some bad people have found them. Found *us*. As a family, we're in a lot of trouble."

"You mentioned you have a son?" Duncan asked.

"That's right, Jack. He's a freshman at UBC in Vancouver where my husband and I live. A couple of days ago, I got an email message from what turned out to be an untraceable IP address. It included a recent video clip of my son walking to class on campus. There was also a video of me getting into my car in our home driveway. Most important, the message mentioned Mom and Dad's real names. Whoever sent the message obviously knows all about us. But my email must have been easier to find than theirs. Now, after all these years, someone is threatening to turn Dad and Mom in to the Canadian authorities. We're fairly certain that we'd be deported back to the U.S. My son Jack has birthright citizenship. But I don't.

"If they expose Dad, he will be turned over to the U.S. Navy and court-martialed for desertion and theft. As I'm sure you know, there's usually a five-year statute of limitations, but I'm told that there are other factors that negate that in this situation. When you're a fugitive, living out of the country and in hiding, as I understand it, the statute is 'tolled' or suspended. It's one of the many things on which we could use some legal advice.

"Then there's the thing with my son. We're afraid that whoever sent the pictures was indirectly telling us that they intend to maybe kidnap or harm him if we don't do what they ask. Why else would they send us that video of him at the UBC campus?" Allison's voice shook as she posed the rhetorical question about kidnapping. "And there's nothing we can do about it. We can't turn to the authorities for protection. Honestly, we don't have a clue how to handle this. Mom mentioned your name and insisted that I meet with you, but the truth is, I don't really see how you can help. The only reason I called your office and drove down here today is because we just don't know where else to turn."

As she had told her story, the composure she'd shown initially had slowly but steadily slipped away. She now looked more like what she was: a woman in serious trouble. Finally, her hands went to her face and she leaned forward, elbows on knees, and went silent as if trying to compose herself.

Duncan got up, stepped around from behind his desk, and took a seat in the second client chair beside the one where she sat. When he reached out and offered his hand, she took it and gripped it tightly.

"OK, so tell me what they want—these people who are threatening you," he said gently. "Obviously it's something big. It must have taken quite a bit of effort to find you."

Allison sighed deeply and straightened up. Then: "They want money. A lot of it. Money I don't have; money my parents don't have. We've *never* had the kind of money they're demanding."

"Do you have any idea why they think you do?"

"The whole thing goes all the way back to my grandfather. My mother's father, Harold Dawson. If it hadn't been for him, none of this mess would have ever happened."

"Before you continue, can I ask why you came to me after all these years instead of a Canadian solicitor?"

"Because you're familiar with Dad's case, and Mom believes you can be trusted, even though it's been years since she's seen you."

The image of her mother, a young vulnerable woman kicked out of Navy housing with a young daughter and no resources came to mind. "OK, maybe I'd better hear more about what's behind this threat."

"Well, we think it started with a recent post in the Seattle Report about Jamison Nowak's passing, but we really don't know for sure."

Could there be a connection between the case Sydney was handling and what was happening to the Ortez family? Perhaps there was some kind of conflict of interest he should be considering, although he couldn't see what that would be. Maybe this was one of those times when a coincidence really was just a coincidence.

"Over the years, Mom and Dad have kept a close eye on Seattle news and especially on mention of anything related to Dad or my Granddad. It was long after the Seattle Report story that I received the email demanding money.

"Anyway, what it all comes back to is the relationship between Grandpa Dawson and my father. After Dad got assigned to Fleet Air Whidbey, right here in Washington, they became really close. Spent a lot of time together. They even went to the infamous shooting range so Grandpa could give Dad advice on how to handle and maintain a firearm. Mom says that they'd talk endlessly about the pros and cons of various hunting rifles, about which one was best for one reason or another. But the real reason for the bond between them was their devotion to my mother. My mom's a pretty special woman. I guess they both knew that.

"When Granddad's business went belly up, he had to sell his assets to stay afloat. And, as I think you know, when things got really bad, he borrowed a chunk of money from a loan shark and used a piece of jewelry from his impressive collection as collateral. It was said to be worth millions.

"By the time he went to the loan shark, Granddad was apparently not just putting off the inevitable—he truly believed the courts were going to save his bacon. Instead, their ruling sealed his fate.

"Meanwhile my grandmother divorced him. That was the point at which Grandpa admitted to Dad that the Tsarina's Spider he'd used as collateral with the loan shark was a fake. That he'd actually sold the real thing long before. He gave the fake to Dad in case the lender sent someone after it—the last thing he wanted was for that lender to lay his hands on the fake Spider and discover that he'd been lied to from the very start. He knew that was the kind of thing that could get him killed. He told my dad to keep the fake somewhere safe and to hang onto it as a reminder of the consequences of bad choices.

"When any hope Grandpa had for digging himself out of the financial hole he was in evaporated, he panicked. The loan shark he'd borrowed from had a reputation for violence. Grandpa wanted Dad to put in for an overseas assignment and take my mother and me as far away from Seattle as we could get. But, as I guess you'd know, that isn't really an option in the U.S. Navy.

"Apparently Granddad's fear was contagious. Dad began losing sleep and looking over his shoulder. That was when he started thinking about ways to save Granddad, my mother, and me from the loan shark. He didn't share his thoughts with anyone because he wanted Mom to have deniability. But he began working on a plan."

CHAPTER 29

Duncan Carmichael
Preston-Martin Building, Seattle
Law Offices of Warren and Carmichael
Current day (continued)

"As it happened," Allison continued, ". . . my father was having trouble with his eyesight, especially at night. He'd never had absolutely perfect vision, but it was good enough to get him into flight training. By the time he got stationed at Whidbey Island and was into Fleet Replacement Training, however, his eyes were getting worse, and his performance as a pilot was suffering. He was about to wash out of the program. If and when that happened, he'd have been given some random assignment as a U.S. Navy line officer. He'd have ended up on a ship somewhere with no control whatever over where he went. And he'd have been completely unable to protect Mom and me.

"Then my granddad was murdered. My mom and dad both figured the loan shark had done it—not his partner Nowak. But with Granddad gone, Dad knew for sure that the loan shark would come looking for my mom and would assume my mother, Granddad's only heir, would have the Spider. She could claim he'd sold it, but the loan shark knew it was worth a lot of money. If he'd sold it after taking out the loan, where was the money?

"My father decided that he needed to do something dramatic enough to divert the loan shark's attention away from my mom and me and to himself. That's when he decided to take off with the fake Spider. He was afraid to tell my mom what he had in mind because she's hopeless at telling lies—he absolutely didn't want her to have to lie to that loan shark. She needed to sound convincing and authentically surprised and upset by Dad's disappearance. And not to seem complicit in it. He knew it would be hard on her, but he figured that once he got settled and she could join him, things would be okay. Spending the rest of his life off-the-grid in the Canadian wilderness didn't sound that bad to him, and he thought Mom, who is pretty self-sufficient herself, would be happy living like that too. Especially given the choices they had back home.

"The key to the whole thing was to make that loan shark believe Dad had taken the Spider with him when he disappeared into Canada.

"Crazy as it sounds in retrospect, that's why he stole a twenty-five-million-dollar airplane.

"He believed that such a public and extreme act would put all the onus on him and draw attention away from my mother. If she clearly appeared to be broke and didn't have the Spider or know anything helpful, and if it looked very much like Dad had left his wife in the lurch and made off with the Spider, he figured the lender would have no choice but to write off the loss."

"I guess I understand his reasoning," Ducan said. "But the act itself was so . . . monumental. It's hard to believe he actually pulled it off."

"I know. It really was a stupid and impulsive thing to do. But you have to admit, it was clever. And it worked. In some ways; it kept us safe and together all these years. He did once tell me that it had taken some real courage to call mom and ask her to join him several months after he took off. She was, of course, furious with him. But in the end, we went to Canada. And he made a good life for us there.

"It wasn't easy though. Having that insurance payout from my grandfather helped. Initially, it paid for two years of being on the run while they figured things out. Then they bought a limited-entry salmon troll permit and a boat. After that, he fished and made a decent living. If someone hadn't found us, we all could have lived happily ever after."

"No matter how you look at it, Allison," Duncan said, "leaving the country with a top secret, twenty-five-million-dollar aircraft was an audacious and foolhardy act. He must have known the Navy would assume he was a defector and a national security risk. And that they'd look high and low for him and for their airplane—maybe never give up."

"Dad says he has relived that choice again and again over the years, but he's never come up with anything else that would have done the trick. And, the thing is, Mr. Carmichael, it was never part of his plan to turn the airplane over to a foreign country or to sell its electronics. With a friend's help, he intended to return the airplane to the Navy almost immediately. But he was betrayed."

"Betrayed?"

"See, Dad had this buddy, Ross Michaels, one of Dad's flight crew, his bombardier navigator at the time. Ross played a key role in Dad's plan, although he obviously didn't tell him in advance that he was going take the airplane because that would have made Ross an accomplice. The day he left, Dad had the fake Tsarina's Spider with him. As he and his crew were getting suited up, Dad showed it to Ross and told him it was a priceless item that he'd been given recently by his father-in-law, the last and only piece of jewelry left from his father-in-law's collection. Then he explained that he wasn't about to let it out of his sight until he could figure out a safe place to stash it and asked Ross for suggestions. After all, they were buddies; he trusted him, right?

"The main thing Dad wanted was for Ross to be able to testify that Dad had taken the Spider with him when he stole the airplane. He figured there'd be a public investigation and that bit of information would be of interest to the Navy and also would filter back to Mom and to the loan shark."

"I get that. But what happened to the airplane?" Duncan asked. "That aircraft never turned up. Your dad sounds like a decent guy. Surely he could have thought of some way to disappear without stealing that airplane?"

"Mr. Carmichael, that's why I'm here. The thing you have to under-stand is that Ross Michaels wasn't the friend my dad thought he was."

Duncan waited.

"Let me put it in context." She paused until Duncan nodded for her to continue. "Unlike my mom, Dad didn't grow up wealthy. He's from Astoria, Oregon. His dad was a commercial fisherman and died in a boating accident when Dad was in college. Given my mom's wealthy upbringing, Dad has always been very self-conscious about his own modest roots. He had to work from the time he was fifteen.

"He put himself through college working on boats. For a while after his father died, Dad crewed on a small, free-lance tugboat out of Bellingham. They towed logs into town where they would be milled into lumber. The logs came from harvest sites throughout Western BC. It was an American boat and crew, but back at the time, that was fine with the Canadian logging firms that needed the services and with the Canadian government that wanted to support their logging industry.

"Anyway, that's how Dad knew of this place in Canada where there was this abandoned private airstrip that had originally been built for a logging operation. When the timber ran out, the landing strip had been lengthened and improved for larger passenger planes in anticipation of constructing some kind of big, deluxe sport fishing resort. They must have run out of money because the actual resort never got built. Over time, the airstrip was basically forgotten. Knowing about that airstrip was what made the whole thing seem possible.

"When Grandpa Dawson was murdered on a Friday, Dad was terrified. He knew he had to act quickly before the loan shark came after Mom.

"He had the weekend off, so early Saturday morning he drove up to Bellingham, chartered a plane, and flew up to a native village in coastal BC called Bella Bella. He paid in cash, which wasn't as unusual then as it is now. He pretended to be a sports fisherman flying in for the weekend. In Bella Bella, he chartered a small outboard powered boat for the one day. He used that boat to get to another boat rental place across the channel in Shearwater. This second boat he rented for a week.

"He towed the Shearwater rental boat some thirty or so miles to the beach below the abandoned landing strip and pulled it up into the woods at high tide and left it there for his escape after he landed the airplane. As you know, those EA-6B Prowlers were carrier-based aircraft with a relatively low landing and takeoff speed. But they're heavy. With powerful jet engines. He needed something better than a typical dirt strip and long enough for the landing. The old airstrip of packed crushed rock was still more than adequate.

"That evening he returned to Bella Bella in the boat he'd rented there and flew home. He wasn't all that worried about the Navy tracing him from Bellingham to Bella Bella because he figured by the time they got that far, he'd be long gone. As it turned out, the Navy never did figure that part out. That's why my folks felt safe returning to the Bella Bella area later on.

"First thing the following Monday morning, Dad was back at NAS Whidbey and reported in for duty as usual. That was the day he took the plane. When he got to the landing strip, he put the plane down, taxied it into the trees at the end of the field, and covered it with branches and brush. Then he hiked down to where he'd hidden the second boat and made his escape.

"What nobody apparently knows is that, as soon as it was possible to do, Dad called his friend Ross, his bombardier-navigator. He gave Ross the exact latitude-longitude coordinates for that airplane. Ross promised to tell his superiors about the call and to let them know where the plane was located. All it should have taken to retrieve the plane was a pilot and maybe a bit of fresh jet fuel brought in by boat or air. If Ross had done as he promised, that plane would have been airborne and back at NAS Whidbey in perfect shape within a day or two.

"Dad said that he told Ross the whole story. Explained why he'd stolen the plane. He figured that when Ross was questioned about it, he would also mention that Dad had that brooch, thus keeping my mother safe. It wasn't till years later that he learned that his friend had never passed the plane's location along to the Navy. Never said a word."

"What about the Spider—did Ross tell anyone about it?"

"Not as far as Dad knows. It left my mom at risk of having the loan shark think she had it and was holding out on him. Fortunately, the lender must have figured out on his own that Dad had made off with the Spider without telling her, because my mother only had that one threatening visit at grandma's apartment not long after Grandpa

Dawson died. Although they worried about him coming back for a long time."

"Well, Allison, I remember talking with Ross Michaels on the phone back at the time I looked into the navy housing issue for your mother. He wasn't helpful, and I recall him saying something about your father being about to wash out of the flight program. What you've told me puts that conversation in an entirely different light."

"Well, even today, as much as my father wants to believe that Ross had a reason for not following through, Dad could never forgive him for putting my mom in danger."

"Which brings us full circle. You said the people who emailed you want money?"

"Initially I figured it was a scam, deleted the message, and blocked the sender. Then he called me at home. I'm an artist like my mom, a painter. My husband Peter was at work at the time. He manages a Safeway store in West Vancouver. He knows some of what I'm telling you, but not all of it. We've never really talked about the details because I've never wanted him facing some kind of criminal accessory charge if any of this became known. I did have to fill him in some to explain why I needed to drive down here to meet with you today."

"So how much money are we talking about?"

"A lot. Way more than we could conceivably come up with. Two million U.S. Dollars. In cash. It's like some wealthy person's kidnapping ransom. We're supposed to have the money ready for delivery somewhere in Vancouver the day after tomorrow. Oh, and, that's another thing. They want the money *or* the Spider. Apparently, they think my dad may still have that damned Tsarina's Spider. The real one, not a fake. Unbelievable. That's got to be why they're asking for so much money."

"What did you tell them?"

"Just that there was no way we could come up with that kind of money. Not by the day after tomorrow or ever. We're just ordinary people. Have normal jobs. My father's a fisherman."

"What did you tell them about the Spider?"

"Well, I didn't tell them we had a fake. I acted like I didn't know anything about the Tsarina's Spider. Just told them we couldn't pay that much. And the guy told me to get it . . . or else. That's where we left things."

"Does your dad still have the fake?"

"Oh Yeah. He's sentimental about it. Not that it will do us any good."

"So, tell me. What would you like *me* to do?"

"Well, since we can't give these people what they're demanding, it's almost certain that my family is going to end up being deported. And my dad will then be facing a court martial in the U.S. Navy. We don't see any way around that. So, it seemed like a good time to talk to a U.S. lawyer who knows something about U.S. Navy law."

CHAPTER 30

Duncan Carmichael
Preston-Martin Building, Seattle
Law Offices of Warren and Carmichael
Current day (later that same day)

Sydney was alone in her office when Duncan knocked gently on the closed door.

"Enter," she said quickly, before he could enter without invitation.

When he opened the door, what he saw were the usual casebooks, hand-written lists on open yellow-pads, miscellaneous paste-it notes, and court documents strewn across her desk. Her hands were hovering over the keyboard of her laptop. And there were at least a dozen white Bankers Boxes piled nearby. Presumably they were filled with yet more documents.

"I'm interrupting . . .?" Duncan said tentatively, although it was obvious that he was. As usual, he hadn't considered how disruptive his visit might be till after he'd entered.

Thankfully, Sydney leaned back in her chair and smiled. "No, it's fine. I could use a break."

Duncan hesitated; some of the cases she handled were large class-action matters with multiple parties and with hundreds or even thousands of litigants. One of her clients was a national voting rights organization. They had a case that involved voting rights violations by the Federal Government which was currently refusing to enforce the requirements of the Federal Voting Rights Act. "If they aren't going to do it," she'd told Duncan a few days earlier, "then, by God, *we* will make it happen."

"I can come back." He knew his voice sounded more like an appeal than a statement. He really wanted to run some things by her.

"No, now's good. Seriously, I really do need a break."

He shut her door, moved a box off one of her client chairs, and took a seat. "I just met with a Canadian by the name of Allison Girard. She's . . ." He beat a drumroll on a tiny bare spot at the edge of her desk. "She's . . . the granddaughter of Harold Dawson."

Sydney blinked and leaned forward. "Really? The Harold Dawson from my murder trial, back in the day? His granddaughter?"

"Her dad and mom are living in a float home up on the north coast of British Columbia. He's a commercial fisherman—goes by the name Vince McDonald."

"Really?" she asked again, this time with even more emphasis.

"Yep, really."

"Did she give you any details?"

"Yes, she pretty much filled me in on everything. I'll give you the highlights later, but here's the problem. Allison got a call from someone who threatened to expose the family unless they give them two million dollars. Or the Tsarina's Spider."

"Someone knows about the Spider?"

"They know everything. They even know she has a son attending UBC, and they sent pictures to prove it."

"Not good."

"Not good," he agreed. "There are two things that bother me . . ."

"Only two?" She gave him a wry smile.

"Two biggies. First, why now after all this time? And second, how did these people find them?"

"Do you think the catalyst was the article in the Seattle Report?" Sydney tapped her fingers together as if to shake a thought loose.

"That seems a bit too recent. On the other hand, I can't imagine that a loan shark would wait all this time to collect. Oh, and did I mention that the Spider the family has is a fake?"

"You're serious?" Her finger tapping stopped, fingers frozen in place a moment before she rested her hands on the desktop.

"Unfortunately."

"So, Dawson did sell it when he was trying to appease his bond clients."

"Then he had a fake one made to trick the loan shark."

"Not smart." Frowning, she added, "And definitely not good."

"It doesn't answer the question of why they waited so long to go after it."

"You don't think someone from the Seattle Report could be involved in the blackmail, do you? Someone who has been trying to locate Ortez, maybe found him, then decided they wanted more than a story."

"It's possible, but I still think it's the loan shark. Or someone associated with him. Maybe the recent posts renewed their interest and they had a lucky hit."

"You said Allison told you he's a commercial salmon fisherman?

"Uh huh."

"If I somehow figured that out, it's where I'd start my search for him. Hard to do, but not impossible. It's limited entry in Canada, just like here."

"*If* you knew he'd become a fisherman."

"And if I was reasonably sure he was still in Canada. Wait one minute." She pulled her laptop closer. "There's a Canadian agency called Transport Canada that is responsible for vessel documentation. I'm going to enter Vincent MacDonald and see what shows up there." Her fingers flew across the keyboard. Moments later she said: "It's here. Vincent MacDonald is the owner of a commercial fishing vessel, 11.58 meters in length, 14 gross tons, maximum speed, 8 knots. His mailing address is listed. Boat's named the *Liza M.* That's pretty much it."

"Easy when you've got his name."

"There could have been bread crumbs somewhere leading to commercial fishing. The limited entry licensing information is confidential. But there are probably ways to either hack in or bribe someone. When you want something bad enough and don't mind crossing the line things are a lot easier."

"I don't think the 'how' helps us locate the 'who' though, do you?"

"It might, but the research could take some time. Which is probably something you don't have. It may make more sense to work from this end—if you can figure out some way to do that. I assume the family can't meet the demands."

"They don't have that kind of money. I've decided to see if we can eliminate the threat by getting them legally back into the US."

"What about his little problem of desertion and the Navy labeling him a traitor?"

"That's actually why I'm here. Do you have time to brainstorm if there's some legal angle to pursue? I'm not getting anywhere on my own."

"You like a challenge, don't you? Okay, let's get out of this office; I keep seeing things that I should be doing. And I'm going to need more coffee."

Chapter 31

Duncan Carmichael
Preston-Martin Building, Seattle
Law Offices of Warren and Carmichael
Current day (evening, same day)

"The reason I've called is that I've given your situation some thought," Duncan said to Allison Girard on the phone later that day. "I need to fly a few things past you. I also need to get in touch with your father. There are some difficult decisions to make."

"You said it, Mr. Carmichael. What do you have in mind?"

"Well, as you know, if you can't pay the money these people are demanding, and if they follow through on their threats, your father's immigration status in Canada will be in jeopardy. Once the Canadian government is alerted, he's likely to be extradited to the U.S. and face a court-martial in the U.S. Navy. But before all this happens, we still have a few cards to play. I'd like to spell out what I have in mind. And if you think it makes sense, I'll need to talk with your father directly."

"Sure. Go for it."

"Well, to start with, even if he gets these blackmailers to agree to an amount he can pay now, they're unlikely to stop there. At some point, they'll come back for more, probably again and again. And if they aren't willing to negotiate, they could turn your family in out of spite. If that happens, you're going to be out of options. We need to get ahead of this as quickly as possible. I think it's worth considering whether your father should contact the U.S. Navy and offer to turn himself in. Unless he's prepared to go into hiding again, I don't see any other option."

"We had a long conversation about exactly that before I came in to see you," Allison said. "We agree that he may have to do that; it's definitely the lesser of two evils, but not by much."

"Well, if your dad chooses to do that, I do think he has at least a little something to offer the Navy that might help."

"OK. I'm listening."

"If we tell the authorities that he's willing to turn himself in, the first thing they will undoubtedly want to know is *why now*. We can explain that he's getting old and wants to set the record straight, and in exchange for favorable treatment, maybe even for forgiveness, there are a few valuable pieces of information he can provide.

"He could, for example, tell the U.S. Navy where their airplane is. If it's still there, that is. Probably isn't worth much to them now, some forty years after the fact, but recovering it gives the Navy some closure and saves them a bit of embarrassment."

"*If* it's still there."

"Right. But if it is, they could get their airplane back—or whatever's left of it. Even without the high-tech avionics, being able to say they retrieved it is not insignificant."

"OK. I can see that. But I'm skeptical."

"Me too. But it's a place to start.

"Secondly, though, we can give them Ross Michaels. Who knows where he is today, or if he's even still alive. But once they learn what he did—and didn't do, they're not going to be happy with him. If he did sell the plane's location or its avionics, it would constitute espionage. Depending on what turned up in our enemies' arsenals after that plane disappeared, they might even already know whether the plane or parts were sold back then. If that's the case, the Navy is going to be *very* interested in talking to Michaels."

"You think they will care after all these years?"

"The government doesn't like loose ends, so, yes, I think they will care. However, there's something else that might play into this. Am I correct in thinking that your dad is perhaps Hispanic?"

"Yes. His family emigrated from Mexico back in the 1960s and ended up in Astoria, Oregon. Dad was born in the U.S. in Providence Hospital in Portland, Oregon. He's a birthright citizen, although from what I'm reading these days, that wouldn't necessarily be enough to keep him out of trouble."

"Well, that goes to my point. If your dad is apprehended, he's going to have to be extradited back to the U.S. And extradition can be tricky."

"I'm not sure what you mean."

"Well, we usually think of extradition as fairly straightforward. But there's a lot of discretion involved. To begin with, your dad and mom have been living in Canada as good, productive citizens for some forty years. In all that time, they've undoubtedly paid taxes. And, I assume they've never had any kind of run-in with the law?"

"Never. They've been careful not to do anything to call attention to themselves."

"Well, none of that would really change the outcome, but it does count for something. And there's one other thing. I hope you won't find what I'm about to suggest to be offensive. But one of the grounds for opposing extradition from Canada is if the extradition is of a 'political character.' Or if a Canadian court feels that the extradited party may not receive fair legal process if returned to the petitioning state—in this case, the U.S."

After a moment's thought, Allison responded: "Ah, I see. Or I think I do. But I don't know, Mr. Carmichael. My Dad's family name may have been Ortez, but in terms of upbringing and culture, I think you'd have to say we are probably every bit as 'white' as any family raised in the United States or in Canada. It seems like that may be something of a stretch."

"It may be. But realistically, we both know that, at the moment, U.S.-Canadian relations are under a lot of stress. And the U.S. immigration process is undergoing some big changes. I don't think it would be at all unreasonable for your father to be fearful that, if extradited to the

U.S. while subject to potential criminal charges in the U.S. Navy, he might get caught up in some kind of deportation sweep and be spirited off to some unknown country or foreign prison without due process of law."

"I do see where you're going with this, but do you actually think that argument would have any chance of success?"

"It's hard to know. The political climate between the two countries is in flux. But keep in mind that we'd be making this particular argument to a Canadian judge, not to an American one. We'd want to keep in mind that, if the Canadians rejected the argument, the American authorities might see it as a political embarrassment and take it out on your father when they finally got their hands on him. We'd need to be careful to keep the request under the radar. And it's something we'd need to discuss with a Canadian lawyer first, if it gets that far. Still, we need to consider covering all the bases."

"I get what you're saying."

"Even taken together, it isn't much, but I think the first thing we need to know is what happened to the plane. If it's still there, if we can locate Ross Michaels, and if your dad offered to waive extradition and return to the U.S. under his own steam, it might be enough to buy some leniency."

"Do you think that would be sufficient to save him from prison?"

"Honestly, I doubt it, but I'm not sure. Granted, the military doesn't like deserters. To them, the longer the absence the worse the offense may seem. Nor, obviously, do they much like people who steal their high-tech military aircraft and perhaps allow it to fall into the hands of the enemy. But we definitely have something to offer, even if it is a reach. A lot might depend on how convincing the story is that your father has to tell. But, if he is to the point of feeling he's backed into a corner, and it's finally time to give himself up in any case, then it seems worth trying this first. If he wants to proceed, I'd be happy to serve as your go-between in negotiations."

There was a long silence on the other end of the phone. Then: "So, even if Dad does decide that he wants to give this a try, what do we do in the meantime about these SOBs who are twisting our arms for some kind of ransom? We can't pay them. And if they follow through on their threats and turn him in, all the rest will go up in smoke."

"Ah, yes, well I have a few thoughts on that as well. If it's alright with you, I'd like to have your father give me a call. It's time I filled him in directly on some of the hard choices he's going to have to make."

CHAPTER 32

Duncan Carmichael
Magnolia, Seattle
Duncan Carmichael's home
Current day

Duncan was sitting on his deck enjoying a glass of merlot and the view from his Magnolia Bluff home. The sun had already disappeared beyond the horizon, but he could still see the outline of the snow-capped peaks of the Olympics silhouetted against the fading sky. The days weren't as warm as they had been, so he'd been forced to put on a jacket. It was worth it to him to be able to breathe in air scented with fir trees and salt water. Just looking out over Puget Sound conjured up the smell of seaweed drying on a rocky shore.

When his phone interrupted the silence with some soft jazz, he almost didn't answer because he didn't recognize the number. Then, at the last moment, he changed his mind and tapped the green button. "Duncan Carmichael," he said.

"This is Vince MacDonald. My daughter gave me your number."

Duncan had been leaning back and immediately sat up straight. "Are you calling from your personal phone?" he asked.

"A burner. And I assume you won't be recording this call."

"No recording. And whatever you say is just between you and me, lawyer-client privilege," Duncan assured him. "Though cell calls are not invulnerable to hacking."

"I guess I've got to take my chances," Danny Ortez said. "Allison filled me in. And I'm interested in learning more. Under the circumstances though, I'm not sure I have many options. If these extortionists have found me, my secret's as good as out. As Allison told you, there's no way I can pay them off, and I can't turn them in for trying to blackmail me and my family."

"That's why there's some urgency," Duncan said.

"Well, I agree with what you told Allison about trying to negotiate with the U.S. Navy, although I'm not hopeful. I feel like my time has come to face up to what I did back then. Even if we can get these guys off my back, it seems like I may still have the RCMP pounding on my door, like soon. Allison says you have some thoughts on that. If so, I'd love to hear them."

"OK, well here's my first question, ah, Vince—is that what you prefer to be called?"

"You can call me Danny. Since I may become Ortez again, one way or the other. Changing names was confusing at first, but even though I've been Vince MacDonald for a very long time, I still think of myself as Danny Ortez."

"My first question is: Do you still have access to that replica of your father-in-law's Tsarina's Spider? The one you took with you in 1983?"

"I do. I'm looking at it as we speak. It's right here on a shelf in our home. Harold told me I should keep it as a reminder of the bad choices he made. To me it also represents the part of his life that he was proud of. Before things went bad. But it's also a daily reminder of how one stupid decision can change your whole life and the lives of those around you—something about which I'm painfully familiar."

"How good is it? Would it fool a non-expert?"

"Who knows? It looks pretty darn good to me. The average person would probably think it was the real thing. It was apparently good enough for Harold to fool that loan shark. Why, what are you thinking?"

"I have an idea about how we can use the Spider to delay things and maybe even eventually capture your blackmailers. We're definitely going to need a delay in order to negotiate with the Navy. That will require more than a few hours or maybe even a few days. So, we have a two-fold goal, two things we'll need to accomplish simultaneously: delay the blackmailers and quickly negotiate with the Navy. I can tell you more about the Navy angle shortly. But first, I need to know if that's the route you want to take."

"What other option do I have?"

"Well, you could take your chances that these blackmailers won't report on you if they fail to get paid. But if they do report you, you'll have lost any leverage you might have had. Or, you could disappear again. But you'd have to be willing to leave Vince MacDonald and all of his possessions and connections behind. And you would probably need to end communications with your daughter and grandson to ensure their safety. Also, your wife would either have to go into hiding again with you or stay behind and take her chances. Finally, you'd have to make that move right away, before the blackmailers got wise to it.

"My fear is that even if you could convince them that you don't have any money, and even if they agreed to keep your secret, I'm not at all sure you'd be safe. It strikes me that no matter what the blackmailers promise, if they can come up with a way to sell your information, they will. And having a family will continue to make you vulnerable to both exposure and extortion. To be honest, I think you have been damned lucky it took someone this long to find you."

"I see. Well, thanks for not pulling your punches. Julia and I have already talked about the possibility of starting over, and we've decided that we are far too old to take off again. Whatever happens though, Julia and I are in this together. So, I guess that means, I'm in. Tell me more about your Plan A."

"Before I do, let me say that I understand why you did what you did, and I'm impressed with how long you've managed to stay out of sight. And I will do everything I can to keep you out of jail."

"I appreciate that. So . . . tell me the plan."

"It starts with the Spider. I think we can use it as a diversion, and if we can pull off a long enough delay, it may give us sufficient time to strike a deal with the U.S Navy. Not that I think making a deal will be any slam dunk. Negotiating with the Navy is risky. But in my opinion, it's your best bet to live out your life without having to constantly look over your shoulder."

"I know it won't be easy. I'm accused of treason; that's the worst possible offense in the eyes of the military service."

"Well, I do think you may have a small shot at reducing your sentence, who knows, maybe even to get it suspended, but we need to act quickly, before these blackmailers lose patience. Let them know that you still have the Spider, but delay turning it over to them. Maybe you can say it's hidden away somewhere and it will take time to retrieve it. That may give us a chance to see if we can figure out who your black-mailers are, but, more importantly, to find out if the plane is still where you left it."

"Well, as far as the airplane is concerned, I'd say it must be long gone, wouldn't you?"

"Seems like a good bet. Although it depends on whether your bombardier-navigator buddy sold its location to some foreign nation or sold off the electronics or parts piecemeal."

"And if the plane is no longer intact, do you think the Navy will want it?"

"They might. We'll need to assess what's still there—if anything— before I approach them."

"If Ross didn't move it, I'm surprised no one has found it. I taxied it up into the trees at the end of the runway, but I only spent an hour or so covering it up with some brush I'd cut and piled up when I was there a couple of days earlier. Given the publicity, I imagine a lot of people were out looking for the plane. And anyone familiar with the area might have thought to search there because of the old airstrip."

"What about your buddy, Ross? Could he have flown away with it on his own?"

"Well, it would have been easy enough to take off. Plane was a bit short on fuel though. The Navy could have coped with that, but for Ross on his own, it would have been a challenge—unless he sold it to someone with the right resources."

"Did you reach out to Ross at any point?"

"By the time I heard that the plane had not been found, I was afraid to get in touch with him. Thought it was better to let it go. It was possible that he'd done as I requested and that the Navy somehow decided to keep the whole affair secret. But as time passed, I started to fear that he might have made some deal with someone, to his own advantage. I thought he was a friend, but I guess you never know about people."

"Finding him is on my list," Duncan said. "Hopefully he's still in the state."

"Unless he took off. He could have a new name and be living it up in some tropical paradise."

"We'll hope that isn't the case. But first, we need to check out the aircraft. Is it possible to drive to the airstrip on logging roads?"

"Nope. It's on an island. No residents. At least not at the time. The logging roads that were there didn't amount to much anyway; they were only built for logging parts of the island that were inaccessible by water. I've never been back, but unless some development went in, and I'd be surprised if it had, both those old roads and the landing strip are probably completely overgrown."

"Well, we need to know the status of the plane. If you'll give me the exact location, I'll see if we can bushwhack our way in to check it out. We can decide next steps after that."

"I still have the latitude and longitude that I gave Ross; I'll send you those coordinates. But, if the trail from the water isn't visible, it might be hard to find the exact spot. If you've got a chart of the Central BC coastline handy, why don't I suggest a few landmarks that might help."

"I don't have a nautical chart handy. But I have Google maps."

Danny laughed. "Hard to believe how much times have changed—Google maps it is."

They both pulled up a satellite map of the area, and Danny proceeded to talk Duncan through how to find the airstrip and where he'd left the airplane.

"Doesn't look like there's much there, even today," Duncan said.

"Not unless these are old pictures. If you get there and people are sunbathing on the beach . . ."

"That could require a Plana B," Duncan agreed. "Now, about the

Spider. You're fairly certain that your blackmailers still don't know that what you have is only a replica, correct?"

"Thanks to Allison's quick thinking. When they called and told her we had to give them the Spider or they'd turn us in, she had the presence of mind *not* to let them know that all we have is a fake. She was afraid that if she told them the truth and they believed her, they'd give up on their blackmail and turn us in, maybe hoping to get a reward."

"That's good. We want them to continue believing that you never sold the Spider. That you've been living off of your fishing income and what you got from selling off the airplane technology. But just in case, you need to be ready with some kind of explanation for why you still have it."

"Sentimental value?"

"Maybe. Though I doubt that would be convincing. Not to some self-dealing criminal who'd sell out his own mother."

"What if I tell them I hadn't realized how hard it would be to sell the Spider without connections in the black market for art. That I didn't want to risk exposure by asking around. So, I'd decided to wait until my little stunt was forgotten before trying to unload it."

"I like that. But it doesn't explain why you took it in the first place."

"I also took the airplane," Danny reminded him. "They don't know that I never intended to sell it."

"That might do it. It's consistent with how these guys are likely to see the world. You were in it for the money. OK, so here's one other question—you don't think these blackmailers are connected to your friend Ross, do you?"

"Hmm. I suppose they could be. Maybe at the time, whatever money he got from the airplane was enough; but now, after all these years, he wants more. Makes some kind of sense."

"Which brings up the possibility that the plane is no longer there. If it isn't, that's going to take away most of your leverage. You'll still have some, but the Navy may not be anxious to make a deal. We may have to pin our hopes on you getting a sympathetic deportation judge—or one that mistrusts the American White House.

CHAPTER 33

Sydney Warren and Duncan Carmichael
Capitol Hill, Seattle
Sydney Warren's apartment
Current (later that same evening)

Sydney loved the look of her older, mid-century wood frame house perched high on the southwest side of Queen Anne. It was on a winding dead-end street away from traffic, making it a calm oasis, a welcome escape from her otherwise hectic professional life. It had been some years since she had gone from renter to landlord. She'd been a tenant, living on the second floor for quite a few years when she learned the house was going on the market. She quickly snapped it up, anticipating eventually taking over the first floor for herself, but somehow, she never got around to making the change. She liked her upstairs apartment. She'd had several long-term renters in the floor below and was happy to have someone there to look after the place when she was away.

She was asleep in her reading chair, a book open on her lap, when Duncan called. It didn't take her long to come fully awake when he told her what he was planning.

"Are you absolutely sure this is something you want to do? Yourself, personally?" She asked him.

"I don't see any way around it. As you can imagine, the Ortez family are feeling anxious about all this. If the airplane is there, they want its location known to as few people as possible."

"If you see that plane first-hand, won't that create a duty to report it? I mean, you're a Navy officer yourself, right?"

"Retired."

"Even so—"

"Anything I see there will have been based upon the confidences of my client. So long as I don't remove, conceal, or alter the evidence of a crime, I should be fine. Just observing the scene of a past crime or evidence that might implicate my client in a criminal charge has to be well within my responsibilities as his attorney."

"You planning to go by air?"

"Flight schedules direct from Seattle are a mixed bag. But there's a 7:10 a.m. flight tomorrow from SeaTac to Vancouver. Then a scheduled Pacific Coastal flight to Bella Bella that will get me there by noon. I've arranged for boat—a 22' outboard cruiser that should do the trick. The location Ortez gave me is only an hour or so by fast boat from Bella Bella. It should all work out fine."

"I don't like the idea of you going alone."

"It isn't my first choice. Dawson's granddaughter would probably go with me, but I don't want her, her dad, or anyone in their family anywhere near that airplane—assuming it's still there. It would absolutely seal his fate if he or someone in his family were apprehended in the vicinity before he reported it."

Something unspoken but hidden in Duncan's tone told Sydney that he'd doubtless already discussed the whole thing with his wife Kate. Perhaps she wasn't available or didn't want to go herself. But if she had approved the trip, Sydney was certain it was only if he took someone with him.

She answered before he asked: "Oh, I'm sorry, Duncan. I'd go with you myself, but this is a really busy time for me. I can't see how I could manage it." But even as she said the words, Sydney began unconsciously sorting through her calendar in her mind. There was actually nothing there that couldn't be rescheduled for something this important.

"I know it's unfair of me to ask. But it's only a quick trip up and back. Two days tops."

She knew that he knew she was giving it serious consideration and that it was something that would be hard for her to resist.

"Come on, Syd. Think of it as a homage to our first days of working together on the Beck case all those years ago. Just another crazy jaunt into the Canadian wilderness."

"No guns or shootouts this time?"

"No one will know we're there."

She made him work at it a bit more to convince her, although she'd already made up her mind. She always loved being out on the water. She didn't want Duncan to go alone. And it sounded exciting. "OK," she finally agreed. "I'm in."

"Good, I've made the reservations."

"You've what?"

"I mean, ah, I'll *make* the reservations."

"Seriously? You made them. For both of us?"

"Okay, I confess—I knew you wouldn't want to miss this."

Duncan picked her up at home early the next morning. They parked in one of the commercial lots near the airport and took a shuttle to the terminal. Even though it was early, there were long lines at security, but it went quickly. They'd packed light, carry-on only, and their plane to Vancouver was right on time.

Sydney was always a bit nervous about timely departures and making connecting flights. So, when two men hurried aboard after everyone else was settled in, she couldn't help wondering whether they had they been delayed by traffic or were the kind of travelers who always showed up at the last minute, oblivious to any inconvenience they might cause to other passengers or to the flight crew. Dressed in city clothes—slacks, dress shirts, and jackets, she thought they might be going to Vancouver on business.

The plane got underway on time, and it was a short smooth ride to Vancouver International.

The Pacific Coastal flight for the second leg of their trip to Bella Bella was a half-full, 34 passenger Saab 340. Most of those aboard looked very much like people you would expect to be headed for a small coastal native village in Northern BC in the summer—a mix of casually dressed locals and a few obvious sportsmen wearing caps with fish logos on them. Then she noticed the same two men who had boarded late in Seattle. She gave Duncan a gentle nudge: "Take a look," she said quietly. "Six rows up. Right-hand side."

"Uh huh. I remember them barely making the Seattle flight."

"What do you think?" she said.

"Well, they don't look much like fishermen. Or First Nation. The shorter guy has a small pack, but no other carry-ons. I guess they could have checked their luggage."

"You don't think we're being followed, do you?"

"It crosses my mind. Probably being paranoid though. This trip was a last-minute thing."

"Maybe," she said. "Maybe not. We need to keep an eye out."

After they landed, they lost sight of the two men. A shuttle took them the short distance into town where their boat charter awaited at the town marina, fueled and ready to go. An employee walked them to their boat and briefed them on what they needed to know, leaving them with a plasticized sheet listing step-by-step instructions for operating the engine as well as a troubleshooting guide. They stowed their carry-ons in the bow and were preparing to leave when Duncan said: "Don't look now, but we have company."

Sure enough, she glanced up just in time to see the two men disappear into the boat charter office at the top of the dock. "Damn." she said. It seemed like ample confirmation. They had a tail. "This looks like a spur of the moment thing for them, or else they would have dressed for the trip. Probably not a phone tap then; more like they had you under surveillance, wouldn't you say?"

"One way or the other, we need to ditch these guys. Let's get out of here." Duncan took the wheel and quickly motored out of the marina and headed south, past the scenic village of Bella Bella—in the opposite direction from where they needed to go. "I have an idea," he said by way of explanation. "I've looked at the map of this area and I think we can shed them not too far from here, but we first need to put some distance between us and them."

The water was calm as he brought the boat up on a plane approaching 30 knots. Sydney kept a close eye on the marina entrance behind them with the small binoculars she'd brought along. They were no more than two miles ahead and approaching the headland south of town when she saw what she believed was another small boat coming from the marina.

"At this distance, it's hard to be sure it's them," she said. After a few moments, she added: "They're definitely headed this way."

Duncan looked back and frowned. "I don't think we're quite far enough ahead to pull off what I had in mind." He had to shout to be heard over the howl of the engine as he pushed it to its limits. "I was hoping we'd make it out of sight around that bluff up on our right. Pull ashore and hide while they passed. Then double back."

He looked ahead again. And broke into a big smile. "Gotcha," he said. "Sonofabitch, this is going to work."

She had no idea what he was thinking, but coming up from the south and heading in their direction was one of the big blue British Columbia ferries. It was already beginning to make its turn over toward the western shore where it would obviously land at the large ferry dock on the west side of the channel. The place was referred to on their chart as McLoughlin Bay. Duncan changed direction slightly so their boat would cross close astern of the big ferry as it turned.

They had to slow down for the ferry's choppy wake. But once they'd passed astern and were out of line of sight for the boat behind, Duncan sharply changed course and pulled up tight beside the huge ferryboat, keeping to within maybe 100 feet off its port side. He backed off the throttle to match the ferry's speed and carefully kept the ferry between them and their pursuers as they followed the ferry in.

There was a large, fender-protected, landing structure to the south side of the dock against which the ferry would come to rest while unloading and loading. It was an easy matter to pull in behind that structure and stay entirely out of sight from the channel beyond.

Within just a few minutes, they caught a glimpse of the other speed-boat as it passed the bay and the ferry dock at top speed headed south. It soon disappeared beyond the next headland in what seemed likely to be hot pursuit of a boat that was no longer there.

Once their pursuers were out of sight, Duncan eased the boat out into the channel and turned back north and powered up, keeping close to the western shore where they'd be harder to see. Soon they sped past Bella Bella once again, but this time headed in the opposite direction. Sydney kept a watch astern in case their followers had doubled back. But when no boats appeared in the distance and they'd cleared Dryad Point and entered Seaforth Channel, they not only felt relatively safe from pursuit but were headed in the right direction. Duncan backed off slightly on the throttle to a more comfortable and fuel-efficient cruising speed.

"Do you think they suspect why we're here?" Sydney asked. "Or were they hoping you'd lead them to your client?"

"They may not have a clue about what we're doing up here. But I don't like it," he replied. "Whoever it is seems pretty determined to keep an eye on us."

"And they could be dangerous," she added, though she needn't have.

It was early afternoon by the time they reached the place Danny Ortez had described. They throttled down near the southern shore of a long, narrow, winding inlet about half a mile from its head.

A high sun sparkled brightly off of glass-calm water. Most of the shoreline was heavily forested with mature trees growing right down to the top of the steeply graveled beach and reaching out above it. Sydney was at the wheel and idled the boat slowly along the shore as Duncan studied their GPS and the chart, occasionally scanning the shoreline with binoculars, searching for the landmark Danny had mentioned.

"There," he finally said, pointing: "Under that overhanging snag."

Sure enough, along the righthand shore not far from the head of the inlet, there were two large, long logs piled neatly atop one another, exactly as described. Even though they were in the late stages of disinte-gration, they had the distinctively artificial appearance of what had once been a bulkhead "That's gotta be it," Duncan said over the soft rumble of the idling engines. "Can you put us ashore there on that gravel beach?"

They looked around one last time. There were no other boats in sight.

"They'll see the boat if they come this way," Sydney said.

"Even if they do, this boat is pretty standard. And getting here was complicated—too many other places we could have gone. If I had to guess, I bet they are back at Bella Bella, pissed as hell, waiting for their return flight."

"I hope you're right."

As the beach approached, Sydney shut down the engines, and they glided in to gently touch the shore. At half-tide, the beach was steep enough that they were able to step off the bow of the boat directly onto the sloping gravel shore without even getting their feet wet. They took with them the two small packs they'd brought in their carry-ons which included their wallets and things they thought they might need if they found the plane.

With the rising tide and calm water, it was an easy matter to simply use the drag-to-shore anchoring technique. They pushed the boat out into deeper water and tugged the anchor off the bow with a long shore-line, thus securing the boat safely offshore. When they returned, they could use that shore line to drag the anchor back into the beach, along with the boat. Sydney strung the long line up to the top of the beach and attached it securely to a large dead snag.

After satisfying herself that the boat was safe, the two of them paused for a moment, savoring the soft silence of a warm spring day on a wilderness beach. Then Sydney scanned the surrounding water with her binoculars. "Still no sign of them," she said.

"Let's go see if we can find an airplane."

The two crunched their way to the top of the gravel beach, hoisted themselves over the slowly disintegrating bulkhead, and spread apart as they searched beneath the underbrush for the crushed rock path described by Danny Ortez. Although it was easy to guess where the trail should have been, thick vegetation had taken over, obscuring what lay beneath. When they did find the trail, it was a steep fifteen-minute climb to make their way up to the ridge where the land flattened out.

At the top, Sydney took out her binoculars and Duncan shielded his eyes from the sun with a hand as they both studied the water for any sign of their pursuers.

"Looks like it's good to go, at least for now," Duncan said.

They turned back to the flat area that ran along the ridge. "This has to be what Danny described," Ducan said. The former runway was now mostly covered by patches of mature salal and huckleberry with a smattering of conifers that had long since pushed their way up through the original surface. If he hadn't been told it was there, Duncan could easily imagine not realizing this place had once been a runway.

They headed east along the outer shoulder of the hillside where the land dropped off toward the shore down to their left, weaving their way through lush salal, stopping occasionally to kick at the duff and dirt at their feet to verify they were still on the former runway. Each time they brought up what looked like crushed rock with the toes of their boots, enough to give them confidence that they were in the right place.

"I hope it's still here," Duncan said. "I *really* hope it's still here. Without that plane, Danny Ortez isn't going to have much to offer the U.S. Navy. Even if the plane's been stripped, it will at least show that he didn't somehow fly the damned thing to Vladivostok."

He and Sydney pushed and bushwhacked their way northeast to where the flat ridge and the one-time runway narrowed and tapered out against a sloping hillside near a grove of taller, more mature Douglas Fir. The place was so overgrown, it was hard to imagine that any of it could once have been the open field his client had described. They poked about in the thick underbrush looking for something, anything resembling a hidden aircraft. Even a piece of the plane or anything to indicate it had once been there would have been a welcome sight.

They'd been searching almost an hour when Duncan called out: "Hey, Sydney. Over here."

She joined him just as he was lifting something off the ground with the sea-weathered "walking stick" he'd picked up earlier on the beach below. "Check this out."

She reached down and pulled at the clump of vegetation he'd uncovered. Only it wasn't just vegetation. It looked like some kind of netting.

Amidst the thick undergrowth that poked up through the mesh, there were also scraps of decaying green and brown fabric—camouflage.

"Is this what Danny told you to expect?" Sydney asked.

"Nope." Duncan looked puzzled. "He said he covered it with tree limbs and brush. Said nothing about camo netting."

Working together, the two of them pulled at the rotten material. It was hopelessly intertwined with mature undergrowth, making it difficult to remove. Finally, they were able to break through a section of it and see ahead into a dark cavity littered with debris from trees and brush. For a moment Sydney couldn't grasp what she was seeing in the shadows. Could that possibly be landing gear? She got out a flashlight. Yes, it was landing gear. The tires were flat and the rubber cracked and hardened.

"It's here," Duncan said, sounding as happy as a kid getting his first bicycle on his birthday.

"Unbelievable," Sydney said, crouching down to work her way closer to the plane. "Look, there's the tail." She shined the light on the discolored silver stabilizers that were splotched with some kind of green moss.

"It looks intact, doesn't it? That's good. The tail houses some of the electronics for jamming and communication."

"I'm starting to feel hopeful," Sydney said.

"Let's take a closer look. Now that we know the plane's still here, we need to find out if it's been cannibalized."

"You said Danny told you how to access the ladder to the cockpits?"

"Yeah, I think I can find the latches, but we'll probably need to pull it down by hand. The ladder has a spring-loaded mechanism, but who knows how operational that will be after all these years."

"That's kinda how I feel about myself some mornings."

Duncan took the lead working his way down the left side of the aircraft beneath the aft canopy. Sydney followed with a flashlight. "At least it isn't a 747-400," Duncan said.

"If that's your way of making me feel good about this, you're not succeeding. I'm afraid to think about what's in the crap that's falling on us."

"Well, consider that at least we aren't in a tropical rain forest and have to worry about poisonous snakes slithering down the sides of the plane." He stopped and pointed. "Here, look. I think this is it."

She aimed the flashlight where he pointed while Duncan pushed aside some brush and pieces of sagging camouflage tarp. After that it didn't take him long to find the latches for the boarding ladder. But then things got more difficult.

"Don't happen to have some WD-40 in your purse?" Duncan asked.

"You mean you don't have any in your fanny pack?"

"I guess we'll have to resort to brute strength. Happen to have a brute handy?"

"Okay, what do we pull on?"

"You pull on this . . . on the count of three give it all you've got. One, two, THREE."

The ladder only moved an inch, so they tried again. And again. On the third try it broke free, and they had to back quickly out of the way as it pivoted out and down toward the ground.

"Not exactly the stairway of my dreams," Sydney said.

"I would have said that the hardest part was over, but now—"

It did look daunting. "Want to flip a coin?"

"He's my client, so I think it's up to me."

"Be my guest. I'll hold the light until you get the canopy open to look inside."

"I'm going to leave my pack here; it might be hard to get out what I need while trying to balance on this ladder." He started up. "This would have been a lot easier about twenty or so years ago." Testing the steps as he went, he pulled himself slowly to the top. "It looks like the canopies are still in place."

"There could be holes here and there. You need to watch out for animals."

"Animals?"

"Whatever might like sheltering in this hulk. Be careful."

He reached down and freed a step plate next to the forward cockpit and gingerly allowed it to hold his weight. Then he pulled his own flashlight out of his back pocket. It didn't help him see inside either canopy. "They don't look any better from up here than they did from down there." He rubbed the side of the pilot canopy with a micro cloth he'd taken up with him. "Both are discolored and covered with some kind of greenish stuff. Smells like mold, musty, like something rotten found under a log. I'd need more than a rag to clean it off."

"But it's all there?"

"There appear to be some cracks in the plastic, but it still looks pretty secure."

"Want me to try one of the release handles to see if we can mechanically open them?"

"Danny thought that would be tricky and probably not doable. Now that I've had a closer look, this plastic canopy has cracks everywhere. There's a hammer in my pack. Let me see if I can bust a hole somewhere."

"You brought a hammer?"

"It was Danny's suggestion. The canopies are some kind of impact resistant polycarbonate plastic. He thought they might not have stood up well over time."

She climbed partway up the boarding ladder and handed him the hammer. Duncan waited until she was down, then turned his head away and gave the pilot canopy a resounding WHACK. Pieces of yellowed, algae covered plastic fell both inside the cockpit and to the ground below. A musty odor of stale air, mold and decay drifted out the hole.

"Whew. I can smell that down here," Sydney said.

"I'm going to hold my breath and take a look inside."

Duncan stuck his head and a flashlight through the opening he'd made. After a few minutes, Sydney couldn't stand it any longer. "What do you see?"

Duncan carefully extracted himself, turned away from the plane, and took a deep breath. "No snakes or wild animals, but I think some bugs and critters call this home. The leather on the seats is dried up. But the instrument panels look whole. I think I recognize a radar system. Danny told me to check out the jamming systems, but I'm having trouble telling what's what. The key thing is that nothing looks disturbed; just degraded by years and exposure."

He looked aft. "The good stuff is supposed to be in the rear stations."

Turning toward the back canopy, he took out his hammer again and struck the side of it as hard as he could. It splintered, but it took two more swings to create a jagged hole big enough to get his head and flashlight through. "More dried up leather seats and disintegrated fabric," he called out. "I see display consoles, dials, knobs, buttons, switches . . . what could be jamming pods. Pretty complicated looking. But no empty spaces. Nothing to indicate that anyone's been messing with it."

He pulled himself out of the ragged opening and looked down at her standing at the bottom of the ladder in the simi-darkness. "I think it's all here, Sydney. I don't think any of this has ever been touched since the day it landed."

"What good news for Danny."

"What incredibly good news!"

"Can I confess that I didn't think there'd be anything here?"

"You can confess if I can confess. Now, take a step back, I'm going to drop the hammer. I need to take some pictures with my phone before I cover these holes."

While Duncan took pictures of the cockpits, Sydney began snapping some of the outside of the aircraft. When he finished, he asked her to hand up a roll of duct tape and some plastic sheeting so he could cover the holes he had made.

Meanwhile, Sydney continued taking pictures to confirm the plane was indeed intact. But why? She wondered who had gone to the trouble of covering the airplane with camo netting if they intended to just leave it there to deteriorate. Had it been Ross? If he hadn't sold off any of the electronics, why hadn't he followed up on Danny's requests? Had someone else somehow stumbled on this site in the years since and decided to claim it for themselves? If so, what had happened to prevent *them* from following through?

In any case, they'd learned what they needed to know. So, after Duncan had duct-taped some lightweight plastic over the openings he'd made, he climbed back down to the ground and they returned to the entrance they'd created in the overgrown camo netting. To once again conceal the aircraft, they put some brush over the entrance, fussing to make certain it wasn't obvious that someone had been there.

Then they made their way back to the path leading to the beach, pausing to see if they had company before heading down. There was no other boat in sight. "Looks like our friends gave up on us," Duncan said.

"Unless they hid their boat down the beach and are waiting to ambush us."

"There's that..."

They hiked the rest of the way wary of potential hiding places, staying close together. Once back on the beach, they finally relaxed a little. And once aboard their boat and underway, the late afternoon run back to Bella Bella was pleasant, though not conducive to conversation because of the boat's noisy outboard motor.

They half expected to see the two men from before lurking in the shadows at the boat charter office, but no one appeared to be waiting for them. After returning the boat, they took a small water taxi across the bay to nearby Shearwater where Duncan had arranged accommodations.

"Maybe they'll be at the lodge," Sydney said. "I assume you used our real names when making the reservations."

"Yes, I did. Had no idea we'd be followed."

When they checked in, Duncan told the clerk about two men they were "expecting to meet" there. "Not sure when they're arriving. Anyone asking for us?"

"Sorry, no," the clerk said. "Give me their names, and I can let you know when they arrive."

"No bother. I'll give them a call. Thanks."

"Well?" Sydney said as they headed to their rooms.

"Maybe they figured out that we made them and gave up."

"Um. Or maybe they guessed where we're staying and are waiting for us to go to dinner so they can search our rooms. Hope they don't finger my undies."

"That's reassuring."

They went to their respective rooms to freshen before meeting up in the dining room for dinner. They were seated by a window facing out over a stunning BC coastal waterscape with forested hillsides and snowy mountains in the distance and a small marina below. Served a tasty pub dinner of fresh halibut and chips, they ate about half before finally feeling relaxed enough to indulge in self-congratulations.

"Truth is, I still can't believe it," Sydney said.

"What? That we found it, or that it was intact?"

"Both, I guess. You really think this will give you leverage to nego-tiate with the Navy on behalf of your client?"

"I sure hope so," Duncan said, sounding cautiously optimistic. "Even though it appears to be in one piece, it's still pretty degraded. No doubt both obsolete and worthless by now. Still, it shows there was no treason involved. And the more Danny has to offer, the more they'll be inclined to listen to us. I'm afraid that the main thing they're going to want to lay their hands on is Danny Ortez himself. And it won't be because they want to thank him for his service."

"Are you sure he really does need to turn himself in?"

"Yeah, I am. I think he is too. When these blackmailers figure out that they can't squeeze any money out of him, you can't count on them to keep quiet. He'll end up in Leavenworth or someplace like it with the book thrown at him. If he first offers to turn himself in, he'll at least have some leverage."

"Are you going to call him tonight?

"No, I don't think our phones have been hacked, but it won't hurt to be cautious."

"Well, I for one will have my door double-locked."

"I may put some pillows under my bedcovers and sleep in the bath-tub," Duncan said.

Neither of them laughed.

CHAPTER 34

Duncan Carmichael
Preston-Martin Building, Seattle
Law Offices of Warren and Carmichael
Current day

T he early flights back to Seattle were anti-climactic. As far as Duncan could tell, no one followed them from the lodge or onto the airplane from Bella Bella. Nor did they spot anything unusual when they changed planes in Vancouver.

"Let's have Kyle check our office and phones for bugs when we get back," Sydney said. Kyle was Mel Marshall's son. Kyle had spent a decade in the CIA before taking over Marshall Security and Investigations when his father retired. Under his leadership, the agency had steadily grown over the years. He now had a team of investigators and specialists working for him, and he had moved their offices from an old brick building near the courthouse to a much larger space in Two Union Square. Duncan and Sydney had remained loyal to Marshall Security and Investigations, forming a close relationship with Kyle like they had with his father.

"I was thinking the same thing," Duncan said. "Have him send someone to check for bugs and see if there's a tail on me. I already asked him to look into whether anyone has been asking around about Danny Ortez. It's a longshot, but I thought it worth a try."

They were back in the office by noon. Duncan contacted Kyle and arranged for the security checks. Then he borrowed a phone from his admin and went to the downstairs coffee shop to call Danny's burner.

"Really?" Danny said. "You're serious. It's still there?"

"Exactly where you said it would be."

"How about inside? What about the SEAD screen in the back cockpit? I mentioned it before, the Suppression of Enemy Air Defenses screen. A big hummer."

"I remember—like a large television screen. Undamaged."

"That's amazing."

"We took a fair number of pictures. Nothing looks like it's been tampered with. Don't get me wrong, there's a lot of deterioration because of the plane being abandoned for so long."

"I can imagine. A lot of years have gone by."

"Oh, one thing though, I don't recall seeing any armaments mounted under the wings."

"There wouldn't have been any. We were just practicing touch-and-goes. The EA-6B wasn't really much of an attack aircraft anyway. Mostly used for electronic warfare."

"One other thing—it looks like someone covered the plane with some kind of camo netting. A very thorough job, from what I could see. At this point the whole thing is completely overgrown. Invisible. My partner, Syd Warren, and I were right there, standing within a few feet of it and had no idea it was there till we noticed the netting wound in amidst the natural vegetation. Do you think Ross could have done that?"

"Well, it sure as hell wasn't me, and Ross is the only one I told. Why would he do that though?"

"I guess there is a certain logic to it, right? You give Ross the coordinates. He knows you're long gone, so he thinks he has a free hand. Maybe he decided to keep the information to himself and to wait awhile. See what happened. Maybe he figured that when things settled down, he'd make some contacts and sell the plane or its avionics to the highest bidder.

"Meanwhile, he didn't want it found. So, he made a quick trip to Canada. Probably chartered a small boat in Bella Bella or Shearwater, just like we did. Brought with him some top-of-the-line camo netting and, with some careful cutting and placement of live vegetation, he made sure the plane was well hidden."

"If that's how he played it, why the hell was it all still there?"

"Damn good question, Danny. Let me see if we can find him. He will be long since out of the Navy, but they should have some kind of home address on his DD-214 discharge form. We can start with that. I have a guy that's great at tracking people. If we're going to offer him up as an inducement in your negotiations with the Navy, it will help to know where he lives. I'll get back to you."

Late that afternoon, Kyle Marshall sent someone to check Duncan and Sydney's law office and phones for bugs and didn't find anything. Then, that evening while Duncan was still at the office, he got a call from Kyle. After their brief conversation, Duncan stepped down the hall to Sydney's office. As usual, she had her door closed, but Duncan figured what he had to tell her was important enough that she wouldn't mind the interruption.

As usual, he knocked but didn't wait for her to answer before opening the door and stepping inside. "I know you've got a lot to do, but I think you might want to join Kyle and me in the conference room a few minutes from now."

"Kyle is on his way here?" She glanced at the clock. Then at the papers on her desk and frowned.

"I can summarize what he has to say for you later, but . . ."

"No, I think I'll want to hear this firsthand. I could use a cup of coffee, anyway."

With a last wistful look at her deeply littered desk, she allowed herself to be led out into the hall and to their firm's smaller conference room. Duncan gestured to a chair and said, "Let me get you some coffee."

"You'd make someone a good . . . husband," she said.

"Aha! You were going to say 'wife,' weren't you?"

"Caught. I'm tired. And I have it on good authority that you *are* a good husband."

Duncan was pleased that the two most important women in his life were friends. His and Kate's daughter Megan, and more recently their granddaughter Lilly, called Sydney "Auntie." He wasn't sure how Sydney felt about that, but he thought it accurately reflected her relationship with his family.

By the time Kyle Marshall pressed the buzzer in the elevator lobby, everyone but Duncan and Sydney had gone home. Sydney went to let him in while Duncan finished getting their coffee.

"My, favorite clients," he said to Duncan and Sydney as Sydney ushered him into the conference room. "As usual, I can always count on something interesting."

"Coffee?" Duncan asked.

"I could use a cup. One sugar."

Duncan had already poured coffee for Sydney and himself and went back to the coffee room to get another for Kyle. When he returned, Duncan said: "You must have something interesting to say if you wanted to tell us in person this late at night."

"Good news?" Sydney asked. "Or should we be worried?"

"Well, sorry, but I guess if it was me, I'd be worried."

"Oh, oh. What have you discovered?"

"Well, it's actually more about what I haven't discovered. I asked you guys to meet me in person because I wasn't entirely sure this was the kind of thing you'd want passing through your email server or landing on your desk in some written report."

"OK." Duncan and Sydney shared a look. This was starting to sound sinister.

"Let's begin with your client who is best known for having made off with a U.S. Navy jet airplane. You asked me to find out if anyone was asking questions about him, particularly up in BC."

"And?" Sydney prompted in her "get-to-the-point" voice.

"So, I have a guy, a colleague I sometimes work with in Vancouver. Someone I knew, um, in a former life." Kyle avoided talking about his time in the CIA, but they got the message. "He's one of the people I go to when I need to know about something happening in his part of the world. In the past, I've found him to be good at what he does, you know? Especially on this kind of matter. And usually very helpful."

"But—?" This time it was Duncan who sounded anxious.

"Well, he's not a guy that always drives at the posted speed limit, if you know what I mean. But I've never before had reason to feel like he was deliberately withholding information. I was expecting business as usual when I sent him an inquiry a few days ago about your client. Just asked if he knew of anyone asking around for this Ortez guy. That's all. Naturally, I didn't mention his current name.

"But rather than sending me an email back, this morning I get a phone call. He was all, like: 'Hey, how you doing? Long time no see. Got your message and figured why not just call. We ought to get together and catch up sometime.' Yada yada.

"And then, like it was an afterthought, he says, 'Oh, by the way . . . on that *little matter*, you asked me about'— Said he had to *decline* the job. 'Too much going on,' he said. But he was happy to 'give me a refer-ral.' That was it."

"And what did you conclude from this exchange?"

"Well, this is not a guy that turns down jobs. A little quiet back-ground check on a private party, finding a missing person—that's stuff right up his alley, something he could delegate to some bright associate. There's no way he's 'too busy' for that. There's something else going on."

"I'm not sure I understand, Kyle," said Duncan. "Why wouldn't he be straight with you?"

"Well, that's the question, isn't it? And I'm not sure I know the answer. But what I *think* is going on is that there's a conflict of interest. I think he may have an existing client that's interested in finding Ortez."

Duncan wasn't surprised; they already knew someone had tracked Danny down. But it did put another wrinkle in their plans.

"You probably know that I'm a member of NCISS—our national professional association," Kyle said. "We have conflict rules in our business just like you lawyers do. The same is true of Canadian investigators. Thing is, I also know this guy, and I'm pretty sure if he thought he could get away with it, he'd bend those rules.

"But he obviously didn't want to do that in this instance. Which makes me wonder *why*. I'm guessing here, but it strikes me that whoever this other client is, it's someone that makes him unwilling to take that kind of risk."

"That's why you think he turned you down."

"Right, and that creates a problem. If I'm right, whoever his existing client is now doubtless knows about *my* interest in Ortez. And given that you two are such longstanding clients, and given your public history with this Dawson-Nowak matter, there's a reasonably good chance they will have guessed that you guys are the ones looking into Ortez."

"This explains why we had a tail on our trip to Canada."

"Sorry about that," said Kyle. "That may be down to me."

Duncan shook his head dismissively. "No way for you to have known. Always a risk when you start asking questions."

"Do you think they know you made them?" Kyle asked.

Duncan looked at Sydney. They both nodded. "It's likely. We weren't exactly subtle. Why? Is that important."

"Maybe. Maybe not. If they're up to no good, it might turn up the heat some."

Duncan and Sydney shared another look.

"I've assigned someone to see if you have a tail here. Just be careful." He looked from Sydney to Duncan. "Both of you."

"For what it's worth, this will be over one way or the other fairly soon," Duncan said.

"Good. By the way, you asked me to check on a guy named Ross Michaels. That one was easy. Michaels died shortly after your client absconded with that airplane."

"Really?" Duncan said with Sydney's face mirroring his surprise.

"Died how?" Sydney asked.

"Nothing sinister as far as I could tell. He was in a flight operations accident. It happened a week after Ortez made off with the airplane. His squadron was deployed to the Far East aboard the Kitty Hawk. Couple of weeks after deployment, his new pilot screwed up. Came in low and slow and failed to power up and abort when they waved him off. The other two EMCOs, somehow ejected and survived. Michaels and the pilot died."

"Damn." Duncan said.

Sydney turned to Duncan: "What does this do to your client's claim that he'd intended to get the aircraft returned to the Navy?"

"Well, I guess it's now just Ortez's word on that. And with Michaels dead, revealing his involvement isn't going to provide much advantage."

"Maybe he mentioned the Spider to someone," Sydney said. "It's possible he cared enough about Danny and his family to have done that at least."

"Spider?" Kyle asked.

"A jeweled brooch that probably belonged to Catherine the Great."

"That sounds like quite a story."

"When this is over, Kyle, we'll have a lot to tell you over drinks."

"Yeah, well meanwhile, you two need to watch your backs."

Duncan and Sydney nodded, saying nothing, but sharing the same dark thoughts.

Kyle took a moment to shift gears to Sydney's case. Turning to her, he said, "So, you asked me to see about getting the trial transcript from your 1983 murder trial and to see if I could locate a couple of the witnesses. There's good news and . . . well, the not so good."

"Good news first," Sydney said.

"The trial transcript was never digitized, but the court reporter is still alive, and her stenographic notes still exist because they were considered of public interest at the time. She is quite willing to do a new transcription. You'll have to pay for it though. And the other side will probably find out that you requested a copy."

"Get it done," Sydney said. "I think it's going to do *us* more good than it does them."

"Done," said Kyle. "Next, finding Grant Meade was a no-go. Meade died in a homicide back in the nineties.

"Also, AA Best Bet Bail Bonds no longer exists. You were right about the loan sharking stuff. Its owner, one Louis Mitchum, was sentenced to ten years for extortion in 2002. He'd completed most of that when, in 2010, he got involved in a prison yard scuffle. Killed a fellow inmate and had another twenty-five years added to his sentence. He died in 2021 in Walla Walla.

"As you may know from Dawson's daughter, her mother, Dawson's ex-wife, died from covid in 2020.

"One of the few original witnesses who's still alive is Lauren Franklin-Keene, the receptionist who testified at the trial. She's retired and lives on Vashon Island. She's some kind of artist. Sculptor. Multi-media. Interesting stuff. I got you her web address."

"How about the Sheriff's Detectives—Small and Brown. They still around and kicking?"

"Both retired. Small in 2007. She moved to Arizona. I have a last known, but nothing more on her yet. Brown was seriously injured in a gunfight in the 90s. He tried to return to work but apparently decided he couldn't hack it and took an early retirement. He lives in an apartment in the Central District. From what his neighbors say, he seems like kind of a recluse. Maybe PTSD, something like that. But he's still around and could probably testify.

"Oh, and that woman with Citizen's Detectives, the one that found Nowak's rifle in the creek after the trial? She lives in an assisted living place in Renton. But she's sharp as a tack. And she still has a copy of the CSI report that linked Nowak's rifle to the killing. It's like a trophy to her. She considers the Nowak case to be a high point in her career."

"You put in some hours on this. I'm impressed."

"Don't be. I personally didn't do much. Put a couple of new guys on it, and they put in the hours. It was all straightforward stuff. And, although I hate to say it, their time is worth less than mine. Cheaper for you."

"Cheap is good."

Kyle grinned. "I didn't say 'cheap,' just not as costly as my time."

"Fortunately," Sydney said, "Duncan and I are horrible about purging records. We do have a modern office archive policy. In civil cases, we try to return files to the client or destroy all paperwork after seven years. With criminal stuff, we keep everything for the life of any client who has been imprisoned or till they're released. But even so, some stuff never gets thrown out. We have a lot of it in secure storage, and I had an associate dig out the witness statements and whatever remains of the actual physical evidence from back in the original trial."

"It's too bad Grant Meade is dead. If the old rumors are true, you used him to some advantage in that trial."

"Yeah." Sydney smiled at the recollection. "Though even if he were still alive, an 80- or 90-year-old ex-thug isn't likely to make the same impression today that he did forty years ago."

"Well, I guess it's a good thing your opponent has the burden of proof."

"Yeah, maybe so. But if that rifle and its linkage to Nowak and the killing comes in, that might be the whole ball game, right there."

"Well, if you need more from me, let me know." Turning to Kyle, he asked, "So, what's next on your plate?"

"Well," Duncan said, "I'd say it's time I made a phone call to the U.S. Navy."

CHAPTER 35

Duncan Carmichael
Preston-Martin Building Downtown Seattle
Law Offices of Warren & Carmichael
Current day

"I don't think so, Special Agent Barlow." Duncan took great care to make sure his tone was calm and confident. He needed to sound as though he was in the driver's seat in this negotiation.

Thus far, his contact with the U.S. Navy had gone about as expected. As a courtesy, he'd made his first call to the NCIS office at Naval Air Station Whidbey—the site of Danny Ortez's original misdeed. Sooner or later, they'd surely become involved. Duncan wanted it to be sooner to minimize delay. The Special Agent there had not been exactly friendly, but he'd at least treated Duncan with respect as he referred him on to the regional NCIS office in Silverdale, WA.

That is where the courtesy ended.

The NCIS Supervisory Special Agent or SSA in charge of their Field Office in Silverdale was adamant: "If you have information on the current location of a criminal fugitive from justice, Mr. Carmichael, you need to give that up right now, or we have nothing further to discuss."

"Special Agent Barlow, I'm sorry to hear that. As I'm sure you know, my contacts and communications with my client are confidential. I have, however, been authorized to tell you that he is prepared to turn himself in to the Naval authorities. And to provide some information which we believe may be of considerable value to the U.S. Navy. There are, of course, some conditions. This offer is in good faith, and it's your choice whether to proceed. At the moment, it sounds very much like you're *not* interested. Is that the answer you'd like me to convey back to my client? Or would you, perhaps, like to first pass this by someone higher up your chain of command?" Duncan kept his voice neutral, but the challenge was obvious.

"All I plan to do, Mr.—what's your name again?"

"Carmichael."

"Well, Mr. Attorney Carmichael, what I plan to do is to send an Agent to your office to bring you in, sit you down, and get some answers."

"Well, I certainly hear your frustration, Agent Barlow. But before you send out an agent on a wasted, unlawful, and embarrassing mission, I would suggest that you may want to consult with your military superiors. I only called you first out of respect for your agency's role in all this. But you might, for example, want to consider speaking with the current Commander, Fleet Air Whidbey. My client was under his command. It was *his* organization's aircraft that was stolen. He would doubtless be the convening authority for any court martial that might be required upon my client's surrender. Even after all these years, I'm guessing the current ComFAirWhidbey might appreciate getting his aircraft back.

"That said, at this point you know my client's offer. You know he has important information to impart that relates to the EA-6B Prowler aircraft taken at NAS Whidbey back in 1983. If you don't want to pass along my client's offer, I can always contact them myself, directly. And note your unwillingness to cooperate."

After the briefest of pauses, he added, "Oh, and for future reference, my full title is *Commander* Duncan Carmichael, Judge Advocate General's Corps, United States Naval Reserve, Retired. You have my contact information. I will look forward to hearing back from you or from whoever turns out to be the Navy's preferred representative. Good day!"

Without waiting for a reply, Duncan hung up.

With that, the die was cast. Supervisory Special Agent Barlow might not turn out to be a friend. But Duncan felt confident that, like it or not, he would get the process started.

Two hours later, Duncan got the anticipated call. It was from a Lieutenant Commander Phillip James, a JAG officer with ComFAir-Whidbey. "So, Commander Carmichael, I understand you have acquired a proverbial pile of, shall we say, feces, and you're looking for someone to hand it off to."

"Well, that isn't exactly how I'd describe it, Commander James. More like: together we have a chance to resolve a long-standing problem. And maybe to right some wrongs and to erase a regrettable embarrassment from the U.S. Navy's past."

"Well, let's hear it. My boss is interested, so you've got our attention. Though I'm not sure you're going to find him particularly sympathetic. Oh, and I'll be recording this conversation."

"The recording is fine. As far as I'm concerned, having the Navy's attention is all I can ask.

"As I guess you've been informed, I represent Lieutenant Junior Grade Daniel Ortez. Mr. Ortez is currently outside of the United States, but he and his family would like to return. I've been authorized to tell you that he is prepared to surrender himself into Navy custody but that he would like to avoid criminal prosecution."

"Ha! I *bet* he *would*."

"There are several things we believe you might wish to consider here."

"I'm listening"

"The first of these considerations is the passage of time. And the fact that, since his original departure . . ."

"*Desertion*, Mr. Carmichael. It's called desertion."

"I know that. And I assure you, so does he. But over the four decades since he left, he has led an exemplary life. He's raised a family, paid his taxes, maintained a clean criminal record."

"All of which we'd expect of *any* good citizen—AFTER they'd completed their committed period of military service."

"I agree. I'm only saying, we're not dealing with some hardened criminal here. We're dealing with a decent guy who made a very bad mistake."

"*Mistake* being a pretty generous way to describe it, wouldn't you say?"

"Perhaps. All I'm saying . . ."

"Yeah. I get it. He's not all that bad a guy."

"Right. A good guy, in fact. And, while *you* may not consider those years of civic responsibility to be persuasive, they *will* be a consideration in any extradition hearing. What Mr. Ortez is proposing is that he would be prepared to waive extradition and turn himself over directly to the U.S. Navy. Without fanfare or opposition."

"What does that mean?"

"It means he's prepared to keep his return out of the public eye. No press. No foo-rah that renews the public recollection of the loss of that aircraft and calls again into question the Navy's basic competence in running a tight ship."

"Right. He stays quiet like a good boy rather than raising hell and doing his best to make the Navy look bad. And reminding everyone of what *he* did."

"That is *your* characterization, Commander, *not* mine. And not my client's, either."

"Very well."

"Also, he will get you back your lost aircraft."

That brought a startled pause. "He has the airplane?"

"He knows where it is. He can direct you to it. You can easily recover it."

"Is it intact?"

"I believe that it is, yes."

"The avionics are there? The electronics? Nothing has been stolen or removed?"

"That is my understanding."

"Not that it makes any damned difference after all these years. But if what you're saying is true, that is a very good thing to hear, Mr. Carmichael."

"You'll be able to confirm it for yourself, once my client gives you the location of the plane."

"OK, I'm still listening."

"I believe my client may also advise you that, immediately after his departure, he provided the location of that aircraft to another person, a responsible person in the U.S. Navy at the time. He asked that person to make its location known to the appropriate Naval authority. For some reason unknown to my client, that never happened." Duncan had decided not to mention that Ross Michaels was dead . . . until he had to.

"You're sounding awfully coy right at the moment, Mr. Carmichael. Are you saying that this other 'person' is no longer in the U.S. Navy?"

"That is my understanding."

"But your client knows where he is?"

"Not specifically, no."

"Still, you're saying that someone in the Naval service knew where that plane was located and kept that information to themselves. Why would they do that?"

"As I said, that's an unknown at this point."

"OK. Well, I'm still listening. What else you got?"

"Only a couple of observations: the first and foremost is that even with everything else set aside, I believe it's in the best interest of the U.S. Navy to get this matter finally and decisively resolved.

"The other observation is this: I think we both know that this particular moment in history might not be the ideal time for the U.S. Navy to be seeking extradition back into the U.S. of someone with the name 'Ortez,' who is a native-born U.S. citizen but whose parents were immigrants from Mexico.

"I'm not in a position to advise where my client is currently located. But if, as I think you probably suspect, this extradition turns out to be from Canada, the Canadian courts have a good deal of discretion. The grounds for denial of extradition include *'unfairness,' 'lack of fundamental justice,' 'lack of good faith,'* the possible *'political character'* of the request and, significantly, *'discrimination.'* Given the events currently taking place in the U.S. deportation of Hispanic immigrants, and given the currently strained U.S. relationship with Canada, you might want to think about how a Canadian judge is likely to see those grounds in relation to the Ortez family. It's just a thought."

"Well, one thing I can assure you, Mr. Carmichael, is that this office and the United States Navy will apply and uphold the law. We have no political agendas other than what's best for our country."

"I'm glad to hear it, Mr. James. And I guess you'll have to hope that the Canadian courts view the world as neatly and cleanly as you do. I can easily envision, however, that a denial of extradition on any of those grounds I just mentioned could turn out to be a significant public embarrassment for the U.S. Navy. It's a prospect that might be worth avoiding."

"I think you've made yourself abundantly clear. I will pass your request along to my superiors."

"Thank you. I probably should add that the airplane and its contents are *not* secure, and that every day that passes, it is vulnerable to discovery and loss."

"Which has, I take it, been true for all of the past almost forty years now. Unless something has changed? Are you saying there is some particular new cause for concern now that hasn't existed in the past?"

The last thing Duncan wanted to do was make the Navy aware that his client's situation had become exigent. "Just saying that it would be unfortunate for all of us, *my client included*, should something happen to that aircraft after all these years."

"How about your client, being the good citizen that he is, in good faith and all, tells us right now where to find that plane. He can offer his willing assistance in mitigation at his sentencing."

"Sorry, Mr. James. We're looking for a much better outcome than a year off his sentence or a more salubrious place of incarceration."

"Fine. Well, we'll get back to you."

CHAPTER 36

Three gangsters
East Broadway Commercial District, Seattle,
The upstairs office of Brunelli Moving and Storage Company
Current day

T hree men were seated at an elegant but worn wooden table that seemed much too classy for its surroundings. They were in a smoky conference room adjacent to a cluttered mezzanine office in the warehouse-headquarters of Brunelli Moving and Storage in Central Seattle. The office belonged to Mitch Brunelli, the proprietor of the establishment, one that was said to be the oldest moving and storage company in the Pacific Northwest. The room's big inside windows looked out over the warehouse floor below where trucks were being loaded and unloaded, and large storage containers prominently emblazoned with the tall, red letters "BMS" were stacked three and four high around the perimeter of the space. Thankfully, the men in the office were insulated from most of the noise below by soundproof multi-paned windows. They quietly smoked while they studied a brief document, copies of which had been made for each of them.

Brunelli was the cigar man. His yellowed fingers held the last remains of what had recently been a nice Cuban but had now been drawn down to a stub that surely couldn't last much longer without the risk of burns. He was a fit older man with neatly trimmed hair. His tailored jacket lay across a nearby vacant chair. His shirtsleeves were rolled, but his tie was still snugged up tightly against his neck in a perfect four-in-hand. He looked up from the report and studied the two other men over the tops of reading glasses that had been pushed down toward the end of his long boney nose. Then he continued reading.

The second man, a chain smoker, had an anxious look. His name was Leo Marks. Leo was Mitch Brunelli's second in command. He had the quick movements of a worrier, someone who was constantly trying to figure something out but was never quite sure if he'd got it exactly right. He, too, was in shirtsleeves, exposing both the slight bulge of good living at his waist and the less convivial bulge of the Rugar semi-automatic tucked into the holster snugged up beneath his left armpit. Beside him was a large glass ashtray filled with bent cigarette butts. While he reviewed the report, he took a long, deep draw on the current fag, and then used it to light another before stubbing the first one out in the overflowing ashtray at his elbow. He was a quick reader and was the first to finish.

The third man was an old-fashioned pipe smoker. A thinker. Ray Barge was his name. He didn't often speak, but when he did, people listened. He was a connected guy, someone Brunelli called on for various special projects when he wasn't sure he was getting what he needed from his immediate staff. Barge was also believed to be someone who could be counted on for the occasional "wet work" when the occasion required. While reading, he gently gripped the pipe in his teeth, relishing the flavor while doing his best to ignore the unfortunate pollution in the room from the less aromatic smokes favored by his colleagues. He wore a comfortable off-the-shelf sport jacket over a knit shirt with no tie. One could not be sure if he was armed. But, given his reputation, it would have been unwise to bet against it.

"You called em off, right?" Mitch asked Leo as he pushed the report away. "Will and that burglar kid, Eric?"

"Yeah, yeah. They were just lookin' for an easy cut. Piece of the action. They're out of it." As Leo spoke around his cigarette, it bobbed up and down in cadence with his voice.

"Good," said Mitch. "Will's OK. Does what he's told. But I don't much care for Eric. A bit too hungry for my liking."

"Well, I got to confess, Mitch," said Leo, ". . . it still seems to me like a kind of dead end. If my guy in Vancouver couldn't find this Ortez dude, I'm not sure how *we* do." He tapped the report on the table. "I don't see anything in here that changes that."

"I know, Leo, but that's what got me thinking," said Mitch. "It's why I asked Ray to take a look. Your guy, the PI? He knew this other guy, right? The guy that tried to hire him to find Ortez? You said his name was Marshall? Kyle Marshall."

"Yeah." Leo nodded, tapping off an ash into the glass tray. "Kent said he knew this Marshall guy 'from back in the day.' I took that to mean he knew him from when Kent was a spy—when he was with the Security and Intelligence people."

"Do we know who this Marshall ended up hiring after Kent turned him down?"

"No idea. But Kent's been paying attention. He says he thinks he'd have heard. He thinks the guy gave up on the idea."

"Gave up?"

"Yeah, you know. Figured maybe it wasn't worth the effort."

"I don't know, I guess maybe." Mitch didn't sound convinced. "That or he got the answer he needed and stopped looking."

Leo took that in but obviously wasn't convinced. "Maybe," he said."

"OK, so the thing is," said Mitch. "I know about this Kyle Marshall. Or, at least I know who he is. His firm's here in Seattle. In Two Union Square. It's a big operation. Provides security services. But he's also a PI and does a lot of work for law firms here in town. That's why I asked Ray to take a closer look. We needed to know who he's working for on this, find out his angle."

Ray removed the pipe from his mouth and held it with both hands while leaning forward with his arms on the table. He nodded thoughtfully at the brief report. "I think I can help with that, Mitch. When you asked me to check this out, I remembered a recent article in the Seattle Report. Maybe you saw it. It was about that murder trial back during the big WPPSS scandal when that finance guy that was killed by his business partner in the woods up I-90. The one where that lady lawyer got the partner off. And then two days later, they found his rifle at the scene and linked him to the shooting."

"Yeah, sure." Mitch glanced at the other man. "Yeah, we remember."

"Well, according to that article, the kids of the partner that killed the finance guy are suing the paper for defamation. They say the Report's wrong and that he didn't commit that murder, even if his gun was found at the scene and all."

"Yeah, yeah, we got that Ray," said Leo, impatiently.

"Well, those kids, they're being represented in that lawsuit by the same lawyer that got their dad acquitted the first time, Sydney Warren. Thing is, her law partner, Duncan Carmichael, is a retired Commander in the U.S. Navy Reserves. The two of them were a big deal back then. They beat the Navy in some high-profile case over arms stolen at the end of Vietnam. Exposed some corrupt Admiral. Front page news."

"I remember some of that," said Mitch.

"OK, so if you were a guy like Ortez and were looking to avoid prosecution by the U.S. Navy, it seems to me like Carmichael's who you'd be likely to ask."

"Lots of Navy lawyers, Ray." Leo was unconvinced.

"I know, I know. Just bear with me. Cause it turns out their firm, Warren & Carmichael, has close ties with Marshall Security. Has had for years. Uses 'em all the time."

"Come on, Ray. How could you possibly know that?" Leo was shaking his head.

"You use your head, Leo," Ray said with exaggerated distain while tapping a forefinger to his temple. "You have to use your head."

In fact, what Ray had used was a couple of the Brunelli Moving and Storage firm's less-than-fully-engaged subordinates to check out the Warren and Carmichael firm. The young men had spent several days following Warren and Carmichael around and asking questions of the people they'd met. They'd chatted up one of the law firm's unmarried interns. They'd looked through the filings with the King County Superior Court Clerk for records of the cases the firm was handling, and they reviewed the public contents of the files that named the witnesses in those matters.

"Anyway," Ray continued. "It turns out that investigators with Marshall Security have been witnesses in Warren and Carmichael's cases several times over the years.

"It made me curious. So, I put a couple of men on it. And just two days ago, the two lawyers—this Sydney Warren and her partner Carmichael—made a sudden trip to northwestern Canada. They flew into a little native town there called Bella Bella. They rented a small boat, and then disappeared for an afternoon. It's all wilderness up there. No place really to go. They stayed one night and were back the next day."

Having said his piece, Ray now leaned back and tented his fingers suggestively. "So, you tell me," he said, mouthing the words around the stem of his gurgling pipe. "Wouldn't you guess that those two just might know somethin' about where this Ortez guy went?"

"Key-ryst, Ray," said Leo, shaking his head. "They probably went fishing. I'm sure you've heard of it. You know, with poles and hooks and lures. They spent a freaking afternoon fishing. People do that."

"They took an early flight, chartered a boat that went fast, didn't have any fishing gear that my guys saw. Most important, they ditched my men. My guys figure they got made. Carmichael and the woman simply disappeared. There's no reason they'd have done that unless they were up to somethin'.

"That wasn't no vacation. That was a business trip. That Bella Bella area . . . that's exactly the kind of place where this Ortez guy could be hiding out. And if he still has that pin thing, we're talking a nice score. Might be worth another look."

CHAPTER 37

Duncan Carmichael
Preston-Martin Building, Seattle
Law Offices of Warren & Carmichael
Current day

"They took her shoe! Her shoe, Duncan! For Christ's sake, who would do something like that?"

Duncan listened with increasing alarm to his wife's frantic voice on the other end of the phone call. "Where's our granddaughter now?" he asked.

"I picked Lilly up at the daycare and have her here with me, at home. I let Megan know so she wouldn't worry. But I'll need to tell her what this is all about. The people at the daycare were really embarrassed, as they damned well should be. Her shoe—just one, for heaven's sake!"

"I don't understand what happened. Could you start at the beginning?"

"I went shopping. When I got back, I found one of those colorful gift bags you use for birthdays and such resting on the kitchen table. *Inside* our home! In our kitchen, Duncan! For a minute, I thought it was from you. Then I looked in the bag and realized that all it contained were two shoes.

One of them was mine—one of those dark blue high heels I never wear. It was taken from our bedroom closet. The other was one of Lilly's cute little rose and yellow sneakers. The ones that have SOOPER and DOOPER printed on the sides in rose colored print. She loves those sneakers."

"Was the door locked when you got home?"

"Yes. I would have noticed if it hadn't been. Anway, I immediately called the daycare, and they confirmed that one of her shoes had gone missing. They leave them on this low bench near the front entrance. Someone has to have come in there, without anyone seeing them, and stolen just the one shoe, one of Lilly's shoes. They say that their front door is always locked. But if it was locked, how'd somebody get inside like that without being seen? And how did they know which shoes belonged to Lilly? You tell me that!"

"You're sure nothing else was taken either at the daycare or at home?" Duncan asked.

"Not that I can tell."

"And they didn't leave a message?"

"The shoes ARE the message. It's a threat, Duncan. We need to call the police. Better yet, call your friend Kyle Marshall. He'll have contacts in the police department."

Duncan hesitated. "If this is some kind of threat, that means whoever it is wants something. Maybe we ought to find out what that is before we do anything precipitous."

"Precipitous?! They've threatened our granddaughter, Duncan! And us! It has to have something to do with that case you and Sydney have been working on. We have to *do* something."

Duncan knew better than to tell his wife to "calm down." That never worked; in fact, it usually backfired. But he wasn't sure what the "right thing" to say was. Suddenly his intercom hummed with a message from reception. They usually held calls when he was already on the line. "Hold on for just a sec, love."

He switched to intercom. "Sorry to interrupt, Mr. Carmichael, but you have an unidentified caller on the line who insists it's urgent that he speak with you *immediately*. What do you want me to do?"

"Put him through as soon as I'm off the line."

Then: "Kate, there's an anonymous caller who wants to talk to me. I'll get back to you as soon as I can. Meanwhile, lock the doors. And stay inside."

"The doors *are* locked Duncan. They *were* locked."

"Good. OK. Let me take this call. I'll get right back to you." With that he hung up and punched the office phone to put through the anonymous caller.

"You get our message?" The voice was brusque. And artificial, as if it was being mechanically disguised.

"Who are you?" Duncan made a conscious effort to remain and to sound calm.

"The point is, Mr. Carmichael, that I know who *you* are. I know about you, your wife, your daughter, your law partner, even your grand-daughter who attends that classy little daycare. Must be nice."

"What do you want?"

"Good. You understand the situation. This is all about what *I* want. And the sooner you provide what I want, the sooner I'll be out of your life."

"And that is?"

"It's pretty simple, actually. I need a location for someone you know —a client, I assume. Danny Ortez. Don't bother denying you know who that is, because I already know you do. I need his contact information. And I need it now. You start feeding me lawyer bullshit about client confidentiality, things are going to quickly turn deeply unfortunate for you and your family.

"So, what's it going to be? A simple address, email, phone number, and current alias? Or a lot of unnecessary unhappiness for you and the people you care about?"

"Well, whoever you are . . .," Duncan replied after a moment's delay. "I'm sorry for your wasted call. But I'm afraid you're under a misimpression. I've been trying to find his location myself, without success. But before you start going batshit crazy on me, if you'll give me the chance, I'll keep trying. There's no need for you to threaten me further. I believe you."

"Sorry, Carmichael. I'm not buying your stalling tactic. You don't get to fob us off so you can call in support and protection. I want an answer, and I want it now."

"As I said, I don't *have* the information you want. I have some leads, but no answers yet. I'm no hero, I assure you. If I knew, I'd tell you. Give me a chance to see if my sources have found anything. Meanwhile, please don't do anything rash."

"It's your funeral, my friend."

The line went dead.

Within moments, Duncan had Kate back on the phone again. "Stay inside; take Lilly upstairs and lock yourself and Lilly in the bedroom. Get the Smith & Wesson out of the closet and make sure it's loaded. Hopefully you won't need it, but keep it and your phone handy. I'm calling Kyle to send over protection."

"What is this about, Duncan? Shouldn't we call the police?"

"You were right; it's about the overlapping cases Sydney and I are working on. For now, please do as I ask while I call Kyle. Then I'll get back to you."

"I'm frightened, Duncan."

So am I Kate, he said to himself as he called Kyle.

Kyle's response to his request was immediate. He told Duncan to call Kate back and to stay on the line with her until he got someone there. He also agreed to send someone to look out for their daughter Megan.

Kate answered on the first ring. "Kyle's sending someone to stay with you, Kate. He's also sending someone over to Megan's. He'll call her and explain the situation. Are you and Lilly okay?"

"Yes, she's watching TV. But she senses that something is wrong. Did you call the police?"

"Not yet. I want to check on a few things first. There are more people who might be in danger. And the police are going to have questions I'm not able to answer."

"Do you know what they want?"

"Yes, and I can't give them the information they're asking for. It would put other people's lives at risk." He paused a moment. "I'm sorry, so sorry."

"I need to call Megan. She's going to want to be with Lilly."

"Let's let Kyle figure that out. Meanwhile, he told me to stay on the line with you until he gets someone there. So don't hang up. But first let me get Sydney in here so I can make some other calls while you're waiting on Kyle's security person, okay?"

He buzzed Sydney and asked her to come immediately. She was there so quickly it felt like she'd teleported into his office. "Here, Sydney, talk to Kate. She'll explain what's happened. Meanwhile, I've got some calls to make."

He moved to the far corner of his office and called Kyle back. "Sydney is talking to Kate," he explained. "I'm going to call and warn the Ortez family."

"Good idea. I talked with Megan. The two people I've assigned are on the line with her and should be there is less than twenty minutes."

"Thank you."

"I've also alerted the two operatives who I've had keeping an eye out for a tail on you to increase their vigilance, but stay out of sight."

"Should I call the police?"

"I suppose. I doubt they'll do more than an occasional drive-by under the circumstances. You can't even tell them who you're hiding from, or why. Still, I think you have no choice but to report the threat. If things escalate, it will be easier to bring them up to speed. Meanwhile, we can try to trace the call you got, but it's likely to have been from a burner. I think our only option is to keep trying to identify those two guys that followed you to Canada. There's got to be some airport security video at SeaTac and Vancouver International that we can access. I'll get on that. Meanwhile, I'm giving you the same advice I gave your daughter, Megan—don't go anywhere alone. And make Sydney promise the same thing."

"'*Make*' might be a big ask. But I'll do my best."

"Tie her up if you need to. I can't afford to lose my two favorite clients."

CHAPTER 38

Duncan Carmichael
Preston-Martin Building, Seattle
Parking Garage, Level A
Current day

Once everyone had security coverage, Duncan called the police. The call turned out to be both time-consuming and, as he had suspected, awkward, since he didn't know who was making the threats and was reluctant to go into detail about what they wanted. The police were naturally frustrated, pointing out that there wasn't much they could do if he wasn't more transparent. Duncan said he would let them know if he needed their support and left it at that.

It was well into the evening before he finally had time to sit down and sort through the files on his desk to see if he had any critical client needs. For every lawyer, there was always work with hard deadlines, absolute cutoffs that simply couldn't be ignored. So, it was almost 8:30 p.m. when he finally called Kate to tell her he was headed home.

In the early days of their partnership, Duncan and Sydney had engaged in an unspoken mutual competition in which each of them had tried to be the first one in the office every morning and the last one out every night. As their relationship evolved and their practice flourished, this had morphed into an effort to always stay later than any of their hired associates; to lead by joint example. Then, Duncan married Kate. Around the same time, their practice had matured to include a growing stable of highly-motivated associates and junior partners. Now he and Sydney only stayed late when a particular case required extra time at the office. Tonight, however, they had agreed to leave together for safety reasons. "Ready to go?" Duncan asked Sydney through her open door.

She looked at her cluttered desk. "Might as well. I'll come in early tomorrow."

As they waited for the next "down car" in the deserted 35th floor elevator lobby, Duncan asked: "Where's your protection detail?"

"Since I'm parked near the exit, they're going to follow me home from there. I just texted them. You?"

"Same. I told them we would be together in the garage."

"Almost like old times," Sydney said, smiling, glancing at the time on her phone. "Although I think in the past it was usually more like 10:30 instead of 8:30."

Duncan smiled back. "Sounds like you miss those sixteen-hour work days."

"Don't miss the sleepless nights worrying whether we were going to meet our payroll."

"At least we weren't threatened by blackmailers back then."

"Any help from the police?

"They don't have the bandwidth to provide serious personal security, especially when I can't tell them who to look out for. I did ask building security to keep a sharp eye and not let anyone into our office area. But they can't be everywhere either."

At the ground floor they transferred to a parking level elevator that took them to the building's underground garage. Owing to their similarly early hour of arrival that morning, their cars were quite near each other, just across a driving lane on the A Level in the garage, the one nearest the exit. It was a short walk from the elevator to their cars.

When the elevator doors opened, they stayed together until they got close to their respective vehicles, her beloved bright yellow Porshe and his dark silver Lexus.

Duncan's car was parked head-in between two other vehicles in a parking slot against a concrete wall. He was standing beside his car on the driver side in the narrow space between his car and the next one as he pulled out his keys and beeped open the locked car door. He was facing his car and reaching for the doorhandle when, out of the corner of his eye, he noticed a sudden movement to his right.

In the moment, all he was able to grasp was that some very large, unfamiliar man was lunging in his direction. Without thinking Duncan grabbed his car door handle, stepped to the left and behind the door as he quickly pulled it open. The open door blocked the space between his car and the next.

What happened then was a comedy of errors; a scene that would have warmed the heart of any Laurel and Hardy or Three Stooges fan.

The assailant didn't realize what was happening in time and collided with the open end of the door, thus pushing it further open and banging it into the adjacent car. In the man's struggle to close the car door and get it out of his way, his unzipped jacket got caught up on the top rear corner of the door. The man briefly lost his footing and tumbled into the space between the open door and the interior of Duncan's car. A sharp clatter of something hitting the ground made Duncan look down, and there, on the pavement beneath the door was a handgun. His attacker reached down for his weapon, but with his jacket hung up on the top corner of the car door, he came up short.

Duncan grabbed the gun. It was a Ruger LC9, like the one owned by one of Duncan and Kate's fellow shooters at their shooting range. Duncan had actually fired one a few times to try it out. It was a newer Pro model with no thumb safety. He aimed it at his deeply angry and embarrassed assailant who had recovered and was backing away.

"Freeze asshole," Duncan yelled as he pushed his car door closed and followed the man out into the driving lane. Apparently, seeing the muzzle of his own gun aimed at the center of his chest at point blank range was enough motivation for the man to rethink his priorities. He put his hands in the air in surrender.

Then Duncan heard another voice.

This one came from across on the opposite side of the open driving lane near the next row of parked cars. "Put the gun down, Carmichael."

About thirty feet away near the rear of Sydney's Porsche was another man. For a moment, Duncan's gun wavered between the two men. Then he realized that the second man had his left arm wrapped tightly around Sydney's neck. The back of her head was held firmly against the upper left side of the man's chest with her body effectively shielding him. The gun the man was holding was momentarily aimed at Carmichael, but he could easily also shoot Sydney.

Given the distance between them and knowing his own modest shooting skills, Duncan knew that the other man had a distinct advantage. It was a classic standoff, one like Duncan had seen hundreds of times on TV and in movies.

The first man now stood with his hands at rest, waiting.

Both men were large and muscular. Sydney, not a small woman, looked like a mere rag doll held in the second guy's powerful grip.

"It's time we had a little chat, Carmichael. I believe you and your partner have some information we need." The four of them stood there for a moment, with Duncan's gun trained on the man holding Sydney and that man's gun aimed back at him. Meanwhile, Duncan was keeping his eye on the man whose gun he had. "As you can see, your choices at the moment are limited," the man holding Sydney continued, reading his mind. "I am perfectly ready to inflict some serious harm on your lady friend here. Lay that weapon down on the ground beside you and kick it carefully over to my friend."

The man nearby began to move forward. But Duncan wagged his gun in his direction. "I said freeze. You even breath wrong, you're going to be the first to die." The man stopped and glanced over at the other man, presumably for instructions.

"This is one you cannot win, Carmichael. Put *down* the gun."

Sydney was looking Duncan directly in the eye when she called out "Law and Order," her voice hoarse and barely audible past her assailant's choke hold. She managed the briefest flash of a grim smile to confirm the significance of what she meant.

Then she continued in an artificially high, frightened voice: "Sorry, I . . . I don't feel well." She tried to cough and took several loud short breaths. She sounded apologetic and panicked. "Please . . ." She moaned and gagged, sounding so convincing that even Duncan almost believed her. Then she completely relaxed her muscles and slumped back against the man who held her, becoming a dead weight, pulling the man downward as he struggled with just the one arm to keep her up while holding the gun in the other. His attention momentarily diverted, his gun wavered, and as Sydney dropped to the ground, his body was exposed.

Duncan fired, twice.

The distance was too great for much accuracy, but Duncan did manage to seriously wing the guy as he let go of Sydney and backed up to take cover. Meanwhile, the man whose gun Duncan held took advantage of the situation to flee. Apparently, he was no hero. Duncan's only option was to shoot him in the back or let him go. He chose the latter, and the man disappeared into a nearby stairwell-exit. Instead, Duncan fired a couple more rounds in the direction of the armed and injured man who was hiding between cars. The cover allowed Sydney to scramble to safety.

Duncan didn't need to call Kyle's men; both of them appeared almost immediately, running down the building exit ramp, guns drawn. "Backup's on the way," the first of Kyle's men called out.

"You hear that?" Duncan yelled. "It's three to one with more help on the way."

Suddenly they heard Sydney shout: "Make that *four* to one. Don't move. Don't you move an inch. *Drop your gun.* Unlike my partner, I have no qualms about shooting an asshole in the back." She'd snuck around the parked car behind which the man was hiding.

"OK, OK," he said. A moment later, the man's gun skidded out from between the cars and into the open driving lane. Then the man followed it out, hands in the air. Sydney emerged behind him. She held the little .22 caliber Ruger that she carried in her purse. It was inches from the small of the man's back.

Moments later they were joined by a building security guard who'd heard the gunfire. Then a Seattle Police squad car squealed to a stop in the street at the top of the entrance. The man Duncan had shot was demanding medical help. Blood had saturated the shoulder of his jacket.

As both armed officers warily approached, Duncan called out: "We need an ambulance. A man has been shot." He didn't mention that he was the one who had done the shooting. One of the police officers stopped to call for an ambulance. The other approached the odd group cautiously, his weapon in hand but aiming at the ground.

"Lay your weapons on the ground and step back," he instructed.

"I'm going to need mine," Sydney said. "It was never fired."

"Ma'am," the officer said. "I'm going to ask you to hand over that weapon. We'll get this all sorted out at the police station."

Duncan said, "We notified the police department earlier about the possibility of an attack. While you're at it, you might want to check on that."

The two officers exchanged glances. The one who'd called the ambulance took out his phone again and stepped away to talk in private. Meanwhile, Kyle's operative was showing his credentials to the other officer and explaining that a second assailant had escaped through the stairwell and was at large.

"You gotta be kidding me," the officer said in response. Just then a howling, flashing aid car pulled in through the garage entrance and shut down its echoing siren that had consumed the confined space.

At that point, the building security guard spoke up. "I know these two," he told the officer. "They're lawyers. From my building here."

"So . . .?" the officer turned to Sydney and Duncan. "The two men that you say attacked you were, what, dissatisfied clients?" It took Duncan a moment to realize the strained attempt at humor. That was when his muscles finally relaxed, and he began to breathe normally.

"Something like that," Duncan said. "Maybe a bit more complicated." Instead of laying the LC9 on the ground, he reversed his grip to the barrel and held it out handle-first to the officer who took out a plastic bag for Duncan to drop it in.

The officer sighed. "It always is. Sorry, but we will have to sort this all out at the station."

Two more police officers showed up. One was assigned to ride in the ambulance with the injured man after Duncan explained he was one of the two attackers.

There was a blood smear on one of the fenders of Sydney's yellow car. "Hope your insurance covers bullet holes," the officer said pointing. Sure enough, there was a bullet hole in that same fender. Then he ordered another officer to check whether there was any damage done to other cars in the area. "How many shots were fired?" he asked.

"I think I fired four times," Duncan said. "For the second two, I was trying to keep the guy who had hold of my partner busy while she got away."

"Did he return fire?"

Duncan looked at Sydney and Kyle's employee. They both shook their heads. "I guess not," Duncan said. "He threatened to shoot her, and both men had guns."

"But you're the only one who did any shooting?"

"With the other guy's gun. I didn't have one with me."

"The officer shook his head. "Why do I have a feeling this is going to be a very long night."

Kyle's second man was nowhere in sight. In all the confusion, it was possible the first two policeman had forgotten he was ever there. Sydney was placed in one patrol car, and Duncan and Kyle's man together in another. While the officers were talking to each other, Kyle's operative managed to let Duncan know that his colleague had gone back outside and was most likely alerting Kyle to the situation.

As the officer had predicted—it was a long night.

The detective taking Duncan's statement laughed when Duncan explained how he got the gun in the first place and then again at how he was able to take a shot at their assailant. "My partner and I are both fans of the TV series, *Law and Order*," Duncan explained. "But it drives us nuts when some bad guy uses an innocent bystander as a shield while holding a gun to keep the police at bay. My partner always says: 'Why doesn't that hostage just pretend to faint or just relax and drop to the ground? Give the good guy an opening for a shot.'

"So, she said 'Law and Order,' and that's what we did."

"You were damned lucky," the detective said.

"I know." It had been a risk taken on the spur of the moment; her call. If he'd had more time to think, he might have hesitated.

When they were finally released hours later, Kyle and his two operatives were waiting for them. "I hear you're quite the actress," Kyle said to Sydney.

"Who said I was acting?"

"Just relieved you didn't shoot anyone in the back. That would take a bit more explaining."

"The police kept my gun," she complained. "I always carry one in my purse."

"I can loan you one," Kyle said. "I have a nice pink Glock that would be perfect for you."

Sydney frowned and punched him hard in the arm as they exited the building.

"Everyone's safe," Kyle said. "So, let's get you two home."

"Do you know if they caught the other guy?" Duncan asked.

"I don't think so. That means by now whoever is after you knows what happened. I'm not sure if that puts you more or less at risk. With any luck, the guy you shot may lead us to who he works for. Although not right away; I understand he's lawyered up."

"No surprise."

"I definitely think I'll have to train my team on the 'ooohhh I feel sick strategy.' Think it works for men?"

"Now I *am* going to be sick," Sydney said as she mimicked putting a finger down her throat.

CHAPTER 39

Duncan Carmichael
Preston-Martin Building, Seattle
Law Offices of Warren and Carmichael
Current day

Allison Girard's voice shook as she told Duncan about the phone call she'd received from the blackmailers. "Like you suggested, I told them we don't have any money. I repeated that all we've got is the Tsarina's Spider. I told them my dad was willing to hand it over if they'll keep our secret. I'm pretty sure they believed me."

"That's good, Allison. Very good."

"They want to make the exchange somewhere in Vancouver, which is fine with me. And they wanted to do it right away. So, I did as you suggested and told them I didn't have the Spider and that it would take me several days to get it. They definitely didn't like that, but in the end, they agreed to call back in three days."

"How did the person on the phone sound? Was it a man? Did he sound angry? How old do you think he was?" Duncan realized he was peppering her with too many questions all at once, so he shut up to let her respond.

She gave it some thought. "Actually, I'd say he sounded youngish. Not a kid though. And he didn't sound exactly sure of himself, if you know what I mean. It felt like maybe he was playing it by ear. Like this wasn't the kind of thing he did every day."

"Did he have to consult with anyone to make a decision about the delay?"

"No, he never left the phone to ask someone else anything. I suppose he could have been on speaker and writing notes back and forth with someone, but it didn't feel like that was the case."

"I think you would have picked up on it if you were talking to a non-decision-maker."

"I could be wrong, too. Or maybe it's an act to put us off guard."

"There are too many unknowns. We need to keep our energy focused on the Spider set-up and our negotiations with the Navy."

"You're right—I just hope the Navy doesn't drag things on too long."

"To that point, I'm afraid we may have yet another problem."

"Oh, oh! I don't like the sound of that."

"Neither do I. Remember when I mentioned that our investigator thought someone may have hired a Vancouver PI to find your father? Well, now we know for sure that there's someone else still looking for him, other than the guy you've been dealing with." He explained what happened and how the police had one suspect in custody. "The man in custody has lawyered up. But he apparently has connections with local organized crime."

"Oh my God," she said. "So, what if those guys catch up with us, too. What will we do then?"

"I'm not sure. The men who attacked us are definitely dangerous. But it looks like they *don't* know where you and your family are located. Their attack was an effort to find that out. So, whoever's been calling you may be some kind of free-lancer."

"I don't get it. How do any of them even know about my dad? Where is this coming from?"

"I have no idea. We're not even sure what these Seattle people are after. It could be the Spider, or the airplane, or something else. Probably they think your father is sitting on a bundle of cash. But why now after all these years and at the same time someone else has tracked your parents down? Could there be some connection with the Navy that we don't know about? Or with the NIS? Maybe tracking him down has been on someone's back burner for years, and the word's out that your dad may be turning himself in, so they want to strike before then."

"I don't see how that's possible. It's all happening so fast."

"Maybe not fast enough," Duncan said.

"There is one upside," she suggested.

"Enlighten me."

"One way or the other, once Dad turns himself in, their leverage will be gone."

He wanted to agree with her, but he knew that no one was safe until whoever was after her father finally realized there was no pot of gold to be had.

CHAPTER 40

Duncan Carmichael
Preston Martin Building, Seattle
Law Offices of Warren & Carmichael
Current day

"If he pleads guilty to desertion and larceny, we'll recommend fifteen years with no parole and a dishonorable discharge."

Lieutenant Commander James sounded supremely confident as he offered up the news. But it was basically the maximum sentence. Clearly, the Navy was prepared to play hardball.

"If we do actually get that plane back, and if its electronics are intact, we'll tell the judge that Ortez voluntarily cooperated to make it happen. If we're also able to identify and apprehend the man he says knew the location of the plane, and if he confirms your client's story, then we'll tell the judge about that as well. You need to know that our CO's dad served under Nate Waterman during Vietnam and considered him an inspirational leader. Your client's caper with that airplane apparently put a permanent blemish on Waterman's otherwise sterling career. Forced him to retire early and in disgrace.

"Bottom line? I think this is the best you're going to get,

Carmichael. And, personally, if it were up to me, I'd tell your client to stuff it. If you turn this offer down, I plan to see to it that we renew our search for him. And when we find him, which we will, I can guarantee he'll spend the rest of his life at Leavenworth."

"I see," Duncan said. "Well, I will of course pass this along to my client. But I can assure you right now that he's going to say 'no.' It's really too bad, when you think about it. My client will spend the last few years of his life in exile. And your Admiral Waterman will spend *his* last few knowing that he lost out on the only chance he'll ever get to recover the stolen airplane that, from what you're saying, I gather was the main factor that ended an otherwise brilliant Navy career. Pretty sad outcome, all around." That ended the call.

Later that same day, Duncan got Danny Ortez on the phone and delivered the bad news.

"Fifteen years! For me that basically amounts to life," Danny said. "It looks like I'm better off turning myself in to the Canadian authorities and take my chances fighting extradition."

"I really feel bad about this one, Danny. It's deeply frustrating that you're being pushed into this corner by some apparently half-baked criminals bent on getting rich."

"I appreciate the sentiment, Mr. Carmichael. But I can't really lay the blame on anybody but myself. My past has finally caught up with me. Let's go ahead and play out this little game with these blackmailers, whoever they turn out to be. You let me know when you think our story has ended—either with them getting caught or when they're likely to discover they've been given a fake. That's when I'll go ahead and turn myself in to our local Mounted Police. Who knows, maybe I'll get lucky."

"It's not over yet; we still have a couple of tricks up our sleeve."

CHAPTER 41

Allison Girard
Vancouver, BC False Creek waterfront
Aquabus False Creek foot ferry
Current day (mid-morning, a few days later)

It was a chilly day. Allison zipped up her jacket before stepping aboard the small Aquabus foot ferry that was about to depart the Vancouver Convention Center from the Plaza of Nations dock enroute to Grenville Island and downtown. There would be several other stops along the way. Probably due to the hour and the cold weather, the boat was nearly empty. As instructed, she took a seat in the very rear. She studied the few other passengers carefully, but none of them seemed likely to be the person she was expecting to meet.

At Yaletown, one person got off, and two more got on. They paid her no attention as the boat cast off again and continued on its scheduled route.

Then, at Spyglass Place, at the dock under the Cambie Street Bridge, she spotted a man she felt confident was her contact.

She guessed his age at early thirties. He was slightly built and was wearing a covid mask. He had on a puffy jacket that she hoped wasn't hiding a gun. As soon as he stepped aboard and saw her, he headed in her direction.

"You must be Allison," he said, taking a seat on the rounded bench beside her but looking straight ahead. She thought she recognized his voice from the phone. She was glad he wasn't looking at her, certain that the expression on her face probably reflected the knot in her stomach created by the knowledge that she was about to hand over a worthless fake to this man who posed such a huge threat to her entire family.

"Yes," she said, her voice lost in the brisk breeze coming in through the open doors. She started to hand over the package she'd been holding on her lap, but he held up his hand. "Nope," he said. "Let's you and me hang out for a while. See what happens." Then he leaned back, looked around at the surrounding Vancouver scenery while the two of them waited in silence as the boat pulled away from the dock and continued along its route.

Their next stop was Stamps Landing. After that was David Lam Park. When no one threatening or suspicious got on at either of those stops, and after the boat was underway again, the man leaned toward her. "OK, I'll take that package now." He nodded toward their destination. "I'll be getting off at Grenville Island. You stay right where you are. Then you can get off downtown or wherever you want." He looked at the package. "This better contain what you say it does."

"It does," she said. "But there are a couple of things I need you to know."

"No talk. You just go on your way. The rest is up to us."

She had worked for hours with Duncan and Sydney on what to say next. Despite all that preparation, she was surprised at how authentically her lies seemed to flow once she made a start:

"Look, I don't want to presume, but do you actually know how valuable this Tsarina's Spider is?"

"We got a pretty good idea, I guess." Under the mask, it was hard to read his mood or tell what he was thinking.

"Well, just to be sure you do, you should know it was appraised back in 1983 when my grandfather owned it at well over a million U.S. dollars. My family has asked around, and we believe that, on the legitimate market, it could be worth at least four times that today. If you're planning to sell it to a fence, it will only bring a fraction of that amount. I guess you probably know that, right?"

"We know what we're doing, lady." But, to Allison's ear, it sounded very much like he might not.

"Well, OK. But there's some stuff you do need to understand. This Spider is the only thing our family has that's of any value. If you come back to us again, sometime down the road wanting more, we're not going to be able to pay you anything. We're just working people. We don't have, like investments. Or own a bunch of valuable stuff. My Dad's a fisherman. You understand what I'm telling you? This Spider is it. There isn't any more."

"That's all right. I hear you. If this is what you say it is, we'll consider it square."

"OK, well, I hope you mean that. Because I'm not shitting you, here. The only reason we even have this thing is my wealthy grandfather was really attached to it. He hung onto it even when he was going broke. He wanted it to go to my mother rather than using it to pay off his creditors. And, as maybe you know, my father ran off with it here to Canada to keep it from being taken by some loan shark to whom my grandfather owed a lot of money."

It felt to her like he didn't really want to hear any more. She could see Grenville Island coming closer up ahead. She didn't have a lot of time.

"The problem," she continued without a pause, ". . . is that this Spider is going to be really tough for you to unload. My mom and dad never sold it partly because they knew that if they tried to sell it on the legitimate market there would have been way too much publicity and attention on them. And if they'd handed it over to some inexperienced, low-end fence for a fraction of what it was worth, there was a good chance even then that word would get out."

"Hey, it's OK. I don't really need to know all this. You've done your part. Now you can forget about it."

"Look, there's an important reason I'm telling you this. If you end up selling this thing to some cheap chiseler of a fence who doesn't have the capacity to pay top dollar and lacks experience with high-end art and antiques, not only are you going to be really disappointed in the price and be more likely to come back on us, but they'll almost certainly get caught. Then you'll get caught. If that happens, you're going to tell the authorities all about us. We don't want that. You understand what I'm saying?"

"Yeah, sure. I hear you. I'm just saying, we got it covered."

"Yeah. Well, maybe you do. Or maybe not. Look, please hear me out, OK? Just in case. My family has done a lot of research on this over the years. And we know the guy you ought to be using. He's here in Vancouver. And if my dad wasn't so concerned about being traced through the sale, we'd have used him long ago ourselves. His name's Martin Buckingham. He's an art dealer. As a matter of fact, he has a gallery right up ahead, on Grenville Island. The Buckingham Gallery. He's the guy to use for this. He has the serious cash to handle something this big and the contacts to move it safely and quietly into the hands of a discreet private collector. You'll need to expect a big discount in the price—if you're really lucky, my guess is he'll offer you something in the range of two million. If he does, you should take it. That's it. That's what I wanted you to know. The Buckingham Gallery here on Grenville Island."

The boat slid up next to the dock and, with a surge in reverse, gently nudged the float and came to a halt. The blackmailer stood. "OK, sure. But don't you worry, Mrs. Girard. You do like I've said and there won't be any problems. Nice doing business with you."

With that, he slipped the small package into the pocket of his over-sized coat, moved to the open doorway, stepped ashore, and quickly disappeared into the Grenville Island crowds. Several other people got on. And as the boat got underway again for its crossing to Hornby Street, Allison pulled out her phone and called an Uber to meet her there.

She'd delivered the package and the message they'd prepared. Now all they could do was wait.

CHAPTER 42

Eric Gee
Vancouver, BC
Chinese Restaurant on Burrard Street
Current day

Eric was grinning as he and Will met for an early lunch at one of Vancouver's excellent Chinese restaurants on Burrard Street. They'd chosen this one because it had booths with tall backs that provided the privacy they wanted.

Once they were seated and had placed their orders, Eric surreptitiously put the jewel case on the table between them, and, after looking around to make certain no one was paying them any attention, he flipped it open for Will to see.

"I don't know Eric," said Will, glancing at the Spider. "Doesn't look like all that big a deal to me. You sure that ugly thing's worth four million dollars?"

"Two million to us," Eric quietly corrected his friend.

"Two million. Four million. Damned thing's just some kind of fancy pin."

"Well . . ., not quite." Eric pointed. "This here's probably an emerald, OK? And these are rubies. And check out the gold." He picked it up and handed it to Will. "Feel how heavy it is."

"You think this is solid freaking gold?"

"Bet your ass it is."

"Well, we'll know soon enough. Soon as we can find a buyer."

Eric took the brooch back, carefully placed it in its box and shut the lid. Then he put it back in his pocket. "One thing's for sure, it was probably smart for us to take delivery up here in Vancouver rather than Seattle. 'Least here we don't have to worry about running into somebody we know."

"Think we will have trouble at the border?" Will asked.

"I doubt it," Eric said. But the border worried him. With his luck, some damned customs official might just pick them out for a full search and think two men with a fancy lady's brooch seemed suspicious.

"Well, I wouldn't want to have to explain to the boss how we came into possession of a four-million-dollar piece of jewelry."

"Two million, Will. A million each, if we're lucky."

"Yeah, yeah."

"And no damned overhead," Eric added. On their burglaries, Will and Eric paid the organization a 20% services and protection fee on their net recovery from every job they did. It was probably worth it. In exchange, they got intelligence on good places to hit. They didn't need to worry about freelancers trying to cut in on their business. And the organization lined them up with a market for their take. Though they wouldn't be using an organization fence this time, that was for sure. The more he thought about that, the more troubled he became. The odds were that a Seattle fence would know the bosses.

"A million each, clear and no overhead," Will repeated. "Not a bad day's work."

"Yeah," Eric said. "Not bad at all."

CHAPTER 43

Duncan Carmichael
Preston-Martin Building, Seattle, WA
Law Offices of Warren & Carmichael
Current day

Two days had passed since the U.S. Navy had turned down Danny's offer. Duncan had retained an experienced Canadian legal team to oversee Danny's surrender to the Canadian authorities and to represent him in the ensuing extradition hearing. Danny and Julia had been using the time to get their affairs in order and to collect some cash to pay legal fees and living costs. Danny made a quick sale of his boat at a bargain price to someone he knew, but he was hesitant to sell his fishing license. The license sale required registration with Canada Fisheries and Oceans, and Danny was nervous that they might question his identity. If they did, it would blow his cover and bring in the authorities before he was ready. The government might also later claim that he'd procured the license under false pretenses and make it worthless. It was too risky.

The Ortez family had similar issues with their modest bank accounts. They hadn't worried too much at the time about using a false name to open an account; they'd only done it in order to make larger purchases that were awkward to pay for in cash. There'd been nothing illegal about the way in which they'd earned the money—except for the phony name on the fishing license—and they'd conscientiously paid taxes on every penny earned. But they needed to get a sympathetic judge that would look at the whole picture rather than zeroing in on each individual unlawful act.

Since their float house wasn't powered by a motor of 10 hp or more, it had required no official registration or title. And it only had minimal value. They chose to stay on it until their fate was decided and then gift it to a friend.

There had been no further calls from anyone demanding money and no more attacks on anyone associated with the case. They didn't know what had happened to the Spider, but they were sure there was more to come when the blackmailers realized they had a fake.

Then, just one day before Danny's planned surrender, Duncan got an unexpected call. It was from Lieutenant Commander Phillip James, the U.S. Navy JAG officer at ComFAirWhidbey. "Your client given any further thought to our offer?" James asked. What was this about, Duncan wondered. Was the Navy going to renew negotiations?

"As I said before, for a man of his age, what you've offered him is basically a life sentence. Not really of much interest to someone hoping to spend his last few years on earth with his wife and family. Painful as it is, he's ready to hunker down and live with his choices."

"I see." There was a long silence before James spoke again. "Well, since you and I last spoke, there's been a lot going on here on our end. Sometimes stuff happens that can surprise you."

"That's for sure." Duncan had no idea what was coming, but it sounded like LCDR James was doing some backfilling. Duncan was brimming with questions, but he kept them to himself. When somebody began offering unrequested explanations, it was just possible that they were about to admit they might have been wrong about something.

Duncan waited.

James cleared his throat, as if he found it personally difficult to come out with what he was about to say. "Well, Mr. Carmichael, are you open to a new offer concerning the Ortez case?"

"I'd say yes, but not if it isn't significantly better than what was offered before."

"Well, we *are* prepared to make some concessions. I must begin by saying that the U.S. Navy feels strongly that there has to be a criminal conviction here. And there must be some kind of penalty paid. The Navy can't turn a blind eye to conduct that is as closely tied to 'good order and discipline' as is a desertion and the theft of a Navy aircraft. Even if it did happen almost forty years ago. And no matter what your client intended nor how well he might have behaved during his years as a fugitive from justice, there *has to be* some kind of court martial. There's no getting around that. You get that, right?"

"I understand what you're saying. What do you have in mind, Mr. James?"

"Well, as I think you mentioned, my boss, the current ComFAir-Whidbey would be the convening authority for any court martial on this matter—"

"Uh huh."

"And as such, he also has plenary review authority after the trial and sentencing are completed. His views on sentencing on this issue are final. So, if we can reach an agreement on the sentence, my boss at ComFAirWhidbey can make it happen. Regardless of what might take place in court."

"And what would that sentence be?"

"Well, your guy, Ortez, will first need to locate and help us recover that aircraft. And the full avionics package will need to be undisturbed and intact. With nothing missing. You still stand by that?"

"We do."

"He'll also need to identify the person that he claims he told about the plane's location and who kept that information from the Navy. There's going to need to be some kind of corroboration that supports your client's claim about this. He will also need to cooperate fully with any ensuing investigation." Duncan and Ortez had strategized about this matter at length. As soon as Danny revealed Ross Michaels' name, the Navy would discover that he was long dead. If the Navy wanted him "brought to account," that wasn't going to happen.

The one thing they could probably argue was that there had been no plastic camo netting on that plane when Ortez originally took off. Someone had to have put it there. Maybe they could track Ross renting a boat in the area. Maybe he even stayed somewhere overnight. Once their deal was finalized and the Navy went to the scene, the hope was that the condition of the plane and the presence of the netting would be enough to convince them to honor the deal.

"We'll need to give some thought to what we can do by way of corroboration. But we will agree to that."

"And, he'll need to surrender himself to the U.S. Navy without going through the extradition process, which, I will concede, might be problematic at this particular moment in history."

"Understood."

"At the time of the court martial sentencing hearing, there will need to be evidence presented that his desertion did not occur during time of war or national emergency and that he did not dessert to avoid hazardous duty. And, he'll need to give testimonial evidence that demonstrates his intent throughout was to see that the aircraft and its contents were safely returned to the U.S. Navy. If he can't testify convincingly and under oath to that, all bets are off."

"I understand."

There was a pause, as LCDR James apparently struggled to actually state his proposition. "In that case, ComFAirWhidbey is prepared, upon your client's plea of guilty to desertion and wrongful appropriation of Navy property, with mitigating factors and a finding of guilt, to guarantee a sentence of Dishonorable Discharge, with no confinement or other punishment."

Duncan wanted to shout for joy. But what he said was: "I will pass your offer along to my client. I can't give you any assurance about the answer. But I very much appreciate the consideration paid to each aspect of the case. I'll get back to you ASAP. Can I also tell him that he will be released on his own personal recognizance prior to trial and sentencing?"

"If he turns himself in as promised, then yes, you can. And get me your answer quickly, Mr. Carmichael. The more time that goes by, the more likely it is that things could change again, and this offer could go up in smoke."

"I'll get in touch with my client immediately and have your answer back as soon as humanly possible."

"Good. You do that."

An hour and a half later, the two men were back on the phone. "My client, Danny Ortez, accepts the offer as you laid it out earlier," Duncan said simply. "As soon as we can complete the paperwork and agree on a time and place, he will present himself as agreed. Perhaps it might make sense for it to occur at the U.S. port of entry at Blaine."

"Agreed."

"And he's willing to do that as soon you wish. How about tomorrow morning. No later than zero eight hundred."

"Agreed."

There was a moment of surprised silence, as Duncan and LCDR James reflected on what they'd just done.

"Are you open for a question, Mr. James?" Duncan asked.

"Maybe."

"I strongly suspect that you personally disapprove of this outcome, and I want to respect that opinion. But would you be willing to tell me what changed to turn things around?"

"Just between us? As Navy men and officers?"

"It won't impact anything except my curiosity."

"You knew that your client was never going to get much love from the Navy's brass. The reaction we got when we sent this up the chain of command was universally the same as what you heard from me when we initially discussed this."

"Uh huh."

"You may recall my mentioning that my CO's father served under Admiral Waterman. After we spoke, my boss had a conversation with his dad. And they were fairly certain that Waterman would want this guy caught and punished like everybody else. Unfortunately, neither of them had actually spoken with Waterman personally. I know that because I got a call from a very determined and influential retired Yeoman Master Chief Petty Officer. Back in the day, she served as Waterman's yeoman for several years preceding his untimely retirement. She heard about this matter, and she *did* talk with Admiral Waterman.

"Her call to me came as a huge surprise. I had no idea she'd stayed in touch with Waterman. She still visits him from time to time. Hell, I didn't even know the man was still alive, but it turns out he is. He may use a walker and live in an assisted living facility near Pensacola Florida, but he is as feisty as ever.

"Anyway, when she heard what we'd decided, she couldn't let it pass. Over the years, she and Waterman had apparently discussed that damned airplane many times. She immediately called him and confirmed what she believed, namely, that Admiral Waterman desperately wants to see that plane returned to the U.S. Navy.

"As you might imagine, it was not the Ortez desertion that created the stir which resulted in Admiral Waterman losing his command. Desertion is unfortunately not as rare as we'd like to think. What really stuck in the Navy's craw was the loss of that high-tech, strategically important aircraft. According to his former yeoman, Admiral Waterman has spent the past four decades mulling that over, rethinking what he might have done differently, and chastising himself for letting it happen. At the time of its loss, they did an extensive aerial search for the plane and came up with nothing. For him to now learn that it was somewhere right there in Canada, quite possibly in the very area they searched, is a matter of grave frustration for him. The bottom line is that he desperately wants to see that aircraft, with its electronics intact, finally restored to the U.S. Navy. The fact that the plane and its contents are no longer of any actual value isn't the point. He is well along in years. And he does not want to die and fade into history with the plane he lost never having been found.

"I laid all this out for my boss. And as far as he's concerned, if that's what his predecessor at ComFAirWhidbey wants, then that's what he wants too. I will say, your guy Ortez had damned well better produce that aircraft. And it better be intact. Or he's not going to like the outcome."

"He will, Mr. James. He absolutely will."

Chapter 44

Sydney Warren
Preston-Martin Building, Seattle, WA
Law Offices of Warren and Carmichael
Current day

For Sydney, like many big things, it had all begun with something very small. In this instance, with, literally, a mere "string." And a dog.

Legal discovery in the matter of the *Estate of Jamison Nowak vs. the Seattle Report* was largely complete. The depositions were finished and transcribed. Key documents had been exchanged. The case had finally passed through the mediation process required by the King County court rules. And the matter was set for trial. But Sydney's preparations were not yet complete.

In complicated cases, it was her practice to do one final assessment in the last days before trial to make absolutely sure she hadn't missed anything—a witness, perhaps, or in a murder case, some detail of the victim's life that might have been overlooked. Also, she wanted to have all the facts fresh in her mind before tackling the trial preparations. As was also her practice, she closed her office door and instructed the receptionist to hold her calls.

Two white Bankers Boxes were piled on the corner of her desk and several others were stacked on the floor beside it. They contained all the files and documents from both the old trial and the upcoming one.

She had the trial transcript as well as police reports and records from the original investigation. She had the Harold Dawson autopsy report along with the testimony of the medical examiner. And, since the Sheriff's office kept evidence in publicly-important death cases indefinitely, she'd been able to obtain photographs of the physical evidence from the original trial as well, including the brass cartridge case the young boy had found under the bridge, the $250,000 promissory note from AA Best Bet Bail Bonds, and Nowak's rifle, the one found in the creek bed over three months after the day of the murder.

In addition, she had re-read the current transcripts of the depositions of key witnesses: the two detectives, the defendant publisher, the reporter who'd written up the story in the Seattle press, and Nowak's son and daughter. And, she had taken a fresh look at the financial records required in her proof of damages. There was a lot to review.

She was examining some photos when she got an unwelcome buzz from the receptionist. "I'm sorry, Sydney, I know you said to hold your calls, but I also know you're working on the Nowak case, and I have this call from a woman who says she has some information about it. I thought you might want me to put this one through."

"That was the right decision," Sydney said. "I'll take the call." The young, earnest receptionist sounded so tentative and apologetic, right *or* wrong, there was no way Sydney would have told her "no."

"Hello, Ms. Warren?" a woman's voice asked.

"Yes, this is she."

"Are you the lawyer involved with that lawsuit against the Seattle Report? The one having to do with the Harold Dawson murder?"

"That's right. How can I help you?"

"Well, my name is Sara-Rose Martinson. And I very much hope you won't mind that I've called. Maybe I shouldn't have. But I recently saw an article in the Seattle Report about your case. I've regretted that I didn't call you at the time, and I didn't want to make the same mistake again. If you decide what I have to tell you is totally irrelevant, please just put it down to the eccentricities of a silly old lady and forgive me for it."

"Well, Mrs. Martinson, as an 'old lady' myself, I doubt you are being 'silly.' And I'm intrigued by the fact that there is something from the past that you want to share with me." She felt a tingle of anticipation; for some reason, this didn't strike her as a frivolous call.

"Thank you. It's about Harold Dawson's dog. You see, back in 1983, my husband Larry and I bought our home in Broadmoor from Mr. Dawson a short while before his death. My Larry's gone now, but I still live in the house. It's a big old place, but I can't stand the idea of moving into one of those assisted-living places. So, I've stuck it out here. Maybe that's why I remember what happened so clearly after all these years."

"I see," Sydney said. She was trying to be patient but was getting anxious for the woman to get to the punch line.

"When Mr. Dawson died, he had a really nice black-and-white border collie that he left behind—Parker was his name."

"Yes . . .?" Sydney couldn't help herself; she glanced at the little "billable hours" clock on her desk.

"Well, not long after Larry and I moved in here, it would have been in June of 1983, Parker showed up on our front porch. And he wouldn't leave. We'd never actually met Mr. Dawson, so we didn't know whose dog it was at first. Larry wanted to call the pound and have them take him away. But he looked like such a nice dog. And I guessed he belonged to someone who had lived in our house."

"I see. And you think this relates in some way to Mr. Dawson's murder?"

"Yes, I do. You see, the thing is I felt bad about poor Parker. He wouldn't let me come near him, but he lapped up the water and ate the food I put out for him. When I asked the security guard for our community about him, I was told that Dawson and the dog were inseparable. That he took Parker to work every day and pretty much everywhere else he went. So, I was sure he'd want him back.

"Anyway, I got his new address from our realtor. And I went there. It was a modest house out toward Sand Point—I guess they call it

Magnuson Park now. Mr. Dawson wasn't home at the time. I didn't know it then, but I later learned that he had been murdered. So, of course, he wasn't there."

"I'm not sure I understand why you're telling me this, Mrs. Martinson."

"Well, it's about what I saw there, you know. At Mr. Dawson's home."

"And what was that?" Sydney felt another tingle of anticipation. Was it mere wishful thinking, or was she about to learn something that would help the case?

"When no one answered, I went around to the back door, the one by the garage, because I wanted to leave a note. It seemed to me that when he came home from work, he'd park in the driveway. Or in the garage. He'd never use the front door; it was too far out of his way. But the thing is, that's how I saw the backyard with the chain link fence. I could see inside Parker's kennel. There was this huge bowl heaped up with dog food. Many days' worth. There were also several big bowls of water there as well.

"Then I saw that there was also a hole under the fence where Parker had apparently dug his way out and escaped. So, you see why I called."

"Well, I guess not exactly, Mrs. Martinson."

"It's like I said. Mr. Dawson took Parker everywhere. To work. Shopping. Everywhere. The two of them were inseparable."

"So . . . you're wondering why he didn't take Parker with him that day he went up into the mountains?"

"Yes! Yes, that's it, exactly. Here he was, headed up into the woods where there were all those hiking trails. If you were going to take a dog *anywhere*, that's where you'd take him, right? But Mr. Dawson left Parker at home, locked up in the backyard with enough food and water to last for days. That didn't seem logical to me.

"Later on, when I heard Mr. Dawson got murdered at about that same time, I knew I should say something to somebody, but I didn't know who to call. And my Larry thought I should stay out of it, you know. And then, when I read Mr. Nowak had been acquitted, I sort of figured things had sorted themselves out.

"We started feeding Parker, and after a while, he got used to Larry and me. We never asked anyone's permission; we just kept him. He was with us for another ten years or so. A wonderful dog. Anyhow, that's what I called to tell you. After all these years of thinking about it, when I recently read in the Seattle Report that the matter is headed for court again, it seemed like I ought to finally speak up."

What Mrs. Martinson was saying did seem unusual, but was it actually significant? As someone who'd never had a dog, Sydney wasn't sure she was coming to the right conclusion. "So, tell me, what do you think it means?"

"Well, leaving out that much food encourages a dog to overeat. People who have dogs know that. I mean, for my money, Ms. Warren, I'd say when Harold Dawson left home that day, he knew he might never be coming back."

Chapter 45

Sydney Warren
Preston-Martin Building, Seattle, WA
Law Offices of Warren and Carmichael
Current day

After the call with Mrs. Martinson ended, Sydney sat motionless for a moment as she struggled to make connections between what the woman had told her and Harold Dawson's murder. He might have known he was in danger, but could he have anticipated his death? When he went to that meeting with Nowak, could he have known or believed that Nowak was angry enough to kill? If he suspected that, why did he go? Did he take a weapon along to defend himself? If so, what happened to it? With a shake of the head, she returned to sorting through the old photos of the crime scene, one part of her mind continuing to work on this new conundrum.

Most photos taken by the CSI team in 1983 showed the wooden bridge deck as it was before they'd collected and bagged up what they found there—discarded paper drinking cups, an empty cigarette packet, a tiny sandal presumably dropped from the foot of a small child hitching a ride on a parent's back. Even a couple of crushed cigarette butts.

In one of the photos, she could make out a length of string sprawled on the planked surface. At the time she had simply dismissed it. It could have come from a package of some kind, from a balloon maybe, or become detached from a child's pull toy. Who knew what some visitor might have tossed or dropped and left behind. Still, a piece of string right there where the body had been found and somewhat spread out like that—it did seem a bit strange.

She moved on to the other photos. Several of them showed Nowak's lever action rifle from different angles. She'd fired a lever-action rifle a couple of times before when target shooting. They were known for their ease of carry and precision. Very popular with hunters. One close-up of the trigger mechanism showed its closed steel loop handle that came up to rest against the underside of the stock immediately behind the trigger guard.

Then her eye landed on another CSI photo. This one had been taken from the center of the bridge facing back toward the shore in the direction of the parking lot. It showed the old, planked wooden bridge deck and the flat two-inch by eight-inch wooden railings along both sides. In this view, she could barely see the long-angled scar in the top surface of one of those railings. Back at the time, she'd wondered if that scar could have been caused by a rifle bullet. But she'd dismissed the idea because its trajectory was inconsistent with the track any bullet would have taken after having passed through Dawson's head at least a couple of feet above the top of that railing.

Suddenly she started wondering *what if?* Suppose Harold Dawson had been bent over or had crouched down at the time he'd been shot. She pictured how that might have looked, imagining him standing by that railing, but bent over and looking back in the direction of the shooter. No, it didn't add up. If the shooter had been on the shore beyond, and Dawson had been bent over looking in that direction, perhaps ducking down to hide with his head lined up with the scar on the railing behind him, the other railing, the one toward which he was facing on the opposite side of the bridge, would have obstructed the shooter's line of fire. Alternatively, if the shooter had been much closer, say standing right there on the bridge a short distance away, he would surely have been upright and holding the rifle stock up against his shoulder to sight on his target. If Dawson had been crouched down far enough for a bullet to crease that railing, the bullet would still *not* have had a sufficiently flat trajectory to have caused that scar.

Could the shooter have fired the rifle from the hip? It didn't seem likely. And even at close range, the accuracy of a hip shot striking the center of Dawson's forehead seemed implausible.

No, she decided, it simply couldn't have happened like that. That long scar in the railing had to have been caused in some other way.

But how?

Then another possibility struck her like a thunderbolt.

There was something suggestive about her vision of Harold Dawson crouched or bending over with his head at the height of that railing as he looked back in the direction of his assailant. Something passive and resigned about the posture. If he'd seen his assailant, wouldn't he have stood and perhaps raised his hands to plead for his life? Or maybe he would have turned away to run.

She picked up the photo of Nowak's lever action rifle and put it next to the photo of the scar on the railing. Then she fumbled through the rest of the photos until she found the one showing the length of string on the planked bridge deck and placed it next to the other two photos.

That's when her imagination constructed an entirely different scenario for how Harold Dawson might have died. One that now, all at once, made perfect sense in view of what she'd been told by Sara Rose Martinson.

As this alternative vision slowly spooled out in her mind, she was astounded at how nicely the other pieces of the puzzle came together.

Here was a man whose life had slowly been destroyed. One by one, he'd lost his fortune, his home, his wife, the respect of his friends and business partners, and possibly the respect of the daughter whom he'd obviously dearly loved. His professional career shattered by his own horrible mistakes. His self-identity tainted by failure. If ever there was a candidate for suicide, it would have been him.

During his downslide, he must have known on some level that there was a possibility of a disastrous outcome because, despite all that was happening, he had retained and steadfastly paid the premiums on a $200,000 life insurance policy with his daughter as the beneficiary. $200,000 was a lot of money in 1983. That policy was the one last shred of dignity that he'd managed to preserve. It was his one hedge against the horrible consequences he'd refused to consciously countenance—the possibility of his own death—very likely at the hands of a vengeful loan shark.

If his daughter was to collect on that policy, however, Dawson needed to make *absolutely certain* his death was not suspected as a suicide. He'd doubtless played out various "accidents" in his mind. He would have searched for something that could stand up under close examination by a suspicious and motivated insurance investigator. He wasn't going to get away with driving his car off a cliff or with some kind of supposedly "accidental" drug overdose.

One thing that could work for sure, however, would be his murder, the fate he'd feared and that had originally driven him to take out that insurance policy in the first place.

Upon reflection, it must have seemed obvious to him what he needed to do. Sydney could almost see the blueprint for how the plan evolved. First, there was that loud and visible argument he'd had with his irate partner Jamison Nowak in the conference room at their office. Then, in the days following the court decision, there were those insistent phone messages from Nowak that went unanswered. It could have been purposeful neglect on Dawson's part, but not necessarily. Perhaps Dawson simply couldn't face another confrontation with his business partner. That too would eventually play into the belated plan.

Without their relationship to the shooting range, he probably couldn't have pulled it off. Sydney remembered that their storage lockers were close to each other. She could easily imagine that Dawson had watched Nowak punch in his four-digit locker combination code so many times that he knew it by heart. And surely he knew that Nowak kept his Marlin hunting rifle and ammunition there.

The why was obvious. As was the opportunity. But *how* had he pulled it off?

The epiphany came as she mentally envisioned the length of string and the scar on the bridge railing from a new perspective. The significance of the two had been lost on the Sheriff's detectives. And on her as well. Until now.

Dawson knew and loved guns. He could have modified Nowak's rifle. She vaguely remembered reading how it was possible to reduce pull weight on a trigger. She didn't know how it was done, but that was something Kyle would either know or be able to research quickly.

One of the hardest things to accept about the theory was that Dawson had set up his partner and friend like that. But he was carrying around a lot of stress and guilt. He may have decided that his daughter's welfare was more important than his friendship with Nowak who had, despite their friendship, humiliated him in front of the entire office the day they'd had that argument. Family, Sydney mused. It always came down to family.

Another thing it explained was why Dawson had picked that location during a weekday morning. Nowak's presence there would look suspicious. Together with the other evidence, that would make his role in the "murder," completely plausible.

She closed her eyes and went through the scenario in her mind. All Dawson had to do was lay the rifle on its side on one of the bridge's flat wooden railings where he aimed it along and across the bridge deck to a point further out, far enough away to assure the absence of powder burns. Maybe he got a heavy rock from among those in the stream bed beneath the bridge and placed it on the rifle to hold it in position. Making sure the safety was off, and using that piece of string, he'd have tied a loop at one end of the string, passed that loop down through the open steel handle of the lever action, then hooked it loosely around the trigger. The rest he would have strung out in the direction of the rifle's aim, across and down the bridge deck to where he'd stand to face his maker.

With the other end of that length of string in hand, all Dawson needed to do was bend over, sight carefully down along the barrel of Nowak's "murder" rifle, and give the string just one firm tug.

Would that do it? Sydney wasn't sure, but it was still early enough in the day that she was able to reach her contact with the with the Sheriff's Property Management Unit, an evidence specialist whose deposition had been taken a few months ago and who had more-recently been subpoenaed to bring the murder rifle and other evidence to court in next week's defamation trial.

"Helen, this is Sydney Warren. The lawyer on the Seattle Report lawsuit. Do you have handy the evidence from the Dawson murder, the stuff that we've subpoenaed for the trial next week?"

"Sure. It's right where it belongs. All packed up and ready to go."

"Is the rifle there? The Marlin 336? The Dawson murder weapon?"

"Uh huh."

"Would you do me a quick favor?"

"Probably. What do you need?"

Sydney had found the office personnel in the Sheriff's Office and Helen in particular to be friendly and helpful. In part it may have been because it was a civil trial in which the Sheriff's Office had no particular interest. But she also got the impression that they were people who were both diligent and caring.

"I could come over there, but I think this is something that would be better suited to your expertise. Could you possibly go take a look at that rifle while I stay on the phone?"

"I can do that. I know right where it is, but it will take a few minutes to walk back there." Sydney heard the faint sound of footfalls on a hard, polished floor. Then, the sound of boxes being moved and opened: "OK, I have it right here. You're on speaker. What do you need to know?"

"I'd like you to check the trigger and estimate how much pressure is required to pull it."

"Hmmm. An interesting request. Give me a moment to make sure this damned thing isn't loaded after all these years." Sydney could hear the metallic clicking sound of Helen working the action and checking for cartridges. "That's interesting."

"Interesting?" Sydney knew she probably sounded anxious. But there was a lot riding on Helen's response.

"Well, for one thing, this trigger is definitely not standard."

"Not standard? How? Are you talking about the trigger pull weight?"

"Yeah. This rifle has been modified. I've heard that there are drop-in trigger assemblies you can sometimes get from a manufacturer that will lighten the trigger pull. But this is something else. Somebody, somewhere, has substantially modified this trigger assembly."

"Can you give me an idea of what that means for someone shooting the rifle?"

"Normal pull weight is at least four or five pounds. Usually more. I know some hunters like it pretty light, so they have modification kits out there for both the hammer and the trigger. I think they can be taken down to as little as three and a half pounds or so. But this feels to me like less than that. A lot less. I bet it isn't over a couple of pounds. Whatever they did to this rifle was pretty extreme. Honestly, given the sensitivity, I'd say this would have been a dangerous weapon to have around. That what you wanted to know?"

"That is exactly what I wanted to know."

"Was this noted at the original trial?"

"No, it wasn't."

"I guess nobody ever figured they needed to actually pull the trigger. They were only interested in the link between the bullet and the gun, right?"

"That's what I think happened. I know it was wasn't something I thought about checking."

"I assume you have a theory about what this means."

"I do. I will need to get official verification on the gun's modifications. Then you will probably get a visit from the lawyers representing the Seattle Report. Or maybe their insurers. Given what you've told me, I think there's a pretty good chance a trial may no longer be needed. But, unless you're asked, stay mum for now, okay?" Sydney hoped she hadn't said too much, but she trusted Helen to keep quiet.

"And you'll fill me in on the details later?"

"Yes, I'll give you the full scoop. I just need to do a little more research first. Thanks, Helen. I really appreciate this."

"Always glad to be of help. Especially if it keeps me from having to testify. And having to shag boxes to and from the courthouse."

As Sydney hung up her phone, she now knew exactly what had happened on that fateful day.

All Dawson had to do was stand back, line himself up with the rifle barrel, then tug on the string. The trajectory of the bullet, after passing through his head, could easily have creased the top edge of the opposite railing just behind him and then disappeared either into the water or beyond into the woods on the far side of the stream. The recoil would almost certainly have propelled the precariously balanced rifle—and the rock or whatever rested atop it to hold it in place—off the railing and into the stream bed. The string would have either broken or fallen loose. Dawson, no doubt expected the rifle to be found under the bridge in the investigation that inevitably followed. And he probably assumed that the string would have simply been collected as part of the public detritus that littered the bridge deck, and then forgotten. Just as it had been.

With Nowak waiting in his car nearby, with their recent history of animosity over business losses, and with Nowak's rifle as the obvious weapon, murder would be the natural inference. And the payout on that life insurance to his beloved daughter was assured.

Before leaving home on the day of his death, Dawson naturally provided for his faithful dog Parker whom he could expect would soon safely end up living with his daughter and her loving husband, Danny Ortez.

The clever audacity of his actions was so staggering that no one, Sydney and her client included, had ever suspected the possibility of suicide, even though under any other circumstances, it would have naturally leapt to mind.

If it had not been for the recollections and stalwart character of an aging widow with fond memories of a loyal dog and a determination to do the right thing, the truth would never have come to light.

CHAPTER 46

Eric & Will
Vancouver, BC, Canada
Grenville Island, The Buckingham Gallery
Current day

I t was just after 6:00 p.m. on a weekday. Martin Buckingham had reversed the small sign that hung against his popular Grenville Island Gallery's glass entry door so it read CLOSED to anyone outside on the street. That did not, however, deter a couple of insistent but harmless-looking young men who knocked on the door and waived at him as he stood behind his counter totaling up his day's receipts.

"Martin Buckingham?" one of the men inquired when Martin cracked the door open to hear what they had to say. "I'm Orville. This is my brother Wilbur. We called earlier?"

Buckingham suppressed a smile at the silly aliases. "Sure. Come on in." Then, as he closed the door behind them and flipped the door lock again, he pointed at the small package "Orville" carried in his hand. "That it?"

Orville handed him the small box, and both men followed Buckingham over to a counter toward the back of the spacious gallery.

Various works of contemporary art were displayed on the walls and on pedestals throughout the large open space, but neither "Orville" nor "Wilbur" showed any interest. Their full attention was on Buckingham as he sat down, opened the box, and placed its contents on a padded mat that lay atop his desk.

"Hmm," Buckingham said, leaning forward in his chair and holding the small object beneath his desk lamp for closer examination. "Impressive."

Orville and Wilbur smiled at each other.

Buckingham pulled out a brass loupe and studied the item more closely. His examination seemed to take forever, Orville and Wilbur anxiously awaiting his conclusion. "Not bad," he said finally.

"That mean you're interested?" Orville asked.

"Maybe. At the right price."

"You know what this is?"

"Yes, I think I do. But you need to understand, under the circumstances I can only pay you a fraction of market. You know that, right?" The two men nodded in response. "So how much are you asking?"

"Four mil. You know it's worth a lot more than that. Four million, cash. That's our price."

Buckingham set the item aside, clasped his hands across his ample stomach, and rolled his chair a couple of feet back from his desk. It was as if he wanted to distance himself from the brooch. He sighed and shook his head sadly. "I'm sorry, boys. That's not happening. We're not even in the same galaxy. Four million is probably a good price, at full retail. If I had this item in my gallery, and if it had unquestioned provenance, I'd probably offer it for somewhat more even. But four million or so is what I'd probably end up having to accept. Given the situation, there's no way I can get that much. *If* I can find a buyer for this thing, it has to be somebody whose ownership will be kept a secret. That, my friends, is a very difficult thing to do. That buyer will not be paying any four million dollars, I can assure you of that."

Buckingham shook his head and stood. "It sounds like we're way too far apart to make this happen. Sorry you made a wasted trip."

"OK, so we get that," said Orville, still seated. "Why don't you tell us what you'd be willing to pay. Give us your top offer—your take-it-or-leave-it offer."

Buckingham squinted his eyes, sat, and rolled his chair back up to the desk to take another hard look at the jeweled brooch. Then, leaning back again: "You said on the phone that you'd need to be paid in cash money, no bank transfers. That still go?"

"Right. Cash. You got enough cash?"

He reached out again and rotated the brooch with his finger as if to see it from yet another angle. "OK, here's the deal. I'll give you one point eight million. Right now. You walk away with the money, and I keep the brooch. How about it?"

"Two point two," said Orville."

Buckingham shook his head. "Two million. But that is it. That's all I've got. And I'm taking a big chance on it as is."

Orville and Wilbur looked at each other. Before they'd arrived, they'd agreed that they would be willing to accept one point six. "You've got a deal." The three men shook hands.

At that moment, the front door rattled as it was being unlocked from the outside. Then it, and a nearby interior door to the Gallery's back room, simultaneously flew open with a loud "bang." Four armed and uniformed officers burst into the room.

"Vancouver police! Hands on your head!"

CHAPTER 47

Seattle, Magnolia Bluff
Home of Kate and Duncan Carmichael
Current day

I t was an unusual ad hoc gathering on the deck of the Carmichael home on a sunny afternoon. Several of the guests had never actually met. Nonetheless, they had a long and difficult history together.

Early the previous Friday morning Sydney had settled the Nowak children's defamation case with the Seattle Report. And it had been only the evening before last when Duncan had been informed that the Vancouver Police had arrested the two men responsible for the Dawson-Ortez blackmail heist. Fortunately, shortly before that had happened, Duncan's negotiations with the U.S. Navy had concluded with Danny's surrender and apprehension at the U.S. port of entry in Blaine, Washington. After a brief drive to the Naval Air Station at Whidbey Island where his saga had begun many years earlier, then several hours of interrogation, and, finally a hurried arraignment before a military judge, Danny had been released on his own recognizance the following morning pending sentencing.

Duncan and Sydney were obviously pleased with what they'd helped to pull off, but Kate saw it as a must-do opportunity for a get-together with everyone involved. "Duncan, these people need to celebrate," Kate told him. "This is a huge moment for all of them. And they don't even know each other."

"There could be some hard feelings about a few things," Duncan said. "Like Julia Dawson having to reveal the suicide of her father in order to clear Jamison Nowak's name. Or maybe the Nowak family just might resent Dawson for having framed their father for murder and pretty much ruining the rest of his life. A couple of *minor* things like that."

"I know all that. And so do they. But these are nice people who have a lot to be thankful for. And their lives have been intertwined for so many years. I think it will provide closure."

Although Duncan had his doubts about whether everyone would feel as enthusiastic about the gathering as his wife, they all accepted his invitation knowing who would be there. Maybe she was right, he thought—maybe talking with each other would allow them to turn the page and move on with their lives.

On the day of the event, Kate and their daughter Megan made enough hors d'oeuvre and desserts to feed twice as many people as invited. There was a table crowded with a variety of drinks, including a large bottle of champagne in an ice bucket. There was a cooler filled with soda and juice for the children and beer for any adults who preferred that to their other offerings. There were flowers and colorful plates and napkins. And enough comfortable chairs for everyone to sit if they wanted.

The Nowak siblings, Bryce Nowak and Bonny Price, were first to arrive, along with Bonny's three grandchildren who were staying with her for a few weeks while her daughter was on vacation. Lilly immediately ran off to the backyard with Bonny's grandchildren while Kate ushered Bryce and Bonny out onto the front deck. They "oohed and aahed" appropriately at the Carmichaels' amazing view while asking Duncan to identify various distant landmarks like Alki point, Blake Island, and the entrance to Eagle Harbor on Bainbridge Island.

Then Danny and Julia Ortez arrived with their daughter, Allison Girard, and her husband Peter. They brought a delectable-looking platter of smoked salmon which they explained had been purchased earlier in the day at Pike Place Market. They were sorry that they'd been unable to personally smoke it themselves from fish Danny had caught on his salmon troller as had always been their family's practice. With luck and despite his advancing years, Danny still hoped to get back to commercial salmon fishing. Maybe in Washington or maybe up in Alaska. Regretfully, the Ortez family was not yet in a financial position to secure the boat and license they'd need to make that possible. For now, they would be limited to sports fishing from a rental boat. But, as Julia pointed out, it definitely beat being in jail. Or on the run.

Sydney arrived soon after, and close behind her, Kyle Marshall. Kyle told Duncan that he had some details about the past couple of weeks that he believed everyone might like to hear a little later. "And by the way," he added, "my guys finally tracked down the two men who tailed you to Bella Bella. I know, it's a little late to be of use, but the police were pleased to get the information. It helps with their case against your attackers in the parking garage."

After all the introductions had been made, it became obvious that Kate had been right. These family members had everything to talk about. And if they harbored resentments, none of it showed.

"You know, since I realized we would finally meet you," Bryce Nowak told Julia Ortez, "I've been thinking that there are some things we really do need to talk about. Mostly, we want you to know that our dad had nothing but respect for your father. Even after everything they went through with the WPPS losses at the company, he felt bad about how things turned out. And he partly blamed himself for not acting sooner."

"Well, that's nice of you to say," Julia replied. "Especially given what we've recently learned about my dad's death. I don't imagine your father would have been happy to know that his good friend tried to blame it on him. Hard to take any joy in that."

"Yeah, that's a tough one," Bonny said. "But honestly, both of them ended up captives of their circumstances. They both lost everything they cared about. And neither of them was able to find a good way out."

The two oddly connected families bonded by misfortune went silent for a moment, staring out at the spectacular view. From where they were standing, they could see the kids running about in the yard below, their shouts and laughter floating upward toward the deck.

Finally, Allison spoke. "I understand you've settled your father's defamation case," she said to Bryce and Bonny.

"We have," said Bryce. "The Seattle Report folks were really blown away when laid out the evidence of our father's innocence. I think they were actually quite embarrassed. They offered us a generous settlement number that we accepted without further negotiation. It will cover what we've spent on the lawsuit and then some. But, most importantly, they're going to publish an apology in a lead article that spells out what actually happened back in 1983, explain the context, including what your father went through to try to help his clients." He paused and shook his head. "I'm sorry that it will make references to your father's suicide."

"It isn't something we can hide, I'm afraid," Julia said. "And, as uncomfortable as it is to admit what happened, the truth needed to be told."

"Well, I can't tell you how much giving our father his day in court has meant to us." Bonny glanced over at Bryce, then back to Allison and Julia. "Got to admit though that the money is nice."

"Both families have suffered," Sydney said. "With luck, one day you'll be able to remember the good times and let go of the rest."

Bonny turned to Allison. "Meanwhile, do I understand correctly that the men who were blackmailing your family have also been caught, and that you played a role in that?"

"Yes," Allison said. "I find it hard to believe that our plan actually worked, but it did. We have Duncan to thank for that." She gave Duncan a big smile

"And I'm square with the Navy," Danny said. "Duncan is a miracle worker." He held up his glass to salute Duncan.

"I didn't do it all alone." Duncan nodded toward Kyle and Sydney. "I'm just thankful it all worked out. We were holding our breath."

Kate stood there beaming, pleased that the get-together was going so well.

"Meanwhile, the Canadians aren't very happy with our family, that's for sure," Allison said. "My son is a legitimate Canadian citizen, so he's going to complete his studies at UBC. We aren't sure yet whether Peter and I will be able to visit him there. But, except for the government confiscating my dad's fishing license, them having to give away their home and losing some of the money they had in the bank, things are looking good." She laughed as Julia and Danny rolled their eyes.

Sydney turned to Julia. "Have you heard anything from the insurance company about the life insurance you received back then from your grandfather?"

"Not yet." Julia turned to the others to explain. "The policy has what they call an 'incontestability clause' that kicks in after a couple of years. It says they won't ask for payouts back after two years. But there are exceptions. Like intentional fraud. Still, it's been so long, and it's not clear that my dad's suicide scheme falls into that category. We're pretty sure they're going to write it off. Which is a good thing, because we've got nothing to give back."

"I have a question," said Allison, turning to face the two lawyers. "It's for you, Sydney, and you Duncan. "It's about those two Seattle mobsters that attacked you in the parking garage. Do you know anything further about them?"

Duncan and Sydney turned to Kyle.

"A little," Kyle said. "I think it may have been me that stirred up things. Early on, Duncan asked me to see if I could figure out how the two blackmailers had tracked down your mom and dad. I contacted a Vancouver private investigator I know to see if he could make an independent effort to locate you. We figured whatever he found might tell us how those two guys had pulled that off. And, indirectly, maybe help us figure out who they were.

"As you probably all now know, the guy Allison dealt with was a Seattle burglar who had a friend with connections to a group of local criminals. He apparently learned about the Spider from a cellmate in Walla Walla state prison. But he had no clue how to find Danny. Initially he handed the job off to the friend's criminal associates—Seattle's own local version of organized crime. As it happened, they hired the same Vancouver investigator to chase your family down. He failed and the Seattle criminals told the burglar guy it was a no-go. So the burglar figured he was good to go and to give it a shot himself. He didn't bother to mention that to the crime bosses though.

"Unfortunately, when I called my friend, the Vancouver PI, asking for the same information, he reported my inquiry back to his Seattle organized crime clients. Apparently, my long-standing professional relationship with the law firm of Warren and Carmichael is well known in some circles. As was Sydney's recent representation on the Nowak defamation case. The Seattle crime folks made the connection."

Kyle directed his next comments to Sydney and Duncan.

"And in all their thuggish wisdom, they decided that, given how you managed to give the two guys they had tailing you the slip, that the two of you must already have known where the Ortez family ended up. Unlike their subordinates who, to give them credit, did actually figure it out on their own, the bosses decided to take a more direct approach. In their own usual and customary way, they intended to simply ask you two directly. And to use whatever *persuasion* might be needed to elicit the answers."

"We were just lucky the one guy ran into Duncan's car door and dropped his gun," Sydney said with a snicker.

Everyone took a moment to chuckle about the image.

"The police think the guy they arrested in the parking lot will eventually fold, and they might get several arrests out of it. But who knows, he may fear his criminal cohorts more than jail and keep his mouth shut."

"Which," Duncan added, "To my way of thinking, rather nicely closes this story in a satisfying circle. Since Walla Walla is where this whole thing seems to have started, maybe all the bad guys will end up there."

"Thank God it's over," Julia said.

"Amen to that," Bonny agreed.

Upon that satisfying note of completion, Kate and Megan poured the champagne, and they toasted "Happy Endings." At that point the children returned in search of food. After eating, they went inside to play, and the adults settled into chairs facing out across the water with the sun starting to descend against a pink-streaked sky and beyond the stark outline of the Olympic Mountains.

Duncan's mobile phone intruded on the peaceful moment. He pulled it out and glanced at the screen. "I'm really sorry," he said guiltily. "I need to take this." He stood and disappeared through the glass sliders into the living-room.

Moments later, Duncan reappeared with the phone still pressed against his ear. "Hold on," he said. "Let me put you on speaker. There are some people here that need to hear this." He faced the group and motioned for them to come closer. "I've got Martin Buckingham on the phone. He's the gallery owner from Grenville Island who tricked the two men who were trying to sell the Tsarina's Spider."

Everyone had heard the story and eagerly gathered around.

"OK, Martin, go ahead. The Ortez family is right here. Along with some other people who'll be really interested in hearing this. You're on speaker. Tell them what you just told me."

Buckingham's voice wasn't amplified much, but it was loud enough for all to hear. "Well, I called because I thought I should ask what the Ortez family wants me to do with the Tsarina's Spider. I talked to the police about the brooch. Since the two men took guilty pleas, they said I can now return it to its owners."

Allison Girard glanced at her parents before responding: "Thanks for asking, Mr. Buckingham. Maybe you could drop it in the mail, parcel post, whenever it's convenient? Maybe send it to Duncan and we can pick it up at his office in Seattle. There's no real hurry at this point. But we would like to get it back. We'll want to keep it as part of our family legacy."

"My father-in-law did emphasize that I should hang onto it," Danny said. "It's a weird legacy, but he wanted us to have it."

"Sure, I see. Well, that's fine. Though I don't think I'll be sending it in the mail. If you change your minds and want to put it on the market or perhaps up for auction, I'd be happy to represent you in finding an appropriate buyer."

That brought a moment of stunned silence. Duncan stood there with a grin on his face, and Sydney raised her eyebrows at him in question.

"Are you saying that you think it has some kind of value?" Allison asked. Her mother and father leaned closer to the phone.

"You're . . . kidding, right? Of course it has value. A lot of value."

Allison looked around at the attentive group. "Really. I guess we just figured, as a fake, it was pretty much worthless."

Martin Buckingham released a brief snort of laughter. "Hardly worthless," he said. "And definitely NOT a fake. What you have here is absolutely the real deal. I spent the morning doing a bit of research on its provenance and its value. There's a strong public record of its ownership right up through its purchase by one Harold Dawson, a resident of Broadmoor in Seattle on March 10 of 1980. I gather that's your father, Mrs. Ortez. I don't want to presume here, but if you do decide to sell, I'd expect it to bring at least four and a half million. At auction, maybe a good deal more."

END

About The Authors

Charlotte Stuart

Award-winning author Charlotte Stuart PhD writes mysteries that fall into a number of different sub genres: cozy mysteries, a lighthearted series featuring a female PI, a laugh out loud comedic series, some deadly serious traditional mysteries—and two co-authored legal thrillers with Don Stuart.

In general, she favors twisty plots with a smattering of humor and a dollop of adventure. Before she started writing full time, she left a tenured faculty position to go commercial salmon fishing in Alaska, spent a year sailing in the Washington and Canadian San Juans, became a partner in a management consulting group and later a VP of HR and training. After living on boats for over a decade, boating and forays into wilderness areas often find their way into her stories.

Awards include: 1st Place in the Chanticleer Mystery & Mayhem

Book Series, Nancy Pearl Finalist, Storytrade Book Award Winner, Killer Nashville "Top Pick," CIPA EVVY Gold, NYC Big Book Award, Global Ebook Gold, and the Firebird "Best Title to Say Out Loud."

Charlotte lives on Vashon Island in the Pacific Northwest with her husband and her imaginary cat Macavity and is the past president of the Puget Sound Sisters in Crime.

OTHER BOOKS BY CHARLOTTE STUART INCLUDE:

- Discount Detective Mysteries (5 books: Amphorae Publishing Group, 2019-2025)
- John Smith Mysteries (3 books: Level Best Books, 2023-2025)
- Macavity & Me Mysteries (3 books: Taylor & Seale, 2019-2022; Quartermaster Publishing, 2025)
- *Bogged Down* (A Vashon Island Mystery, Taylor & Seale 2020; Quartermaster Publishing, 2025)
- *Raven's Grave* (A Jonah St. Clair Mystery, Vine Leaves Press, 2023)
- *Raven's Legacy* (A Jonah St. Clair Mystery, Quartermaster Publishing, 2025)
- *Sham Shamus: Soft-boiled Noir – Where Shadows Laugh* (Quartermaster Publishing, 2025)
- *Forget or Forgive? NEVER! Suspense, Dark Secrets, and Revenge with a Twist* (Quartermaster Publishing, 2025)
- *Midnight for Justice (Warren and Carmichael Legal Thrillers, Book 1)* by Charlotte Stuart and Don Stuart (Quartermaster Publishing, 2025)

Non-fiction:

- *Disastrous Interviews: The Comic, Tragic & Just Plain Ugly* (CreateSpace, 2013)

You can visit her website or contact her on social media:

- Website: charlottestuart.com
- Twitter (X): @quirkymysteries
- Facebook: charlotte.stuart.mysterywriter
- Goodreads: 19305587.Charlotte_Stuart
- Instagram: @cstuartauthor
- BookBub: authors/charlotte-stuart

DON STUART

Award winning author Don Stuart, JD was a U.S. Navy JAGC officer during the Vietnam War (1968-72) and later a partner in a Seattle law firm. In 1978, Don and his wife Charlotte quit their professional jobs to cruise the Pacific coastal waters of the U.S. and Canada and then personally built a 47' commercial salmon troller and, during the 1980s, earned their living commercial fishing in Southeast Alaska. Don later became a non-profit manager for the commercial fishing industry, then for conservation districts, and finally for a national organization working for agriculture and the environment. In that work he gained 20 years' experience as a legislative lobbyist.

Don draws upon his years trying court-martial cases in the U.S. Navy and in the practice of law for his depiction of JAGC Lieutenant Duncan Carmichael whose assignment to the criminal defense of an unlikable client requires working with independent-minded civilian ACLU volunteer lawyer Sydney Warren.

Don's books have earned 1st place in the BookFest Award, the Incipere Award for Exceptional Writing, and the Pinnacle Book Achievement Award. He's received 2nd and 3rd place or a Bronze Medal in the Outstanding Creator Book Awards and Global Book Awards. And he was a Finalist, Top Pick, Short Listed, Distinguished Favorite, or Recommended Read in the Next Generation Indie Book Awards, Killer Nashville Best Books, Cygnus Book Awards, Author Shout, New York City Big Book Award and the Eric Hoffer Book Awards' Montaigne Medal.

Don lives and writes in the Pacific Northwest on Vashon Island with his wife Charlotte.

OTHER BOOKS BY DON STUART INCLUDE:

Fiction:

- *Final Adjournment: A Washington Statehouse Mystery* (Epicenter Press, 2017)
- *Suspension of the Rules: A Washington Statehouse Mystery* (Northwest Corner Books—an imprint of Epicenter Press, 2021)
- *Censure and Repeal: A Washington Statehouse Mystery* (Northwest Corner Books—an imprint of Epicenter Press, 2024)
- *Darwin's Dilemma: A Story of Humans, AIs, and the Future of Intelligence* (2023)
- *Secret Places: A Southeast Alaska Mystery* (Epicenter Press, 2025)
- *Descartes' Shadow: A Story of Humans, AIs, and the Future of Intelligence* (Colvos Publications, 2025)

Non-Fiction:

- *Barnyards and Birkenstocks: Why Farmers and Environmentalists Need Each Other* (Washington State University Press, 2014)
- *No Farms No Food: Uniting Farmers and Environmentalists to Transform American Agriculture* (Island Press, 2022)
- *Small Claims Court Guide for Washington: How to win your case* (Self Counsel Press, 1979, 1989)
- *CLEDEX: The Index to Continuing Legal Education in Washington* (CLEDEX Publications Inc., 1986-1991) (Originating author)

You can visit Don's website or contact him on social media:

- Website: donstuart.net
- Twitter (X): @DonStuart14
- Facebook: don.stuart.7359
- Goodreads: 534936.Don_Stuart
- LinkedIn: don-stuart-4a874747/

A Few Thoughts

The forty-year time gap in the storyline for *Bad Day for Justice* not only poses the dilemma of what constitutes true justice, but is intended to challenge stereotyped views of aging.

We usually assume that discovering the truth even after the passage of time is still a cause for celebration. However, William Gladstone is credited with saying: "Justice delayed is justice denied." In *Bad Day for Justice*, it is the children of the victim and alleged murderer who grapple with this issue.

From our experience with our prior book, *Midnight for Justice*, we know that some readers find it difficult to accept a forty-year story gap after which the same adult characters reappear and are still robust and fully functional. Many people live longer, healthier lives, and retire later than they used to, and it is not unusual for people in their 70s and 80s to be actively engaged in their professional lives. We wanted to present that point of view rather than the more common image of elderly amateur detectives.

On a different note, we often have people ask: *How do you write a book together and stay married?* Actually, we have had many occasions to work together in the past, but writing books together has been by far the most fun. We discuss plot and characters on our afternoon walks, share essential research, play constantly with "what if" ideas, and celebrate milestones together. Our main disagreements are about comma placement!

THANK YOU!

First, we have our two "production" colleagues to thank: Sue Trowbridge for doing our interior and putting up with last-minute changes and Chris Holmes for creating a cover that we love. Thank you both for your great work and for your patience!

We also want to thank our friends who read our books, especially those who don't normally read genre fiction. What a test of friendship!

Finally, we want to wholeheartedly thank you, our readers. We hope you enjoyed *Bad Day for Justice* and will continue to read our books.

We do have one request: we would deeply appreciate your feedback in the form of a rating and/or review on your favorite retailer, Amazon, or Goodreads. This is much more important than you might imagine. A star rating or a brief review of a sentence or two is all it takes to satisfy a retailer's voracious algorithms that influences both search engines and promo placement, the lifeblood of the publishing world.

Please feel free to contact us with questions or comments.

www.ingramcontent.com/pod-product-compliance
Lightning Source LLC
Chambersburg PA
CBHW030242120726
47903CB00005B/1586